THE MEMORY ADDICTS

THE MEMORY ADDICTS

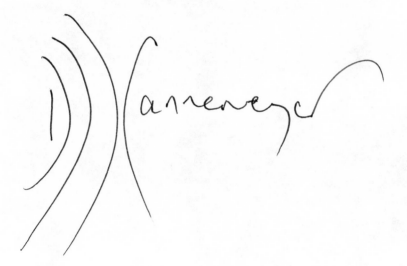

DEREK KANNEMEYER

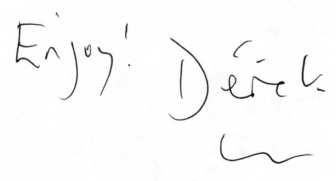

Enjoy! Derek

atmosphere press

The Heartwood Chronicles

"Remember us. These are our names and who we are.
Together we will survive, and we will remember."

Andrew Barker, *35. Aka: Andrew Borrendong.*
Troubleshooting and oversight; short and long-term crisis planning; maintenance management; field crops; armory; State of the World board; State of the Farm board.

*Edie Driscoll, *34. Blend elements: Tiffany Driscoll (deceased).*
Pharmacy; a.m. check-in and scheduling; household upkeep and oversight; household inventory.

Elise Barker, *13. Aka: Red(s); Redsy; Elise Oswald.*
Homeschool classes. Some p.r.n. assistance to Andrew Barker. Also to Edie Driscoll and Lisa Huttongold.

Jeremy Jaronsky, *25. Aka: Jemmy.*
Machine maintenance; small buildings; property line; field crops; p.r.n. manual work.

Jenna Brower, *circa 62. Aka: Sarah Oldchurch (superseded).*
Kitchen management; household upkeep; routine small animal care; market supplies.

Jody Barker, *30.*
Apiary; gardens and orchards.

Lisa Huttongold, *30.*
Animal husbandry; veterinary work; medical care; barter management; SNAG board.

*Matt Simmons, *58.*
Storm cellars; construction; large buildings; stock rooms; ponds and waterways; large vehicles.

*Millar Kearney, *30, "Heartwood Chronicles" editor. Aka Brian Everett (deceased).*
Colony history; records room oversight; logging room; p.r.n. manual work.

Nicholas Trifflett, *26. Aka Nick; Big Nick; Nicky.*
Crop husbandry management (gardens and orchards); p.r.n. manual work.

Ages are as of the colony's expansion, 2/17, Year Three.
(* Founders, 10/20, Year Two.)
Year One marks the arrival locally of the EEMLV & the X7 drug.

PROLOGUE: YEAR FOUR

"Mercy on us, we split! We split!"

William Shakespeare, The Tempest, Act 1, scene 1

"Almost every such colony prioritizes the persistence of identity and the preservation of memory. To some, the distinctions between lived and constructed identity and true and false memory seem critical; to others, more pragmatic, what has most mattered is to cohere. Within every community, however, the range of individual strategies has been broad. On which topic, the Heartwood Farm, to whom (full disclosure) two of us have ties, may merit its own docuhistory: both digitally and on paper, the colony kept astonishingly full records."

Library of Virginia Commission, The 5 Year Report

YEAR FOUR, HEARTWOOD:

Elise, Jody, Matt

Jesus, another one down. Elise stops, tugs out the flashlight. A yellow pine. Sixty yards away, yet the shudder of its fall thunks through her bones. No lightning, no thunder, except from the crashing trees, but such wind! Shrilling through the branches, and this rain belting and flinging at her. Well, fine. Elise is foolhardy, but she's not a fool. So. Plan B. She was bivouacked close to the south storm cellar—or what a foolhardy teenaged girl calls close—and she's been scrabbling zigzag toward it, in the drenching dark. Nobody knows this terrain like her. She swings her flashlight beam. It finds the bunker. The direct route would take her through thorn bushes and poison ivy and a double bend of the creek. A ten-minute crawl if she goes around—or with a fool's guts she could just cut through. Either way, someone will be down there. Matt Simmons, at the very least. He'll let her in.

Debris gusts by her. Small branches, yard clutter, then suddenly these sheets and sheets of paper. Ghost-white in her light's frail glare. She snags one just as a second one strikes her outstretched arm and wraps there. Brian's work, obviously. Wet through but readable. Bloody *how*, though? The records room is in the damn basement. Is the whole house down, was a window left open? Did someone toss the dumb stuff out the door?

The page clinging to her rain slicker mentions her nutty aunt Jody. She loses it to the wind. The one in her fist lists all their names. A title line: *The Heartwood Chronicles*; a cast of characters with thumbnail descriptions. There she is, two people below her father: *Elise Barker yadda yadda, assistant to Andrew Barker, yadda yadda.*

The rain stripes into her. She raises her arm a little, what the wind will give her. It snatches the sheet up, gone. She gets lower; gulps air; peers out into a scour of leaves, twigs, papers. She picks out the storm cellar again. She'll make it. She shuts off her lamp and crawls.

Up in the house, Jody's eyes squint open, then flinch shut. Reams of paper thrash about the ruins of a room, with wet leaves and bits of tree debris caught in their whip. Where the window once was a dislodged blue curtain sags and twitches, pooled with busted glass. A chunk of the ceiling is down—is that crawl space above her, is that a tree she sees hanging over her?

Her head hurts. She's naked, sprawled crookedly on the rug. Scratched up. Can she move? She can move. Ow, she would prefer not to. Except not this time. This time, she refuses to lose herself. Stay *alert*, Jody. Take *action*, damn you! *See!*

A naked man lies nearby. No. No, no—not again. She calls his name. Croaks it, rather: "*Brian!*" No, not Brian. *Not* Brian. She's Jody. He's *Millar*. This is *Heartwood*. She rasps: "*Millar!*" Does he hear? Did he just stir? Half-toppled boxes, gashed open, empty themselves into the air, draping his back and his legs with a scurry of papers. She drags herself toward him. Something white and sopping slaps at her. She tears it from the dark and flings it. "*Millar!*"

Matt Simmons has pulled a novel from the storm cellar shelves. *Slaughterhouse Five*. He's read this one—read it dog-eared, in fact, he sees as he flicks through it. The Dresden air raids: that's right. Ha. Like out there, right now. And Billy Pilgrim, unstuck in time, is the Jody Barker story. Or aunt Jilly's... He was wrong, it strikes him, about if he were the last one left standing—that he'd be equipped to handle it. Sheer dumb bravado. He has lost too many people. They have all lost too many people. *Hello? Could somebody rap at the hatch, please? Now, please!*

He repeats the last part out loud; it comes out as a scream: "*Now*, please!" But all the answer that gets him is more storm. And the first throbs of a tension headache. He flips the pages, looking for a line to catch his eye and anchor him. Nothing does, since the story he's unstuck in is *their* story—from the start of the plague to now, to this life they have made for themselves at Heartwood. Once a week for the last year, the ten of them have gathered to master their ten variant catechisms, each with its set questions and its fumbling, evolving answers. Tonight, as he finds himself reciting his, he feels the edges fray. Matt Simmons is not a fanciful person, but he swears, the howl of the storm outside is battering at something in him—it has damn well come to breach him. Just wind in the trees, he mutters, not that other howl. But it *floods* through them, into shipwreck.

Which he is *safe* from, down here: *his* here, he mutters. Only *this* crisis; no *survived* ones. He is not like Jody. Matt's memories know their place. Let the old pandemonium shrink back in its corner. Barely to tweak the thrum of his tension headache. The low strafe of his fear.

Huh. There's a maddie by his lamp: the other half of the

last pill. What the heck, why not swig it down and fly, ride its Superman cape wherever it elects to carry him? Maybe touch down somewhere better in the Matt Simmons story? It was mostly better. He could ask the memory pill to pick a pretty back chapter and deliver him.

Yes. He could. Perhaps he will. Because whatever the fuck they're up to, the others aren't coming, are they? Or should he give them, what, five, ten more minutes, maybe? Just in case.

Rap at the hatch if you're alive out there, anyone!

Edie and Jenna are alive, huddled in the farmhouse basement. They *felt* that tree hit. Andrew, Lisa, Jemmy are alive, probably, on their trek into Eastdon, gambling with their safety to keep Big Nick alive. Jody is alive and praying that Millar is also, that she can wake him with a kiss. His chronicles of them flap about the room. They gauze the nakedness of his body.

There's a ritual tag of prayer, written by Millar, with which they end their group memory sessions: *Remember us. These are our names and who we are. Together we will survive, and we will remember.* Jody, like Elise, skips more often than she attends, so that for a moment she can't identify how she knows these words or why they rise in her now, unbidden. But then, as she wades through the clutter and feels for Millar's pulse, quite suddenly and luminously, a plea is answered. Because she finds that pulse; it beats. And (as has happened before, which has always hurt too much to endure) in that moment, she remembers—astutely; *coherently*—everything.

This time, she swears, if Millar makes it... So. Will. She. Listen to that simulacrum of her, limply praying Millar's name! No more coasting—no more letting him or anyone else carry her! What he *needs* from her, starting right frigging now, please, is to be *Jody*.

Wind-snatched from Elise's hands as she began her crawl toward the storm cellar, the first page of Millar's *Heartwood Chronicles* turns suddenly in mid-air and hangs there, as if forgetting what impulse had set it on this course and debating the need to stick to it. It loiters for a moment over the storm cellar hatch. It wheels, and somersaults off into the dark.

Elise is alive. Should she risk standing and running? She raises herself into the hunched shape of a sprinter at the starting blocks. She is a quadruped; she is a wolf. She lopes.

Andrew Barker, ...
Troubleshooting; oversight chores and long-term ...
amory; State of the World board; State of the Seas ...

Edie Driscoll, 54. *Bird darren & Tiffany Driscoll (deceased)*
Pharmacy; a.m. checkin and scheduling; household upkeep and oversight; ...

Elise Barker, 13. *Aka Red(s); Redsy; Elise Oswald.*
Homeschool classes. Some p.r.n. assistance to Andrew Barker. Also to Edie Driscoll and ...

Jeremy Jaronsky, 25. *Aka Jenny.*
Mobile maintenance; small buildings; property lines; field crops; p.r.n. manual work.

Anna Drover, circa 62. *Aka Sarah Oldchurch (superseded).*
Kitchen management (household upkeep); routine small animal care; market supplies.

Judy Barker, 30.
Apiary; gardens and orchards.

Lia Huttongold, 30.
Animal husbandry; veterinary work; medical care; barter management; SNAG board.

Matt Simmons, 58.
Steel alloy; construction; large buildings; stock rooms; ponds and waterways; large vehicles.

Millar Kearney, 30. *'Heartwood Chronicles' editor. Aka Dean Duval (deceased).*
Colony history; records room oversight; lending room; p.r.n. manual work.

Nicholas Trimnel, 26. *Aka Nick; Dr Nick; Nicky.*

CHAPTER ONE: YEAR ONE

"Today, I will live in the moment, unless it's unpleasant, in which case I will eat a cookie."

The Cookie Monster, *Sesame Street*

"So this, we can now say definitively, was the first year of our Great Forgetting. And for how many months of that year did we fail to notice? The woman I lived with worked at the Eastdon Clinic on the breakthrough X-series trials; she was exposed daily to some of our first wave of casualties; and yet, like the vast majority of Americans, I remained oblivious. Oh, we had been told what was happening in Eastern Europe. But what did that have to do with us?"

Library of Virginia Commission, *The 5 Year Report*

YEAR ONE, EASTDON:

Millar, Jody

I.

The walls and cabinets of Jody's kitchen were painted a layered yellow, with gold and saffron swirls peeking through the ragging. Her refrigerator was pink; her table a lacquered scarlet; the pair of coffee mugs she set down on it were a bright sky blue. Pink curtains. A red vase sprigged with rosemary. She bustled off to the pantry, and Millar sipped. This was one gaudy room. A *Go for the Gusto* room. Or possibly *I'm kind of crazy*.

Millar liked it. As well as he kind of knew Jody, he liked how she could still spook him. Well: surprise him rather. And quirky; she wasn't crazy. Whatever, she was what he needed; he'd always known that. Finally, some things had fallen into place, and look! Here they were in her kitchen. Her colorful, crazy-spooky kitchen. Cool. Through the tipsy jangle of his nerves, he felt something deeper in him, a knot in his uptight core, untensing.

It was late, the nightcap hour of their third dinner date. The first one—they were longtime work friends—that had felt like a *date* date. They'd danced, they'd kissed, he'd come back and met her cat. Hello, Eggy! She had found candles and was now arranging them, in an apparent pentacle, around the sky blue mugs. Peach candles, mauve candles, lilac. She turned off the lamps, and the colors softened and began to throb. Woooh. Floaty! Maybe he'd hallucinate.

In the apartment Millar rented, the kitchen was shades of beige. The whole kitchen, now he thought about it. His mother had favored beige. Beige, he'd been brought up to believe, was the truth, the word, and the way.

"You know," he told Jody, sipping his decaf, as she stood at the counter, unscrewing the lid of a cookie jar, "I think I've been under a curse of beige."

"What?" she answered. "Cookie?"

"Sure. Beige has been my problem."

She clinked cookies, synchronizing their first bite. Almost too late he realized—oh cripes—that the white bits he'd taken for macadamias were the cut halves of a pill; and oh God, he knew what *crazy* pill; and the beige heck with it, why the beige heck not, he found he was sucking a chunk to the brink of his throat; that it was down, and he was swallowing.

He simpered at her. She showed her half-eaten cookie: a cut pill. She ate around it, four fat bites, and chewed. She popped in the pill, the stolen X7. He watched. She licked a thumb; she drank some coffee; she narrowed her eyes at him. Eggy the cat narrowed his eyes. Hi, Eggy!

"Finish it, Millar," she scolded; so he did.

II.

At work, they were break buddies. Nothing more, although people kidded them. But come on, there was no flirty touching. It was a contained heat.

Jody had a live-in boyfriend then, Danny, and sometimes in the snack room or at lunch, she nitpicked about him. He left the bathroom a mess! He was without style; he had redneck proclivities! He was such a fusspot! But perhaps, jealous of Danny, Millar inveigled her to? Theirs were such blah little problems, and Jody vented about them so breezily. On reflection, Millar did find himself guilty of some slight over-supportiveness; of a certain inner purr as Jody caviled. As to Jody, oh possibly he imagined it, but might she not have let slip, sometimes, a hint of an *Are you interested, I may be...*? Or even an *I'm involved but it's doomed don't rush off...*? Anyway, he didn't rush off. When had Millar ever rushed anyone? Perhaps she took his habitual passivity for a declaration of intent; perhaps it became that; or they were break buddies, and to claim anything more, now, was the revisionism of memory.

If not the boyfriend, they discussed work, or movies, books, the weather—nothing out of the ordinary, except that work was. And, of course, their local history fetish was. It was flat-out geeky. Arriving in town as new adults, seeking their place, they had each, separately, been drawn to explore Eastdon's rococo chronicles. Somehow, this came up during lunch.

"Wait! What, you too?"

"Me too what?"

"The local history thing. Because me too!"

"You too, like what?"

Till they exchanged stories, and they shrieked with amazement and declared it a sign or something. Until, together, in genial, one-upping combat, they pledged to truly discover this town, to become the Eastdon illuminatus and cognoscentoid, to unearth what made it *it*—that past Eastdon's present was uniquely built upon.

To visit the theater where the fire of 1886 began, that razed Old Town and made it new.

To tour the site of the Colonial revolt that ended in the hanging of a child.

To climb the hill the city once tunneled a railroad through—which caved in when the first ceremonial train rattled into it; to picture the festive wreckage buried there, unreachable...

Millar had majored in history; he loved history, but honestly? Less the window displays than the backroom gewgaws—

you know, *wow*.

"Dude!" said Jody.

They put together lists of their top ten local attractions.

"Gosh," said Millar. "Almost all yours could be disaster flicks."

"Mine?" said Jody. "What about your Civil War blather? Those damn statues?"

So they made alternative lists, our *non-violent* top ten— which proved to be surprisingly fun—there was even some oddball sex history if one needed to inject some spice. "Got a new place," they would say, crossing paths in the hall; then later, in the cafeteria: "So listen to this!"

Even when they weren't at work, the spark of their fancy jumped; periodically, they *felt* together. Visiting a city site. Glimpsing some woman grocery shopping, some man parking his car: who was that, was that his office buddy, was that her history homie? Phantasms fattened pleasantly in the corners of their consciousness, catching and casting shadows.

Work was a medical research facility. Jody was a nurse technician, Millar an office clerk. She had ditched med school, years back, for a life less pressured; he'd dropped out of college, years back, one term shy of his degree. Since when, a dash of this, a dab of that. Filing, flunkying. C'ville, H'burg. No hurry, but maybe he'd, you know, start over? Perhaps in español. Or Pharmacology. What did Jody think?

Jody laughed. "I think you're a goofball." She enjoyed— playfully, surely?—calling him a goofball. Bertie Wooster. Lloyd Christmas, from *Dumb and Dumber*. Well, she overdid it. "But sure," she said. "Working *here*. The pharmacology here can seduce the poo out of you..."

"I guess. If I had *your* job," Millar responded, fishing. "Some of us aren't in the loop..."

A Phase II clinical trial had been accelerated. Which they weren't supposed to discuss, but one picked up on things. The

X7, Millar had heard, might yet prove to be a triumph or a disaster. The X7 was a memory drug, hush-hush in its arcane details. An explosion in amnesia cases—in the Baltic, mostly, but getting buzz—had flung wide a window of demand, and the stakes were high. But the trials, the murmur was, were barrel-riding through rough water.

He said, "Not to breach confidentiality, but I do hear things."

She said, "Like what?"

"Stuff," he said. "The Madeleine effect, and such? These doctors were talking across me like I was the desk furnishings? So I said, *Like in Proust...?* Not that they answered. Actually, they got huffy. But it got me, you know, curious, so I skimmed this file..."

Laughing, Jody fended him off. He accepted the redirection. Two weeks passed during which she was perpetually busy—lunching on the run; cutting out the coffee breaks. But when she re-emerged, she raised the topic herself. In sideways fashion, as if still too skittish to reveal quite all—although what she did say was titillatingly erotic!

"There's this woman," she had begun, but then she broke off to chew. For a moment, she seemed to reconsider, backtracking to shift the tack. Oh, did I tell you—that doofus Danny is claiming he grew up near this weird, wild animal cemetery out by Westvale—can you believe he never said? But Millar wasn't having it. He knew the animal cemetery. A weed-bedraggled old hippie vet clinic. Come on, Jody, the X7!

When she resumed her tale—about a patient who had largely forgotten her marriage, until the pills (intimately!) hullabalooed it back—Millar found it fascinating.

He also had the distinct impression it wasn't what Jody had started to confide at all.

III.

It was Jilly Simmons she had nearly spilled the beans about.

"Please don't turn me in, Jody," the old dear had said.

They were in Jilly's bathroom, whispering. For added privacy, Jody had turned on the faucet and was running water over their four hands.

"Jilly, we have to document it. You're a test subject in a clinical study."

"Yes, yes, I know, but what if they kick me out of the test group—"

"You want to be in it? Then take what they give you—"

"Jody, you *know* why! It's a... temporary failure of nerve. If I could *ease* my way..."

In truth, Jody couldn't say she did know why. She knew what Jilly had told her: that this last burst of recovered memory had been too much for her. Jilly was yet another of the "anomalous" test subjects, whose memory loss, "not Alzheimer's" and mostly recent, was deep, narrow, and jagged. But she had blotted out the time surrounding her infant son's death long before her disorder had set in. She had *worked* to forget those months, and now this drug was breaking them wide open. What Jody didn't get was how after fifty years, any memory could achieve such power: as if, to hear Jilly tell it, one were reliving the real experience.

Other patients had made similar claims. To Jody, the most vivid of memories was a mere after-image, a perfumed contrail of the event itself. Jilly Simmons made her X7 restorations sound like doors in time, an authentic way back.

Of the two deaths that had once devastated Jody, there was one whose circumstances she would give anything to recall. She envied Jilly—both her second chance to come to terms and the cool, safe distance of it, stripped of the terrible call to act.

But Jilly was less sanguine. She got squirrelly and sly. "Fluff my pillow," she had asked that day, then behind Jody's back she had switched the X7 tablet with an ibuprofen.

And distracted by her patient's apparent fluster, Jody had administered this wrong medication. Tidying up, though, she spied the real pill, folded in Kleenex by the open ibuprofen bottle, and would have loudly remarked on it, had not Jilly clutched her off into the bathroom.

"Jody," she pleaded. "I thought we were friends."

"Look, sweetie, I know that last treatment was hard on you. But Jilly—"

"It was. You've no idea."

"So maybe it's time to step away..."

"I'm trying to save my life here! It *is* hard, but this drug is saving my life."

Fine, Jody decided with a sigh (refusing, as she so often did, to think the choice through), *what's the harm really?* She nodded; she made a full-throated gagging noise above the toilet to set up the cover story, and she flushed.

"Let's wash your face, sweetheart," she called out in an old people are such simpletons voice, signaling Jilly to comply.

"All right," she continued more quietly. "The ibuprofen stays our secret. Here's our play. You felt sick; you threw up the medication, we flushed it. No deceitful intent, just nerves and a screw-up. Can they hold off for a while till you feel better? Can you restart at a lower dose?"

"You make holding off for a while sound reasonable," Jilly whispered back as Jody blotted them both dry. "Not one of my talents."

"Hey, it's cool," Jody answered. "You freaked."

The plan worked fine. The doctors were a bit miffed Jilly had flushed the emesis—we have to measure and document *every*thing, Jilly—Jody, you should have stopped her.

"I'm sorry, Dr. Corrigan," said Jilly. "It was my fault. I went all, I splashed some, water over my, to calm the, but it... And then it got worse, this wave of nausea, I didn't think..."

"No real harm done," said Dr. Lee. "Half-dosage it is."

All that was left was to dispose of any incriminating evidence. Jody rewrapped the X7 in its tissue and pocketed it. Dr. Lee motioned her out with him; she'd flush it later.

At lunch, as Millar rambled, it struck Jody that she might take that pill. She changed the subject, barely hearing herself talk. Her hand was in her lab coat pocket, fingers inside the Kleenex, chafing at its embossed X7, its swathe of cloud cover. *Why not? Tonight, when Danny leaves for the club...* Circumnavigating its rim, and gauging her angles of approach, she began to shred the tissue paper, as she imagined the dangerous parting of an old veil of mists.

IV.

Jody shuddered. A shadow had fallen over her. It was her own shadow.

It felt both familiar—just the touch of a memory too faint to place—and very wrong.

We exist, after all, as thought. As memory, regret, intention, a whole flit and caboodle, that races and goes slant, as we lose bits of what was, as we fudge and tinker with *if only*. We barely notice. They fuel the story vehicle that we call a *self*. We drive it.

This shadow, though? It was as if today—Jilly; this lunch; her first X7—was a corner she had already taken. Jody was bracing—not now, somewhere else, yet to come, where she was steering far too wildly—to retake it. She felt, if such a thing were possible, the frisson of a mind echoing backward; remembering *her*.

Strange, but only a shadow. She shuddered but shook off the fear. There was no need, yet, to believe in such things. They weren't real. How could they be? *Here* was *now*.

Preoccupying her now was a past day: "*The* Day," as her

friend Lisa called it. She knew the gist, the sensational headlines. There was a car wreck. Jody, perhaps by design, had caused it. Her brother Andrew's car was hit; her fiancé Brian died. Left in a coma, waking with a wiped memory, she'd been tossed guidebooks—newspaper reports, a will—but sorry, no visa. Except now here she was, working at the wrong place at the wrong time, and her need to risk returning to the site—to force her way in—was back; she could feel the tremors building—the shifting plates of hope and terror. She would be rocked again to her core. Her place of ash and lava.

Pumpkin, said her daddy's voice (or a shadow's voice, or a chorus of such voices, telling her her friends will die unless she, chop chop, stops fooling around and *acts*—unless she steals, lies, and drugs the lot of them) *you don't flirt with danger. Danger's not that kind of relationship. You decide, and you commit. You slam the door on it, or you go in all the way.*

Jody left it ajar: not yet. Since she wasn't crazy yet. Until the sea and sky of the X7 pills breach her, and she's adrift in time, in the Jodyland ether, the voices couldn't harry or hurry her.

Only her own need, here, now, might. And Jilly's.

Yeah, you and Jilly are screwed either way, probably. But we might not be; you could save us, Jody. Lie, steal, go all the way for us. Take your desperate, duplicitous best shot.

V.

She carried a clipping in her purse about the strings trio Lisa booked for her coma room. Three of Brian's musician friends. Jody rarely read it. But sometimes she caressed the picture. Six years ago, brandishing champagne: the party her parents threw them before med school. She was twenty-two, and quite the princess, styled to astound. She had that same scrubbed skin now, those same bright teeth; her face was no older, really, just less open and more knowing. But she had shed the trappings: ugh, those clothes, the signals they sent; that short, chic hair; the aura.

Brian's death had remade her twice, as a damaged spirit, and then as a freer, fiercer one. (How few years it took to become someone else!) Her hair, back to blond now, had gone, in her rebel phase, through too many dye jobs to ever quite regain its gloss or fullness. Her feistiness, too, had sought new textures. She became the couldn't-give-a-fuck bitch, rather than the sweet, tough little rich girl. For a moment, a shiver of pity shook her, for the sweet, tough innocent in this photograph, who had every confidence she could get and keep whatever she wanted.

And Brian. A glance sufficed. A nicely opposite type to Danny. Clean-shaven, trim black hair instead of kinky red. Slim oblong glasses, more fashionable today than then. He was shorter, if stockier, than Danny, lips no higher than her brow when they stood embracing barefoot. By contrast, that first time she met Danny (Lisa introduced them), she had called him "Mountain Man." He'd been kind to her, though, Danny had. And she'd needed that he wasn't Brian.

Nor, of course—the idea was laughable—was Millar (that goober) like Brian. But as long as she didn't start dating him, it was nice how much he *looked* like him.

VI.

"So they're caught between."

Once again, Jody was the one to broach the matter of the X7 trials, and today she had trouble keeping her voice down; Millar found himself worrying about eavesdroppers. Why the volubility he didn't know, but the topic fascinated him; she'd got him peeking at files again.

"The drug is spectacular, there's no question. It works absolutely across the board, it turns out. Most of this memory loss increase is officially undiagnosed, did you know? They claim they can't get a fix. But it doesn't matter what the disorder is, or maybe even if there *is* one."

"Yeah, I read that, about the etiology. The file was evasive about it, actually, I'm not sure why. But what, the drug would spit-polish a *healthy* memory?"

"Well, there's a theory. But it's... capricious? Even at low dosages, there are restorations, but they're temporary. As you keep upping the mgs, they get huge, but they're also less reliable."

"It may not work."

"Oh no, it works. And then you're worrying about dependency, chemical even, though they do seem able to limit chemical dependency, you have to cocktail it. Anyway, you boost the dosage, and well, shazam."

"The Madeleine effect."

"The Madeleine effect, but the hitch is, you can't *trust* it. It *lies*. Not at first. Spectacular memory retrieval, authentic memory. Unpredictable in nature and in scope—from petting some childhood dog to major, months-long sagas. Recent or ancient. Discontinuous, even—"

"Sex with your husband—"

"Right, Mrs. Radowicz, the sex lady who forgot her entire marriage of forty years, and then, boom, not just the last time but a montage of times—and not just the sexual act, the whole now of it, the *circumstances*. Everything she was feeling, and why. The like, total context of the, the *life* the sex came out of—"

"I wish I could have seen her face, I mean, yesterday you said—"

"Oh, my God. *Un*believable. Of course, I didn't know why, yet—what she'd remembered—but unbefriggin*liev*able."

"But I suppose any really personal memory—"

"Oh, sure. No question. It's your way back in. The intimate *self*—"

"God, yeah."

"Her own intimate self she'd gotten back."

"Still, it would be like your personal epic porno movie—"

"Yeah, yeah. And the *life*. Enough with the sex thing. The point is, well, firstly, *Wow*, but secondly, the whole composite could be a massive *lie*. Probably not on a first go-round—"

"The first Madeleine effect—"

"Yeah, and not the small dosages, the polite smacks—"

"They reserve the term for the wallops, then—"

"Yeah, and they subcategorize, into true Madeleines and false—"

"So sometimes, it's a lie?"

"With the wallops, anyway. For one guy, the *second* wallop. The first one was a nice retrieval, confirmed as authentic, his graduation week; the second time, his wife dies in a fire at the river house. It never happened, but he relives it, they have to show him her. 'You *died*,' he says. 'I *saw*.'"

"I guess that's why the recommendation I read—"

"I guess. Recall, huh? Recalibrate? Sure, what choice do they have?"

Millar sighed in agreement and checked his watch. Lunch was almost over. A hyper one! Jody had had so much to say she'd hardly touched her food. She looked thinner lately and paler, the blond wisps across her face less casually modish, more unkempt. He wondered, not wanting to ask, if this meant the trouble at home, with Danny, had reached a crisis point, if she might soon be unattached. He hoped so; yep, this was a hope. Actually, he'd had a hot dream about her. But it wasn't just that. And it was but wasn't *just* the sex talk, flashing him Mrs. Radowicz's fleshy memories as they leaned into their whisperings; the shiver of Jody's scent; the meeting of their breath. The Mrs. Radowicz Millar pictured was young, had Jody's face. He was following her down to a multiple shared dark, where he woke and was lying with her, in an allied life.

"Unfortunately, a recall alone won't do it. They have to understand it to fine-tune it."

"She had to twist his arm, it read like. Corrigan's lab boss? To make the call?"

"Oh, Corrigan's all in. He'll push for more testing. Why not? They've got a great formula to spark the Madeleines, the what my oldest old dear is calling her MGM's. The thing is, how do they preserve that power while keeping the memories from shifting into fictions?"

"Yeah," Millar replied. "But what a ride either way, right?"

"Sure, they'll probably market it both ways once they reconfigure the triggers. X10 to remember; X11 to plunder your subconscious and screen your movies."

"Party time in the R&D cages. I'm Mr. Stoner Lab Rat, buzz me."

He launched into the rat impression that had made her laugh once before. *Squeak squeak!* he went, with scampering paws and big, wild eyes.

She smiled politely. She had other things on her mind.

VII.

That afternoon, Millar snuck a longer peek at Mrs. Radowicz's file. For the sex details, mostly. Disappointingly, there were no sex details. *I am,* Millar thought, *such a goober.* But it's a rough ride, the mid-twenties doldrums. He'd been single too long. Like a snake that don't know where it's slithering, he'd missed some right turns, and he just kept dithering. But he would shape up! A girl would help! And you know, a feeling of purpose... Meanwhile, he read:

The patient avers that she is "mortified" by the rush of memories prompted by her third treatment. While her husband reports that <u>all retrievals seem to be authentic and accurate</u>, Mrs. Radowicz resisted recovery of the core experiences because "there were people in the room." They were re-integrated despite this. She expressed shock that the earlier events were pleasurable—remembering, before the treatment, only one recent, dutiful act of congress, which, with some relish for her husband's discomfiture, she designated as "grim."

Of interest is how, to evade the core retrieval, she <u>focused her attention on its tangential elements.</u> She was thus able to recover a wealth of secondary material with as much assurance and accuracy as she did the ostensibly central event. She knew the circumstances in which each sexual act occurred; she could recall much of what she was thinking. "My mind did tend to wander," she noted—this clearly for the benefit of her husband, to whom her stance is spiteful. Her post-session mortification was certainly genuine. But she was also so vividly rediscovering her own history, including this difficult marital one, that she seemed, and still seems, more a creature of their vanished worlds than of our present time.

In short, we will need to work on <u>reassimilation therapies</u>, but the breadth of today's retrieval was immense. I <u>recommend training other patients in a like technique</u>.

The wizardry of this research dazzled Millar. The flimsiness of the record-keeping galled him. Could the patients' unfiltered statements be on file somewhere else? They weren't in the charts. Surely they mattered? Millar was fond of recording his own memories, and if he chose to tweak and shape, having no responsibility to any public record, he wasn't entirely cavalier about it—there *were* times to document matters more scrupulously! He kept, for example, a folder of "significant conversations"—if not transcribed, recollected as faithfully as he could. For publicly significant, potentially groundbreaking work like this, he would *insist* on transcripts.

And something in the researcher's note struck a chord. He was reminded of an outing with his old flame "Then Girlfriend." When he got home, he fished out his account.

Yes indeed. The sex, but also the deliberately decentered gaze. They were hiking: a mild winter's day in the foothills, some passages of thick snow, but the going more comfortable as they climbed. By mid-afternoon they reached a shelter with a table and wood benches, where they stopped to set down their packs, strip off some clothing, and eat fruit. Millar skimmed his intro to flip to where TGF began to grill him. Why was he dropping out so close to graduation?

> Millar: *It's just... All the hoop-jumping. It's bullshit. What's the point?*
>
> TGF: *See, that's the bullshit. The fact is you don't finish things. You'd rather have the fallback of not trying than risk the finishing.*
>
> Millar: *Psych minor girl!*
>
> TGF: *And rather than confront hard truths—*
>
> Millar: *No, it was cool. A romantic insight.*
>
> TGF: *Don't get snarky, boyo.*
>
> Millar: *I wasn't being—*
>
> TGF: *Millar! You're so dishonest with yourself! Be hostile if you feel hostile. We can fight if you like. But don't act charming when you're pissed off; it's icky.*
>
> Millar: *Snarky's how I fight. Snarky's how most couples fight.*
>
> TGF: *When they're old and desiccated. Let's not be your parents.*
>
> Millar: *My parents? You know nothing about my parents!*

TGF: *Millar! It's all you talk about. Your life story. Your history, you call it.*

Millar: *No, it isn't!*

TGF: *Fine. Everyone's history. You get off on everyone's friggin' life story.*

Millar: *I like a lot of things. Baseball. I like movies.*

TGF: *I guarantee you, though. Eventually, you'll half-forget me, you may even forget my name, I'll be your Then Girlfriend or whatever. But you'll have made your story of me. I'll be something you've picked over to say about yourself.*

Millar: *Because you fascinate me.*

TGF: *Because you don't live in the present. You collect it.*

Millar: *You don't want me to remember you?*

TGF: *Sure, I do. But right now I want you here, I don't want to be a story.*

Millar: *I love stories.*

TGF: *Fine, but wait till they are stories! Let them happen first.*

Millar: *You think if I drop out, I won't give us a real chance either.*

TGF: *Arggh! That's not what I'm saying! If we're talking about what I want, well, it's not some commitment or what have you. I like having stuffy boyfriends and psychoanalyzing them. I'm happy dating a screw-up who's about to dump me. All I'm saying is: "Don't drop out of school—that's dumb."*

Millar: *Doesn't that depend—*

TGF: *It's counterproductive! And the reason you'll do it anyway is you're a memory freak who won't let anything play out because you hate closure. Who would rather haul your past about with you and not move on anywhere.*

Millar: *Okay.*

TGF: *Whereas I am a here-and-now aficionado.*

Millar: *Not a freak?*

TGF: *Fine, I'm weird. But about this, not so much. Me fan; you addict.*

Millar: *Fair enough. So for yuks, explain how I'm doing the here wrong. How I should let us "happen."*

TGF: *For starters, see this place. Be in it.*

Millar: *It's pretty.*

TGF: *No talking! Look! Okay... Now, pan—in very, very leisurely fashion— around to me... Wait, there'll be touching shortly. But first, you be! Here... Slower... If you find yourself drifting— most people daydream forward, or sideways—*

Millar: *But I'm a memory addict—*

TGF: *So you daydream back. So refocus. Reboot. See this space. Tongue the air... You smell that? And listen... No rushing it, Kearney! ... Out; then center... Muster the, the gestalt of it ... Take your time... ... ... Good... ... Better. ... Now move in... Where I am: so check me out... Slowly... Slower... Oh, lasciviously is fine, take your... Oh, yes... Oh, kinky... Nice, keep... slowly... taking the time... we need... So... Ooh! ... ... So... Now I check you out... And I'm reeeally good... at looking, so... ... Oh yeah...*

And a conversation grown rich in the muteness of eyeballing, of gesture and body language, of sniffing ("kinky" et seq.) and light giggling, shifted into its ellipses; so that the subsequent love-making—even to the dampness that rose through the sheet (she'd brought a sheet!) and the ground's roughness, even to the exhilarations of the cold—felt like a part of it, its necessary slow punctuation. Not transcribed, but oh, he remembered.

And she was right. Her way was better.

Let the record state, incidentally, that TGF dumped him, not he her. And he recalled her name, just chose not to use it.

(Her major, Chemistry; her birthday; her then cell number. Her smell, as he closed his eyes to nuzzle. The fact she'd relocated, last August, to Eastdon.) But the being dumped was okay. *(Liar.)* That one February day was their story. *(Sure.)* He'd changed a lot since her, though; because of her, in some pivotal ways.

And in many ways, sure, he was still that memory freak guy. In others, though—how she rarely seemed wholly *with* her boyfriend, the Danny boy; the way (from what she'd let slip) she treated Lisa—that description now sounded less to him like him, Millar, than it did like Jody.

VIII.

The notion Millar was having trouble framing—what her friendship with Lisa encapsulated for him—was that he some-times found Jody self-involved.

If he had put this thought into words, he'd have laughed at himself: *Millar! Who are you to call anyone self-involved?* But although he was an introspective and private person, Millar was considerate of others in a way that Jody wasn't. Professionally, she was warm, kindly, and efficient. They'd both chosen a service profession, after all, being more drawn to issues of social equity than to money, more intellectually and emotionally questing than they were ambitious. (Millar, a clinic flunky, also did some volunteer work in grassroots local politics, and had begun tutoring immigrant kids at a shelter.) But Jody, Millar thought, could be careless of her friends; he thought maybe she used Lisa.

~ I was supposed to go Saturday with Lisa, but I stood her up. Well, I texted her, but she'd already got the tickets. So Danny went. He loved it! I'd expected it to be just *her* thing.

~ Oh, she's fine. I don't worry about Lisa, she worries about me.

~ Danny was gone, so I whined to Lisa and pretty pretty pleased her to come over and paint each other's toenails.

Nothing major, in short, and often there'd be a self-deprecating laugh to accompany such confessions; still, it made Millar (who had no friends close enough for such presumptuousness) squirmy. Without much grasping why he was curious, he made a mental note to ask about Lisa, to get a handle on who Jody was with her; what kind of best friend Jody might be. It wasn't a burning issue, though, and soon there was one that *was* burning, as, within a week, Jody was fired.

They didn't have a choice. The memory drug was being recalled—its formula demanded a recalibration—and a box of top dosage tablets had been raided. Jody had signed off on it as full, locking it up with the sealed 30mg stocks she left on the counter when Mr. Gruber fainted; she'd not realized it was unsealed and had not verified. Perhaps nothing else was provable against her. She was distraught, perhaps the fall guy only, but who else could be held responsible, who else had failed to follow procedures? All employees had now been interviewed, and warned against ingestion of the medicines; had been threatened, if liable, with criminal and civil prosecution. Should new evidence surface... Meanwhile, they were grateful for Jody's contributions to the work of the clinic. She should know (regrettably, one had to say it) that they were watching her. And if any information at all should come her way, it was urgent that she contact them.

Jody went to shake Millar's hand but quickly thought better of it, hugging him; a fierce, distraught embrace. "I'm so sorry," he told her—sorriest he might never see her again. But three months later, she called. She and Danny had broken up, finally, after she was fired. Danny had moved out, and she was doing some trainee work in real estate. For a friend of Danny's father. It had taken a while, but she was back in control of her life.

Millar said, "Let's grab dinner."

They went out three times that week, talking as easily as if they'd never stopped. Some about the X7, how could they not, given the alarming and global news of memory loss flare-ups; given the fear that this was becoming something massive. Given, also, Millar's dutifully restrained curiosity about whether it could possibly, actually, have been Jody who...

But no, of course not. Say rather, his curiosity about how it had felt to be accused.

"So, having any trouble with your memory?" was one of the first gambits he used to fill a conversational pause. And then, "So, taking anything?"

And Jody had laughed, both times, and asked, "Why, are you?"

Then, after that third date, when he came back to her place for the first time, she made him coffee and fed them each the pill. He swallowed his, and as he did so, he knew what he had done; he gaped at her, as he digested everything the knowledge meant. She watched his re-evaluation of her cloud his gaze and clear again. Oh well, his shrug said. She gave him back a barely apologetic smirk, and ate, tonguing the last fallen crumbs from her palm. "Finish it," she chided him, "there's another chunk of the tablet." He obeyed. She nodded. She turned on the stove's hood light and blew out the candles—to be on the safe side, she said.

The safe side? he thought.

The psychedelic wall colors darkened. They sat facing each other across the lacquered scarlet table. They sipped coffee from the sky blue mugs.

"Should be soon," she said.

She toed off her shoes and pushed them away. He kicked off his and undid a second button of his shirt. The lids of his eyes began a slow morse flutter.

She pressed his hands between hers and said, "It's starting."

He nodded. They waited for the Madeleine effect to overwhelm them.

CHAPTER TWO: YEAR FOUR

"Does green mean *Stop* or *Go*?
Is plastic good to eat?
Should I put a hat
On my head or on my feet?"

Dan Bern, "I'm Not From Around Here"

"By the fourth year, we had found ways to cope. Our watchdog groups were well-organized, and we had shored up the essential social structures. Out in more rural areas, small cooperatives, some set up by us, some wholly independent, were establishing functional colonies. There was evidence that the infected, or most of them, were no longer deteriorating. The contagion itself might be abating. But then came that series of climate disasters."

Library of Virginia Commission, *The 5 Year Report*

YEAR FOUR, HEARTWOOD:

Jody, Millar, Edie, Andrew, Elise

I.

When Jody wakes, she has no sense of where she is; nor is she clear on who is this person doing the wondering, or when; or why more possible answers keep coming at her, as if hers is now a multiple-choice life. A slew of vivid data streams, of memories more like sense impressions, all apparently recent and actual, vie for dominance. She struggles to sort them into a rational chronology. She fails: too much of it is contradictory. She feels a mounting panic.

Fortunately, she appears to have prepared her room to welcome her back into its working present tense. She discovers, trusting the reflexes of her sense memory, a light switch, and triggers it. The first thing she illuminates is a whiteboard message, scrawled in her own handwriting. She understands without knowing how that her location, given as *Heartwood*, is not a town but a house. Or an estate? Fixed to the dresser mirror, she spies a signed photograph; she rises to compare the images, and confirms that she is who she believed herself to be. Older than she might have hoped. The whiteboard advises her to visit the records room downstairs and read in detail about herself and her housemates. Her bedmate's name, it adds, is Brian. Or he answers to Millar. She checks the bed's other half: slept in but empty. Perched atop a disconcerting array of sealed cardboard boxes, stacked three deep from the window to the door, is a smaller whiteboard. Wiped clean, but the photograph pinned to its frame is of Brian. Also older. Something off about it. His features bleary with fatigue.

Around these guideposts, Jody begins to reorient herself. It's a more rational process than it should be: she is assessing the land's lay rather than settling into it. And there are too many gaps, and yes, still too much contradictory data, all of a vibrancy that she finds alarming. But she begins to recall why—an outbreak of memory loss. No, no longer unexplained, a contagion; she can't come up with the details. But a pandemic, as it's turned out, though the percentages of the affected defeat her. (Ninety-five percent? She refuses to believe that.) But they've weathered it, her friends and she, by medicating themselves. She remembers with what, and that she's taken this drug longer than any of them, and that once, or at times, she did so recklessly; it comes to her that she's a little messed up. How messed up? Well, many of her memories are false, almost as many of them as are true. It hurts to examine *which* exactly, so she doesn't, yet. It's as if a sign posted in her mind says, "Beyond here be dragons: back off now."

So is this the case for everyone in the house? Why wouldn't it be?

Okay. Why then, she wonders (as she does most days, and does not know she does), do they bother with the drug? Is the only choice between no memory and a fiercely unreliable one?

She supposes that yes, that must be the case.

Sitting in her bathroom, she works to put names and faces to the people she will meet downstairs. The images flicker and riff, presenting more conceivable candidates than there are slots. She hopes Lisa's here. Splashing water on herself, dressing, she sorts the mental file of them, her available information and her instinctive responses, idly selecting a housemate dream team. But she stops. Best not to take such imaginings further; what good can they do?

To refocus on the here, the now, the necessary realities, she parts the blue bedroom drapes and examines her surroundings. A pretty enough morning. Late spring? Early summer? She's in the country: there are fields; trees; barns; an apiary. She recognizes the apiary. One of her jobs involves the apiary. And she and her bees (the welling of her pride is immediate) matter here. It's a working farm, after all—it would have to be—and whatever grows and flowers needs to be pollinated; honey is pleasant to eat and good to barter. Oh, and beeswax. Beeswax candles, she thinks, not sure if it's a word association or if the farm manufactures them. Another word pushes itself to the forefront, in connection with the honey, it must be, and this is *excipient*; for the moment, she can't place it. Almost no short-term memory, she decides. But surely it'll revive as she awakens, she can't possibly relearn everything she needs to know in the course of the day, only to lose it all again overnight.

So what does she remember? What facts can tentpole this world for her and keep her efficiently traversing it? Well, her sense memory seems fine. As do her grasp of language and function: she knows towels are for drying you, shoes are for your feet. A song lyric pops into her head. She suspects she may know a fair store of popular songs. Geography, history, great literature, the current culture? No, not so much. Yes, shards and shreds; then more, as she probes harder. Her physical health seems good. It's only that her head is thronged, bustling, jostling with discrete anthologies of her personal stories—more *present* than memories ought to be—and so urgent that they compete for her attention with what her senses tell her is the actual world, the shared and physical one. What's more, the tales they spin her are in conflict—combatively so, if she doesn't back off—and how is she to know which ones are true, which false?

All slightly annoying, but things could be worse. It occurs to her to check her gut feelings, and yes, she decides she feels fine. Better, in fact, than in most of the memory montages spooling in her head. She suspects that she likes living in this world, and nothing in her gut contradicts this.

She's hungry. It's with more curiosity than anxiety, finally, that she opens the bedroom door and makes her pleasantly familiar way down to the kitchen.

II.

A woman is drinking coffee at the small round table. Petite, brunette, assured. Mid-thirties? She looks up from her yellow pad and smiles.

"Edie," the two of them say simultaneously.

"Morning, Jody," Edie adds.

"You're the one who calls Brian *Millar*."

"I am."

"Why is that?" Jody asks.

"I've known him a long time," says Edie, which really isn't much of an answer. "Coffee?"

Jody pours some and cuts herself some bread. "Where are the others?"

"You're the last. They're at their chores already. Word is there's a storm coming."

The weather has been difficult, Jody remembers. Heat waves and drought, lightning and late blizzards, hurricanes. (And this isn't coffee. Nuttier and grainier, more bitter.) But they cope.

"What do I do first?"

"You go to the records room. Check some message boards, study some logs. Start with your log. Lisa's, Andrew's, Red's— the ones that orient you. But read some snippets about each of us, put our pictures with our names. You usually like to spend time with the State of the World log, but not too much time today, please, we need you to pitch in. Do take a peek, though. Check the front page of the News board and the SNAG board. And the first farm pages, the basics of what we do here to survive."

"Have you been waiting here for me?" Jody interrupts to ask. Because it comes to her that, of course, this is one of Edie's jobs.

"It's one of my jobs, Jody. I get up first, and I check everyone in."

"Why you, is your memory better than ours?"

"Yes, in fact. I have no false memories—I took just nine maddies, my luck held, and I quit while ahead. And for some reason, the virus hit me less hard. I still have good cumulative recall. Nothing pre-pandemic, though. For some reason—I don't probe why—I don't much care."

"But you remember Brian. Millar."

"I got lucky with my trips. One of them was Millar, at college, the time we were together. I got back that whole year of my life. Most of my maddies worked like that." She checks the wall clock. "Please don't ask for details."

"I'm sorry if I have questions."

"We talk a long time some days, which I like, honestly, because, after the first few, you do come up with fresh ones. Keeps me on my toes. You're my morning brain exercises."

"But today?"

"You need to get to the records room, and I need to get to the lab. Here." She hands Jody a to-do list; it looks like the same instructions she just gave verbally. "Take forty minutes. Then ten for your chores list. Then go do your chores. Big storm coming."

"Okay. So you and Brian were together?"

"*Were*, Jody. He's all yours now."

Jody isn't sure this is so. But she finishes her sandwich, swigs her quasi-coffee and tops it up. She loiters at the door.

"So, where *is* Brian?"

Edie rifles through her yellow pad. "With Matt Simmons, in the south storm cellar. Maybe the orchard after that, if you go looking. But we need him back in the logging room by this afternoon."

"He chops the wood?"

In her roil of encodings, Jody finds nothing to make sense of this notion.

"We all chop the wood. But Millar's our record-keeper, Jody."

Jody nods. Of course. The historian.

"And what will you be doing, Edie?"

"Well, for one thing, since you're kind of an addict, you'll be happy to know that supplies are in, and I can get busy compounding you some drugs."

She smiles at Jody. Jody doesn't find the smile particularly warm.

III.

"Hey, Brian?" Matt Simmons calls.

Or that's Brian/slash/Millar's surmise of it. A case of water bottles needed hauling; Matt watched Brian fetch it. Then waited until they were as far apart as possible, without one of them exiting the cellar, to initiate a conversation. His barely raised cry, its thin, breathy huskiness amplified into a cawing wheeze, is less like speech than the distress call of some sea animal.

Okay, that's unkind. But everything about Matt Simmons is just slightly off, from his faintly crossed eyes and spasmodically tufted hair to his speech rhythms, replete with pauses and unexpected emphases that freight everything with meaning. Brian's cumulative recall is decent—he has a grasp of the last twenty or so days—but Matt's tics and quirks are stashed in some fuzzy sock pile of his memory laundry. He *knows* him, their lives have intertwined for years, yet the man's oddities surprise and grate on him. He wonders if this is new, or a daily irritant that he shucks from storage, or if by day's end he is used to Matt again and no longer bothered.

He returns unhurriedly to where there's no need to shout. "Yes, Matt?"

"Should we move your backup crates in?"

"More to trip over. Let's see what space we have after we lay the cots out."

Matt nods. "Won't be much. Could we stack them between as privacy walls?"

Brian laughs. "There aren't *that* many!" The storm cellar is immense. "We're good."

The farmhouse basement is their main records room; its loss would be catastrophic. But it's solidly built, and it hasn't flooded yet. The north storm cellar, once finished, will house the backup records, which for now are in boxes in Brian's bedroom. He has digital storage too, but none of them at the colony is capable of fixing computers, nor of salvaging compromised data; there's a heck of a lot they suck at. Including farming, which is likely to become a problem!

Ten addle-memoried patchworkers can only do so much, even with the help of handbooks and encyclopedias and the unreliable resources of the web.

And while the old social order isn't wholly kablooey, how can it remain viable if folks don't start remembering? About which, prognosticators are divided. As Andrew loves to remind them, whatever the conventional wisdom—that this is a shock to our human systems, not the end of us; the contagion will run its course, contagions do—no cure has yet been rumored; children are still being born infected; and there was a period of breakdown, a year and a half back, that verged on a final collapse. Miraculously, heroically, the national and regional governments—run as they are by the coteries of the immune—did reimpose a degree of peace and order. A wing-and-a-prayer order: there is fuel, but it is rationed; there are stores, but they are downsized, scattered, and almost all government-run; utilities companies and hospitals continue, erratically, to semi-operate; there's PSA television; there are help forums on the radio, although the talk show crowd has moved in on them, competitively unhinged, sputtering windily on. Andrew, the house survivalist, assures them that this respite cannot continue and that they are all doomed.

Even, Edie asks, if they can find their way to his fully armed and supplied secret compound whose location he's forgotten? At which Andrew does not laugh. Brian suspects there might be such a place. Well, the reality that they possibly *are* doomed is not that funny.

But the raging and smashing, at least—the outbreaks of mass insensate mayhem—the Rampages, people called them, or Hellfest, or even, not ridiculously, the Zombie Apocalypse—those seem to have ended. This plague is by its nature inimical to sustained aggression. Most of the survivors they've seen are too like them: patched up precariously on maddie home-brew; struggling to remember who and what they are.

The true danger, Brian feels, is not from despotism or anarchy: nowadays, only the cooperative approaches work. It's that the patching will fail. However crucial the large systems—the regional, the national, even the global—it's at the local level that the world must be mended. Here, at touching distance: with a dozen people you know, and partly remember, and somewhat trust... Building yourselves back up, from the ground up, if you'll only be given the time to do so. If your hobbled group can remain in balance. If you're savvy enough to suffice.

"Is this storm warning reliable?" asks Brian.

"Radar hasn't quit working. Access is open."

"You've looked?"

"Yep. It's big. Could miss us, but the size it is, I doubt it."

"So it's a hurricane right now? Category 3 or something?"

"Bigger, but when it reaches us, if it takes the easterly track, a cat three sounds about right. We're a hundred miles inland; I'm told that helps? A genuine tropical storm, they said it is now. Maybe a four or five?"

So Matt is clueless: Situation Normal, Addled Guesswork. Brian pushes for anything else he has. "We've gotten through a bunch of bad shit. Why will this be worse, you think?"

"I don't think anything. I can't tell a hurricane from a tornado without a scorecard. I was a building contractor, for shit's sake. All I'm saying is what I read on the scroll. Big winds. Major flooding. Violent lightning. Hail. Bad like the apocalypse, they made it sound. The last storm made an impression. I say we prepare for anything."

Brian calms his impatience. That storm (the logs say) was an April blizzard, not this improbable hybrid. (And they *did* agree to quit using that overblown word *apocalypse*.) But hey, he's no luminary either. It's the new imperative: be blunderers together. They have a Wind Events fact sheet. For the protection of buildings, equipment, animals—when the storm's not some weird hundred-year outlier. But it was written for more competent, more experienced farmers. What's worse, there's no certainty that it's sound advice. The maddies turn some people into crusaders for batshit ignorance, so that passionate blowhards have overwhelmed the wikis. So you trust your instincts, and you hope. You prepare as best you can for the worst.

"But we have all day, right?"

"And on into the night. Work till it's at our doorstep; that's my vote."

41

They wiggle the water barrel into place. They look around. This is the men's locker room. The women's locker room is set off by a tunnel, which doglegs out to a second door. Except for mopping, and the towels, the laundry baskets and such, they're done in here, and the women's room *is* done. Men's room prettifying can wait; the men won't tell.

It was intended as a joke, Edie said at breakfast, calling them the men's and women's lockers. Fancy-pantsless latrines, she thought they'd be—but genuine locker rooms are what they have become. Rather than a storm cellar, this is an underground network. It was already here, in miniature, when Matt Simmons brought them to the farm, but he's worked on it every day since, as if what gives his life meaning is to keep McCellaring. He's been amazing. Brian knows all about it because he keeps the daily logs and reads them, and because the essence of it is in the first paragraph of Matt's profile, right after the Meet Me bio: "Matt is convinced we need two fully finished storm cellars. He works every day to realize his vision."

"Fine," says Brian. "Let's see to it that we leave room for everyone's self-centering kit. It's likely to feel very wrong in here. We don't want to wake up too disoriented."

"Sure. But we need the place cozy, so they get their butts down here; no balking? None of that, *Oh, I'll stay in the house* crap. Or some of us might not wake at all."

Once again, Brian is disconcerted. Can a hurricane just take the house, like a tornado? He seems to remember, now, that Matt Simmons can be a terrible alarmist. (Which is the kind of assessment you don't document: the profiles are chiefly for their subjects. Time for a second set? Warnings about each other?) But what if this time Matt's right? If they lose the farmhouse—even if they themselves come through— and the barns are intact, and everything they can pack into the basement and the storm cellars is cataloged and preserved—

how could the colony withstand the loss of the house? And then what might become of them?

"Course, if the house and barns go, it'll mean starting over anyway." Matt laughs at the prospect, a wheezy, cawing cackle. *Just try me.* "Two or three of us might make it through that transition."

As functioning selves, Matt means. Abruptly, Brian recalls a vacuous face, two teetering bodies—it's their expedition to the lodge at the Cricket Club after the riots, to pick up Jody and Andrew and the rest, and the truck is weaving through a gas-tranked horde of zoms, vague-eyed and shambling, clutching and slumped—he feels the bile rising again in his throat, he is clawing his way out, anywhere but here—damn the maddies, that force him to reinhabit such days. Although they also offer, bless them, the blazon of their exit doors, true scene or false...

His memory skips and shifts. It's a crisp Sunday morning of wooded islands and white river rocks, fall leaves and blue sky. He is hopping boulder to boulder with Then Girlfriend, with her laugh so much like Edie's...

Matt's hands cup Brian's face. It's the grounding gesture they all use to bring each other back. He chucks Brian's chin and lifts Brian's gaze toward his own.

"You all right? You with me?"

Brian nods and grasps Matt's arm. Even late-stage amnesiacs, in fact, even the shufflers and slumpers who have lost their last anchors to the world can be brought back. (The *cattle*, short for cataleptics. The *zoms*, short for zombies. Bad jokes seem witty longer when your memory is feeble.) With luck, maddies, and a support system, it's possible to remake even the mindless, although not into their original self. But finding the support team—a colony like this one, a smartish group of willing people, still strong and barely sane enough to buoy you up with them, in this sea of the drowned and drowning—that's the long shot. The ten of them here got lucky.

And with luck comes responsibility. You owe it to the less lucky to stay lucky. If there are enough strong and sane selves in it, civilization, too, will figure out a way to survive the crisis. So you latch on to your raft, and you don't drown. You don't let Jody, or Edie, or any of these half-selves you've pledged your allegiance to, drown either. You weather the damn storm.

The storm cellar's main room, thirty feet by thirty-five, was an astonishment when he got here this morning; it's evidently been a while since he's seen it. Ceiling lights, wall lights, floor lights. A working sink, a refrigerator, a stove. Furniture, stocked bookshelves, and enough canned and steel-barreled goods stacked on pallets to see them through a month of refuge. Decorative knick-knacks. Schlocky paintings. A spindly plant. Six bunk beds and four still crated cots. Brian surveys the busy disorder of it. Well, he's helped bring in most of what needed bringing. Matt can handle the rest from here. Andrew and Jemmy will come and help once they're done. Or Big Nick, or whoever—they can't all be swamped.

"Matt," he says. "I'm sorry, I've got to get to the logging room. If we lose the house, we'll need some first response notes. And if we make it, we'll need some dodged-a-bullet notes. For the next climate horror."

Matt sighs and nods. "Oh, sure. I couldn't agree more."

He jerks a thumb toward the door as if all he's been waiting for, ever, is for someone to take this crisis as seriously as he does.

Yep, decides Brian. *A big old alarmist. We'll be fine.*

IV.

Edie is in her lab, adding yesterday's new jars to her store of powders and pills, chemicals and creams. Supplies, it turns out, are *not* all in. She's missing no key ingredients, just lowish on two, with no idea how they'll eventually replenish them— the critical stuff is barely to be had. But this is going to be an experimental recipe. No telling with those. Well, they'll get their fix, at least, for a while yet, the addicts she lives with. She won't guarantee it will agree with them.

Jody is the only one making no effort to wean herself. Supposedly, Andrew, Lisa, Matt, Nick are down to three pills a month; the others claim they're already clean, that their two tablet stash is for emergencies. Edie knows better. They indulge plenty. Their memory seems worse, and they panic, or a withdrawal migraine nails them to their bed. Take this month: Jemmy, who had been doing so well, spiked all the way to eight.

"I'm unexpectedly out," they'll confide. "Top me up, please?"

(Later today, Edie will blush to remember this thought. *Eight? And I took that at face value? No doubts about his lack of physical distress—how he just asked and signed?*)

She shouldn't judge. She's luckier than them. Her house-mates are recurrently skeptical that she remembers back six months; in fact, though—apart from some very patchy weeks before and after the fire, when she lost Kitty—it's close to two years. Since the day, in fact, of her second to last maddie—so she's counting on no further deterioration. But they don't get it, do they: if they don't detox *now*, one day, maybe soon, they will have to go cold turkey. What if Edie walks out on them? Or they get separated? Or their supplies run out, and she can't restock?

Down the hall, she hears the barking of the dogs. Since with everyone but Lisa and Reds, who rescued them this winter, they remain quite wild, Edie guesses Lisa or Reds is out there too.

"No. Stay," she hears, and the dogs go quiet. Good. Edie

can't have them in the lab.

Then Lisa and Andrew are at her door. They have Jenna Brower propped between them, half walking, half dragging her. Her skin is an even pastier white than usual. (Chocolate Lisa, vanilla Jenna, coffee Andrew: good old, who-else-remembers-them ice cream sandwiches!) They set her down on a bench. Andrew brands Edie's forehead with a brisk, lord of the manor kiss.

"Bye, loves," he trills, patriarchally. "I've got Elise up a ladder, wrassling plywood."

Edie swipes the man's mark from her brow.

"You okay, Jenna? What happened?"

"Panic attack," Lisa answers. "We were debating—okay, I was laying it down and she was *losing* it—whether to leave the horses out or bolt them in the barn."

"To keep them safe!" Jenna protests.

"Untethered and running free is safer, sweetie," says Edie.

"But there's a storm coming! A big one, Matt says!"

"Well, I need to safeguard the feed supply. When you're ready to do as I say, plus leave me the heck alone so I can get our work done, you come assist, okay?"

Edie reminds herself, yet again, not to put Jenna and Lisa on the same team. Lisa has a hot button, and Jenna pushes it. For some reason, Edie forgets this until it happens again, a weird little blind spot in her amazing memory—which is disconcerting. What other blind spots might afflict her, and who in this blind world might help her see them?

"Anyway," Lisa continues, quieting as quickly as she flared up, "she got to wailing and rolling into a ball. So I fetched Andrew."

"She's okay, though?"

Lisa is their doctor as well as their veterinarian. Like Jody (much good it does Jody), she trained as a nurse. But it has always seemed to Edie, who admits that she doesn't know Lisa well (Edie's alliances with very few of her housemates rise to the intimate), that she cares more about her animals than her people. Certainly more than she does about Jenna Brower, whom she clearly wishes to foist off on Edie, *now*.

"She's fine. Might need a valium or four. Got?"

Actually, no one except Edie ever has much patience with Jenna. Edie likes her. Edie's the only housemate who even calls her Jenna. They do housework together and cook; they talk.

"You good if I leave you with Edie, Mrs. Brower?"

"It's fine," says Edie. "Get back to the beasts. Incidentally, what happened at the barter market? I don't have all my supplies."

"Oh, we cut the trip short. Some cooperative trying to help the helpless brought in zoms, they were overrunning the place. Well, overshuffling the place."

"Mmh. We could use a zom. Just one is probably all we could manage. Might get a real farmer, or *train* one to be."

"Well, Mrs. B. was spooked. She had your list, though. I thought she got everything."

Lisa waves goodbye. Jenna puts her finger to her lips, *Sshh!* They hear the happy yelping of Lisa's dogs; the hall goes quiet. Jenna Brower pulls out a bag of what looks like animal treats.

"I got these instead," she whispers. "For Eggy."

Jody's old cat and Jenna Brower have adopted each other. Eggy is creakier nowadays, but he can catch a critter when it suits him, and Jenna cooks for him; he doesn't starve. Jenna loves to find ways to spoil Eggy. Eggy worships her.

"Oho!" exclaims Edie. "You rascal, Jenna!"

Jenna gives her a rascally chuckle. She seems better already, no pharmaceuticals needed.

"You don't mind? Lisa got something for her dogs."

"I'm sure she did."

"Lumped it in with the animal feed, but I noticed."

"No worries, sweetie. Go get your knitting. Bring Eggy—Eggy's no trouble. Put your feet up and keep me company."

"Chores, dear heart. There's a storm coming."

"I'm the chore scheduler, remember? Keep me company."

"Work, work." She smirks, smirks. "I could finish the tam. I'm knitting Brian a hat. Millar. He placed an order."

"Perfect."

"Listen. I'm sorry about the horses. It wasn't the horses. I... I lose myself."

"No worries, Jenna."

"It's how she looks at me. Our Dr. Lisa? That look she gets like she wants me gone. Like she's *hoping* for when I become too big a burden. Which is karma, isn't it? I should have—"

She's going to lament the abandonment of her parrot again, her African grey. Edie waits to console her, wishing she didn't always know what her friends were about to say. Weary of being the one who remembers the stories they repeat. But Jenna surprises her.

"I miss me. I miss feeling competent. And the dependability of the world, if that makes sense. I should have... New Year's, at the lodge... Made my stand. Oh, I'm grateful to y'all for not letting me die, whoever I was. It's this... it gets to you. This feeling that I've... lived long enough. Well. I expect you miss things too."

And she goes to collect her knitting.

Edie begins, startling herself, to cry.

What would I miss? she thinks. *I'm a here-and-now aficionado.*

And since this is the truth she swears by, she refocuses. She blows her nose, she wipes her eyes. She gives a moan and she shakes it off, like a dog throwing off water. And she is great.

V.

Andrew Barker is not Jenna Brower. Up on the house roof, he is feeling—as usual— nicely competent. All the windows are now boarded. He keeps a log; he knows when he last checked these shingles. In a moment, he and Elise will recheck them. Anything loose they will nail down. There have been other storms; they've planned for storms. One sunlit week in September, Andrew and Matt screwed hanger bolts into the window framings and readied the plywood. The first hurricane they hung it for missed. After it passed, they put Elise up their ladder and trained her in the drill: a task that requires two emergency personnel to perform needs three who know how.

It's Elise's first time as wingman, but she has practiced and observed. She knows when to ask for help. For example, there's some plywood starting to warp. Some nuts and washers are rusting and not tightening well. Andrew checks behind her, knowing that she's less strong and less experienced, so that sometimes she believes a nut that resists a little to be tight enough. She has done well today, though; she is, after all, his kid.

So now a moment of repose. She claims her place beside him, and they look out together on the green world beyond Heartwood. From his backpack, he retrieves his binoculars and her telescope, ruffling her hair as she takes it, which she affects to dislike. An obligatory grimace and squirm. He laughs and ruffles it again. She wiggles to the roof's edge and sits dangling her legs over the drop. He grins: his ballsy daughter.

Legs swinging, Elise focuses her telescope on whatever moves. Birds, she's been reading up on birds, but the skies today are quiet, only crows and cardinals. Some scattered housemates below: Big Nick, up to God knows what among the vegetables; Jemmy, idly hither-thithering between the chicken run and the north storm cellar; aunt Jody, intently skittering, as if following a scent of bees. And forests, fields, and foothills, the far mountains. (The town, what passes for one, is behind them, blocked by the swell of the gambrel.) Her father says little, and she answers less, munching on her spring carrots. If there's a storm brewing, there's not yet any sign of it.

Andrew is looking for other dangers. Smoke, fires, people. They'll come, eventually. He takes, he assures himself, no pleasure in the knowledge. But none of this can hold.

His daughter's telescope has found three deer drinking at a lake. She slips into the trees upwind of them, steps out, lets fly her heart's fierce arrow.

I'm coming, she promises the path into the woods. None of this can hold.

CHAPTER THREE: YEAR ONE

"I love the passing of time."

David Byrne, The Talking Heads, "Naïve Melody (This Must Be The Place)"
(music: David Byrne, Chris Frantz, Jerry Harrison, Tina Weymouth)

"At the time, the clinic's security breaches were a scandal. The consequences would surely be appalling. Yet whatever the dangers they did in fact bring, where, ultimately, would we have been without those security breaches?"

Library of Virginia Commission, *The 5 Year Report*

YEAR ONE, EASTDON:

Millar, Jody, Edie, Jemmy, Jilly, Mrs. Radowicz, Dr. Lee

I.

What could a memory addict remember, prompted by an X7, which he hadn't already sifted, sorted and resorted, recollected and collected?

Unlike Jody, Millar suffered from no crucial gap in his remembering. There were no people or events that he ached to see more clearly, nor was he ill at ease with how time worked to muddle the view. He liked the little arrangements he and his memory had come to. He knew full well that what Then Girlfriend had said was accurate: that he reshaped his days even as he lived them, into a stock of stories, into the narrative of how he wished to remember them. So why risk the careful anthology of his past, its phrasings and stylings and manipulations, to the fiddly light of what claimed to be *fact* or *truth*?

So his Madeleine effect came, and he surrendered to it warily. But surrender he did: he was a lover of his history, and gradually he let the fresh experience of it seduce him. He was a sulky seventeen. His father's voice was saying, "Yes, it's hard, but there's nothing that can be done. The company's downsizing. The one way to keep my job and put bread on our table is to go where they send me." The scene was enough as Millar had pegged it to reassure him—but then this was a standard conversation; six times they had recited its lines, in four different states; and at six years old, and nine, and ten, at thirteen, at fifteen and at seventeen, it had hurt neither more nor less. If he had loved the first home longest, where he was born and lived the longest—and which he'd carried in his memory the longest—he loved each subsequent place as dearly. He was good at locating the parts to claim and at sculpting memorials from their quarried stone. Loving a place meant readying it for his museum: how to angle it, in what postures. And quickly. Because he'd quickly be gone from there. He had learned not to submit to the loss, that's all. He got his memory maquettes ready. He packed them up and brought them away with him.

Under the drug's influence (Millar was relieved to see), his version of *this* story wasn't, at its core, cast into question. But because its physical particulars were now as vivid as his heart-held abstract, he could look around, as TGF had taught him, and assess the tinkering he had committed. Over the years, he saw, he'd fully transposed it, setting it in a stretch of parkland his memory had made totemic—the one where he and his friend Pete used to go to fish. (He and his dad went there also; not often, but often enough to validate the transposition.) But in reality, they were in quite another park, a smaller one, where painters' studios budded in clusters on the hills, and a public gallery and arts cafe rose out of the valley, among a grove of shade trees.

Millar stopped listening to his father; stopped feeling his own wrench of grief. Instead, he studied the groupings of the picnic tables, and how the sun made its shadow paintings of the trees and bent in and out the dapple of the leaves. The factual setting was as lovely as the one he'd deleted it in favor of, but the factual setting *meant* nothing to him; he'd seen the signs for the artists' colony often, but other than this day, he'd never come here.

His mother was present also. He had forgotten that. Sometimes she was, and sometimes she wasn't, and when she came, she rarely spoke. Her deletion from his memory of this day struck him as instructive. As his teenage gaze passed over her, he found himself able to slow and pause the film reel for a moment and frame a snapshot; to see the tightness in her lips, and to understand, at last, what she would not say, but wished to. Not only that Millar was being lied to (he knew that: his father was being transferred, again, because he was a trouble-maker, and retained because he was a brilliant one) but that his mother was tired of it; and exactly how tired.

At seventeen, still leaning on her for steadiness, Millar may not have allowed himself to know the extent of her discouragement. She'd hung on until his senior year of college, then stayed where she lay when her husband took off again, so that all three of them at once, as if in choreographed disseverment, spun separate and free. Millar had visited each of them once or twice a year since their divorce, but their two lives, the dances of their feelings for the other—which he knew his presence set again in motion—were simply unimaginable to him.

Ultimately, he found this whole drug trip (although why Jody had felt the need to impose it on him, he had no idea) surprisingly involving and rewarding. He knew its story well, having worked to tell it to himself the way he judged most satisfying. But there were always other lines of narrative, revelatory in their own way, to be mined; he'd never doubted that. As he sat in this parkland with his parents, together again at last, outdoors in Jody's candlelit kitchen, he found himself, for once, putting aside his own well-burnished version of the tale for theirs. For the course of a sunlit night, he reimagined their unimaginable lives.

II.

Evidently, Millar had gone under before Jody had. When he came out of the trip, the first thing that caught his eye was her quilt-curled shape through the kitchen's open door, sacked out on the futon in her den. She was twisting, crying out in little gasps: clearly, she was still wherever the X7 had taken her.

The side of Millar's face hurt—it had smooshed against the kitchen table and his arm, mashing the latter numb. His ass and the base of his spine felt painfully out of alignment.

Whereas Jody—look at her!—had gone and gotten herself as cozy as you please.

And in any case, the *nerve* of her!

So was he sufficiently vexed, on the whole, to up and leave, right now?

He thought about it. *Ouch, yes!* he decided. *Beige, yes!*

Yes, but don't worry, he wasn't going to.

Yes, but he was also curious what all this was about.

And perhaps a bit concerned for her; her futon looked unfairly comfortable, but Jody certainly didn't. He shambled over to her side and studied her. She was having a bad trip; serve her right.

Five minutes later, though, when he came back from the bathroom, he felt less grumpy, and Jody looked more relaxed. Or at least less restive. He trusted—another brief surge of irritation—that she was not now simply peacefully asleep.

He pulled up a chair to watch her. Gosh, the mess of hair, the just pursed lips, the cat-purr little snore, but was she ever a cute little bedbug.

She opened her eyes. Millar said, "So. How was it for you?"

III.

Not only did Millar and Jody compile their lists of top ten, non-violent, historic Eastdon sites, they wrote out their separate accounts of them and had them bound into a booklet. How differently they'd approached the task! Millar's were more formal, arranged by reverse chronology, with an eye for the forward lunges of a larger history; Jody made idiosyncratic leaps, in clumps of preference, until she climaxed at her favorite. He removed himself from most reports, or kept his presence discreet; hers were chattier and seasoned with personal anecdotes. Jody hadn't expected him to take a slant so academic. It was lively enough writing, but why? Millar couldn't tell her. Later, he decided it was because he still lived here. The first task was to document the facts; afterwards, in the poetry of his remembrances, he would sing them into his private Eastdon, in notes by distance made more sweet.

Three places had made both their lists. They began their reading with one.

Here's some of what Millar wrote:

#5. *The Lawn Tennis & Cricket Club, 1910*

Like every history buff, I stand in awe of what makes it through the centuries fully preserved, but what I love more is the history of vestiges. The park now known as the Eastdon Lawn Tennis and Cricket Club is a preserve of vestiges—like the jumble in the attic, it's a memorial to the everyday nothing much—to three hundred and fifty years of our grown-like-a-weed America. Yet it's also a wellspring of tangled mysteries, in a setting to tease the dark imaginings. Those unconsecrated graves; those vine-snarled woodlands; their high crowns quick with whispers...

It is thought that what stood here first was a tavern, conceived as a plantation but begun too small and too close to the town, which slopped sideways after the 1667 floods. We know that in 1726 the main building, the ordinary, was burned to the ground by the Pamunkey, and its ninepins green "desecrated." (No video, more's the pity.) But the terrain was reclaimed, and when the Gover-

nor, in 1752, needed a hideaway for his wife's demented mother, he acquired the property, which is why for a hundred years it was known as the Mad Mother-In-Law House. It's with her that the place became an enclave. Stone walls rose to separate the house from the grounds: bulwarks that endure, buttressed and patched, although the house itself is gone. The Confederate Army set up a field hospital within them to erect tents and charnel huts.

The modern name dates from 1910, the year of the Club's founding by a maverick freemason—and it's here that the more Gothic mysteries begin. Because, sure, tennis and golf resorts were coming into vogue, but cricket? In the début-de-siècle South—in Eastdon, Virginia? Who did they think they were kidding? And why behind such ramparts? Such high, high hedges?

Still, over that way was the clubhouse; back here, the tennis courts; out yonder, a round field ringed by woods, with at its center a standard twenty-two yards long cricket pitch. And there you can see them all still, if you look. Or at least the vestiges of them.

The best guess is that, at first, the Tennis and Cricket Club was exactly, crazily what it claimed to be—until, with scant interest to sustain such use, it evolved into a site for other kinds of games. By the mid-1920s, women, no one's wives, were rumored to be admitted in groups and to remain at the common leisure. There was some notion the Beale treasure was buried there, or that the Club was a headquarters for the search for it. There was talk of cults.

Whatever its business, the Club failed to survive the Depression. A single family, the Wolkers, took the place over: a father and bastard son, prominent among the old membership and very protective of Club secrets. They became the estate's second and third mad hermits. Their only well-publicized venture was to archive and seal the club records. For two hundred years.

In 1992, a decade after the bastard son's death, the property was offered to the city.

The city doesn't seem to know what to make of it. No signs say it's a park or a historical site; it's barely visited. Should you plan a tour, you may pass by its main lodge,

*boarded up and of no architectural interest; you can pluck
dandelions from its tennis courts; you might apply to buzz
the acres of undergrowth for relics of the Civil War. But
do make sure you take the path that zigzags through the
trees. The one that ends in a wildflower meadow, and a
cricket-pitch-shaped strip of cropped grass, meticulously
rectangular, thirty yards by fifteen—ringed round by
whispering, thick woodlands, that hover in perfect sym-
metry at the meadow's frontier...*

Jody wrote:

*My father was a wonderful man. He died during my first
semester of med school, which I let strangers assume was
why I dropped out. It wasn't. His death was devastating,
but I'd braced for it. Oh, I'd been coached in how to deal.
"Big waves, pumpkin," he used to tell me. "The good ones*
live *to ride them. You brave them, they pummel you, and
you learn. You wade back in for more."*

*As I got older, I began to wonder what catastrophes
had brought him to this philosophy, but clearly, he'd made
it work for him. He was an entrepreneur, constantly
launching businesses. When they thrived he'd start another, or if they didn't thrive, the next one would, or the
next one, double or nothing till he was riding high again.
Until the cancer, a rare and vicious kind, dug in to kill
him, I never questioned his invincibility, or my place atop
the rollercoaster. My parents loved each other, they loved
me, and all my life, we were either rich or confident we
were about to be. But then came that long sickness, the
false remissions, his body and his energy wasting.*

*I went pre-med when he was diagnosed. Rescue
fantasy. By the time I got into med school, we both knew
he would die. The week before I enrolled, my parents
threw us a party. Dad was amazing. He put on a show
and rode that wave...*

*It was his last hurrah. Not that he made a huge deal
of it, there was no farewell speech, no "Big waves,
pumpkin, make me proud!" But of course, that's how I took
it. He passed three months later; I missed a week of school.*

But I was ahead with what I could be. I judged the trip home nicely: in time to watch him die. Stayed busy with my coursework, got mom to push back the funeral and memorial service, zipped off to nail my semester exams. Did daddy proud. Then, when I was good and ready? Goodbye, daddy, God bless, and rock on.

But whoever is really gone? Glimpses remind us and unlock histories. And in Eastdon, at the Cricket Park, a grief opens in me, and out wades my father.

I'm a New England girl, but Dad grew up in Australia. It's where he learned to surf. He came back to the States for college. His grandparents' idea, I guess. He gave up surfing, but for years he maintained a membership in a Sunday cricket league, gathering to him the flotsam from the old British Empire: at my parents' parties, there they would be, the Aussies and the Kiwis, the South Africans and the Brits, the Indians and the West Indians.

So no surprise that my first year in town, on the anniversary of Dad's death—for ceremony's sake—I went to check out the Eastdon Cricket Park. Man, though, that place is eerie. A bit because of the age it has on it. There are a few Colonial residua that still cast shadows, and there are heavier Civil War ones: it was a field hospital; death must have been rampant. But the real spookiness feels recent. It feels rooted in the decay of the club—in what their freemasonry became a cover for. (Fight clubs, war games, knife-hunt tourneys? The black arts, prostitution, the Lost Cause white supremacies?) Whatever secrets those men swore to, and clung to, even as their den of iniquity withered into an old coot shrine. It's the very not knowing, finally, that unnerves us. This is the city's wilderness, its gallbladder of darkness.

Then there's the cricket pitch itself. You could cut through the woods—they're not impenetrable—just gnarled, shadow-haunted, and eerily devoid of wildlife. But the path is clear and emphatic, and it's forged of crooked turnings: not a maze, a geometric figure. The thickest, oldest trees mark the figure's corners, so that as you turn where they steer you, your view is blocked. Then you round one last bend, and ta-dah, you're at the meadow. The central strip is cracked and brown now—

*adays, but it's kept rolled flat. And you're staring at two
headstones, set face to face, twenty-two yards apart.
Exactly where the cricket stumps would be, if it were still
a cricket pitch. Instead of what it has become.*

*The artful ruin of one. A dual stance, or a duelists'
stance, of graves.*

*Just as I arrived at the first headstone to check the
inscription and discover there was none, a bird cried out.
I don't know birds, I don't know what kind it was, but it
wasn't sweet or melodic, and I can't say it felt familiar.
When I reached the other headstone—no name or date
there either—another bird answered, from somewhere
else in the woods, the same call.*

*I was the only person in the park that day. My return
visits have been free of drama, yet I still feel the shiver of
that first haunted emptiness, that sad call and response.
I've gone back once a year. Every year I say to him, Well,
so, goodbye, Dad. And I think: Well, maybe it's enough
now, maybe the old ghost's laid?*

But so far, each next year, it hasn't been.

They sat in a cafe one Friday after work—something they
hadn't done before or since, but this was an occasion—to
exchange and sample their dossiers. Scanning Millar's list,
Jody noted what topics they'd both picked, and he said, "Let's
compare!"

After reading his Cricket Club one, Jody said, "I'm surprised, it's well done, but I thought you'd be more personal."

After reading hers, Millar said, "Hey, we both have father
issues."

"Oh, you've no idea!" said Jody.

Millar was interested. Jody clearly had some kind of secret
history—she could be quite evasive—and perhaps he was about
to learn something of it. He raised his eyebrows and waited. A
polite invitation to elaborate if she so wished.

She didn't, but nor did her flurry of ugly memories much
fluster her. This was back when the X7 trials had been

announced but hadn't yet begun. She was doing okay, at last! It was more out of habit than need that she shifted the subject. "The lodge only *looks* boarded up, actually. The caretakers *want* you to pass it by. It's my favorite park in town now. I began to visit so often, researching and writing this piece, that I made friends with them. You never met them? Harlan and Sarah Oldchurch. Her especially I like. She's quite spiky! But Millar, really, what a dream job! Nothing much in the way of duties, except to occupy a nice quiet back corner of the lodge, them and their goofy parrot. They have five big, empty, really rather striking rooms, did you know? It could be a downtown B&B goldmine. But it's all for them."

IV.

In Jilly's last new X7 memory, she was Jody. It was the day she got her braces off.

Even as she raised her hand at the start of English class, though, to say, *Hey, Ms. Bilyard, look!*, and flash her fresh dazzle of a smile, she knew she wasn't Jody. At about 8mgs a shot, the movie magic had lost its oomph. Such bells and bright whistles; but a part of her held back its faith. And for her panic's sake, they had extended the lower dosage by two weeks.

Well, she had been cautious long enough. It was nice being Jody; it would have been pleasant to believe the memory. And if the other memory came instead—the little dead son, floating face down in the dusky blue water of her neighbor's swimming pool—maybe this time her feet would unfreeze and carry her to him, and she'd kneel and reel him in, her arms wet with the dead, wet weight of him, to hold him, weeping, until the ambulance and firemen came. She would ask for no larger falsehood—no miracle of revival; no lock on the gate; no cat to deflect the dog who had nosed it open—nothing that in its desperate need would seem a desecration; only to be in her actions who she was in her heart—to be the one who stretched her arms out. At least she *knew*, now, why she'd failed to go to him: loving too much, not too little; and she could almost, if not quite, forgive herself. Reliving it had taught her she could live through it again.

Which told her it was time.

Which meant that tomorrow she'd go back to requesting her full 20mgs.

But tomorrow never came. They discontinued testing. Thank you, Jilly; we'll check back in six weeks. Contact us if you have anything to report, though. Don't, ha ha, forget us.

But she did forget them, of course.

Not by the six weeks check-up; it took ten months. And she never lost a single memory, true or false (she no longer knew the difference) which she had recovered under the influence of the drug; and because of it, she retained many of the big tentpole facts about who she was, how she had lived. Otherwise, though, Jilly's memory took her back two or three weeks, a blurry, always shifting horizon. Still—compared to those with the virus who had never had access to the treatments? The husks, the howlers, the mutants? She was queen of the country of the blind.

In Mrs. Radowicz's last new memories, she was eating salmon. She rarely ate fish—she had tried salmon exactly a dozen times in her life—and now she was granted the recollection of every single one of those repasts, tidily sequential, fish by fish. No other of their subjects, said the doctors, had reported the "list" experiences that were her trademark. Other patients had had collage recoveries, but they were more haphazardly connected, less of a catalog than her own.

Now she heard her sister—her sister!—saying with a false smile that salmon was "delicious, and to my mind less fishy than most fish—I think you'll like it, Joanna!" Or rather, Susan couldn't be bothered to prepare her a separate entree. The invitation to a dinner with her hoity-toity friends was all the charity Susan could muster; she certainly must know she had served her salmon before. As she took her first bite, Joanna Radowicz caught sight of her own face in the dining room mirror. It wore a grimace. And immediately she could feel her visage changing, becoming younger, its grimace morphing into a twelve-year-old's sour *blech*. Frantically, she concentrated on the dimmed mirror: who was beside her, was there someone she could salvage the memory of before the time change took? But there was no one, only her sister's lover's wife, a woman she had never known well. Still, until a few moments ago, she had had no adult memory of her sister (no friend to her, perhaps, but kin), so not a bad haul. Six moues and scowls of salmon so far, beginning with one from her second day at the research facility, which she hadn't even forgotten. And even *it* had retrieved for her a little bit of her history: the memory that, good sport that she was, she had politely tried salmon an even dozen times. So six more contortions of disgust, each with its whole rich story, still to come.

Fish memories, perhaps, because hadn't she remarked once how she saw this wonderful drug as a kind of fisherman's net, the way they dropped it in her darkling sea, and up came this wriggling teem of silver? And she was just halfway through her month, with eight doses to go!

But then the trials were suspended. Dr. Lee, reading through Mrs. Radowicz's florid last report, wondered if a single item on its list of memories were genuine. He knew, for example, and checked to be certain, that she had no sister, only the two brothers. And he remembered quite well what she'd said when selecting the salmon lunch—her *first* day, it was, her admission meal: "What *food* here! Oh, she loved salmon, one of her favorites!"

Oh, he had said, he was from the Pacific Northwest, yes, he'd fished for salmon, in the Deschutes River, with his father, big chinook!

He sighed. It would be his responsibility to dismantle her false memories. A tough but manageable task, if undertaken immediately—a matter of three or four sessions; but always unpleasant. This drug, though, had so much power. It only remained, somehow, to *harness* it...

If one day they succeed in doing so, Dr. Lee will never know: he has monitored his lab rats without once entering their maze. By the time, much later, that he does essay the X8, it will be in the vain hope of it reteaching him his name. There are people in his life who love him, who will fuss over him for a while and risk any remedy, until they too forget their names.

V.

At that time, Edie had just moved to Eastdon, although she wasn't yet aware she had.

She'd come to sleep on her sister's couch and think. Or not think. To get up, drink coffee, lounge. To walk to a nearby park and not think, the leg bone connecting to the foot bone, the foot bone connecting to the patio, the patio contiguous to the crabgrass, that collected in spirals about the plum tree, which fluttered its new greens. And touched its limbs to a picket gate, which maybe she would open. To pass through, and veer left down the alley, across one street then another, till the trees of the park broke into their greens around her, their smatter of white buds.

A new marriage had at once gone wrong, and Edie had lost herself. Which was what she thought about, mostly, and strove to rinse from her, from both heart and head, to let melt into the sod. Till the grass yielded to a gravel lot, that connected in a shift of grit to the soles of her shoes, to the roll of her instep, ball to the arch, left then right, as the weight of her foot compressed and released, as the rhythms of her breath compressed, released. Her kid sister was an older soul than Edie—so present and unruffled. Edie had acquired the things, the doctorate, the marriage; her sister seemed cheerfully indifferent to things. In the evenings, when she got home from work and they hung out—mostly the two of them, sometimes the three, on the nights when Tiff's sweet, gawky semi-ex-girlfriend Kitty visited—Edie wanted to talk and not talk; she wanted to efface herself and listen. Their stories, Tiff's and Kitty's, scrubbed away at her and made her clean.

She passed through a mixed grove into a broadening sky. On the right, grey granite steps descended between green ranks of trees; which fluttered; and had budded; into white, pink, pink, white smatters.

They couldn't say if they were on a break or done: the jury was out, said her sister. But Kitty brought by her peace offerings (a nice meal, usually; these were the rare days that they ate well, since neither of the Driscoll sisters much bestirred themselves to cook), and Edie could see her sister softening. Her sister, or Tiff and Kitty together, told her the stories of their two lives, wry, ridiculous, and raunchy, until Edie began to laugh and to turn into herself again.

And down the grey steps to a lake, to take its circuit. Where the cattails connected to the red-winged blackbirds; who disconnected, releasing tra-la into the sky—their cry of air to air.

The park, Forest Ridge it was called, wasn't much peopled, but she began to recognize a few of the faces: dog walkers, joggers, mountain-bikers on their rough, dangerous trails through the woods. One day, coming through a coppice of redbuds, she came upon a curious mound of granite blocks, twice her height, in the shape of a pyramid, overgrown with vines. She was pausing to try to make sense of it—it looked for all the world like a cairn—when she heard a halloo. It was Kitty, over among the trees with a distinguished-looking older man, who turned out to be Kitty's father. They were weeding and planting. He was a Friend of the Park or something. "Look," he said, and broke off a single magenta redbud blossom and showed her it.

"Oh," she exclaimed appreciatively. It was the exact shape of a hummingbird.

"Edie's just moved here," Kitty told him.

"Welcome to the neighborhood," Kitty's father said, "you'll like it."

She smiled. It was Easter Sunday afternoon. She said, "I already do."

VI.

There was the evening that Jody took her first dose of the memory drug, which was the same day Jilly Simmons tried to switch it for an ibuprofen; and there was the evening two weeks later, after a brace of chattering lunch dates with Millar, during which he told her the company was about to discontinue the X7 and reformulate: when she took the second.

If Millar, finding her busy and frazzled, could have found a way to ask Jody what exactly was going on with her, she might have answered, fiercely meaning it, "Nothing." For her it was a time of sheer nervous abeyance. There was a decision to be made, and she was resolved to not yet make it. Was she on the verge of a crisis, or an abnegation, or a breakthrough? Ought she to plunge herself into deep shit and drown, or let her dumb, desperate hopes and hungers twitch and peter out? She had, admittedly, made one wholly ridiculous commitment, in the matter of Jilly Simmons and her concealments, the slivers of pills they had colluded to hide; but really, Jody's forbearance during those two weeks was terrific. She gave herself wholly to her work (wanting the distraction); skipped or gobbled lunch (fighting off the temptation to drop hints to Millar); made Danny's home life insufferable with her heightened irritability; and studiously tuned out the self-whisperings. If she were to think, it would be about the X7. About acquiring it, and about taking it. For two weeks, she strove to shut her mind to it.

Except that she worked with it. Not, thank God, all the time, but too closely. And Jilly Simmons—God, how difficult she made things! Because Jilly, needing to feel more in control of her experience, had perfected the art of taking just less of the drug than was prescribed—and Jody, how could she get out of it now, had made herself her accomplice. For three days, Jody hadn't even realized what Jilly was doing. Which was, as she popped the pill into her mouth, to bite it; detaching a neatly intact sliver, the size of a fingernail's rim, along the fault-line of its trademark's indentation; removing it with the withdrawal of her hand; and concealing it in a tissue she kept folded by her lamp. The third day, Jody caught her in the act. The first two chips were still in the tissue. Jody glared at Jilly, summoned her willpower, and flushed them.

But on every subsequent day—which amounted to five, since the test patients got their pills on alternate days—Jilly used the blade edge of a spoon, and Jody pocketed the jetsam.

By the time Millar told her they were discontinuing the tests (immediately, in fact: the very next day, they sent those patients home and warehoused their supplies, at which point Jody became one of the people responsible for the storage), she had amassed five crescent slivers. A tad more, she estimated, than one standard 20mg dose.

And working in the lab late that night, she imagined how, when she got home, she'd lock the bathroom door behind her, run her bath, and light the window-ledge candle. Swallow all five at once, and do the time-travel mash.

VII.

Two weeks before, on the evening of Jody's first self-medication, Danny had taken forever to get out of the house. It was a transitional time for them. Was it a bad patch? Or should they write off the relationship and move on? They each had days when belief, hope, or stubbornness outweighed their lassitude, and one or both of them would make a real effort to reconnect. This was one of Danny's days, which was terrible timing. Jody could think of little but the chalk-white pill: when would he *leave*, so she could try it? It became impossible to quiet the voice of her impatience—its sharpness, stropped by her interior whispers, became physical; she could feel her words punch the air out of him, see his spirits sag.

"I don't suppose you want to come with me tonight? Say hi to the band?"

This was the bar band they had met two years ago as friends of. The drummer was Lisa's cousin Nick, the bass player was Danny's brother Jemmy. They had recruited Danny to sing back-up and strum. There had been some always terrifying, always exhilarating weekends when she sang back-up alongside him.

"They paying you yet, Danny?"

"Jode, you know they're not."

"Well, then."

"You know they don't make enough to pay me in anything but bar tab."

"Well, *that* makes it worth it."

"*Tonight* it might," he muttered. He normally didn't drink much. He was loud and a terrible driver when he did. She relented a little; guiltily, worried.

"Please be careful, sweetie. I don't want you..."

"Yeah, I know. Sometimes I don't want you either."

"Ha ha."

"Think I'm kidding, huh?"

"Sorry if I've been a bit of a bitch tonight, Danny. It isn't, you know, you."

"Yeah, yeah... So, last chance, coming or not?"

"Just go have your fun, will you."

He nodded, gave a little wave, and left. Twenty minutes later, Jody was in the bathtub, stoned as she'd never been stoned. Lucidly, calmly stoned, sitting in a second-grade classroom, three feet tall. She knew all about her adult self, she remembered that she was in a bathroom, but physically, *actually*, those things were shucked: instead, there was this smallness of her bones, the smell and scrape of chalk, the classmates she hadn't thought about in decades. Today was story day; she adored story day! First, Mrs. Coelho read to them, and then they wrote. Some girls needed to be rowdy before they could begin—Windy and Dara and Meredith, jostling at Mrs. Coelho's desk, all talking at once about their animals—but Jody didn't mind, when she was creating, mommy said, she was as deaf to you as that dog there on the TV. Today she was writing about the brown bunny from the story and drawing him, his round white tail, his hoppy paws, his pink pointy ears. She held the page to the window's light and admired it. When she got home, she'd show it to Mommy, and Mommy would fix it with a magnet to the refrigerator, and when he came home, Daddy would see it, and he'd like it and give Jody her hug.

Little Jody scrunched her brow and thought about her father. Which was hard because Daddy was Daddy; no thinking needed. Let the world come at you, peaches, he said, and ride the waves. But big Jody had climbed small as she could inside her, was forcing her younger self to swivel her child's eyes: *Come on, sweetie, look!* Big Jody could barely breathe inside that space, all elbows, shoulders, knees, but somehow she squeezed the words out in a wheeze and a gasp into the other's ear: *Come on, sweetie, show me the Daddy you see, I'll do the thinking for us, who he is...* But it was too hard, he was lovely Daddy; only some days he got home late, after her bedtime; and Mommy was lovely Mommy, who was there always.

Soon, Big Jody stopped fighting and relaxed into the innocence of her tiny blithe self, of the girl holding the crayons. Drawing with bent concentration the green grass of the meadow, its wavy waving waves... Then a house on a hill in the distance; a face in the upstairs window looking out, its crown of princess hair, yellow as the sun above... She found the brown crayon and a pink one to color his arms and face in, and she placed Daddy in the meadow, kneeling near the bunny, holding something out to him, two bright, thick curls of grass...

When Jody's twenty-eight-year-old self came to, that picture and two more like it done, the bathwater had grown cool, and she was sunk in it so low she rose sputtering for breath, splashing the bathmat with her body's run-off. She climbed out and stood for a while, disoriented.

I pushed, she thought.

Had her girl-self put her father in those three pictures, or had adult Jody required her to? She shut her eyes and looked hard at them. Whatever the truth of it may once have been, it was now revisited; an official version had been scanned and burned to back up.

Why did I push? she thought. *Why couldn't I just watch?*

Oh well. Next time (*hell yes, next time*), she would do better.

VIII.

Jody was confident her second retrieval was also genuine. The drug-memory overwrote the blurry original, but there *was* an original memory, she could feel it clarify and brighten. In any case, for a few years, she had kept a skimpy journal, and she checked it; everything fit.

She was in the car with Lisa, driving back to Eastdon from her mother's house. It was before her second year of nursing school, so almost two years after dad died; twenty-one months post-Brian. Mom had sold the house and left the town Jody had grown up in, although she didn't move far, barely forty miles south. Just far enough, Jody guessed, to start fresh but not feel rootless. Lisa was from the same hometown as Jody. They hadn't met till college, in another state, but now Lisa was her only reason to go back. The only soul she still wanted to know from there, and Lisa's far end of town the only part of it she could linger in without feeling faint.

So they had spent a last summer week at Lisa's house and packed up her college stuff, and then a weekend at Jody's mom's and packed up Jody's, four days of which Jody had relived, and now it was pre-dawn on the interstate—light traffic, no moon, not long after a longish burst of rain—and they were trying to make it back in one day, taking turns at the wheel.

It was a simple, pleasant memory, as the first one had been. Too uneventful to expressly choose, but the intensity of its last movement, as it turned out, thrilled her. For this was now a true MGM in all its technicolor rapture! What is there usually to see on a pre-dawn car ride along the interstate? If it had been real-time, she'd have said, "Not much." In Madeleine time, with its vivid, immersive heightening, the car's interior became a cunningly lit movie-set, every angle of vision as if a camera were fixing it. One window—on Jody's side; Lisa was driving—lay halfway open, and the wind on her face was just a little sticky, just a little sharp, reinvigorating. What was the music?—with the window's noise, Lisa had it too soft—oh! it was "This Must Be The Place," the Talking Heads. She loved that song. "Sing into my mouth..."

To her delight, she found she'd turned it up to sing along: in the car she was singing it; and here in Eastdon she could feel herself, inside her head, with a whisper of her breath also, sing with it again—for a moment she was lying in the bathtub in her candlelit dark as well as in the car; and then in another moment, she was singing along with it a third time, in a second place that she was remembering—with her *other* memory, her then-memory, as she rode in the car—singing it in a frat house bedroom, Brian's bedroom... As Brian sang off-key with her...

She jarred out of herself as if scalded. She could still hear Lisa saying something about their two mothers, about how Jody took hers way too much for granted, and then, "Hey, jeez, Jody, are you all right?"

And then she was crashing out of the tub in a hiss of water and damped candle flames; finding the bedroom and the bed and collapsing on it, water draining off under her onto the violet bedspread; as Egghead their cat, hers and Danny's, who'd been dozing and waiting for her, ran from her squalling; and because the drug was still working on her, she was also in a car and saying, "No, I'm fine," through a blinding headache that came at her from years later.

She lost track of how long she foundered there, in both places. Except that it seemed interminable. What she remained aware of was the noise and the blur of a persistent overlay, persistent in spite of her best efforts not to be in either place, neither in the car on the interstate with Lisa, nor on her bed in Eastdon without Danny. "Danny!" she heard her voice moan from very far away as if *she* were Danny, thick with sleep, and someone from very far away was rousing her:

"Danny, help me, please, Danny, come *home*, fuck you, come home and hold me..."

But eventually she blanked out, as her automatic functions kept processing; suffering and calling out for help; because when she came to, Danny was there and holding her, saying, "Shhh... Hush, baby... Shhh..."

IX.

"So your *theory* is that the X series has rewired their perception of time? How exactly?"

"It's not *my* theory, Danny," says Joyce. "It's broadly held."

For a moment, Jemmy doesn't know when he is. Well, this is clearly the club, in the backroom after a show, but that's his girlfriend, Joyce, and that's his brother, Danny, and when Joyce and Jemmy were together, which was for a few weeks, tops, he had never even heard of the X series drugs. But it seems Joyce and Danny might have.

"Because in some trips," Joyce is saying. "The subject will re-experience a whole year of her life in less than an hour."

Danny says, "Yeah, but aren't dreams like that?"

"With that kind of detail? Verifiable, meticulous, and sensory? And an entire year of it! The X7, X8 trips aren't stories, they don't just *show* or *tell*."

"They're the real-time re-experience."

"Or the hyper-experience is the coinage now. They *brand* the experience *into* you."

"What the fuck's an X7?" Jemmy asks Nick and Lisa. Yet he *knows*, of course!

But the cousins are sharing a family story. They shrug, and laugh, and turn back to it.

"You don't know what an X7 is?" says the new girl. Sita, yeah?

"Others, for the same fifty minutes, can lock the user in a one-minute span."

"Which sounds like torture."

"But is more like this big mystical enlightenment deal, apparently."

"This isn't real," says Jemmy. "Has someone slipped me a maddie?"

"According to what Millar posted a couple of weeks ago on their wiki—"

"Who the fuck is Millar? How do *you* know Millar?" says Jemmy.

Joyce, confusingly, hears and laughs. "Do *you* know Millar, or don't you yet, Jemmy?"

"It's not X series, Jemmy," says Sita. "You're in an induced dream state."

"What? Why?"

"When are you, buddy?" asks his brother.

"At the club. The night Jody took her second maddie."

What? How can he (he *is* Jemmy, right?) know when Jody took her second maddie?

"See?" says Joyce. "His brain's been rewired. Give him the right stimulus, and—"

So they're *experimenting* on him? Right now, Danny should be protesting. He should be saying, "So to you, Joyce, my brother is just some kind of rat in a maze, then?"

But he doesn't. Ergo, that's not Danny. It can't be. None of this is legit.

"Well, then," Danny says. "It's time I head home so Jody can sob on my shoulder."

As he rises from the table, he passes right through Nick and Lisa. They notice nothing!

"Sorry about that, Jemmy," say Joyce and Sita in unison, like they're the same person. They strap him gently down.

He re-enters the story, observing it. From the wings still, at a slant where it stars Jody and Millar. The narration picks up its pace, tell not show, till he's caught back up.

X.

They broke up. Jody told Danny her version of why she'd been fired, and because she was lying, Danny didn't believe her. And because if she admitted the truth, he'd do something about the drugs, Jody wouldn't budge. And because she wouldn't budge, they fought. But it wasn't because they fought that they broke up; it was because they stopped fighting. Tired of it, he slipped from her grasp, and she from his, depleted in both their anger and their tenderness.

Because there was more residue of tenderness than anger, they didn't know, as Danny drove off, if he was really gone. He had lingered at the door, saying he was scared for her, pledging his help. She *had* money, Danny, it was her house, she didn't need his help. Goodbye. He wasn't talking about money, and she knew it. Thank you, Danny, but she was fine. Just go. The worst thing, he said, would be to shut yourself away here. Promise me you won't do that. Look, I'm fine, it's fine, fuck off now. Maybe Lisa... Oh, fuck Lisa! So what *are* you going to do, Jody? You *are* going to find a job? Oh, I don't know, Danny, quit worrying about me! Jesus.

But Danny did worry. So he had his father call in a favor. And rang Jody to tell her, and kept ringing, until she picked up and he could ask again if she was all right. There was this friend of his dad's—Jody had met him, in fact—he really liked Jody. She'd be so good at real estate—and having something new to learn would be great for her, didn't she think? Before she knew it, she'd be able to start over, start fresh.

Since, in fact, Jody was as scared for herself as Danny was, she heard everything he said, or almost everything. (She stayed off the drugs, but didn't turn them in or dump them. She didn't go pick up the stashed ones.) She called Lisa, and reassured her, and they talked; Lisa had the grace to act as if she believed her. So Jody acted as if she believed herself: she *was* fine, things would *be* fine. She applied for the real estate traineeship and got it. She called to thank Danny; they went out to dinner, and broke up more nicely, although if anything even more sadly.

She tackled the dull puzzle of her job. She came home to her cat, to let him minister to her. She fetched the pills from her scrunchie drawer and counted them; she planned what to do better, more sensibly, once it felt safe to try again. She readied herself to ride the next high wave.

XI.

So why hasn't Millar contacted Jody in the interval between her firing and her phone call to him? Has the dude even thought about her? Danny has, and what's more, he's been figuring out a way to help. Should Jody be turning back to Danny rather than to Millar? Or can she go it alone, or get what she needs from Lisa, or perhaps her cat?

Jody honestly doesn't know, and Millar honestly can't decide what to make of the Jody thing. He misses her at work quite a lot, and fantasizes about her in bed, quite a lot. What *was* the X7 story, though, exactly, and did she even *like* him? Anyway, right now—temporarily—he isn't much geared for action. How long has it been since Millar had a girlfriend? Well, those three quickie relationships about two years ago. Two months, two weeks, five weeks. A few dates since, but just one followed by a second. He's twenty-eight, damn it, he's getting too old for the bar scene and what have you, and his friends' girlfriends seem to have run out of friends to set him up with. He's not a hermit loser, he has his peeps. There are card games, there are dinner parties, movies. He plays rec league tennis, and the season's started, he's been working to get in shape. There *is* this one girl, she reminds him of Jody, volunteering with him at the shelter, he likes her; isn't sure, actually, if she's involved. Though she's not as pretty or as interesting as Jody. Nor as off-kilter, he supposes. But honestly, is Jody that off-kilter? People don't always get her.

Damn it, he thinks, I'm an idiot, I should call Jody. But before he does—no, really, he was about to—she calls him.

So why does Jody telephone Millar? Well, why not, after all? She misses him; the new job doesn't interest her the way the old one did, and Millar's a part of that, especially all that dorky local history stuff they were getting into—jeez, that was fun.

But mostly, it has to do with pills.

Her third trip was her best so far. It was wonderful, it was perfect, except that she didn't revisit the scene she had been hoping to revisit, the one that she so needed to revisit. Still, just as well, perhaps; when that memory came, she had to be ready to meet it. So far, she hadn't done too great with the readiness part.

In her third trip, she remembered how to do two things she'd been really good at as a girl, that she had mastered, and since let her tongue and her hands fall wholly out of practice with. She remembered how to speak Italian and how to play the cello.

No candles this time; no bathwater. She fed Eggy and climbed into her nightgown. She put on a selection of Chopin nocturnes—not too loud, only to get the mood right—the player carefully under the bed, where if she jumped up, she wouldn't step on it. She took the pill and carried the water glass back to the kitchen. She rolled down the top layer of bedspread, the violet one, leaving only the pink one and a single cream sheet, so there wouldn't be too much to fight against should she start to panic. She got in, turned off the light, and waited. Everything calm and safe and soothing. Eggy sauntered back and settled near her feet—cautiously off to the side, though, Danny's old side. She closed her eyes to let what came come over her.

She was in Italy. The third of her three summers at the music camp; three days, a thought informed her, before she would be leaving. *Always intending*, a more adult thought intruded and admonished, *to return*. Neither her cello playing nor her Italian would ever seem as easy as this again—and they were easy!—perhaps only for this single day of grace, but right now, right here, her mastery of them felt like accorded gifts, as forever as a godmother's in a fairytale. Why on earth had she abandoned the cello? Had she declared herself sufficiently good at it; had her interest in non-pubescent music flagged? Either way, she regretted it; and though her Italian didn't match her musicianship, it too had grown impressive, considering how her schoolbook French was such a struggle— it had become not a construct but a language. But by college, it had grown ragged again, and then there were scheduling conflicts, so she persevered instead with French, of which she acquired a stubborn dominance. More studied, less free a grasp than this, though! The boy with her was Marco, he was Italian and her good friend, they were talking animatedly and practicing a single subtle flourish, first trying it one way and then another, for this evening's duet at the concert. His hands smelled of strawberries, she could still taste them in her mouth, the strawberries and the hands with which he'd lifted strawberries to her mouth...

Which was only some of the remembering, but what was truly glorious was that when it ended, she felt, as sweet as strawberries, *come le fragole*, the *Italian* in her mouth, and spoke it to herself as she hadn't known how in years—her voice cracking into a squeak or three from lack of practice, but only at first. And her cello, too, was in a closet. She tuned it without strain and she played—and if the bow had some issues and her fingers hurt, such difficulties could be remedied, if only the sense memory would linger; and amazingly, it did, it did!

And so now she played her cello every morning, and it was wonderful.

But then there came the fourth trip; and the fifth.

Till now, Jody had been unlike the test group patients in that she took the drug with far less regularity and frequency. She had observed an interval of two weeks, then another of four. She wanted it that way, because her results had proved interesting, her three retrievals had all been authentic, and she could say she was demonstrating clinical control.

But then she grew impatient. Honestly, a two-week wait was excessive. The clinic schedule was alternating *days*. So how could a ten-day interval, for example, be called reckless?

In the event, it became nine.

And if, this time, she skimped a little on her preparations— for it had been a spur of the moment decision—she was still relatively careful. She'd used the bathroom, checked to see if the stove was off, avoided the candles and pulled off her jeans. Sat on the futon with a quilt across her knees, in case she went too quickly into trance and spilled her coffee. Which in the event she did, although fortunately there was hardly any left in the cup, and the comforter absorbed it.

The problem was more what happened afterwards. When she woke out of the trip (and in her trip she was in a coma and could make no sense of anything, could barely feel her presence in her body, only a nightmare flicker of how what happened, happened, and the faint struggle of a self toward an impossibly high surface, through an almost maroon darkness, writhing like water—or what she construed as water when she woke) she carried every bit of that with her, the way she had brought the Italian and the memory of the cello and of strawberries up from the third trip. And since what she brought this time was the double wish to die and to fight back to full awareness, she must, she thought, have stumbled to the kitchen, and found the pills, and ingested a fifth one, to help her: to achieve either outcome, to achieve both. Thank God, just *one* pill.

And then she had plunged back into the untime of the coma, which she woke from eighteen hours later. In a scared sprawl on the den floor, a little chug of vomit on her tossed-off jeans. No memory of anything at all for a few moments. Barely a half-life of the cello or the Italian would come back ever. Although gradually the rest of her did, together with not much new: only the consciousness of a word; the name she had been calling. *Brian! Brian!* Who was her fiancé and whose arms she wanted about her; who looked a lot like Millar.

XII.

That morning, Danny ran into Lisa in the supermarket. Jody wasn't all they had in common, but today she was who they talked about. Though things seemed better this last month or so. But no, neither of them had seen Jody since Friday at the club. Still, she seemed better recently, didn't the other think? They did, they did! And how about you, Danny? Oh, Danny was fine, Danny was hunky dunky dory, you know? Well, Lisa was glad. Well, anyway... See you around? You bet, see you around, babe.

That day, Mrs. Radowicz and Mrs. Simmons were at the clinic. There were follow-up evaluations. "Tell us," asked the doctors, "who you are, and what you remember."

Dr. Lee (fifty-seven, avuncular, third-generation Chinese American, four adult children, terrible dress sense, department head) observed to Dr. Corrigan (thirty-four, whip-smart, un-principled, vain, meticulously shaggy and half-shaven, clinic/research lab liaison) that the true memory retention was encouraging. Dr. Corrigan agreed but remarked that con-versely, some of the false memory had proved less easy to eradicate than one might have hoped. All subjects were still losing memory—although nothing that the X7 had retrieved for them, which was interesting. Disturbingly, most of their people, both the control group and those receiving the X7, were now presenting as anomalous. Across the clinical test age range, even. Equally disturbing were the lab's commissioned reports, had Dr. Lee read them yet, on the exponential increases in memory loss in Eastern Europe. A new strain, if EEML was indeed viral? Happily, there were differences between EEML and what they were seeing in Eastdon!

Dr. Corrigan scratched his stubble, Dr. Lee raked his fingers through his thinning hair.

Mrs. Simmons asked where was Jody, and although she was not told the truth, appeared to the nurse to suspect that something was being left unsaid. For her part, Jilly almost mentioned how Jody had given her something for safekeeping, a package she thought Jody would probably want back... But she knew, vaguely, that Jody wouldn't want her to tell.

Mrs. Radowicz came in with her husband. Dr. Lee caught them holding hands. She hoped they were serving salmon that day (the post-medication therapies had turned her back into a fan of salmon); their salmon was almost as good as Mrs. Radowicz's sister's.

That night, Millar woke in Jody's kitchen from a drug jaunt. "Jody, Jody, Jody," he said—his Cary Grant impersonation. He sat by her futon and waited for her to wake.

And that night, Jody, Jody was finally in the delirium trance she had pursued, revisiting the day Brian died. But it was a fever dream of it—not the reality; even in her hypersensual *now* she knew this, because mostly he had Brian's face, but sometimes it was Millar's face. The rest, though, so vivid, surely *some* of it was real? They were at the Cricket Pitch, she and her brother Andrew, and Brian. So Brian had visited her in Eastdon! Andrew said to his buddy, *Keep the gun on them,* and handed it to him, and went and pissed against the headstone of their father's grave. The buddy—Ben—was laughing; Brian launched himself and had the gun; he had it trained on her brother Andrew and would have shot him—but *Brian, no!* Jody said and barreled into him, spinning off to knock her head against the headstone, which Andrew's piss had made a stream down like a crack. And as she blacked out, she heard the gunfire and knew Brian was dead and that she'd killed him.

She woke, and Brian, no, it was Millar, was watching over her.

"So," he said. "How was it for you?"

CHAPTER FOUR: YEAR FOUR

"If the bee disappeared off the face of the earth, man would have only four years left to live."

Attributed to Alfred Einstein

"We are an adaptable species. We had better be. Because the ways of our doom keep coming at us, and almost never do we take them seriously enough, soon enough. 'Oh,' we say, 'it won't be that bad. And if it is, we improvise pretty well.' Which is true for a while. We break out our dodgeball moves, and we make a good game of it."

Joyce Banerjee, Library of Virginia Commission, foreword to *The 5 Year Report*

YEAR FOUR, HEARTWOOD:

Millar, Jody, Nick, Jemmy, Andrew, Lisa, Elise, Edie, Matt

I.

Brian is at his station in the logging room. It's a converted rec room at the top of the basement stairs, big enough for each of them to have a cubby, with side tables and armchairs to bring their breakfast to and read about themselves and the world they live in. Brian's space is the largest. Here, he roughs out a record of everyone's day, based on schedules, eyewitness reports, first-person interviews. Those he can't catch in the lunchroom he seeks out. They report back before or after supper: confirming, effacing, refining; filling in the evocative detail. Some changes will be large, others will give color. The goal is to reflect and to inform. Brian will make his adjustments, they'll check his copy, they'll make their own polish. When it works, they use a community wiki, meaning anyone can contribute to, or monitor, anyone else's log. (God knows, Brian sighs, how they'll manage when and if the computers die. The printers even.) But it's holy writ that each individual has his or her own last word.

It's a delicate balance: say enough to be useful; keep it crisp enough to be useful. But what you choose not to report will eventually be forgotten. This has always been the world's way, but not the self's way, or never so rapidly. Before, you, whoever you believed yourself to be, could keep secrets. You could harbor an inner life. Now, you record it or you lose it. Mostly. If you're not too far gone, the maddies can give you back days, whole years, big, scattershot collages. You can and will hold on to a few bonus glimpses, rich silvery shoals and flashes; the drug boosts your capacity to. To a never predictable degree, you can even will *which* bonus glimpses, if you don't mind the lies and the wishes-so that ride your little truths like remoras. Possibly you won't mind. Don't most of us lie to ourselves routinely anyway, to create a nobler, more coherent self, a more interesting, more right self?

But it's a matter of practical intention and what serves it. Is your choice sustainable? As you read your logs, one day when you're lost again, is it yourself you need to find or some fudge of you: some lush or pallid shadow? The question isn't rhetorical! Nowadays, if your community assists you, as the Heartwood tribe is doing for more than one of its number, you may tinker with your identity, or even craft a brand new one. *That* measure is quite desperate, but it may be called for. Of course, all distortions, whether intentional or careless, have their risks and their cost. Jody's example has been salutary. It isn't at all that she has no useful memory; it's that her memory has grown so wild, indiscriminate, and overstuffed that she can't trust it. And yes, he, Brian—or Millar—has committed his own falsifications. But only, he hopes, in a strictly limited fashion: precisely to remind himself that he is not who he was, and that he'll never again be that guy. He wishes he could be; but let this diminished version, this tougher and more purposeful him, soldiering on through the valiant succinct accountings, the essential fussy convolutions, be renamed as the man whose place he has taken; let him be Brian.

Today, he has begun by logging what he promised Matt Simmons he would. He has proposed action should the colony survive the current crisis: to ensure, moving on from here, the integrity of its identity. He has proposed action should it not: to make possible its members' survival during the first days after the rending of their social fabric; to ensure, on a micro-level, the exact same things.

It's meticulous, exhausting, necessary work. The kind that is almost all he does with his life now. But all of them in this house have their similar tasks, their similar mission, their crucial part in the exhausting and necessary machine. These tasks, this mission, are who they have become, are what they have of self; to what else in this reconstituted world might they lay claim?

Only to this cog self; and to some degree—cog and cog and cog of it together, while they conjoin to maintain its motion— to their mysterious, greater, more rickety whole; this whoever they take for each other.

II.

Jody is at her apiary. How could she not be? She took a maddie once while with her bees, the way she used to in the bad old days (oh, she remembers)—to steer herself into a vision of them. This was months back, one day when she'd forgotten how to care for them, as she had been doing, for who knows how long. Weeks and weeks. For some reason, the notes she'd been given didn't make sense that day. For some reason, her sense memories of what to do failed. And she needed a maddie anyway. (Well, perhaps that was the reason.) So she took one, and she willed herself to relive a good day with the bees.

It worked, splendidly and improperly. It achieved, she would claim, what she hoped. Finding that trip inside her still, fresh and vivid, she can recognize, with the double seeing the maddies trade on, that the vision she experienced was as impossible as it was utterly real. Of the bees coating her like nerve ends. At first, naturally, simply, on the mesh surface of her suit, but already she was arms outspread to welcome them in; and patiently, meticulously, they fingered it apart, and sieved through the holes onto her clothes; they pried open her work shirt, and fumbled in droves through the gaps, coating her skin. Once they had encrusted her—though more and more next ones came, pushing through the writhe—they began to taste her, as if suckling, and then to seep into her, oozing their store of honey. There was no sensation of being stung—for she was their honeycomb and their queen. It was natural and simple; it was splendid and it was meet.

All very foolish, no doubt, but since then, she loves her bees. They are hers and she is theirs. So once she has read her records room profile, and the memories have begun to pool into more coherent shapes, the realization of what may happen to them, her bees, when the storm hits, quickens her with fear. She fails to spend forty minutes with the logs; she spends fifteen. She hurries out to the apiary, which is on her chores list anyway, to move the hives into the shelter of the north walls and re-anchor them, to shift them closer together and ratchet them down. She finds the boxes deserted. For a moment, only a moment but a long one, she is dismayed and afraid. Then she understands: the bees know about the storm. They have swarmed off in search of shelter. Which means, if at such distance they already feel it, that this may be the big one. Which means she needs to find them. Where they are, for one thing, there'll be safety.

Yes, but what if, having tested their options, they return here, home, trusting her to have made it safe? First, she must secure the base. Box by box, she repositions the hives, all twenty-five of them. Then she locks them down. Her body knows how to do this. It takes a while. It feels wonderful to do well what she knows how to do. She sets down the bee smoker where she'll look for it, although she rarely needs the bee smoker. She rakes the site; she's stalling now. Reaching the limit of her muscle memory's competence, her bees still nowhere in view, she begins to drift. A favorite memory beckons. She savors the taste in her mouth of tipsily exact Italian. *"Di vino e divino,"* her friends would say. *Jody speaks beautifully when she drinks.*

When she returns to the present moment, a half-hour has passed that feels like hours. Her throat is dry and scratchy. She has a faint need to pee. And the bees, where are her bees? She lumbers after their scent for a while—or it feels like a scent—zigzagging in their wake. But somewhere, right about here, they uncluster and fly severally, and she loses them.

Two boys whose names escape her are tending the vegetable garden. In the records room, she neglected to look at the boards or the housemate logs; now she searches the film library of her memories, and a jumble of reels falls off the shelves at her. They're *in* there, in there a *lot* even, but the *how* and *who* clatter by her. The very tall Black guy has spotted her; he waves; she waves back. He may have seen the swarm, but she can't untangle the threads of him, how can she ask? She flusters away toward the fishpond. She sags down on the grass slope to regroup.

To find the bees she has to think. Or feel. She needs a maddie, and she's out of maddies. How does she know that? She saw the pill case in her bathroom cabinet this morning, and it was empty. She was remembering Lisa, a drive down I95—singing, with the windows open—as she shook it and unscrewed it, just to be sure. None left; a now-time's twinge of disappointment. But in then-time she was turning up the Talking Heads, to sing with, and it passed.

She wonders if Brian is out of maddies. She bets not. She feels the frisson, rarer these days, of a presentiment whisper. *Hello, future me,* she tells it. *So I'll still be alive, then?*

She'll go look for the bees, but first, she needs a fix. She heads back to their room.

III.

By late afternoon, even Nick, the tall Black guy, who has always had more energy than he knows what to do with, whose nickname until late adolescence was "Puppy Dog," is utterly done in. It's not, he's sure, that his jobs are inherently exhausting. It's his situation that is.

Look, work is different when you can settle into its rhythms, when your familiarity with it allows you to prioritize and accomplish its tasks without thinking because you know enough to bypass the snarls. At Heartwood, for much of what's on the bustle and to-do list, they are all equally inexperienced; there is no one to train or supervise them so that they might acquire the right kind of experience; and even if there were such an instructor, his students would forget, over and over, almost everything they were taught.

Which explains, Nick reflects bitterly, the rush to claim the jobs most like those they had pre-virus, the ones they have a chance of being competent at (work that needs doing, but still!)—because the way this virus affects you—if you've been lucky enough to inoculate yourself against the worst of it—is that your body remembers what you don't. What's more, with a solid enough course of maddies, you'll *consciously* relearn it as you grab back swaths of yourself. Swaths of false selves might accompany them, but unless you're crazy-reckless like Jody, or he suspects like Andrew, they're minor impediments. Hence Jody's Brian gets to be their historian. Thus Edie is their pharmacist, Lisa their vet, and Matt Simmons their builder. Whereas he, Nick, having no such skills to vaunt, shall get him hence to the odd-jobs lot, to fetch and to carry, to till the soil and scoop the chicken coop. Accruing not much sense memory of anything.

Except for the foul clucking stench of barnyard drudgery. Except of *bumbling*.

Take the last hour or so. Spent botching his specialist job, these days, that of tending the garden. God knows how one is supposed to preserve a vegetable plot from a hurricane, but Nick has been laying out sandbags in a mystical protective configuration, and praying the wind won't simply divebomb the seedlings with them. (As that gibe turkey Jemmy, lolling over to wave a pulp paperback at it, immediately suggests it will.) For all that Nick's a city boy who never so much as grew his own pot, he is now expected to blossom into a boss horticulturist! To plan, plant, weed, and reseed the beds; to bend, tend, and produce the produce! Nick, *you* pick what to put in where. How much. When. Oh, and the tastier *pests*, Nick? Quit shooing away the fuckers and *shoot* them! Lure and snare those bunnies! String up some deer and *stew* them!

Well, like Elvis's hound dog—Elvis sings in Nick's head sometimes, he is a pitiful excuse for a hip urban Black man—he ain't never caught a rabbit—though he did once hold a stake-out for a particularly vexatious deer. A day so traumatic he half-recalls it: *Don't be a cowboy today, Nick,* a sign by his bed says. *The deer legend is true.* (Short version: the gun bucked, and he slew a nightgown hung out to dry on a tree; Andrew turned up at the last minute to dispatch the actual animal; then to skin and butcher it, forcing Nick to sidekick; until at the so-called venison feast Nick threw up all over himself. *I ain't never caught a rabbit, Andrew ain't no friend of mine,* as his head canon has it, his mondegreen of Jerry Leiber as rewritten by Freddie Bell.)

There is apparently also a mole story, which he declined to record for posterity and has no personal recollection of. Jemmy, who, of course, did log it, tries to tell it to him sometimes. Why must his housemates archive such *drivel*? "Today, after the bellicose chickens, I dodged rogue bees. I dragged out sandbags for the breeze to bop my beet beds with and cackle."

His *job*, by the way, only because he and Jemmy brought

in the rhubarb and asparagus and that spicy green whatever it was from last year's garden. A garden that was already *there*. Then from the beds that *Andrew* laid in, while "instructing" him but mostly instructing his kid. All that had been required of *Nick* was to nip out and *nick* some. And raid the orchards.

They are a shadow of last year's crop these days, the vegetable patches, the fruit trees, and he's not sure anyone has noticed. (Or only Andrew has, and is gloating, that only I-can-save-you-from-doomsayer, that woe-and-gloom seer.) Perhaps, Nick thinks guiltily, he should report on it to Brian, at the logging update. But there's a storm coming, right? Can't it wait a day or so?

Oh, jeez, all his life it's been hard for him to let people see he's floundering. To flounder about, and slick-talk the suckers into not seeing, that's what his body recollects how to do, apparently. That and play drums. He could drum to wake the dead if he had a kit. Not much call for kick-ass drummers, is there, though. Or for music store clerks. Not that he ever eked much of a livelihood from being a kick-ass drummer. Or a pretty damn sensational music store clerk.

He turns to Jemmy, his rhythm section buddy, his never-stymied compadre in crime. No bass guitars here either, no wooable women—Jemmy *always* has some new woman—yet Jemmy *still* works the angles. He got his duties shifted right fast, to the farm machinery. In his stead Nick's somehow been saddled with Jody, who is never around. Vague as she is, as besotted with her bees as she is, as arcanely at one with them. (He saw her for perhaps sixteen seconds today. *After* the bee bombardment, which she might actually have been of use with. He waved. She startled away.) But Jemmy hasn't felt any more call than usual to incant over his equipment, which is routinely (so he claims) primped, primed, and put away where the wind won't blow. So here he is instead in the vicinage of Nick, parked under a tree with his Neil Gaiman, ready and able—at need—if hollered at—to (engage air quotes) "help." Off and (conceivably) on. Off as in off-handedly. Off as in officiously. Conceivably as in *not*.

"Are these popsicle sticks in the right places?" Jemmy ambles over to ask now, as if either of them has any better idea than the other. "Those are the peas, dude. These over here are the lettuce. Were you looking at what it said on which packet?"

When Nick, digging a trench to divert the run-off from the storm waters, answers only with a low mutter—a succinct, dyspeptic neologism roughly signifying "offer *corporeal* help or eff off, you effing effluvium of offal"—Jemmy begins to make jokes and sing.

"Lettuce pray you mustard seed," he intones.

Nick sprays a shovelful of dirt at him. It falls well short.

"Mary goes into the garden, among the beans and pees," he sings with a music hall leer. "Mary goes into the garden, among the beans and leaks."

"Jemmy, speaking of peeing, could you piss off and haul a bucket of water from the stepwell for me?"

"It's going to rain, dude, it's going to rain buckets and buckets! What the fuck you want to pour water on for?"

"The ground's moderately too hard to dig here, in fact? I'd like to soften it a little?"

"That's more work than just *digging*, dude." The stepwell is a football field's length away. It's a converted swimming pool, converted by Matt, in fact, in his old life as a contractor, which is how they knew about this place and the absence of its owners, an Indian American family who got trapped back in the homeland and had to abandon it. "Just put your back into it, bro."

"Oh, for God's sake," Nick says, slinging down his shovel. "I'll go get it myself."

And he stomps away.

"At last!" he exclaims to himself as he goes. "At last,

what?" he doesn't bother to ponder. Because who in perdition cares? It is enough, for now, to clomp on down the road and scuff dust, savoring the sour flap of his exasperation. To let the surge and fume of it carry him to his place of dudgeon, of resentment and martyrdom and toil.

But he is tired and not always that coordinated to begin with, and when he arrives at the wellhouse, he finds that all four of its inside lights are out. (It's Jemmy's job to change them, but light bulbs have been in short supply.) So it's dark in there, and all Nick manages to do is stumble around until he topples in.

IV.

Jemmy is dawdling after him, rounding the corner and almost at the wellhouse door, when he hears the tail end of this mishap: a kind of a thud and an ouch, then a second yelp and a faint bucket trawl, or perhaps a splash.

Fuck, was that a splash?

V.

Andrew was once mildly nuts. Life in America has supersized the attribute. A bop on the knob, a hoedown of hallucinogens, some government head-meddling, *et voilà!* But he'll own it: he's the Andrew he needs to be. His housemates, however extreme they find him as a prognosticator, are blind to the extent of his derangement, because he *is* high-functioning—and because their own more rational thinking, dark with memory loss, is moth-riddled.

But nuts he is. Which doesn't mean he's wrong in his public pronouncements and private reservations. About the shape of his world, both macro and micro, and what needs to be done about it, he's the sanest person in the room. Admittedly, there was a nanosecond when he wondered if his survivalism *were* nuts in the same way, if what was happening to his perceptions may have led to a corruption in his understanding. But he soon learned to distinguish the two new strains of him: the unseating of his reason from his sharpness of foresight.

It had begun with a car wreck concussion, but it quickened with the drugs. From his first experience of it, the X7's effects on him were divergent. Oh, his memories, as advertised, were restored and vivified, and in the usual way, they admixed the authentic and the false. He has good middle-term *access*, in fact—blotchy, but in spots almost as good as Edie thinks hers is. But the trove itself was made hallucinatory. A new world lit by prophesy attended the old one, dimension upon dimension. He entered it clumsily, at first—the experience of it external— but something mystical began to open within him, easing his passage. He wanted, he needed to know more, and he pursued that more, in the shape of the traditional hallucinogens, as many different kinds as he could procure. Often he wound up taking them with the maddies, to boost and season them. He is more circumspect these days, but they have left their mark.

For example, like the poet William Blake and the occultist Aleister Crowley, he sees angels. Extremely helpful angels! Because, unlike anyone he has ever read about, he also sees temporal shadows: a second and third present tense beside the actual one, a clutch of near futures that arise from them—and his angels hover over the true path and steer him.

Or over the wiser path when the actual path is about to prove disastrous. Which might be extremely helpful if they weren't as fallible in this regard as he is. His angels tend, he notices, to foresee exactly what dangers he sees, except with even more passionate intensity.

His chores done—when he and Elise are focused, they

work well and fast—Andrew has sent his daughter off to do whatever it is she does. To walk Lisa's dogs, or so she claims. He's not her keeper, fortunately; the job would be beyond his capacities. And now he has slipped into the barn to spy on Lisa; he likes to gaze upon Lisa, and the angels help him evade her attention so that he can. Also to sip some scotch. The farmhouse came with scotch. The group came with only two scotch drinkers. And unlike him, Edie is moderate in all things. The scotch, he finds, tints the temporal shadows: a kind of color-coding that lets him sort more quickly through the dimensions and settle on one. Where he lets his eye settle—by no means always where his angels are pointing, he is not himself an angel—there is a vividness and sharpness of focus that's as sharply cinematic as with the maddies. Where the angels are pointing at this moment, some of them at the chore Lisa is actually doing, some of them out the doors, in the direction of one that they would prefer that she do, interests him less than this other-dimensional hot day he has conjured, where Lisa has stripped to work in her bikini top. There appears, unfortunately, to be no scenario where she is more naked, but this one is very satisfactory. In a while, he'll descend from his hiding place and tell her what his angels are suggesting; also and more importantly, what he himself has to suggest. But for a little while more, he sips his whiskey, and he leches.

Oh, lovely. Ah, yes.

VI.

Nor is Lisa entirely in the here and now. Not that she really needs to be. She is good with the animals, and knows with her whole self how to do what is required, in order to love and care for them. These particular two—a ten-day-old foal and his mare—have been occupying as many of her days as she can remember; but the mare seems well now, standing and hovering, and the foal is nursing normally, and bruising Lisa with the occasional kick, though he's still a mite weakened by the diarrhea. Considering how hard it is to worm these horses adequately, she's very happy with how she's seen them through the crisis. But she's keeping them separated from the others a bit longer out of caution, and for the pleasure of their company.

In truth, there are too many animals on this farm for her to tend to well, and of too many species and genera for her level of experience. Fretting about it, however, does neither her nor them any good. She will relinquish such worry. She does the maximum she can, and her grunts (Red and Nick, who help muck out and feed) do almost the minimum that she asks. The estate's owners had farm hands and managers to work the place. Ideally, for the animals' sake, a few of those professional types would have remained: healthy, dedicated, and compliant. "How wonderful of you and your colony to absorb and rescue us!" Instead, Matt, Millar, and Edie had found Heartwood empty of its people. A not unusual scenario, as the virus strengthened its hold. But to inherit one such as *this*, without fight or fuss? A miracle!

Not the best outcome for the livestock, though, who suffered months of virtual neglect. Her challenge has been to restore their health and to become their good steward; she is not so stupid as to think she has been adequate. How could such a thing be possible?

Still, she has done as well as almost any one person could, considering.

And her work, especially when she is called on to touch a particular animal in her charge, warmly to know it, calms and centers her. Which is really all she's up to at this moment. Calming herself, and centering herself, and without the help of drugs.

Unlike her dear pal Jody, to whose far world Lisa's mind

has again been wandering.

If they can't wean Jody off the maddies, they're going to lose her. She'll keep adding and adding layers of psychosis until she drowns in them; whereas if she stops right now, there's still a slim chance that she can sort through the waves and swim back, whole enough, to the surface. As genuinely as Millar loves her (in her head, or one on one with him, she *never* calls him Brian), and as disgusted as Edie is to keep supplying her, no one but no one seems to see, or to wish to acknowledge, the urgency of this problem but Lisa. If there's to be an intervention, a forcible detox, a twelve-step program, it's all on Lisa.

Well. A full plate keeps the soul and body fed.

She needs to come up with a plan. She has a sheepish sense of previous resolutions to do so; this time, though, she makes a note in her notepad. Soon, tomorrow if she has a spine, she vows to begin her formulations earlier in the day; so that she may push through into action.

VII.

A scrawny red-haired girl is across the brook at the far reaches of the west meadows, Lisa's dogs in tow, watching a storm of bees wheel and bank. The dogs mewl, suggesting that she might like to back off a ways. When she pays them no heed, they slink off a little themselves, behind her into the swamp field where her father put in his wild rice, to nose half-heartedly about for birds. But there are only the bees today, in their circling, predatory cloud—high over Elise's head now, to dance over the dogs, who nervously decline to notice them. She hasn't followed the bees here, this is just where she comes when she's fantasizing about running away from home. But it's interesting that they seem to be doing the same thing as her, isn't it? They hover and cluster as she has witnessed birds doing, from one clump of bushes to another and back again. She thinks they're mostly restless; they act like they're restless. She has no sense of having seen so many bees out of the hives at once before. It's pretty cool.

Here's where the hiking path goes through the trees that mark the farm's border, to cross the country road that you can see on their far side, or could see if it were winter, and climb up into the forest and the foothills beyond. The Gingerwoods are her favorite mountain range. She's never, as far as she knows, laid eyes on any other mountain range, but she's fourteen years old; she likes to have irrationally favorite things.

It wasn't until the last few years that it went plague, but the EEML virus, or so she has read, made its initial appearance around fifteen years ago, in Eastern Europe. Her father suspects it got loose from an old Soviet lab—and who knows, it may have done. The point is it's older than her, which makes her a native of the Memory Loss Era. The other Heartwooders are its refugees. Her father claims to see little significance in this difference, but he's wrong.

She, for instance, is not a memory addict. She's glad that Andrew gave her the drug because it did ease her transition into the new age: unlike the kids now coming into the world, she was born remembering. (Lisa and her contingent may be correct in supposing the lack to be temporary, that eventually memory must return to the world. Or they may be wrong.) But she no longer needs it, except perhaps as a bargaining chip with her father, who, with her consent, pilfers her supplies. As she sees it, her task is not to shore up her attachments to a dead world, but to strengthen herself for this one. And that means learning to live like an animal. An intelligent animal, better able than most to manipulate her environment but less dependent than old-world humans on systems that must be maintained.

Physically, she's not yet fit for such a life; hers is a transitional generation, the one that must learn to adapt. She must stay with these people on this farm until she's strong enough to survive without them. But already she is preparing herself for a less technological, a more practical existence. For instance, she rarely sleeps in the house—Andrew is too poor a (traditional) father to notice or much care. Actually, she's lucky he *is* her father because what he does notice, of her activities and her propensities, he tends to admire. She has not told him, since he might care about this, that she has no sense of being his daughter—oh, she has no reason to doubt his word, but it is a matter of indifference to her. He was a means, once, apparently: he got her into this world. But that was the past; it is her own responsibility to get through it.

So she toughens her body by going barefoot, and when she can get away with it, half-clad. She's been studying how to live off the land, to forage, to build fires, to trap game and make full use of the kill: to feed off it, but also to wear its skins, to shape its bones into weapons, to learn from it how to be the predator and not the prey. She'll master what's available to her in their armory, of course—she's not an ideologue. But she must marshal those resources, conserving her firearm as a tool of last resort; must be prepared for when things break down or are lost—know, for instance, how to fashion a replacement knife, or a better spear.

And knowing *about* isn't knowing *how*. She must *practice* these skills, remake them as instinct, as reliable sense memory. Not just as notes in her three-ring binder.

If she's lucky, she may have another year, or two even, of the protected, pampered life she's come to enjoy here. Which is good; she'll need that time. She'll do what they ask her to do, answer to the names they call her, Red, Reds, Redsy, kid; her name is Elise, but a name means nothing. Eventually, though, sooner rather than later, she suspects, these people's time will be past. And she'll make for the beautiful hills.

She sniffs the air. She can feel the storm coming, the way the bees can, without knowing how. An atmospheric restlessness. She's picked out a place to ride it out, if so required, in the lee of two rocks, although it's not near where the horses have chosen to gather, so she may have to rethink it. The difficulty is in preparing for both high wind and flood. *(Add that to the binder file on weathering bad weather.)* For the moment, she'll head back to the farmhouse. And ha! The bees are beating her to it, rising in their dark swarm like a great, blurry erasure, blotting out the swell of the barns; as whistling the dogs to her, she turns to follow.

VIII.

In the event, Edie and Jenna have spent most of the day together.

As they are wont to do. Because after Edie's work in the lab, there is Jenna's in the kitchen. They keep lunch simple here, but it still has to be made. And after lunch and log call, they clean up and wash clothes and tidy, starting in the kitchen and moving to the other common rooms. Since, by habit and by discipline, the Heartwooders use most of their prelapsarian gadgets sparingly—their clunky wind turbines generate power as fitfully as do the utilities companies, and Andrew keeps a strict eye on the rest, in expectation of leaner times—the need for manual household maintenance is nearly constant. Supper alone, if they're without power, can take many hours. Most of the colony has no idea what Edie and Jenna do. Even the boys (as they call Nick and Jemmy, full-grown but permanently infantile), whom they call in often to lend muscle, seem to be pretty clueless, and the others are rarely around.

When their work brings the two of them together, and talk is possible, they talk.

"Jody missed lunch again."

"The circles under Millar's eyes are as dark as bruises."

"Don't you find Andrew even crazier than the rest of us?"

"Well, not crazier than Matt Simmons, if he thinks I'm going to spend the night in his storm cellar when there's a perfectly safe basement right in the house. Could you give me a hand setting it up later, Jenna?"

"Oh, of course! Though I don't know if I'd call Matt crazy..."

Matt and Jenna have occasionally courted. Edie doesn't see it herself, but it's not her business, and there are not, after all, a lot of fish in this sea.

"Oh, Matt's all right, *generally*! He and my sweet Kitty were great pals."

Edie shivers. Odd how the memory comforts yet unsettles her. Something wrong there.

"And as for Jemmy," adds Jenna, her mind also apparently wandering.

"Jemmy?"

"Oh, don't mind me, Edie, I promised him I'd be discreet. For now. It will come out shortly. I agreed that I'd let him announce it."

Jemmy is the Heartwood songwriter. They all, without exception, like to sing. He doesn't have his guitars here, but there's a piano. He likes to bang on it sometimes and try out new things he's written, and they often have oldies sing-alongs—for entertainment and because it helps the memory. Jenna has him play hymns on Sundays, has even written a couple of lyrics for him to set. Edie imagines that it must be something along these lines she's being coy about.

"Do you remember if you were always religious, Jenna?"

Jenna has less memory than anyone. And is less the person she once was. But she never completely lost herself, as far as Edie understands it. The crew of them who were there, at the

101

lodge during the riots, helped to reconstitute her, but not from nothing.

"I'm told I was; I feel I was. I don't believe I could be otherwise. Why?"

Edie doesn't understand religion—not the appeal of it, she gets *that*. How, rather, to have faith in it. Matt, Lisa, they claim to still, in the face of everything. And so, most fervently of all, does Jenna, who has so little left of the schoolgirl self she was, molded by confirmation classes. And whose reprogramming last year was entirely secular! And yet her faith came with her. Edie has a hard time believing even in the essential self—that there's any real hard-core *her* to her, who could withstand the kind of knocks and shocks that Jenna has, and come through them even mildly recognizable. Or that *should*. While Jenna writes hymn lyrics like:

"What keeps me whole
Is my Christian soul,
Steadfast in Christ
I will persist."

And there have been Sundays where Edie has belted out these words with the rest of them. Well, sure. She hopes to persist.

"Oh, no reason," she answers. "Because you impress me, Jenna. Your persistence of self."

Jenna smiles. They are outside, briefly, fetching in the laundry hung out first thing this morning, before she went to Lisa; today, mostly sheets and towels. The sky is innocently dappled. The boys are headed toward the stepwell, it appears—Nick as if he's pissed at the world again, Jemmy sauntering behind him, no worries, no hurry. They wave, but the boys don't see.

"Edie," Jenna says suddenly.

"Yes, Jenna?"

"May I tell you something?"

"What do you mean? Yes, of course you can."

"Because he did ask me *not* to tell anyone yet, and I did promise, but perhaps I was wrong to promise. Don't you think so?"

"Well, I don't know, love. Who asked you not to tell what? Tell me, and I'll tell you if you should have told!"

"I'm serious, though. She needs more attention than he's giving. If I say nothing, and she... suffers, it will be on my head, not just his."

"Tell me."

"Okay... Well... There's a zombie girl living in the north storm cellar."

Carefully, Edie sets down a clutch of washcloths, still unfolded, on top of her full laundry basket. She drops a couple more pegs into the pocket of her apron. She turns to face her friend.

"Tell me."

IX.

Jemmy grabs the flashlight from its shelf by the door. Apparently, Nick was trying to draw out water in the dark. What an asshole!

"Nick! Hey, Nick!"

No coherent answer, but a noise, at least. A wheezy little caveman groan. Pitiful. The flashlight finds him on the far side of the pool, which was probably where the last person in here left the bucket, because the bucket's in the middle of the pool now as if stumble-flung. And Nick has banged his head, and it's bleeding. Not profusely, thank God, and not into the water, he's only in the water up to his knees, thank God, but over a section of the third step. That big crazy motherfucker! Jemmy has no idea how he's going to pull him out.

He puts down the flashlight.

"Ge tha thi ou a my face," Nick moans.

"Sorry, dude." Jemmy adjusts the angle. "I'll grab your shoulders and tug, okay?"

"You? Gimme a brea. I'll dra mysel."

But he can't. It's so pitiful to watch him try that Jemmy laughs.

"You're gonna bellyboard down the steps and drown, dude," Jemmy tells him.

But when he leans to lug Nick up from under his shoulders, the result is no better. It's like trying to haul in a big-assed tuna. Nick full-on screams. Jemmy backs away fast.

"Go," Nick spits out. "Ge. Hel. *Now*."

"Okay, okay, big fella. I'll go find Andrew."

He hesitates but turns off the flashlight. Gotta conserve, man.

"Sorry to leave you in the dark, buddy. Kinda your native habitat, though! Back soon."

He does at least leave the door propped open to let in a bit of natural light. A low, grim muttering follows him out, a kind of caveman cursing. He chuckles.

Jemmy doesn't mean to be mean to Nick. Really, Big Nick is his only real friend here, if you don't count Lisa and Jody. He sometimes counts Lisa. He may have counted Jody once. He doesn't altogether recognize Jody any more. So he hopes Nick doesn't think he's mean. Because he's just teasing, dude; it's a sign of affection.

And for the record, he'd have gone to fetch the well water in a few seconds or so, if Nick hadn't been so testy and impatient.

And now, if Nick can hold on for a few minutes, he'll go fetch Andrew.

But Andrew isn't where he was. The windows are boarded up, the ladders and toolboxes are put away. Nothing around back either. Jemmy supposes the roof must be finished also.

He doesn't know how Andrew does it. Or why in such solitary fashion, except it's true, he *does* work more efficiently alone, or with just a little kid he can boss about to help him.

She's gone too.

So Jemmy goes looking for Lisa. She's with that new foal, right? But the mare says neigh.

Crap on it, he's pussied around too long already, he's going to have to try to get Nick out himself, if that's even possible. *Crap* on it. He hurries off instead to the north storm cellar.

X.

Up in Lisa's room, behind boarded windows, by the light of two beeswax candles, she and Andrew are on break. Everybody needs a break. They sometimes take theirs together.

How many times have they broken up, because they are fundamentally so unalike, so opposite in everything they stand for? How many times has Lisa sworn never again? She knows, with the kind of removed knowledge that comes from reading their records, that they have done these things, over and over, but she has been lucky with her grasp of detail, and happily, she simply doesn't remember the worst of it. And sensibly, they don't log the specifics. Of course she knows he's a swaggering rifle-toting bird-hunting sexist who maintains that this, right here, is the apocalypse. (It is not the goddamn apocalypse.) Of course he knows she's a sappy prey-hugging mother bloody *ostrich* who believes that the brunt of this mess is behind them. So? So?

So their attachment never, apparently, lasts very long; but how nice to have someone perpetually new enough in your life to fall head over heels for, over and over, without baggage, without restraint, without breath, without regrets.

Until Lisa's furious, bilious regrets about two weeks into their relationship. Right before the limit of her short-term memory. At which point they break up again.

For the next length of her short-term memory, anyway. What's nice is it doesn't take.

XI.

Matt Simmons pokes his head out of the storm cellar and takes a peek at the sky. Nothing yet. And he's ready. If the rest of them are doing their jobs as well as he's done his, they'll make it just fine; they will be one well-oiled machine.

He thinks he has time for a nap before supper. He needs it, and later on, he may be very thankful to have grabbed some rest.

He goes back in, finds his cot, takes off his boots, puts a hand on each of his totem items, what Brian calls his self-centering kit. He checks the pillbox in his breast pocket.

And maybe half a maddie will help his sleep be sweet.

CHAPTER FIVE: THEY REMEMBER

"What seest thou else
In the dark backward and abysm of time?
If thou remember'st aught ere thou camest here,
How thou camest here thou mayst."

William Shakespeare, *The Tempest*, Act 1, scene 2

"Every cell in my body has it all writ down."

Mike Heron, The Incredible String Band, "All Writ Down"

Selections from "The Heartwood Chronicles"

Andrew Barker, *36. Aka: Andrew Borrendong.*
Troubleshooting and oversight; crisis planning; maintenance management; field crops; armory; State of the World board; State of the Farm board.

*Edie Driscoll, *35. Blend elements: Tiffany Driscoll (deceased).*
Pharmacy; a.m. check-in and scheduling; household upkeep and oversight; household inventory.

Elise Barker, *14. Aka: Red(s); Redsy; Elise Oswald.*
Homeschooling; assistant to Andrew (maintenance) and Lisa (animal husbandry).

Jeremy Jaronsky, *27. Aka: Jemmy.*
Machine maintenance; small buildings; property line; field crops; odd-jobbery.

Jenna Brower, *circa 63. Aka: Sarah Oldchurch (superseded).*
Kitchen management; household upkeep; eggs and dairy liaison; market supplies.

Jody Barker, *31.*
Apiary; gardens and orchards *[to be revisited & re-assigned? barns and dairy?]*

Lisa Huttongold, *32.*
Animal husbandry; veterinary care; medical care; barter; SNAG board.

*Matt Simmons, *60.*
Construction and repair; storm cellars; stock rooms; ponds and waterways; manual.

*Millar Kearney, *31, "Heartwood Chronicles" editor. Aka Brian Everett (deceased).*
Colony history; records room; logging room; planning and policy review; manual.

Nicholas Trifflett, *27. Aka Nick; Big Nick; Nicky.*
Crop husbandry (gardens and orchards); barns and coop; odd-jobbery.

Ages are as of this update, 4/20, eighteen month anniversary of the colony's founding.

1. *What childhood memories have you retained or retrieved?*

Matt Simmons

Comic books. My teddy bear. Called William, if you can believe that.

This model racer. I collected those, you know, hand-machined miniatures? There was one car I fell for from an auto race on TV. Not because of how it ran or such: I liked the *colors*. It was deep purple and lime striped, with a red 4. Painted so pretty that the number 4 is to this day my favorite number. Oh, Brian—the pantywaist predilections you have when you're a young 'un!

Well, I wanted it. And I was made to *wait* for it because we were not in any way rich in my family. But I got one!

There's a maddie clip where I tip that beautiful toy out of its box and perch it on the table. I hover it over my plate, going *vrrm! vrrm vrrm!* at it. And as soon as I finish my mac 'n' cheese and my fresh juice—the way they tasted when you were a *kid*, Brian—I have taken *off* with it. *Vrrm*, straight into the street.

Now, this was a quiet cul-de-sac. We played there all the time. So that was no biggie. But what was big was to see how far I could get number 4 to roll from our driveway down toward the wasteground at the end of the block. No car had ever on its maiden run gone further than the first lamppost, and no car, any run ever, had reached the second lamppost.

This one does. I give it a good snappy launch, and it rolls, and it keeps rolling. So sweet to see! I stand shading my eyes like so, and I peer after it, gaping with my mouth as round as a damn pie plate. *Wow! wow! WOW!* Until it starts to tail off right. Down the camber toward the gutter. And yep, into the black mouth of a drain, and *gone.*

Man, who ever felt such a mood crash. I am bawling at the top of my lungs. I go pelting after it. I bawl all the way to the drain.

But no. It's gone. And I cry, and cry, little pantywaist

that I am, but eventually I wipe the tears dry, and I put my hand over my heart.

"Well, number 4," I say. "You went out a champion."

Edie Driscoll

I have a kid sister: Tiffany. I know because she's in my maddie cache. I hope she's alive and happy somewhere. Who knows when I last saw her. Not in two years, since I have two years of live memory. I have a sense of her as being out there growing up, during later maddie trips, such as when I was with you, Millar, for my sins. And with Kitty. Such an angel before the virus claimed her. I have Kitty with my real memory, but the beginnings of us are courtesy the X7.

But for Tiff, other than some such incidental fuzz, all I have is when she was in first grade, me in third. Ten months of vivid, paltry maddie cache. She's six. She's my kid sister.

I'll commemorate Tiffy, if I may. Something typical and everyday...

As necessary as they've proved, I'm not a big fan of the maddies, because they rewrite you, and they make addicts of you. But I'm fond of how they refocus your perspective on the small ordinary moment; they turn that trick quite well.

Tiff coveted my bicycle. A sea-grey Schwinn, with pink accents. Pink seat. Mom told her she wasn't old enough yet, but shh, be patient, cutie, because here's a secret: you'll get a bike for your birthday. But meanwhile, I loved mine so much it made her miserable. She told me so; she wasn't one for closet resentments. I'm sitting astride it, and she's by the roadside, looking down at the ground, confessing. She's barefoot, and she's inscribing spirals in the dirt with her big toe, mumbling that she's sorry. Such a cute kid she is. Puffy little pink cheeks and stumpy legs.

"Tiffy," I say. "We'll share. I'll give you lessons."

Her chin lifts into a haughty tremble.

"No, thank you," she says. "I don't need your charity."

Ugh, when I say it out loud, it doesn't even feel real. It's like a sticky *story*—like I made it up. Even real memories, I'm sorry, but I think the maddies gimmick them. They gimmick them.

Jenna Brower

Oh, honey, I have no childhood memories. The drug wasn't able to fetch them back, or it needed help none of you folks doing the rehabilitating could offer. This artifact, that memento. A visit home, wherever home was. I have the wear and tear of my body, I have my Dixie accent, I have the marks that were left on me. I believe I have the soul I am. But no, dear, no videotape.

Brian, are you sleeping enough? You neglect yourself.

I do have some later stories, which could all be lies. Plus a good thirty or forty days, or parts of days, from the end years at the lodge. Pottering about the Cricket Club grounds, home-making. Fussing at my husband or our parrot. True days, I think. Could be because those times were fresher in my mind. And those of you who knew me at the Club could prompt me some.

Elise Barker

This *is* my childhood, though, right? So yeah, a lot. Childhood's the only place a maddie has to go.

A half-dozen from Oz, with my mother or with Dad's grandparents. One horrible one on the plane. True, I guess, but I don't get how that's me. Most of Connecticut. A lot in Eastdon. The coolest being a three-month stretch when I'm eleven, and which is mostly lies. I can tell because it overlaps three true trips which swear otherwise. So weird.

Just one, the last maddie I took, from this farm, Mostly I don't want to be about... You know? Time passing any more? I attune myself to this place to become part of it. I expect you don't get that, do you? I absorb its feel.

No, not that attached. I don't expect to live here much longer, actually. Do you?

Not as good as I want, but I'm getting better at it. I'll adapt quicker next time.

Nick Trifflett

Jemmy and I have talked about this, Brian. We have our personal records. It's fine for you to keep an official record also, but not everything should go in the community log, because who we are is private, and who cares?

I understand. I understand but forgive me if I'm terse.

My cousin Lisa's family saved my life. My mother is worthy of being remembered also, and I have a few essential vignettes, upon which I expatiate in my journals. But since Lisa is part of this community, I'll declare *publicly* that her parents were saints, and that her father helped mold me into a drummer.

He was a jazz poet. In a jazz combo. He sang Tin Pan Alley standards mostly, and he played keyboards. A little trumpet. But some of their material was also his: spoken word pieces mostly, with full band arrangements. Their drummer was a head case, and once I was old enough—I was twelve, in fact—I started to fill in.

I maddie-remembered one of my first shows. It was at a nightclub; they admitted me with the group; I was a celebrity. Nick the Kid, with his tongue hanging out! Puppy Dog!

I'll recite part of something if you like, it's called "Blue Pen." It's one of Lisa's dad's pieces. For the public record. In honor of my fucked-up childhood.

> There'll be a time when everything in your life goes wrong.
> The washing machine breaks down, or your job, your marriage;
> Or you just couldn't hold your liquor or your tongue,
> You came under the influence of Uranus and did damage;
> It will be hard, then, to be simple. But sit.
> In this blue room, with its one chair, and be still.

Take up your blue pen and uncap it.
Let its little vein of music spill.

Chilton, his name was. And I trust still is. Chilly
Huttongold.

Jemmy Jaronsky

Oh, man, I wish! You'd think by the law of averages, as
young as I am and the mads I've inhaled, I'd have scored
some legit kiddie trove, right? Wrong. One *fib* is all. My
folks said I got it off the TV. The earliest which isn't
bogus, I was, like, thirteen. I keep ride logs, man, and
you don't forget trip tales. I pen ditties. Not much at the
lodge, those months got fuzzy, but yeah, *songs*, even. All
teen scenes and twenties. Music and women. Jobs,
family. No kiddie clips.
    But listen, I've got this private hoard, dude. Yeah,
that photo album! But also my second-grade
composition book. An authentic diary with entries
lavishly illustrated in crayon—yeah, *exactly* where, it's in
my room. I'll fetch it, and you can copy out a couple of
them.

> 22nd Jan.
> Yesterday I made my name in the snow. When my father came
> home, he swept it away.

> 28th April.
> This morning my brother felt sick and stayed
> home. I don't believe he does feel sick, though.

They're good, right? Simpler than the mads, yeah?
Hand-printed, at a time, I'd not long learned how to
form my letters. You should scan them in. Include the
artwork, bro.
    That April one's about my big brother Danny. You
knew him, right?
    Really happy to have that composition book.
    I keep it in my backpack with my song lyric

notebooks. That backpack has made it through some wars, man.

Lisa Huttongold

Family dinners, Sunday after church. *One* dinner, *one* Sunday, I suppose, but a big part of the pleasure lies in my awareness of it as a ritual. Roast root vegetables; baby Brussel sprouts, crisply undercooked; rice with gravy. A choice of two meats, though all of us but my mother always want both. Part of the ritual was to serve ourselves from the meat porringers, whereas the rest was placed on our plate. Mama wasn't a meat-eater herself, and I think would have liked it if I had taken after her more, in this and in many other ways. I did become a vegetarian for a while, later, as much out of love of her as for my love of animals; but it didn't take. There was too much of my father in all us kids: the hungering carnivore.

I must be eleven or just turned twelve, guessing from the hulking half-presence of my brothers. Their last year of high school: they rise from the table without permission, before the dessert course even, and are gone. They are huge and dangerous and jolly, genial predators utterly at ease with themselves, about to set off to college on a pair of football scholarships. We love each other dearly but without closeness.

Nick is with us, as is the Sunday custom: I take him with me to Sunday school. Both my parents attended church today, which is not commonplace for my father. There's some talk of the sermon, which dealt, I gather, with covetousness and was found amusing and a little risqué. The allusions are discreet, for my sake and Nick's, but now, with my adult ears, I pick up on them.

It interests me to study Nick. Not only how young he is, but how untroubled. He laughs at the faces we make at him; he chatters, loudly and easily, with his mouth half-full of food. When a tune he knows comes on—we have music playing in the background, a jazz station—he scampers to stand next to the radio, drumming with his hands on the mantel. I haven't seen that Nick in too long. After lunch, my father and my brothers always used to take him up to the attic studio to coach him in the art of jamming. My brothers aren't the musicians my father is, or Nick is—we already suspect how good Nick will be— but they had some fun with it. They've moved on by this time. Today, and for only a few months more, I believe, there'll be just Nick's drums and my father's keyboards. Alone, then over a soundtrack of old records.

By next year, dad will have Nick playing in clubs. Only to look at him, even then, I am suffused with pride. The world, I believe, will be at his feet.

Jody Barker

Mmh! Mom's baking biscotti. I'm nine, almost. Daddy's away again. If I ask where, or suggest by some flounce of behavior that I miss him, I'm worried I won't see him again, Mom makes biscotti. Even the biscotti *smell* is mmh. Like mmh, almond crunch. But with a sour tang that wells up from my gut. At ten, at eleven, the scent of warm biscotti. Its knife cut of sourness... I'm six. Winter, the zoo. *Do not feed the animals*, the sign says. *Dougie!* Mom yells. He's pitching a fit again, he's naughty and he's mean. *I'll feed the animals if I like!* He hurls his sandwich over the bars... Liar, I have no brother. Oho, Daddy teases me, how d'you *know* you don't. Coz if I have a brother, where's he hiding? Where's his bed, the attic? Somewhere still blacker. Darker even than the crunkle-dark of his mommy's crinkle-black hair. Deep, he whispers, in the dark of the clonk-crick coal bin, which I don't know what that is. We had a coal bin, back in Oz, he explains, when I was five like you. He makes the sad face. I left him there, he says, left him playing in the coal.

Andrew Barker

Listen, I want to insist on some things. I know most of us will prefer oral interviews, and I get why you might also: e.g., b/c that's how we already do the logs; e.g., so you can weave in material from the logs, if you like, and not have jarring tone shifts. But I've looked through your questions, and I choose to answer in writing, thank you.

You've explained that you aren't merely fleshing out our personal profiles—that you're compiling a history of the colony. Which is admirable. But I have concerns about the narrowness of your focus. So I aim to broaden it.

I'll write my answers under your topic headings, but I won't necessarily address your questions. E.g., I'm not going to discuss my childhood. And sure, I must have done so somewhere in the logs, and you could edit out my written response and switch that material in, but I have a request: don't. If you must incorporate something "on topic," I grant you permission to *add* it.

But I mostly want you to use these responses. Agreed?

So I'll start by saying that I don't believe everything I've been told. I want to warn any future reader of this document to adopt the same approach.

Maybe some people's narrations aren't always to be relied on. I'd have to lie some myself, were I to tell my stories. At the very least, I'd need to go heavy on the spackle.

Maybe I should declare that the whole supposed history of this virus, of your famous Eastdon clinic—of this colony, to a degree—smells fishy to me, and I don't always trust my records. There are ways they could have been got at.

E.g., perhaps I should point out—I got poison ivy; I took a prednisone and tried it—that pills crumble when you bite the edge off them as we were told Jilly Simmons did. So did Jilly have unusually sharp, slender teeth? But then I recall that manufacturer's stamp—that off-center) (with its two seams—so maybe this particular pill split easily along them.

The point is, I have my suspicions, and I have my unanswered questions.

Here's what I know, and here's what I ask myself:

i) *The virus is real, and its effects are real.*

Could it have been bred? Given its peculiarities, isn't this, in fact, the most likely explanation? If so, who engineered it, and did it escape, or was it released?

ii) *The drug, the anti-virus, is real, and its effects are real.*

Was its discovery fortuitous, or was it designed as a defense against this virus? Was it perhaps formulated in *concert* with this virus? Who arranged for its release and for the subsequent wider release of its purported formulae: a drug company, the Russians, the US government, wild card environmentalists? (E.g., maybe this contagion was concocted to combat overpopulation and depletion of the world's resources. As it has, in fact, done.) Were Jody Barker, Jacob Corrigan, etc., acting on their own initiative, or were they knowing or unknowing agents of the drug's propagators?

iii) *The nature of this drug, despite what is widely believed, has not been proven.*

How much of our induced memory is real? How much is a useful construct? (Is the drug a memory micro-regenerative, or does it merely excite the guess reflex?) It *is* a palliative; is it also a purgative? Why, if it was developed as a memory drug, does it shield users from *physical* deterioration? (Do you know why the Rampages stopped, Brian? Drug usage prevents catalepsy. What's more, early adoption of the drug with consumption in sufficient quantities stabilizes you; you don't reach the 'wild dog' stage. *Meaning* it's a partial antidote. *Think* about that, Brian.)

iv) *The world as we know it has been brought to its knees; it has not yet collapsed.*

Is the outcome thus far an unintended consequence of an accidentally created or an escaped contagion? Or is it the intended consequence of a designed contagion? Or something in between? Is the worst now over, or are we waiting for the other shoe to drop?

Can we afford not to plan for the worst? To this one, I think, we know the answer.

Speculation and analysis to be continued in my next response.

My childhood, btw, was somewhat idyllic and somewhat appalling. Wasn't everyone's?

2. *What, as far as you recall, was your life like before the EEML virus?*

Jemmy Jaronsky

I played music. My day job was in an office, a temp agency. I placed the temps. But I always liked to tinker around with ye old toolboxes, you know? Home repairs and cars and carpentry. I was looking to move more in that direction, back before.

Here I am, I guess.

I do wish I had my guitars, though, man. Piano will keep me on the roadway, but for the engine to hum, I at least need me a nice little acoustic. Couldn't be that hard to snatch one.

Elise Barker

I'm not about that.

Jenna Brower

How do I know this? But I'm sure it's so: I've spent my whole adult life in Eastdon.

As of a while back, anyway, I can't say when, my husband Harlan and I are the caretakers of what used to be the Wolker estate, or the Eastdon Lawn Tennis and Cricket Club, to give it its formal name. We live quietly in the back section of the lodge—most of it is locked and boarded, and it appears to be abandoned, though it's not.

We're modest people, and we don't occupy very much of it. But we're also working people, not hermits, and we do encounter visitors to the park. Sometimes we introduce ourselves. Sometimes the more curious ones ask. There's a girl called Jody, whose daddy died, bless her heart. From Connecticut. She's conducting research about the estate. We speak often enough to invite her into the lodge. Once with two friends of hers, Lisa and Nick. They're real excited to meet the parrot, who they call Loulou, though that's not her name. It turns out they once knew another woman with an African grey called Loulou.

Now that my husband is sick, he and the parrot spend a deal of time together. Vaguely communing. My husband is losing his memory, I regret to say. And I'm not so confident in mine!

It can grate on the nerves, truth be told, dear. You know how parrots and memory loss people both repeat themselves? When I say "communing," I'll let you imagine what that might be like. "Did you turn the heat down, Sarah?" "Did you turn the heat down, Sarah?" Then usually he chuckles. "You hear, Sarah? Even the parrot thinks you got the heat too low." Then the parrot chuckles. Ten minutes later: "Did you turn the heat down, Sarah?" Yep. Both of them. So I get fed up, I nudge up the thermostat. "How high you got the heat there, Sarah?" Yep. *Both* of them.

And even without the parrot. He tells the same stories over and over, like as not about some girl he saw with tattoos or piercings or an acre of skin showing—any pretext to be shocked and ogle her. I learned to tune him out, mostly back then; but surprise—now it's all stored in maddie memory. Seems to me if you get to remember so little, you could weed out the tiresome parts. *Edit* Harlan for me—make him suave and studly! An old broad can dream, right?

Well, to get back to my point: Jody is intrigued enough to worry about us, how we're forgetting things, and she says to stay in touch; she might be able to help us. I've no idea what she means by this, but she's a polite, kindly young woman, so I see no harm in the friendship.

Lucky for me, I guess.

The work's still manageable. We have groundskeepers. The city doesn't expect much of us. Our positions are funded by the Wolkers. The Trust appointed us, I don't recall the details.

My name isn't yet Jenna Brower. If I admit that it's Sarah Oldchurch, I trust that you won't begin to call me by it. I miss Sarah Oldchurch, but I can't be her. Should I try to be, it hurts.

I still wear her wedding ring, look. I have no sense of how I acquired it, or of most of the years I wore it, but I cherish it as a tribute to her and to the man she shared her life with. During those last years, we weren't the best of pals, but I have faith we once were... There's a very lovely November evening I see so sharp... It's two days after Thanksgiving, which we've spent alone. We have a child who is difficult, and a not normal grandson, bless his heart, but this year they've not visited; we're less disappointed than we are relieved. We're eating tin roof sundae ice cream by the fire and watching the *Antiques Roadshow*. All day it's rained or sleeted; now it's shifting to snow. November snow! We don't wish to be anywhere else in God's world. This comfortable sofa, this snug, warm room. I make a joke about one of the presenters, how he looks like and talks like this crazy old buddy of ours, and it's weirdly true, and Harl laughs and laughs.

There. I believe that is all I care to tell you of that.

Matt Simmons

I was a regular guy. I did my job, and I went to church, where I was a deacon. I loved my family. No kids. Berry, my wife, she didn't want them. But there was us two. And our siblings and cousins up and down the east coast. Nephews, nieces. Aunts, uncles. In the end, it was just me and my uncle Rip and his wife living in the Eastdon area, though, and when Berry died and so did uncle Rip, within a few months of each other, aunt Jilly and I, we leaned on each other.

Write that it was a quiet, honest, working man's life.

Whatever else I got up to, and small-time, regular guy mischief is all it was anyway. I don't believe anyone needs to know.

Andrew Barker

Before the world changed, hereinafter BTWC, I was a numbers cruncher and consultant. Accounts, business planning, estate planning. Long before the writing was on all four walls and the ceiling, my consultancy moved into massive disaster preparedness—MDP Consultancy was our name. After my father's death, I managed three of *his* companies. I inherited part-ownership. I sold out to Ben, who had a similar deal, when I moved south. We part-owned with Jody and her mother. Brian had helped us talk the old man into an arrangement that would treat us equitably.

My turn. Let's address the enormity of our faith, BTWC, in drug manufacturers and drug treatments. Assuming they weren't in bed with some still more sinister organization, like terror groups, or a foreign government, or our own government, what can we say drove such firms? By the most generous judgment, were they getting off on the research or its efficacy, on its efficacy or its profitability, on helping people or on getting off?

The research at the Eastdon clinic, as you and Jody tell it, seems particularly cavalier—granted, I don't know the whole of it. The control groups and the placebos; the parameters of the tests and the screening of test patients; the more solid, more modest results already documented at Phase 1. The drug's origins, and the hoops to jump through. Still, how did it get itself "accelerated," and on whose say-so? Were Doc Corrigan and his ilk rogue cowboys, or were they required to be? False memories all over the map, and they're pretty much *fine* with them if they can assess and tinker!

And wasn't their research at an oddball angle to the responsible treatment of memory disorders? Of Alzheimer's, anyway, if that's really what they set out to treat. I understand Alzheimer's to be primarily a problem of misrouted attention—where you're lost in your interior stories, unable to distinguish between the true and the false ones—rather than of real memory loss; and a drug which made both kinds more *vivid*, without helping you to tell the true from the false of them—well, wouldn't it exacerbate the problem?

I have in my records that I raised this objection with Jody. She tried to fob me off with talk of a *jolt* theory: the *Madeleine jolt*, which isn't a radical idea, it's not unlike a jump-start to a car or the shocked heart. As for Alzheimer's, there are aspects of mnemonic function which our treatment may, in fact, engage and realign, so that blah and blah...

All *that* accomplished was I began to have my doubts about Jody.

I'm not yielding the soapbox yet. I have a chore to do, but I'll continue shortly.

Nick Trifflett

Before the virus, I was a semi-starving college grad selling shiny new musical instruments and accessories at a strip mall, and a good drummer in a blandly adequate college town bar band. I've forgotten most of that life. Here's more of the tune "Blue Pen" instead, by the Gold Cards, which by contrast I've had stuck in my head.

> *When you have no money or time, and in another country,*
> *Your brother's in the hospital, or your old man's gone AWOL,*
> *Or your aunt has died, or all that and more, to put it bluntly.*
> *And at the shop, business is slow; they want you off the*
> *   payroll—*
> *Same old, same old—*

> *It will be hard, then, to be simple. But sit.*
> *In this blue room, with its one chair, and be still.*
> *Take up your blue pen and uncap it.*
> *Let its vein of music spill.*

Piano and bass, with the band coming in on the breaks. One horn solo. Fat drum fills.

Edie Driscoll

My active memory chain starts sometime after you show up with the X7. I show no signs of infection, but Kitty does. It's a great big blur before then. I should know more; I knew more then; things must have come up in conversation. But somehow it's all smeared out.

Here's a secret, though: I have a wedding ring. It fits my ring finger; it has to be mine. Weird, huh? No impression of it on the skin, so perhaps I didn't wear it long.

Which I so would have done if I were tragically widowed. A short, unhappy marriage is my bet? No, Millar, if you know anything, *don't* tell me! I suspect I don't want to know.

Jody Barker

I'm a first-year resident starting a rotation in family medicine. They have me in the clinic, where I have no clue. Lop off those wiggly whatchamajigs with the pink excrescent tips and call me in the a.m. No, thank God, scratch that. That's *her*. Nursing's scary enough, grazie. Telling dumb first year residents they're *wrong*. Hey, I'm a wild thang. I am way too hot to be so cold, babe. "As far as I recall," huh? You're funny. Hey, there are mice in my hat! Nine newborn white mice, blind and wriggly as toes. Cool! I'm supposed to keep them alive with an eye-dropper. Simpler times, Lisa. I need my eight, my shift's at seven, is it six, I don't get five? What's it for, conquistador? A question without answers. My life's all rush. My life is a rush. Hey, lilac and gold hair! So, I maybe did a terrible thing once, who she was once, I don't recall, but I'll come to terms, I hope, with the not knowing.

Lisa Huttongold

I was an R.N. and a do-gooder. I was warily optimistic
about the world. It appeared to me that, in some ways, it
might be getting better! Not that I was blind to how we'd
befouled it and were exhausting its resources; how we
liked to exploit and massacre each other in the name of
trumped-up principles; how soon we forgot, excused, or
glorified the abominations of the past while
congratulating ourselves on our more enlightened
present. But it's possible to have a rosier view of such
things if your own life's going well. And it did seem,
politically and socially, that there might be an inching
away from some precipices. From some old sour
attitudes.

So the rapidity with which the crisis swept over us
caught me by surprise. For instance, I was the last of us,
other than Jenna Brower, to partake of the memory
drug. I understood that the *rest* of you needed its help. I
fussed at you to get it. But me? No consequential
symptoms. Tiny lapses, little cracks and earth tremors so
teeny they might be imaginary. So I continued to live
my workaday, hang-an-evening life. When things fell
apart, pieces of them fell on me hard.

For instance: I had two dogs. I loved those dogs. To
be honest, I still can't let myself think of them. Because
then, one by one, I picture the animals in the shelter
where I volunteered; or I picture my neighbors' pets.
Every abandoned, dependent bird and beast I might
have met...

When we fled to fetch you folks from Mrs. Simmons'
house that last day before the lodge, it somehow never
occurred to me that I was fleeing my dogs, I was *always*
back within a few hours, right? At the lodge, I *screamed* at
Danny—"Let me nip home and GET them!"—I have *that*
memory. Right as the second wave broke... It was weeks
before we risked leaving the park. Nick tells me it was a
sight out there; I don't recall. We hit each of our houses,
grabbed and got out. But there had been body heat in
mine. So it was ash and char. Or so I'm told.

Is it terrible to say that of all the things I've ever

done, this strikes me as the worst?

I don't much remember our life at the lodge. I was taking the maddies by then, so I have glimpses of it, the way the drug opens you up to that kind of awareness. The memories feel more wiped than they should, but I do have *some* access to the context in which I medicated. One glimpse I have is of Jenna Brower, or whatever her name still halfway was. That day you come to fetch us. Mrs. just born again Brower and her parrot. Of Nick saying, "We have room, don't we, can't we make room?" And that silly woman's utter and appalling lack of interest.

Of course she wasn't herself. Of course she wasn't. But the parrot got left there, and I blame her. Of course it isn't rational. Of course it's a deflection.

I could have taken that parrot cage onto my own lap. Yes, Millar. Yes, I do know that.

CHAPTER SIX: YEAR ONE

"Tis in my memory locked,
And you yourself shall keep the key of it."

William Shakespeare, *Hamlet,* Act 1, scene 3

"The X-series drugs were never intended for targeted recovery. They were broadly administered jolts. What particular memories might be retrieved was neither predictable nor manipulable. The test subjects, not knowing or not accepting this limitation, routinely sought to circumvent it: they pursued some particular memory, and they did so with a degree of success! However, the risk of creating false memories increased exponentially. And there was a second slight risk, which was known in advance, but which became significant as the consumer used the drug less passively: that the memory jolt would affect the broader limbic system, resulting in wild mood swings—perhaps, even, in prolonged emotional instability. When bastardized versions of the X-series formula became public, the drug both saved us and unhinged us. Clinical controls were no longer possible. There were no protections against psychological and chemical dependency. As the pandemic raged, more of the population was able to remain functional, but at what cost? For many, the past tense of trip became *trap.*"

Library of Virginia Commission, *The 5 Year Report*

YEAR ONE, EASTDON:

Lisa, Millar, Jemmy, Andrew, Edie, Jody

I.

"Hey, Lisa?" Jody shouted. "I'm seeing someone!"

"New guy!" Lisa shouted back. "So *that's* it, yo. Bounce in your booty!"

"Yeah, more to it though, babe!" shouted Jody.

They were at the club, the one where Nick's band had a weekly gig. The band would be playing shortly. At the moment, there were discs being jockeyed, and Jody had pulled Lisa out onto the floor to twirl and talk.

Lisa and Jody were family. They could tell each other anything and hear it. Ducking out of a squabble in their freshman dorm, they had discovered over bowls of cafeteria chili that they shared the same far-off hometown—a speck of commonality that felt like a life raft. *Twins!* they shrieked. True, on Mars, any earthling might be your home girl, but it turned out they were well suited. Graduation stretched their connection but didn't sever it; Lisa would have been a bridesmaid had Brian lived to marry Jody. His death and its aftermath redoubled their bond.

Lisa was helping out her folks at home that winter, and she'd been with Jody that very morning. So after the wreck, she ran at once to sit in vigil, and throughout Jody's stay she stopped by the hospital daily. The solicitude wasn't one-sided; Jody would have done no less for her. If in the event Jody knew little of her ministrations, her spirit being a lost raggedy bit, straggling back in tatters from the void, what mattered was that Lisa was nearby when Jody woke; that they had some free and frank discussions, as Jody worried at the truth of things; that Jody began to depend on Lisa, and Lisa liked it that she did.

Lisa was four months older and had grown up in a nice, stable family, with parents who were actually good people. Oh, Lisa had met Jody's father. Way before she knew Jody. She'd had dealings with his *minions*. Hired to adore him and do his gofer bidding. To humiliate anyone who crossed him. The man sent out minion *signals*. A tilt of the chin. A narrowing of the eyes. Yeah, no. Lisa was never her baas daddy's little princess. But she was still Jody's elder sister and Jody had better listen; Jody was still the kid twin, and she mostly did. In public, they might say "girlfren" or "sista", but the truth was "sister."

So as they danced, Jody fessed up about Millar. Lisa knew about Millar, the history buff. She'd already teased Jody about him, then teased her more when the girl got indignant.

"Millar! Millar the *goofball*? The guy Danny needn't worry a New York second about?"

"I know!" The girl was *giggling*! "But we didn't break up because of Millar!"

"So who's this Millar dude?" asked Danny, coming up behind and embracing them in turn. Danny was a teddy bear; Lisa adored Danny. "Is he here? Do I need to punch him out?"

"Danny, I'm seeing someone," yelled Jody. "You don't mind too much, do you?"

"Hell, yes, but why is it my business? So am I, sweetie, but it sure ain't yours." Danny and Lisa had gone out to a movie the night before; did he mean her, had that been a *date*? He caught Lisa's eye and winked: *shh*.

"Danny, you're a sweetheart," Jody shouted and kissed him on the cheek.

"Anyway, I came over to invite you to sing with us when we do 'Calico,' if you remember it. Fourth tune, right after 'Proof's in the Pudding.' Interested?"

"Hell, yeah! The guys are okay with that?"

"Hey, Big Nick's idea, his and Jemmy's. I'm the messenger."

"Yeah?" She looked, and Nick waved. Poor Nick had a Jody crush. "Then fuck, yeah!"

So Lisa danced, as Jody sang, and stayed onstage, and it was the most fun Lisa had seen her have in months. And afterward, maybe one or two a.m., she sat in Lisa's van and dished about the memory pills, and Lisa said, "Holy shit, Jody!"

"Lisa, I know. But if anyone can understand where I'm coming from..."

"But nurse to nurse?"

Meaning, was there any chance it could *work*? Because there was a big difference between degenerative memory loss and brain damage from a car wreck.

"Lisa, I really think so. You should see what this drug can do..."

"Yeah? And the memories are reliable?"

Instead of answering, Jody teared up. Lisa cradled her to her motherly bosom.

"They can be," Jody said eventually. "I'll give them at least a dozen tries to be. More, depending on how many pills I split with Millar."

"Holy crap, Jody... Okay, so talk me into this. You realize it could get you jail time, right? Which is already... Look, can you trust this dude?"

She waved that one away. "Not an issue. I can handle Millar. And I need his help, so it works out nicely."

"All right. Before I give my okay—because I get it, of course

I get it, but sweetie, the question is if *you* get it. Apart from the *why*. Rank the *people* for me. Who is your priority?"

"Ben, not that much, frankly. I know, I *should* care. But I'm being honest."

"That's all right. Ben gave up on you a good while back."

"Not just the why? The *people* who...?"

"Yes! Countdown."

"I count four, in fact... Brian. Brian was perfect. I know in my gut that what... went wrong was nothing to do with him. But there's still the question, I guess, of what exactly that was, *how* we killed him. Because it makes my missing him, my mourning him, not... complete."

"Okay. Next."

"My father. I'm way more confused about Dad than Brian. So yeah, he was *already* dead, but he's still on the list. A *lot* about my father."

"So why not talk to Ben and Andrew? Start over with them?"

"I don't want to talk to Ben. And I don't know..."

"You don't know how to talk to Andrew."

"No."

"So Andrew's number one."

"Well, I'm up there too, right? I need to... Me next."

"Sorry, absolutely. The why. But for seeing the *people* right, Andrew's number one?"

"Well, the priority is more... *Us*. But yes. Me and Andrew."

"And this is not to appease me?"

"It's not to please you. And yes, it's a way to Dad. But to him too. To my brother."

"All right then. If it'll help... Because you have to deal with Andrew, Jody, it's gotten ridiculous. This is big-ass craziness, mind. More like a moon shot with a BB gun than actually dealing. And why *Millar*? I think Millar's a mistake. Better him than me, but a crutch."

"So you'll approve it?"

"It's a dismal idea! Dismal, Jody. But I get the need. I do. And I do see that desperate measures may be all you have to get you past this, this *block* you have. So—*reluctantly*, mind you! And for God's *sake*, be careful... I won't say *approval*. But blessing, I guess. Jody: I give you my—reluctant—blessing."

"Oh, thank you, Lisa! Thank you, thank you, thank you!"

"Yeah, yeah, yeah." She turned the key in the ignition and pulled out to make the night ride home. "Jody, to change the subject: do you think Danny thinks he's *dating* me?"

Ben, Andrew, and what Lisa called "The Day."

Lisa had known Ben since she was four. His church adopted them when they arrived from Jamaica. But they were only ever casual friends—he was just a dorky shy guy from the hood. She did know Jody's father was with Ben's mom, though. Who on the block didn't? They were the *talk* of it. *He's buying her that Horry house, Latisha says. No, honey, ain't you heard, the White man who owns The Breadbox!* Ben must have been about nine. What Lisa had no idea about—not till she temped there one summer—was the Breadbox man's other *White* family; nor did she put one, one, and one together (Jody's name, his name, their physical likeness) till the day Jody led her to him, junior year, and she was shaking her ex-employer's hand.

They weren't yet blood sisters; just close friends. So Lisa only dropped hints, she initiated theoretical discussions to probe what Jody knew; to determine she knew nothing. And instead of broaching this taboo topic directly, Lisa called the man; she invited him for coffee; she begged him to talk to Jody and asked, *How could you?* While appreciative of "the discretion" of her approach, he retorted that it was none of Lisa's business. He agreed it was his *wife's* business; his wife had always known. He was not persuaded, however, that it was his *daughter's* business. But given the circumstances—meaning

131

Lisa might gab?—he would think about it.

And he may, perhaps soon, have come clean.

But then he was diagnosed with cancer, and that became the revelation that mattered. So Jody found out about Ben the same day she learned of Andrew and heard her father's will; the day of the goddamn *wreck*. Too *late*, Mr. Breadbox! Our "discretion" damn near *killed* her.

Jody did remember the half-day before. A late breakfast, fruit and cereal. Brian with his feet up, reading the paper. (As she waited for Lisa, in point of fact: there was a morning escapade Lisa needed help with.) The phone ringing. Her mother smiling a tight smile, saying, "You get it, dear, I suspect it's about the will." Which it was, but all the lawyer voice wanted was to confirm the appointment. And all he revealed was there would be other heirs present. Not who, or why. And that's where her memory fell into its pit. Dragging the rest of Jody in after it. To clamber back out or let some duppy contrive the feat, usurping the shell of her.

Months later, Lisa was in the room when Jody's mother showed Jody the documents. It was Lisa who fetched Jody the newspapers she demanded. *Crosstown expressway, three hospitalized, Brian Everett dead, etc.* It was Lisa who said, "Jody, this is Ben, this is Andrew": a stranger who called himself her stepbrother; a stranger who said he was her half-brother. It was Lisa who got them both out of there after Jody asked if they knew what had happened. And Ben said, "No, not really." And Andrew said, "You drove your car at us. You tried to kill us."

Jody—or possibly Brian—because Andrew did see Brian grab at the wheel, whether to steer away or into him, whether to save Jody from herself or to enable her—veered, he said, quite *deliberately* across the path of his larger vehicle, and spun, and rammed it.

"I'm so sorry, Jody," said Lisa, once the men were gone.

"That fucking asshole!"

"I did ask," said Jody, her quandary sharpening. It was still the *how*, but even more, now, it was the *why*. It was what that *why* might say about her. Its summary judgment of who she was.

And oh yeah, Brian was dead. And she had a brother. And a... a Ben. And her father was... whatever the fuck her father was. And Brian. Was. Dead.

Andrew didn't level his charge officially, thank God. Officially, it was "bad luck": there was a "simultaneous change of lanes." Jody was held responsible anyway because it wasn't quite simultaneous, after all; but she was unconscious, and there was no call to ask harder questions.

But those are the questions Jody was stuck with. How, at her private core, had she taken the soap opera news? That she, Ben, and this man Andrew were each, equally, her father's heirs. That this man Andrew was her half-brother, by an aboriginal girl in Australia—her father having been sent to America to scotch that liaison. Each summer, while Jody was at camp, when her dad returned "to see the relatives," people he assured her she'd meet one day, he had, in fact, as a letter he left her phrased it, "spurned the relatives you know of" to devote his visit to this elder child. Since Jody turned three and Andrew eight, he had striven to be a loving father, or a loving summer father at least, to Andrew; as your mother, pumpkin, has always known. And no sooner, baby, did your dad fall ill than Andrew flew in to be my loving son... To be installed, across the tracks, with the old man's *third* family, his crosstown clan: Ben's family.

So just who *is* this Jody, Jody asked then—still asks—who may, in grief and abnegation, have done so vile a deed? And who was this man, her father? About which Lisa was frank, and Jody was uncomprehending. To befriend Ben might have helped, but she missed that boat. And who was this Andrew, who had made such a terrible charge against her?

"You've known him some time, haven't you, Lisa?" she asked back then.

"No, Jody, I've met him is all. The first time not many months before you met him."

"And what do you make of him, Lisa? Is he a scoundrel?"

"Yes, dear heart, he's something of a scoundrel. And unlike Ben, he has resented you, I think. But I'm not sure what that means about The Day; you'll need to let him into your life, Jody, to answer that. But not only for that, as you must know. Because he's your brother."

"And to discover if I killed Brian," she said then. "Brian's *dead*, Lisa."

"Yes, sweetheart."

"Well, I killed him either way," she repeated now, years later. "But if I murdered him."

"Not a useful way of thinking, darling. You were in no fit state to drive. Brian shouldn't have let you. We've talked about this." More than twice.

"But I still won't *know*, will I, though? Not until I remember for myself."

"Possibly. But do be careful, won't you? Because I don't think it works that way. Sweetheart, I just don't think you're ever going to remember."

A silence.

"I have to, though. I have to."

"No, darling, you really don't. But it's okay. I understand that you have to try."

II.

It wasn't that she wouldn't sleep with him. During those first weeks they split the pills three times only, rationed to six-day intervals; whereas Jody had rather missed sex and liked sharing her bed. It was more that the nervousness and the excitement of their encounters had the pills at their bedrock and as their backdrop: Millar felt as if she'd settled on him as a "you'll do"—because he knew about the drug; because he was crazy about her. It was a tidy trade-off.

When she wasn't taking it, she was talking about taking it, or about having taken it: about the memories she had reawakened, or the slightly false ones that had become hers— which Millar did and didn't mind. He loved her voice. He loved how she talked. He only wished she would talk about other things more. And yes, sure, he wanted to feel that he mattered.

The last time, the night of his third pill, they were in the bedroom, they were naked, he knew pills were on the agenda for the weekend, but it was only Friday and they could surely wait. She'd uncoiled from his embrace and said, as if the idea had just struck her, "Hey, Millar... What say we take the pills first and see what it's like to make love during?"

He hesitated.

"With some of that red wine you brought to wash it down," she suggested. A hand in his hair, a hand tightening against his back.

"I'm not sure," he said at last.

Her hands slackened, removed themselves. Her body went still, and her hands got sulky; the left one lightly clenching, the right thumb fidgeting with its fingertips, counting to four, to eight, to twelve.

"All right, fine, then," she said.

They lay in silence. There was a ceiling to look at.

"All right, then," he said at last. "Fine."

So she fetched the wine. And for Millar, the rush of the pill came almost immediately, as if it had been waiting at his consciousness's threshold, to barge in and take him.

They were at her doorstep, Jody and he, fully clothed but locked in a goodnight kiss that made the ride of their clothes, the tautness of the fabric's lifting, twisting, the tug of rumple and breach, into a candid and mutual foreplay. It was their first kiss: that third date.

"Come in?" she asked, her key in the hand under his shirt, scraping his spine, descending. The flat of it cupped the small of his back. It made, in the heat of her palm, a shiver. And at the top of her thigh, his own hand slipped under her panties' crinkled rim and gave her ass its squeeze of answer.

It took two minutes of embrace to get inside the door, one to close it, ten to shuffle beyond the funky hat rack.

There was no hurry, not yet—the hat rack was patient, could find room on its hooks for anything they chose to hang on it. Many of these clothes were of styles and shapes with which it was previously unfamiliar, but that was fine, they could keep 'em coming.

They kept 'em coming.

There was no dialogue, or hardly any, merely as seasoning.

"I hear there may be orgies," she had said, her key entering its lock.

"Can two people constitute an orgy?" he had asked, a minute or so later, closing her door behind them with the swiveled and pressed weight of her, the heavy conjoined angle of his body against hers so close they were a single toppling line.

"Oh, I think so," she answered, some of the last words they spoke for several hours, though there were noises. In his false memory, he heard them, made them, one by one, discretely, cataloged them with the sensual rest of it; the restless and many-consummated rest of it; took gloriously slow note of, was made replete and desolate with, the wonderful slow lie of it.

When he came back to the present, naked next to naked Jody still in her altered state, her bed and its bed sheets hardly ruffled, their wine barely sipped, their skin at no point touching, he knew the memory must have been a false one, because he also recalled his real first entry into her house, the one the drug had so embroidered and brought to other climaxes, and he knew, who could be so stupid not to know, which account was the truth and which only the wish. But since it didn't feel as if, he asked himself if he really cared.

Yes, he answered himself experimentally, *I care. I care and what I need to do is get up, scrawl a note, and leave.*

No, he said, *maybe I care, but who am I kidding? I'm not going anywhere.*

He leaned over her and kissed Jody on the brow and on her slightly parted mouth. He brushed her hair aside as he had so often watched her do. He cared but didn't care. That was enough, for now. He knew but didn't care to know which true answer was the truer.

III.

Danny was his brother; Big Nick was his bro. Jemmy hung out with both of them way too much not to have mixed feelings about Jody. Oh, she was all kinds of fun. A little careless with a guy's feelings was all—a bit too much of a user.

She sure had a sweet, ragged voice, though, and he always wished she'd sing for them more—she and Danny blended great too, which helped when your actual lead singer's voice, his job purely because he was the main songwriter, was such watery tea.

They played a gig once when Rhino was sick, so that he confined himself to guitar and frog-croak harmony. Danny sang lead that night. Surprise! They were *way* better. Rhino soon put a stop to that! The next time he was sick, they canceled.

But that was Danny in a nutshell. The talent to be front

man, the mindset to be back-up. Somehow, improbably, he was dating Jody. But the lady obviously liked him less than he liked her, and she radiated heat and charm. Sending out vibes to guys like Nick that maybe he could steal her away.

Course, Nick was even more of a wuss than Danny.

Man, like that double date when he was with Shannon, and Nick invited himself along? Talk about *awkward*, dude! What an embarrassing big puppy dog! Even Danny got ticked off.

So when his brother and Jody broke up, Jemmy had serious concerns, even more for Nick than Danny. He went round to see Jody one day, bringing the new live CD, featuring her voice somewhere in the mix on a couple of songs, as a way into the house.

"Damn, Jody," he said over coffee. "This is one wild kitch-en."

"Thanks, Jemmy," she said. "So you're here on behalf of Danny?"

"More of a heads up about Big Nick, truth be told. Can you be aware of him a little more? Either set him straight or give him a chance?"

"Wow," she said. "You're quite the friend. Actually, Jem-my, I'm *with* someone now, you know? Someone not Danny or Nick?"

"That's fine, not my business. But could you talk to Nick?"

"Nick will be fine, dude. But sure, if you like, I'll talk to him. Listen, though, are you up for something?"

"Me? What the fuck you mean, Jody?"

"I've got some of this new drug. Millar's not as into it as I am. I mean, he'll take it with me, but not necessarily as often as I need."

"What the fuck you talking about, girl?"

"From the hospital. I swiped some pills. Don't look at me like that, dude; they're not for sick people, and they're really safe. They just make you remember stuff, stuff you've forgot-ten..."

Long story short, she talked him into it. He split one with her, just half a tab each, but wow, man. Holy fuck.

His first maddie.

IV. From "Letters To My Sister," a folder of journal writings by Andrew Barker

I've always known about you, Jody, and I've always wanted you to know about me. I'll agree that our father was as impressive and charismatic a man as you thought him. But he led multiple lives, and he guarded secrets. Not from his wife, he assured her; not from me, he said; merely from the world. And for whatever reason, from you also. I wish it had been otherwise.

I have been, in my biography, very like him.

I had, too young, an illegitimate daughter in Australia, as he had had an illegitimate son. Her mother, a red-haired beauty with the athleticism and lean strength to match most men, kept my girl from me at first, then foisted her on me when she married. Then I, in my turn, abandoned her: my father fell ill, and I came to America to be with him. Or this was a chance I seized to try out a new life. What boy my age would find it easy to be a single father? My grandparents took Elise for a few years, but I kept faith with her; I brought her over to America, eventually. Of course, in part, I wanted to meet my sister: a new life with you in it intrigued me, and I thought a pretty niece might thaw the ice. As it turned out, Elise had ideas of her own about what I was and was not entitled to ask. And since I have never understood how to treat her, if not as an independent, autonomous being, I have made very few real demands.

Anyway, I had begun badly, what with the matter of the car accident between us. About which I know little more than you or Ben: the witness reports and the physical evidence indicate that your car hit ours, as we both changed lanes, and yes, I did indeed see Brian reach for the wheel. The expression on his face was not grim and purposeful. It was aghast and panicked. So I foolishly accused you of veering deliberately into us, as a result of which I don't believe you have ever trusted me. Although, yes, you may have done just that terrible thing.

The truth is that I doubt it. I think you were in shock, *frozen*, and should not have been driving. Naturally, you had been struggling with what you felt, and protecting yourself by masking your feelings. But at the meeting with the lawyers, I saw no sign of hostility. You smiled at Ben and me. With wet eyes, in confusion and disbelief, but not (yet?) blaming us for any of it. Later, when I attempted a conversation, you did your best to listen politely. But you couldn't focus. I left you alone: you were not angry, but you needed to be left alone. Your expression reverted to an appalled blankness of regard.

I was angry, though. At our father, mostly. And I would have liked a more immediate rapprochement with you than a reasonable person might think possible. Then, later, I was angry at you for almost dying. Hard to explain, perhaps, but true. So that shortly after you came out of your coma, I lashed out by implying you had murdered your fiancé. So uselessly, uselessly stupid.

What I didn't tell you, what I may never tell you, until the day that you feel able to read these journal musings—I hope charitably?—was about the effects the concussion had on me.

Because although I wasn't in a coma and didn't suffer from memory loss, I too was affected. I began, at first quite often, to have visions—vivid, unsettling visions—and they have persisted, irregularly, for far longer than the effects of post-concussion syndrome usually persist. Rationally, I dismiss them. But I am not a fundamentally rational man.

Sometimes, they're apocalyptic. Or post-apocalyptic; the nature of the catastrophe changes, but it is global, and you are with me, Jody, as is Elise; we are helping each other survive. Oh, these visions may be ludicrous—they are so luridly cinematic—but why do they revisit me so? Typically, I watch the three of us making our escape, camouflaged among hordes of empty-eyed automaton people, out wandering the streets without purpose. We elude the occasional outburst of violence—the wanderers are in turns listless, belligerent, and erratic, as if punch-drunk. Bright, person-shaped lights, with wings, I am afraid to put a name to them, hover and lurch above us, as if selecting and rejecting. Where they pass, they cast something like shadows, distortions of the image that shift it into variant, shifting scenes.

Usually, I'm awake. A brief, blaring headache summons me to attention; it sucks me into a kind of betwixt place. Sometimes, the pain wakes me into it, out of a deep sleep. The visions' plots are dream-weird, but they are more coherent than dreams: they are sustained as well as insistent. One particularly fierce one came upon me while I was drinking with Ben. I was telling him goodbye, in fact. I'd been explaining that Elise and I were moving to Eastdon, that I hoped to be a real brother to you. Ben, of course, is no blood sibling to us, and our bond, though always cordial, had been loosening as his memories of our father weakened. So he wished me luck, but he'd long renounced interest in you, and the wish was pro forma. As we spoke—and yes, I was impaired by drink—I watched his face, in cadence with a thudding at my temples, empty itself of personality and of spark. Until he looked through me like one of my automaton people and turned and strode into a lake that submerged the world; and drowned. I didn't so much as call his name. I watched him slip under the water. I waited, and he failed to rise.

When I returned to the present, we were seated at our table in his neighborhood bar, laughing at some story he'd been telling, which I had no sense of having listened to. We shook hands, and we pulled each other into a firm embrace. I said goodbye.

Jody, I was never a survivalist until recently, and even now I find my survivalism absurd, patently ridiculous. But it's the visions, you see. I have acquired, some people might say quite stupidly, this need to prepare myself.

V.

"How would we manage, do you think," Millar asked, tickling him. "If we were *Freaky Friday* body-switched, you into me and me into you? Could anyone tell?" Millar doubted it. He would make, he thought, a pretty good lazy puddycat, and Egghead, with his air of shrewd serenity, of wary luxuriance, might pass for a rather more formidable Millar.

Eggy was a lanky and sinuous all-grey animal, as slippery and voluptuary as his slippery, voluptuary humans. His name derived from the scrambled shadings of his face and pate rather than his air of contemplative mystery, but he did stop a lot and muse. In truth, Millar thought him a poseur rather than a genuinely thoughtful creature, because these sudden pauses and prolonged fierce nowhere-stares were routinely followed by a bout of scratching. Millar's guess was that he had been busy identifying what part of him itched. Who knew, though? Maybe the scratching was a self-reward, the treat he granted himself in the wake of some hard thinking.

Millar liked him a lot and dutifully offered him his hand to gnaw; but although Eggy accepted the offering and chomped with compliant gusto, it wouldn't be long before he moved away, around Jody's corner of wherever they were sitting, to lie flat with his head tucked in, looking for all the world as if he had given it his best and come up disappointed.

"Eggy misses Danny," Jody said one time.

Danny had spent long hours at home with Eggy, letting him out into the yard and calling him back to feed, sleeping with him on his chest and at his chin, batting the tangles of Danny's red-black beard. Millar wasn't, not yet, Danny.

"Do *you* miss Danny?" he asked.

"I needed a break from Danny," Jody answered, which was not precisely the phrasing Millar wished to hear.

"Mmmh," he grunted.

There was a silence. Jody stretched a hand down to Egghead, who sniffed it, gave a little lick, and turned half-over easy; paws still stretched around her fingers—paler belly showing, then the fluffy tuftings of his side, and back again, a purring little riff and roll of greys.

"I'm not sure who I am right now, I mean," Jody said.

Millar smiled sympathetically. Or piteously. She giggled a little.

"Relax, dude, I like you."

She withdrew her hand and sat up straighter, stretching, yawning. Egghead resettled.

"Mmmh," he said.

"Still five pills left," Jody said.

"And all of them," Millar continued firmly, "are just for you."

VI.

"It's not really in Eastdon. It's out your way. Four miles past the docks down 219."

"So it's an island?"

"A vast one, for a river island."

"Okay," Edie said. She liked big goofy Kitty. She didn't mind hanging. Though she suspected this was about more than visiting Foghorn Rock and chilling to local bands. Kitty had split from Tiff again, which saddened the elder sister. She didn't see what she could do to fix it, but she was back to being the captain of the good ship Edie, cheerful and resourceful; she would be glad to lend an ear or a shoulder.

So that Saturday, brighter and earlier than she thought necessary, but fine, she was a morning person, Kitty picked her up at her new place, a little jewel of a Hale County cottage, in the woods of a rich gay couple's estate, and drove them out to Foghorn Rock. And sure enough, when they got there, it was swathed in a glittery mist. They parked, and there was the river, and here an elaborately wrought footbridge that kettle-spouted into nothing halfway across; only treetops like leaf clouds to let slip where the over there was, over there, in the beyond.

"Yay, high five!" said Kitty.

It was considered good luck, she had explained when she called, to see Foghorn Rock for the first time in the fog, and she'd been quite anxious to get Edie there before it lifted.

"Maybe," she had said, "your luck will rub off."

They followed a few other early birds across the footbridge into a hover of mists, which timorously disrobed to reveal a reedy field, and ooh, a score of port-a-potties. The lanes forked three ways: sharp left back by the water; a wider, loopier right-hand trail up top to the Visitors' Center; and a well-trodden path into the gauze-girt trees beyond.

"The concert area's that way." She was pointing at the gap into the woods.

But the tunes weren't scheduled for an hour yet, so they turned left toward the riverbank.

In a meadow of milkweed and thistles they startled up a flock of goldfinches. "The Rock totem!" Kitty exclaimed. "They love it here!" Edie pulled out her phone and took pictures. She got a cool one of her and Kitty with a goldfinch rising over them as if emerging from Kitty's hair.

"Edie," she said eventually, "there's something we've been hiding from you. Your sister has started to forget things. A lot of things, in fact. And here's the other thing, Edie. So have I."

They'd had a good hike about the island in the melting mists, keeping the conversation casual. People-watching, surveying the scenery. The trees; the river that broke into whitewater around flat, slabby rocks; a bedraggled interior lake, fast food detritus and squished beer cans speckling the reeds. Up the hill was a hulking Visitors Center, with a pugnacious foghorn thingy straddling the roof. They mused upon it from across the lake and mocked its looks. But once the feedback and the warm-up noodling started, Kitty steered them toward the closest of the three stages, into the mill of music freaks and picnickers. They spread their tarp. An acoustic trio was up; good for hearing themselves talk, and enough privacy cover to feel comfortable doing so. *Sorry, sensitive harmonizing folkies, don't mind us.*

Because Kitty, finally, was getting down to her agenda.

"You know those memory loss outbreaks that have been in the news recently?"

"Kitty, all that's in Eastern Europe, isn't it?"

"Well, apparently not so 'all' any more."

"What are you saying, that you guys have begun to forget stuff—"

"Really forget stuff. Like a slew of stuff."

"—and you think you've *caught* something, some *bug*? Whatever that Eastern European mess is, Kitty, I'm pretty sure there's nothing you can *catch* that makes you lose your memory."

"Well, apparently there is now."

"I'm sorry, but I don't believe it."

"You need to start watching the news."

The song ended. The front row fans clapped and hollered. A blarier, jazzier horn noise wafted over from the main stage. Edie poured two coffees from the thermos. Kitty unwrapped them each a croissant with cheese. They ate. Edie let the next song simmer awhile.

"Okay, you have me provisionally anxious. But even so, why here, why would it have infected you here in Eastdon? And why are you telling me this, anyway? Why were you hiding it from me in the first place? What exactly has changed?"

"Why here, because there's a clinic here. Memory loss

patients have been coming to Eastdon for a while for a drug-testing program, from all over the east coast and beyond. The feeling is, Edie, that this is now memory loss central, USA."

"What, Eastdon is?"

"Eastdon is. And what's changed is your sister has become convinced that what she has is contagious. She pushed me away, Edie, I didn't walk out on her. But apparently, I've got it anyway. So we're back together, just letting you know. Yay. But now we want you to leave."

"You what? You're pushing *me* away now? That strategy didn't protect *you*."

"We kiss. We exchange bodily fluids."

"So you're saying it's sexually transmitted? Then I'm safe with you guys."

"You don't have to catch this, Edie. It's not too late. Leave Eastdon."

"Not going to happen, Kitty. My sister, whom I need to go see like right now, is sick. Her partner, of whom I have grown quite fond, is sick. I'm staying. Tell me what I can do to help."

"Well. I still hope you'll rethink that. But if..."

"But if?"

"But if it gets as bad as we've talked about it might get—if it spreads here the way it has in Europe, and not just Eastern Europe, lately—"

"In which case, nowhere to leave Eastdon for."

"Then things are gonna get bad. We'll need somewhere... secluded... to hide out..."

"What? Foghorn Rock? You're thinking Foghorn Rock?"

"No, not Foghorn Rock. Though someone will probably try that. No. We were hoping maybe your—not yet, but when it starts to get bad, and after you've gotten away, far away, hopefully—your rental cottage?"

The sensitive harmonizing folkies hit a three-part *Ooooh*. Edie opened her phone and googled the memory loss news. The pages and pages of it. Including some stories about the Eastdon clinic's drug trials. She clicked on one and she read.

VII. From Millar's set of top ten Eastdon histories:

#1. The Foghorn Rock Visitors Center, 1960s

There existed no James River island called Foghorn Rock until the 1960s. This amazes folks. "What? I thought John Smith wangled that foghorn from Chief Powhatan himself!"

The official name is now, and has been since time colonial, Shaw Island. But when it was decided, in 1823, that Shaw Island was a shipping hazard worthy of a lighthouse, it got dubbed Lighthouse Rock. Railroads made the shipping traffic obsolete, and the lighthouse fell into disrepair. It was torn down; the island became Old Lighthouse Rock. In 1932 Cornelius Shaw IV donated it to the state. After the state and the WPA got busy, we wound up with two bridges, a Visitors Center on the granite hill, and an annex to display the lighthouse's exposed remains and its salvaged foghorn. Let's tout the rock's historical significance! Let's ballyhoo those river-rinsed forests! Oh, and why not place, no, not a new lighthouse (too costly) but a new foghorn, how expensive can a foghorn be, up on the VC roof? A giant antiquey foghorn might be an attractive curiosity!

And so, luckily (for it was expensive, and is grotesque), it has proved.

The design is whimsical: an obese, rainbow-speckled black trumpet shell. To be decorative and striking is all that's required, since there's no longer any merchant shipping, nor much real fog. Just morning mists, persistent all year, but scrubbed clean by the sun. (It's said there were once thick smogs.) Still, the diaphone built into the sculpture is functional, as, on ceremonial occasions, it emits a honk to prove. Commentators have been impressed by its lugubrious bass resonance.

The VC itself is a mixed bag. The annex, which has a

reading room, a balcony overlook, and a display room for other artifacts, is charming in its modesty. The island actually has no historical significance, apart from the lighthouse and one bloodless Civil War skirmish, between five shipwrecked Confederates and two shipwrecked Yankees. So modesty is appropriate, and I applaud it! The non-museum part, the fleece-the-visitors-with-snacks-and-trinkets part, is by contrast immoderately tacky. There are plate glass windows with good views, though.

And then there's the Foghorn Rock Film Library, which is the best!

At least three movies, not counting the VC documentary short, have been filmed on Foghorn Rock. The Film Library screens scenes. One was a Civil War pic, where six different battles were recreated on this one five hundred-acre site. (Since its release, the island is sometimes used by re-enactors. But not often. The movie was quite bad.) One was an indie coming of age story, for which the filmmakers built an eighteenth-century village in the fields. And the third was a zombie apocalypse flick. And this film, once a week, every week, they show in full! It is a HOOT! Two of my tennis friends play zombies in it. They still dress as their zombie selves at Halloween. With some cohorts, they're now planning a big re-enactment of their own, in fact, of the film's zombie banquet, for this coming Halloween. On Foghorn Rock itself, if they can get permission. I hope to be there, munching on a leg or three!

(Jody, I know we agreed to exclude mayhem and violence. But gloriously fake mayhem? C'mon! Maybe, October 31st, you can join us, even? C'mon, let's drink some blood to that!)

VIII.

Down to her last three pills. Even Jody was reluctant to take them; she knew, as Millar didn't yet know, that after this batch there could be more if she liked, when she liked. But the knowledge unsettled her; she balked at seeking out that fresh supply, at needing it, and at having that much more drug to feed her need. She couldn't just traipse off to see a flick and sit, which is what Millar wanted to do. So she tried to dissuade him, but without confessing why.

"The local paper gave it a pretty bad review," she said instead.

"The only bad review I've seen." Millar shrugged. "I don't dislike Charles Finchley as a reviewer, but about some kinds of film he's an idiot."

"He said it was boring. All yak and no yeti."

"Yes, I'm sure he meant that line as a putdown. Whereas to me, it's an enticement. Films that *intend* to be all talk are often my favorites."

"Mmh. I'm not sure they're mine."

"Oh, I can see it alone some other time. I just thought, you know, since it's a relationships movie, it might be nice..."

"I don't know. I don't really see going to a movie as doing something together. You're in the dark, sitting separated by the dark, each having your own experience."

"Which you then *discuss* together, over dessert and coffee. Getting to know each other more intimately, using the issues the film raises as a touchstone."

"If the film *raises* issues."

"Precisely why I prefer *talk* movies. Or one of the reasons."

"Okay, I'll bite. Why else?" Almost despite herself, she'd begun to enjoy this conversation. Not because of its content exactly; it was more to do with Millar—the person—the intensity of his quirks, his squealed enthusiasms. It was like moving to Eastdon and learning to see it, feeling that she was discovering it.

"Well, the major one is that I think intimate conversation is what film does best. There's no other medium as well-adapted for that kind of authentic eavesdropping. In theater, there's the stage, and there's the audience, the actors have to talk loud, and there's all that blocking, it's inevitably more of an artifice—"

"In books, they have all those interpolations of *he said* and *she said—"*

"Well, that too—"

"They do, though, there's a distancing effect—"

"Well, sure, you're right, no doubt that's true too, but—"

"Most people would say film is a visual medium, though; that action is its essence."

"Those are, um, those are two completely separate issues! There's, well—though, *yes*—" Millar seemed to have too much to say now to control the saying of it. His words glugged out in a stumbling rush: all stop, start, gesticulate; it was quite the entertainment! She decided to shut up and let him go at it—more to *observe*, truth be told than to listen all that closely. So okay, he was being pompous, but it was a very bubbly pompous; it was rather endearing.

"In the first place, there's the, there's the *visual* aspect—which is true, film *is* visual, it's the other reason why film does intimate conversation better than books, the *major* reason—because you can *see*, without being told, the whole physical context. The body language. The relationship to a space. The, well, this is more auditory, but it's still essentially cinematic, the hesitations and the intonations, the context that often *undercuts* the text, that shows what's being said to be a total *rationalization*, or else emotionally just *wrenching*—you see, it isn't just the *surface*, which may be quite *banal*, it's the *under-current*, the, the…"

"Okay, okay. And in the second place?"

"In the second place, what?"

"I don't know! *You* were the one who said 'In the first place.'"

"I don't know either."

They laughed. He brushed a stray hair from her brow. She said, "I give in. Let's go."

"Oh, I remember!" Millar said. "*Action.* I actually think books do action better than films because books work with the imagination, and films, especially action films, so often just worship spectacle, which is much more tawdry and less telling—"

"Okay, o*kay*! I already gave in. I said, 'Let's go,' already!"

"I know, I was just saying what, um... Let's go to the *movie*, you mean?"

"Yes, Millar, let's go to the movie."

"Cool!"

So they went to the movie and sat side by side in the no longer quite so separate dark. They had dessert and coffee, and she said, "I really liked it," and told him why.

And he said, "Oh, I thought it was *wonderful*," and why, and she found him a bit pompous but so endearing, and it struck her that maybe after all she *was* falling just a bit, or more maybe, in love.

IX. From "Letters To My Sister," a folder of journal writings by Andrew Barker

We have met twice now, you and I. And reconciled, I hope?

Momentous news, right? How we have struggled, each of us, for our different reasons, with the other's absence from our lives. How much we have counted on such a reconciliation resolving. So come on, muster some giddiness, Andrew. Say hooray.

Well, it was certainly interesting. I will say that; interesting, in fact, is a pale epithet. And I'm certainly glad that we're "friends" at last, even if the precision of our accord feels more like a treaty than a breached barrier. We agree to use the terms half-brother and half-sister. We agree to grant the other a measure of intimacy. We agree to listen to what s/he has to say about the State of the World and acknowledge the extraordinary wisdom of his/her posturing.

The first time, you came to my door with your boy-friend, Millar. Elise and I, co-kinfolk, had signed the invitation together, and for whatever reason, you had decided that it was finally possible to accept. You waved to your niece, who was across the room, but asked if it could just be the two of us, this first time. I suggested that Elise go down to the TV room, where she could watch whatever she liked. You gave Millar a peck goodbye. Before leaving, he crossed to shake my hand, and glare into my eyes, and decide if I was or was not a nutjob.

(I was, of course, but not glaringly. Not yet.)

It was a business meeting, at least at first. Your terms, less baldly stated but in essence as I have described them above. Your demand that I tell you everything I could, from my perspective, about the day we met, from the reading of the will to the accident. I complied without accusations this time. You will, I hope, by now have read my earlier entry on this topic, and we will have learned to trust one another. You will know that I told my whole truth.

But then it got complicated.

"Okay," you said, "now, in exchange, let me tell you something. I have begun, quite illegally, to take some experimental medication. I stole most of a box of pills from the clinic. They restore—let me finish, please, if you interrupt with questions, I may not be able to get through this. They restore lost memories, and burnish existing ones. They are very, very effective. But they aren't pre-dictable—meaning, partly, that the memories come from anywhere in your life they like, rather than where you might wish them to. Also, I won't lie, the drug has been known to create false memories, memories that are as powerful and persuasive as the true ones, and which, without treatment, are very hard to unmake. This has happened to me two or three times, I can't be sure, in the dozen times I've self-medicated. Only a few small false details, except for the one time. Even the exception was harmless; enjoyable, to a degree, even; a kind of enter-taining, very vivid, waking dream.

"All right. Now to it. I have three pills left. I should explain that Millar has become reluctant to split them with me—he's had nothing but good experiences, but he worries more than I do about the psychological and mild chemical dependency. Or so I believe. You will have guessed that I don't like to take the pills alone. There's something in the nature of... that way of doing things which, I don't know why, unsettles me. Which creates, frankly, a poor climate in which to try the drug. But it's got me thinking. I've been thinking that, under the right conditions, I might, possibly, be able to direct and focus my attention more—perhaps so that I'll remember what I wish to. You can guess what I wish to."

You left a pause. I took a chance and spoke.

"Jody, allow me to recap. You're asking me to be your accomplice in an illegal act. To take an experimental, you say mildly addictive drug with you—which you have stolen—whose effects are dramatic and unpredictable— in order that you may remember things which—I'm assuming that you know the difference between brain injury and simple memory loss—you probably have no serious hope of recovering?"

"Yes."

"Because this would help us connect? Or are you using me?"

"Both, maybe? Well, I *am* using you."

"Do you think I owe you, Jody? Because I don't believe that I owe you."

"Maybe. Honestly, maybe I do. Does that matter?"

"Perhaps not. All right."

"You don't need to answer now, of course, you can think about it."

"I just did answer. I said 'All right.' But not now, not with Elise in the other room."

"No. No, of course not. But you really will? Sometime during the next few days, do you think you could? At my place?"

"All right, your place. Why not tomorrow?"

And *that* became our second meeting.

CHAPTER SEVEN: THEY REMEMBER

"Without memory, there is no culture. Without memory, there would be no civilization, no society, no future."

Elie Wiesel, "This I Believe"

"Anon, who'll live when we're all dead,
How did you write this song?
He told her rhyme to them,
And I remembered it all wrong."

John Boggenpoel, "Anonymous's Tale"

Selections from "The Heartwood Chronicles"
continued

3. Describe the experience of losing your memory.

Jenna Brower

I do have some recollection. The frustration of having
something on the tip of my tongue and it not coming.
Thinking I'd find it if I groped awhile, since I could sense
it in the shadows.

I guess I went into the shadows after it, huh?

The remaking I have more of. What images re-
awoke first, and how I couldn't tell truth from lies. Best I
can figure now is most of the lodge ones were true, and
most of the rest was a useful fabrication. I knit it all
together equally to make Jenna.

The blankness between, I have this residue of how
cold it felt. Brutal cold, like the chill in my blood's too
fierce to ever rise to the human again. Unearthly cold.

Nick Trifflett

I think my memory's getting worse. I know what Lisa
likes to write on the SNAG board, that the contagion
must be running its course because we're not seeing new
outbreaks. But who's left to be outbroken? And is anyone
getting *better*?

She may be right about the world. I hope she is. And
maybe I'm going through a bad patch, or I'm atypical?
But I can't say I expect my memory ever to be what it
was.

I'm terrible in the garden, Brian. I have multiple
gardens, in fact, I try to do everything in multiple ways,
in multiple beds, so that no single half-assed action will
derail us. But I can't tell you what I've done where, and I
can't recall from day to day what mistakes I've made or
learn from them. I know we're not on a mission to feed

the world here, that it's more just us and for barter, but it's a sniveling relief that Andrew has taken charge of the field crops, and is giving me clear instructions in the orchards, or I'm afraid I'd starve us. At least Lisa's not still a vegetarian. She'd be a skin and bones one. And why we have Jody partnered with me is beyond me; she's the one person here less competent than I am.

I forgot where Jemmy's room was this afternoon. He got filthy fixing some pump or other, and he washed up in the creek. *Nick,* he says, *can you get me some fresh clothes from my room?*

Sure, I say.

Ha. I got *lost.*

Our little sallow-skinned red-haired lass can't grow up fast enough for me. So that you can put me out to pasture with the cows.

A couple of them are quite attractive.

Elise Barker

That isn't one of my hang-ups. Sorry. I'm a native of the Memory Loss Age.

Andrew Barker

Okay, on to memory loss. I'll address this actual question.

The thing is, we can explain, or explain away, anything. Coming up with explanations—our truths, our tests of truth—that's what we humans do. Starting out, they're *theories*; spun through our embroideries, they're *stories*; deceive ourselves with them (we are all self-deceivers) and they're *rationalizations*; dice and strain them into a stew of value judgments and spicy data, and we have *interpretations*; frame them as about our rightness and your wrongness, and they're *articles of faith*; prove them to be objectively verifiable, and that's *science*; and when they're the interior touchstones to the lush seethe of our subjective pasts we call them *memories*.

As there are all kinds of forgetting, there are many ways to remember. It's not the mechanisms, axons signaling to dendrites, that trouble me or interest me; my sense memory and working memory and ongoing memory will do what they will as well as the disease allows—I've no control over that. What I love most but trust least—my drug-peddler, my rationalizer, my storyteller, my articulator of faith—lies deeper in the floodplain, where the hippocampus swims and swallows and spits up anything that shines. To measure the *nows* against the *thens*; to ask the *who I ams*. As I shift and explain my meanings. As I sift; select; divert the data streams...

Okay, so I've lost most of my long-term memory. But I've enough of it still—thanks to the restorations of the madeleine drug; thanks to our warehouses of community records, and my private notebooks—to exploit what I do have. Enough to want, and to fear wanting, more.

I'm a conspiracy theorist, after all—I know that as well as anyone—and as passionately as I might swear I'm *right*, I know I can't trust myself.

Because as our memory's stories codify, jewel, and calcify, they begin, inevitably, to lie. Conspiratorially, like all our explainers—creators as we are of pattern—they begin to *plot*.

It's possible not to be appalled by this. It's possible to prefer our arts of conjecture to the truth—as they *become* our truth, more and more elegant. You, Millar—may I call you by your name?—might agree with me on this. The truth, wouldn't you say, is clearly too complex to be knowable? What one requires, rather, is an organizing principle; a set of theories to steer by.

It's equally possible to find such arguments repugnant.

Or like Jody, three, four years ago, to be in quest of one clear revelation, counting on it to be transformative. Or like all of us amnesiacs, of ways to repair ourselves by a great reconfigured seeing; to reimagine our world's story. Until around the gaps we begin to *draft* one, to establish its pathways, to travel its map of plausibilities.

Do we focus on the mystery? Deceit! Intrigue! Or on the romance? Perhaps it could be Gothic? Oh, it will have to include the tragic. But make it make choices, or it'll be so large it has no archetype; it will be shapeless, and anchorless, and shifting.

And *this* is how my memory loss affects me: it pushes me into blind leaps and barely supported risk. Oh, I make those leaps; I take that risk; but I'm less confident than I hope I sound. Too often, I feel blocked and frustrated in my quest for clarity, my need to *explain*, to have some *answers*. Which, I secretly know, are two gut-wrenchingly different things.

We can probe for the *truth*. Or we can just *explain*.

Of course, once we trump up an explanation, we'll surely buy into it hook, line, and sinker, and lay *claim* to it as truth. As our ego prefers we do. And as every lying maddie expects us to.

Edie Driscoll

My memory was fine until the fire. Until Kitty burned. I'd taken a half-dozen or so tablets back in Eastdon, my lab notes say, counting both the X7s and my own first effective ones—but that was precautionary, and it was an ethical choice. To test it on myself, not just my friends.

Shortly after you and Matt brought me to Heartwood, I fell ill. Stress; PTSD; exhaustion; the flu— who knows? But I had a fever, I was delirious, and I slept. When I felt alert again, the first thirty years of my life, minus what those maddies had conserved—including you!—which, remember, I had laughed about remembering, since I had never forgotten—were simply gone.

And because of the fire, of course, I don't even have that much of my stuff. A few boxes which I'd stashed out in my car to make room. Mostly clothes. One really nice photo I'd pinned on the bulletin board above my lab equipment and snatched up with it: a day trip we took to Foghorn Rock. Each with an arm about the other. Kitty with a goldfinch over her head.

I don't really recollect the illness, but I recall the time leading up to it. Me and Kitty. You arriving, with Matt, to get away from Eastdon and to help me with her, her being sick. Kitty getting sicker. Losing Kitty... The fire... After which, coming here, I took a last maddie, and I, well, remembered what I needed to. Kitty. Our whole holy damn me history, of how we became to be, and who we were for each other. And God, what if I hadn't? But I've had an unbroken chain of memory since.

It wasn't a particularly difficult discovery, then—the fact that I was now, in duration of memory, about two years old. Two years are plenty. Two years were about all I could cope with.

Jemmy Jaronsky

I lost my memory? Remind me again, what's a memory?

Nah, there's a joke about this guy who's losing his memory. And in the joke, he likes to *tell* jokes, and he's really bad at it, meaning he'll nail the set-up, but when he gets anywhere close to the punch line, he realizes he can't remember the punch line. So he says, *Okay, forget that one, here's a better one*, and he gets into it, it's going fantabulous, he's doing the funny voices, the fart noises, the big wacky gestures, the imitations of drunken sheep, he's got his crew rolling around clutching their stomachs—and he forgets the punch line. He forgets the general *vicinity* of the punch line, like where whatever he's leading up to was last time it passed through town.

So he starts, oh yeah, no, it's his buddy who starts *another* joke. You know, Oh shut up, dude, you're useless, let me show you how it's done. But now the *buddy* forgets the punch line. And the next buddy takes over, and yeah, he's trying to tell the *first* joke the *first* buddy was telling all *over* again, which it's like none of them even remembers at *all*—and *he* forgets the punch line, and he says, Wait, wait, wait, I've got another one, a better one...

You know, one of these jokes that keeps going and going.

Someone made it up when everyone started losing their memory, I guess. It was a routine, you know?

Yeah. So it was like that. Losing my memory.

As incredibly fucking *irritating* as it was incredibly fucking *tedious*.

Jody Barker

How long? *How long?* Sleep, wake. Name? *Dunno dunno don't KNOW*. Lisa! Squeeze Lisa's hand till eyes go mumbly. *Lisa, bits of me not there*. Parts of me not there, nurse! Mom! Mom, I love you. Squeeze bye bye, Jody. *Lisa!* Hello, sweetie. I'm *Jody*, Lisa! Yes, dear, you are, you are! *Shh! Parts of Jody aren't there. I can't find them.* Wheelchair. Sun in my eyes, close the thingamabobs, please. Blinds. The blinds. Mom, the machines? Suction me more gone or to find me? *Lisa, shh, where's Brian? Why isn't he, is he, oh God, he is, isn't he?* What do? I? No, Mom, I need to sleep. No, *sleep*. No, *later*. If I. G'night, *g'night*. If I sleep... No, *not*! Lisa, *help*... ... It was like that, I guess... Where...*were* you, Brian?

Lisa Huttongold

If you don't mind, I'll pass on this one. There was too much else going on. Forgetting things was a terrible inconvenience because how could I get done what needed doing?

That's still how I feel, in chief. I wish that I could have been more competent. Then *and* now. That in spite of it all, I might have learned more thoroughly how to be more competent.

Matt Simmons

I was having a beer with the Southside Bowling League boys. At that alley with the two karaoke bars? Or a bar at one end, and at the other, more like an ice cream parlor.

So we're in the adult bar, and it's my turn at the mic. Now I sing pretty good, as you well know. I'm a karaoke fiend, truth be told. So I'm singing away, "I guess you'll, my girl," and I look out at my buddies, and one of them is a complete stranger to me. I mean, I know I've known him for years, and I have a feeling maybe it's even been since high school, but I cannot for the life of me tell you one thing about him. I mean, not even if he owes me *money*. I'm wondering who the heck might have spiked my ale because I just haven't drunk that much.

So I fake my way through it, but as the weeks go by, it keeps happening. Someone will be clean gone. Or some place or some period of my life. As if someone's wadded up a wet paper towel and blotted them away. That's what it was like for me.

I did get some of it back. When we started splitting aunt Jilly's maddies, it was sometimes the lost stuff, sometimes things I already remembered. I would recall them so much sharper.

4. How did your initial experiences of the maddies affect you?

Lisa Huttongold

Confusion and fear. Delight for what I retrieved. I hadn't believed myself infected—I was conscious of no slippage. So that first three-week chunk was a shock. It could be the ins and outs had smalled free of me in the normal way of things, the way anyone forgets, but this period of time was *recent*. And I'd lost moments that were *memorable*!

There was a dinner party, for instance, at Jody and Danny's. I'd brought a guy. We'd been dating for a while, to our moderate mutual pleasure. We weren't going to wind up together, or be best buds for life the way Jody and Danny and I had a chance to be. In all honesty, I can't say I was that upset when he started hitting on Jody—that's how guys *got* around Jody: they hit on her. No doubt you recall. And anyway, Danny and I were flirting too, the way we did. It didn't mean anything, only that we adored each other, which we liked to let each other know. So it may have felt to Vinnie that he was fitting in. That this was how things were played here. But for some reason, it made Jody bristle. Oh, it always did, I guess, when someone failed in the sufficient appreciation of my worth—which I loved, loved about her. (Huh. *Sophomore year*, I remember remembering. *Bet she didn't even realize...* Wherever that thought once led, it's gone now.)

So the conversation had turned to illegal immigration, on which only Vinnie had firm opinions. He was spouting them, going so far as to ask what we wanted the US of A to look like: like *Jody*, for example— or like—and his eye fell on Jamaican American *me* for an instant before he caught himself—well, like Juan Carlos, or Li Po, or Sanjay.

Danny began to quote Li Po. Danny was capable of surprising you like that. "Alone with my pot of wine under the flowering trees, I lift a toast to the moon, inviting her to share my cup and drink with me..." This failed to derail Vinny. "I mean, like Jody, right?" he said.

No real friend will suffer this kind of nonsense for very long, of course. "Like me? Like, like *this*, you mean?" Jody asked. In an instant, her visage... *transformed* from sweetness to howling rage. There was volume. There was sustainment. There was legitimate spittle. He had to wipe it off himself. And then she switched back, and we permitted ourselves to act as if it had all been in fun. Continuing our evening in a civilized, careful, three-fourths amused state of truce.

I enjoyed retrieving that memory.

Edie Driscoll

I wasn't stricken yet. I expected to be more interested in monitoring the effects than in the trips; if you recall, I was studying how to synthesize the drug. But I was staggered by their fullness and clarity. Their sheer scope. In hours, I relived months. I actually began to hope that I might, in fact, manage to restore my sister to health. My girlfriend. Wow, I really said "sister"?

Sorry, Kitty. I'd have been her raunch lackey for a week for that one.

Matt Simmons

The first three tablets I took, it was like God granted me three brand-new home movies of Berry and me, three great days in the life of. Except not a movie: it was like the real, true *days*. That was the wham, woah, wow of it. But sure, I can tell one as a story. Since you like stories.

We're on a bike ride out by the Williamsburg Road, aiming to reach one of those colonial-era plantation homes and tour it. In the event we don't make it, we stop for lunch and linger too long so that we wind up heading back, a smidge tipsy.

But that's not the story yet. The story part begins with us doing this on a *tandem*.

My wife, Beryl, we all call her Berry, decides we need to go on a proper date, so she rents this tandem, and she organizes an excursion. I pooh-pooh it as a matter of form, but it turns out fantastic. Just honest, cornball fun. Sometimes I do the pedaling as she coasts, but more so, we both do it, steady and easy together. She pedals for me even, which is adorable and hilarious. Puffing and wheezing, her round little ass waggling. I sing her "Daisy, Daisy." And on the way back, a touch wobbly from the pie and ale, so taking it nice and slow, we steer through the trees and off into a field. You know, after dinner, rest a while? Except rather than rest, we have ourselves an old-fashioned, teen-geezer, frisk-fest in the grass, if you can believe that.

Well, if you can or can't, the point is that right off the bat, I refreshed my memory of some terrific times. Or relived, really. I got to feel in love with my wife like new again. And for years, I did take her for granted, and I ran around on her a little maybe, but I never did quit loving her. Or resent her or anything. She was always my girl. And it was like she was back alive, you know?

So this was pure, pure pleasure for me.

So in a word, *Holy hot damn.* That's how those first maddies hit me.

Jenna Brower

Without the maddies, I would have no memories. I had no other recourse to be a worldly person. That is how we fashioned me—not the soul me, but the temporal one. They were my rag and patches therapy sessions. I have no feelings about this; it's just the way of the world to me.

Jemmy Jaronsky

Jody turned me on to them. I didn't even know people were losing their memory. I wasn't losing mine. Yeah, you know how the mads preserve the circs under which you took them—the bonus bang, Nick calls it? So yeah, at Jody's, but after Danny split. She'd redone the kitchen.

I do wish, not that every ride was the boo, but that I knew which was which, right? If you knew what was and *wasn't* bogus, you'd love the mads, right?

That first clip was like an A major 9 groove, though. Me and my uptown girl Ilsa at the Nascar track, my first race day. Right *by* the action, man, and I didn't know to bring ear-plugs, right, so at the time it was like, *excruciating* thrills—like what are you doing to yourself, dude, you're a musician, save the destruction of your eardrums for the workplace! But in mad mode, it didn't matter. You could take it all *in*, and it was *more* real, larger than freakin' *life*, man, and it was like you were *immune*. Meaning it's so loud you're like, hey, there's a bomb going off in my hat, man, but you can step away from it, and slow it, and ease out of and back *into* it, and know it, and when it's over, hey, there's, okay, this tiny bit of residual deafness, but no actual hurt at all.

It was a rush, man. It was like, mad love.

Nick Trifflett

I don't recall taking my first maddie. That is, I recall the nice ride, but not the dull why or where of it. Who gives an outhouse crap about all this, Brian?

Elise Barker

I wasn't even gapping when I first dosed, was I? It was preventative.

No, it was good. Like my dad says, I liked it better than TV or video games. Luckily, or I'd be a zom.

I'm over what I've lost or haven't *lost*, though. Or what I've *shed*, to be lean and mean about it. Because I do have what memory I need, Brian.

Uh, no. The maddies *did* their job. Why would I still be taking them? You can ask my dad, he uses my supply more, but I'm pretty sure it's been a good long while.

No, Brian, because I want to learn how to live *without* that kind of memory. I want to remember the way that animals do. They do remember, you can tell they do, but it's not memory like with you guys. Old style.

No, it's fine. I guess it's too late for you to learn anything new. Who knows, the world may change back to how it was. You can dream.

Andrew Barker

Now, this is interesting. I have had the routine retrievals, both true memories and false. But they're not my norm. More often, I'll watch narrated scenes, as in a documentary film. I may be peripheral to it or the protagonist. The memory may be true, false, or approximate, on which topic, the voice-over, in my own voice, will invariably offer its reflections. The commentary is broad, however, and as pontifical as I am here, except with pictures.

And sometimes—not narrated—vividly or less vividly—I eavesdrop on *future* memories. My POV shifts; I'll become some future me, thinking back to now, from a time that may or may not come to pass. Of the memories I've since lived through, none has been spot on, in the way the credulous allege the rearview visions to be; still, the discrepancies tend to be as revealing as the resemblances. Some bore no real resemblance, and for some others, time will tell.

In one of my earliest trips, which affected me deeply, I witnessed the death of a future housemate, a person I hadn't as yet met. I'd rather not discuss whom—I don't wish to provoke the event into being, somehow—but here's the kind of detail I am able to observe. My daughter Elise is present. She has spent her recent homeschooling hours learning about birds, and there's an ornithological paperback, *Birds of Virginia*, poking out of her pocket. Of the other people gathered about the victim, I knew only five at that time, but I am now familiar with all of them. They live *here*. Only two of those present in my vision—my stepbrother Ben and a woman I was seeing back in Eastdon—are not, in fact, members of this community.

And yes, I've looked for it, and that book is indeed in our library.

Jody Barker

Hope. Or its possibility? With those first maddies, I began to hope for hope.

5. Describe a maddie retrieval you believe to be authentic.

Edie Driscoll

Authentic? I believe they all were. And I was healthy enough to make that call.

The best thing I safeguarded, present company excepted? No, seriously, I was delighted to have that one, Millar. Okay, because I'd personally compounded the pill, and it was the same high-speed, narrow-focus narrative I'd been getting with the X7s. So bebopalula, who's my baby, right? But also because we had fun together, babycakes. I enjoyed being with you.

The most useful, though, was my doctoral program. The whole last year of it, and some scenes from before; two X7 collages. So I still know science we need, and I know it fresh!

There was also a man. Sandy hair, dimples, with slyness and charm to burn. God, I hope he wasn't the one I married. I've a horrible feeling he was, though. Oh dear, he was so lovely.

Odds are, I would have cut off his dick and lit out for the hills.

Jemmy Jaronsky

Another true one was in high school, playing soccer.

If I could have petitioned the gods of the mads, right, to cherry-pick my game of the ages? This one was like the boo. We won in the league semis, 4-3. I scored twice and set up Piet Gilray for the winner. A high curling cross, left-footed. I thought I played awesome, man.

But it was better in fuzz memory. I didn't, in fact, play that hugely great. And yeah, it was fun times to be out there on the turf again and all, but I kept wanting to fast-forward it, you know? The game felt fairly ordinary. And one of my goals was overwhelmingly lucky, and yeah, Piet *was* offside. And there was... other stuff.

I wrote a song about it, not a ditty, a proper one.

Which was better because I could shape it into a highlight reel. And when I put in the other thing, which I scrupulously *did* do, about listening to myself spout crap in the car after, and her breaking up with me, in the song it became like, poignant, you know? Because reality is reality, but art has to stir the soul, right?

Nah, I never sing that song, dude.

Nick Trifflett

Let's see... Okay. April 7th in sunny Eastdon. My twentieth birthday. My girlfriend has purchased me a consultation with a psychic—the funkiest birthday present ever. I got that day back, no skips. From before breakfast in her bed—or brunch, more properly— through the walk from the parking lot after the Ali Farka Touré concert. Exceptional concert. But the psychic—a truly interesting experience to revisit. Partly because she hazarded some predictions, including some now unverifiable ones about my girlfriend, and in ways I don't wish to divulge, I consider them droll. Partly because she claimed I was the hardest person she had ever been called on to read, which was gratifying. I was intent on remaining inscrutable. No cheap leads. Partly because of two predictions I *am* able to make a determination about.

One, that the band—we were very recently formed and Caitlin had told her about us—would at some point be offered a recording contract and that we should think very carefully before accepting it. No, and never going to happen. And two, that I would one day be *cornered by a tediously chummy interviewer*, who would ask me a series of *intrusively personal questions* and possibly *become quite insistent*, and I should remember that I was under *no obligation to answer*.

No, I'm serious.

No, I am; that's how she put it, verbatim. Yes, Brian, *tediously chummy*.

Jody Barker

Charlottesville. You and me, babe. It's winter. Monticello is all school groups. One from France with their American *correspondants*. I eavesdrop. Does my French still work? A French boy tosses a glove onto an iced-over pond. His friend's glove. Just fooling around. His friend is so exasperated. *Get me my glove!* The teachers are thirty yards away, chattering in a gaggle. Kids swarm to the pond's edge, swatting at it with their scarves. Nope. Oh! almost! But nope. *T'en fais pas, hein*, says the first boy, and he steps out on the ice. The ice breaks. He's in the water. He has the glove, he is waving it in triumph. Big splashes as he wades out. Oh, how he is soaked through. Uh oh, here come the teachers. *Quel petit con!* Meanwhile, in my coat pocket, I'm fingering a vial. Should I tip it in Thomas Jefferson's little Monticello pool? But then who could it ever infect, save the occasional asshole French boy? Wait, is this the *virus* I want to infect people with? Am I some kind of *agitator*? In a few hours, we'll be hiking by the Ragged Mountain Reservoir, you remember? So gorgeous this time of year and so unguarded. A *much* better spot!

(*Tu me crois, chéri*? Coz my brother would. In a heartbeat, he'd believe it.)

Jenna Brower

My African grey was called Luther. It seems a peculiar name now, and I'm curious as to how he came by it. He was very attached to us, especially to me. He'd preen my hair something furious. What he loved, though, was to make his noises. In imitation of us, or of the kettle, or a train passing, or a phrase out of the Sunday sermon on the TV—it made no matter, it could be any noise. Right often, it was our own agitated voice-raisings, he liked a dash of querulousness in the mix, like that made it spicier—mostly, he'd do his call and response with Harlan when Harl got peevish on me. But he'd come out with about any of them at just about any time.

Some afternoons, he'd go through the whole repertoire.

One darn noise after another.

That's what he was doing the day y'all came knocking that last time. Well, not you, but Jody and Lisa, Nick. Jemmy. That redheaded boy. I thought he and Redsy were kin when she turned up. Luther was doing his dishwasher noises. Y'all knocked, and he stopped, and he cocked his head, and he said, *Uh oh.* My own voice, I reckon, though I don't recall ever much saying such a thing. And real drawn out, almost like it was two separate pronouncements. *Uh*, then *oh. Uh. Oh.*

Lisa Huttongold

It interests me how I can't tell. Maybe I only hope some of them are authentic; maybe I only hope that others of them are not. I suspect we've all remembered things there's no one to dispute or to corroborate.

Do you recall when Jody introduced us? You. *Millar*: the *not Danny.* The not even Nick. Which, just as well for Nick, maybe, but may have cleared his puppy love sinuses. Do you recall what I took you aside and said? *I* remember it, I think. The maddie *claimed* I said it.

But who knows, maybe I just thought it. And nope, sorry. Much better forgotten.

Andrew Barker

"Authentic," in reference to the madeleine drug? That's a slippery word. I'm skeptical about the reliability of any and all drug-induced memories. Let's not mistake plausibility and ballpark proximity for proof. But I'll address this question too—in my way.

Here's a scenario from a future memory, set, oh, ten years hence. I may take, apparently, a maddie to come back and warn myself. Yes, yes, absurd, but may I present it as a *possibility*? Rather than narrate it, let me engage in the logical speculation it provokes: as something I suggest we prepare for, once we come through, if we come through, the current round of crises.

What our world will have is a problem with truth. Oh, we've always had one, but formerly we could build smart defenses—we need not be easy to deceive. But then came this contagion. And now we must *lean* on deception, most of us, to not lie broken. We have been made, perhaps irreparably, vulnerable. Remember, the official claim is that roughly one person in twenty is immune. We've had one such person in our ranks! *Are* there such people, *is* Danny one, why they might exist I cannot say, but let us accept, for the sake of argument, the claims as fact. When the call was made for these allegedly unaffected folks to come run the country, some, like Danny, heeded it. They now rule our local, regional, and national governments.

What, in madeleine mode, I was warned of was a world where the zones of government will have become heavily armed enclaves. Places of refuge, from the perspective of those within their walls; bastions of privilege, for those excluded from them. Attacks against them will be ineffective, b/c how much can the undermemoried do? Nor will the numbers be in our favor—far more of us than them will have died.

OTOH, not all the unaffected will embrace their life of privilege. There are always those who go out among the less fortunate, proselytizing and administering hand-outs. We'll be the less privileged, you and I. We'll despise our benefactors, as the less privileged do, but we'll need them. Not all the aid they offer will be material; it will be in unpolluted knowledge. There'll be, by then, a general recognition that the maddies have destroyed our capacity to tell the difference between truth and falsehood. More of us will have lain down with the husks. More of us will be like Jody, swimming through a half-world of the here, the then, the never-nowhere, and the who the hell knows. Let go and let gaga. As the immune ones among us, licensed as "objective truth-tellers," make themselves indispensable and become our overlords.

If they're honest and hard-working and smart, hallelujah. But how many of them will be? In this vision of mine, I was escaping from a zone whose objective truth-teller was hard-working, smart, and a con man. I strove to expose him. I failed.

Maybe none of this will come to pass. But something of its ilk will. We have no defense against it—except that when it's upon us, we needn't be psychos or simpletons. Let's keep doing what we're doing now, only better. We're barely surviving, but we're learning survival *strategies*, and I hope getting better at them. B/c, at some point, we will have to be.

I'm very fond of Lisa; you know that. But even if she's right, and kids are about to be born remembering again, shinier and more the shit than we ever were, when exactly might they be ready to take charge? And why will the powers-that-be just let them?

You want "authentic"? Read the warning signs.

Elise Barker

I'm not that into the maddies, Brian.

Matt Simmons

Our last month in Hale County. Tiff's in sad shape. Edie's had the drug right for a while now; our stash is stretched, but why isn't it helping more? Maybe Tiff was too sick when she got started. And she went months with the X7 dwindling and Edie not yet cracking the code?

Oh, that's right, the good Doctor Corrigan had muddled some of the details. I'd forgotten that. On purpose, didn't Andrew believe? No, you're right, Brian, how could Corrigan *know* the formula that well, when you think about it.

Anyway, we're with them for quite some time. My aunt has passed, it's the start of the Rampages. The way I back-gather it is: we abandon ship, Eastdon's a mess, we're all fleeing to the cricket park lodge, but you and me swing by to fetch the pharmacy girls. Because to survive, we need to stick together. But the lodge crew calls, "For God's sake no, lay low!" So we're *still* at the woods cottage. Edie's rental place. *So quiet here!* I'm thinking when the maddie blossoms in me. *Except for the damn foghorn.* Eight minutes from now, my watch says. Then *doom, doom, doom.*

You're spending time trying to record Tiff's memories. Kitty and Edie fuss over her. But let's face it, Tiff's headed for that, what, rabid dog mode that the medicated too late ones go through. Enough real self left to resist the catatonia, but not the rage stage. So y'all are saying goodbye as best you can, and I'm leaving the pack of you to it. Most days, I go out into the woods. I take walks to settle my nerves—because they're shot, frankly. I stand vigil where I dug her grave.

I dug it slow. It was clear we weren't going anywhere. And it was just birdsong back then, but nowadays, here comes the Foghorn Rock siren, off through the trees again, ten minutes at a time of it, on the hour, on repeat. *Keep away, keep away, keep away.*

It was a week before I got her in the ground. Goodbye, sweet, stubborn aunt Jilly.

We had a nice ceremony, all five of us at the graveside, if you recall. No? Kitty's Lakota flower ritual? To sanctify the ground? To this day, I commemorate Kitty in my prayers for that.

By when the maddie hits, there's been a third wave. Eastdon's bracing for the fourth. And us, here, we're scared for Tiff, but hey, Edie and Kitty aren't doing too wonderful either. Their short-term's half-shot. You and I, we make them pay attention to themselves, we up the dosages. Edie's like her sister—we have to bully her into medicating. We pretend we're making progress, we discuss what next, if the lodge won't work, try Heartwood, you girls come too. I'm loading up the truck off and on as you tinker with your logs and you negotiate. I walk in the woods. I wait.

Then on *this* day, you come out to aunt Jilly's grave to find me. You've brought drinks, which is nice. Kitty and Edie come out too. We're all four at the edge of the woods, with a glass of wine, cheering me up. Until we look around and see the house is in flames.

Kitty barges into the fire. Edie follows her. You too. Tiff's inside already, of course—she's the one setting it. I yell, "Get the hell out, you morons!" And all four of you do make it out! You have your arm around Tiff! But she wrenches free. Edie grasps, she writhes away, Kitty grabs her and holds on tight. I mean, *tight.* You're coughing and choking, "Urgh," you say, "the *smoke* in there." Then *Edie* darts back in the cottage, there's *stuff* she needs, and you holler, and you gag yourself with a towel and hightail it after *her.* And after *your* damn stuff that *you* need!

Tiff's joining in with the foghorn now, the way she would sometimes. I back off to make for the grave again. I'll say a prayer, I reckon. You two will be smart, right? You won't just grab and grab? Tiff's straining at Kitty's leash, but she's wrapped up safe, right?

No to my second proposition. Tiff's gone rabid. Tiff *bites.* Back in she hies.

And then once a-fucking-*gain,* all four of you are inside a holy Jesus burning *building,* and I'm *alone* out here. And I'll be honest to God sobbing before just two of you make it out.

In the moment of the clip that I keep coming back to, I'm cowering beneath the trees, looking to find some quiet. If those folks quarantined out on the island are like Tiff, I'm thinking that Foghorn Rock must be one loud, loud place. But look, new leaves, like it's the spring, and all this bright August blossom. Yeah, I know, we *got* there in August, the fire was in *October,* but the moment is genuine, Brian. I've just *shifted,* right *then,* I mean, into maddie-memory. Like, oh, do they have a fig tree—yep, those little knobs there are baby figs. When do figs come ready to eat?

I thank you, Lord, for the bounty of this world. For all its beautiful, sweet things.

This is not something ironic, Brian. I know what's what. But I do thank Him.

6. Describe a maddie retrieval you believe to be false.

Jenna Brower

I've thought about this. Those false ones, they came out
of something. If there was only a blankness to me, what
could I bird's nest them up from? This one, for instance:
this has to be a concoction, but I'll bet there's some true
Sarah in it. Leastways I've used it as if—to make Jenna.

I'm at the seashore with my beau. There's no beach
to speak of, just cliffs that fall sheer to the water. The
gulls are wheeling up high away from the waves and
cawing, there's something there that's got them spooked,
or that's what they act like. I peer down, all I see is the
frillery of the whitecaps and the wash and spin of lace.
Now it's a beautiful day, mind you, blue sky and barely a
speckle of cloud, and by the same token, the boy and
me—we're young, maybe mid-twenties—we *seem* to be
getting along just fine. He's a sweet-talker and a toucher,
and I'm smiling. But I know, if he doesn't, that it's a grit-
toothed smile—that I've had about enough of all this
pawing and pecking, thank you. When he leans over the
cliff's rim to see if he can make out what's in the water,
I'm saying, *Oh, be careful*, but all along I've got my foot
poised, waiting for his butt to raise itself up just a mite
higher, and when it does, one nudge is all I need. And by
the time I inch up to the edge to peep over, I see nothing
again. The waves have taken him.

Now if that were real—I guess it could be, though,
couldn't it?—I should feel terrible because who could do
such a thing and not feel terrible? But in my memory, I
feel satisfaction, and I feel good. I'm *free* of the man.

Now what *that's* about, I'll let you imagine. But let me
tell you how I used it, for Jenna. Because I know Sarah
loved her husband; she did. Sometimes she loved her
parrot. But more covertly? The free, independent
woman below the surface, inside Sarah? We'll keep this
between you and me and your posterity project there,
but Jenna has her look-back-and-mope days, and she has
her kick-the-caboodle-off-the-cliff days. There's times,

maybe, Jenna doesn't much regret how a couple of details turned out.

Nick Trifflett

I took a maddie today, in fact! I was feeling oh so sadly incompetent again, and I thought it might prove therapeutic. Unfortunately, it did zilch for my memory since it was quite nakedly mendacious, but you can still color me buoyed. It was frickin' hilarious!

Now my research has revealed that some people favor the "my whole life or five fat years of it flashed before me" rides, and some people prefer the statelier "ooh, I've been gazing at this groovy daisy for two astonishing hours" ones. I'm more of a "week in the life of" man, and that's what today's clip was. Not too scant of story, and not too laden. Picture this, if you will:

Jemmy and I are on tour with the Stones—only as the support band, of course, but we're summoned up every night for the third encore. Danny too, actually—so good to see him again!—but he prefers not to do the encore thing—you know Danny—so they quit petitioning him. Anyway, it's now the last week of the tour, which means that it's time to prank Jemmy before he pranks me. So... You're not really listening, are you? You find all this boring and juvenile. In fact, that's the point, Brian. This is not an "I guess you had to be there" story. I'm well aware of the fact that even *I* wasn't there. It's a "please God get me out of this hellhole for an afternoon" fantasy. I used to be a very mature, astonishingly jolly adolescent. I'm now a morose and inchoate little old man. I don't *remember* asking for that.

I need some damn frivolity in my life, God damn it, Brian. I need Mick Jagger and Keith Richards to depants Jemmy for me in front of seventy-five thousand screaming classic rockheads. Is that fucking asking too fucking cocksucking much?

Elise Barker

I'm not that into the maddies, Brian.

Matt Simmons

Well, what's ironic—I guess "disquieting" is a better word—is that I acquired another maddie memory of that period. We've compared notes on this, Brian. All three of us relived that stretch of weeks, I believe, after we got here—in one manner or another, it was going to prey on our minds. Edie's version went off course more, no question, but I got my own false vision. Which began by reconfiguring the day Tiff and Kitty died.

Now unlike Edie, I know full and well which way the tale forks true. But I have to work to not let the lie co-opt it. The way my lie goes, you and Edie follow Tiff and Kitty back into the flames and you don't come out.

I wait, and I holler, but in the end, I pick the salvage from the yard, I hop into my truck, and I haul ass out of there. From Foghorn Island, the siren's calling; I pay it no mind. I don't pass Go, I don't acquire supplies, I don't so much as think of swinging by the lodge. It's straight to Heartwood, and I've been living here alone ever since. Making out just fine, too.

Hey, lookie, here, here's a hundred of Edie's maddies stashed in the truck, all for me!

What I despise about the maddies are the lies. Sometimes the true memories can hit you hard, but the way the fake ones want to rub your face in the worst side of you, sometimes? Like they're saying, here's who you are in the private dark of you? I can't abide that, Brian.

Edie Driscoll

Please don't push this with me, Millar. I've chosen to assume I have no false memories. If I do have some things wrong, so be it. I've integrated them, so leave it. I'm a stable working self.

Lisa Huttongold

Here's a coin toss one. I slept with Danny. Oh, Lord.

I told Jody, who *thinks* we actually had some kind of full-scale torrid *affair*, which I've forgotten. Oh, I do hope so. If we didn't, Jody says, why didn't you? *How* didn't you?

If I've forgotten, that's just cruel. If we *didn't*, and I've forgotten? Mmh.

Jody Barker

Oh, Brian. Beyond here be dragons. When I *think*. And I think you know that.

I can try, if you like. There are a few that are so *obviously* fake that I don't get lost... trying to figure out true from false. But then I turn a corner somehow, and I'm—

Fuck it. Sorry. Could you just kiss me, please, Brian? Just hold me and kiss me and give me a fucking maddie, please, Brian?

Andrew Barker

With the madeleine drug, as (arguably) with everything, true memory and false are a blurry continuum. The greater part of every life, after all, is imaginary.

I may have told you that I've had visions since the day Jody almost killed us? I was concussed in the car wreck, and the effects lingered. Even BTWC, I saw the world in ways more grandiose. Once I started taking the drug, the dimensions of my visions expanded.

I won't write about or discuss this on the record. I don't want my ideas discounted b/c I have unorthodox ways of thinking and perceiving. We'll talk off the record. You'll be interested.

Jemmy Jaronsky

I don't personally remember the Z.A. Or Hellfest, the Rampages, if you prefer. None of it.

Not the lodge, not our convoy out of there, through the aftermath. The bodies and shit? Which I wish I did, believe it or not, or some of anyway—because Danny. The Danny part.

But I have this, whatever you call it. In its stead. This like, three hour, handheld, home movie *ride*. With the *cattle*, man. Fuck, man. I mean, as a for real fucking *zom*. You know?

I don't get any of it, even. First of all, I'm not Jemmy; I'm someone else. How does *that* happen? I don't know his name—he's way too addled. Then, second, the dude isn't me, right, but is he like, a real guy? And if he is, is what I have of him true? How would I—Jemmy, yeah?— be conversant enough with this crap, for real, to make even an authentic *fiction* of it? According to those who recall the lodge invasion, which, admittedly, none of us do that much, we skulked inside with the heat turned off. Big Nicky says I wouldn't even peek through the slats. But it does feel real.

Yeah, *every* ride feels real. *More* than real. Like, how do I step away and keep it at arm's length like it's just some regular memory? Not get trapped in it? Yeah, we all know about that. But this one wakes me in the night, Brian. From the chill of it. I feel that chill right *now*, Brian. Even if a maddie made it up. Or if my own head made it up. Hey, I surely did see *some* poor fuckers going rabid—like, so I'm told, at Rhino's place, that very first day the cattle all woke up. So I could have, what, extrapolated? Intuitively assessed, extrapolated, and internalized it? Made a shrewd, synthesizing postulation.

Truth is, my bet is that this exact ride *happened*. This dude *lived*. He got sick, it flaked his brain into dust. It bit by bit crazed him, and it killed him. Somehow I, what, hitched a ride and observed. Like a war correspondent, yeah? Embedded, it's called, right? That.

Except "observed" is detached. You keep an emotional distance; you process *information*, right?

Whereas this is pure feeling, and it's immediate, and nothing makes sense. Not your senses even—because nothing connects. It's like the mechanisms of your body, the mechanisms of your thought, have become this all-consuming, gut-roiling incoherence.

If that tells you anything.

This is hard, man. It isn't *in* words, and all I have to *tell* you it is words. It's not in pictures either, it's interior, but I'll try to say what he sees. Which isn't much because of how the light dims and the connection to your brain dims: for whatever reason, you're like half-blind.

There are like, knots of standing cattle literally on fire, and you can't find where! Or am *I* on fire? Could I even tell? I squint at my hands. No. Charred and singed is all. *Was* I on fire?

So you crowd up to who blocks the way back; you're so damn cold; you need to touch, to clutch. And also to seek out if anyone—someone competent—is there. You do know you need help. That this is wrong, that *you're* wrong. But wherever you turn, the other shapes are *like* you, except maybe they're even worse off. I mean, *they*'re crowding up against *you*, they want *you* to help *them* —as *if*, right?—you're *all* grabbing, you're all *howling*. So are you maybe one of the least far gone? All anyone is, is this need to grab and howl.

Until woah! Shapes just stop and fall. That one, this one, this one who just now had her hands on you, they keel over like, *I've been gassed!*—which we are being? She's howling; she's whimpering; she's dead silent. Her eyes two tiny votive flames: dimming, then gone dark.

I'm at the edge of them. I've withdrawn, to observe. Like there's some Jemmy in me.

Now it's their breath's turn. Because they're not dead, not clinically, it's more like Death called and left a message to stop breathing and he'll be right along. Slower breaths, smaller breaths, stop. Yes. Almost nothing makes sense to you, but this does, that it's time to give up.

But when two zoms at once yowl into me, I'm barreled out of the gas zone. A megaphone barks. I do *hear* okay, without the sound connecting to a sense. Or to a purpose—it's like what's a howl *for*, what's a car horn *for*, why care? What I'm *called* to do is *make* noise. Back here among the roarers (there's this staccato, hoarse as hell barrage of us—stopping; starting; no hint of unison), we are this need to roar. What we are saying, not coherently, is, "I am broken. My connections aren't sparking. I am reaching to connect. Connect what? I don't *know* what."

And since my connections are down, and the *this* doesn't link with the *that* the way I desperately know it should, I am really, friggin', *clumsy*, and we hurt each other.

He does die, my one. And not by going blank-eyed or burning. He falls in the path of something. I'm guessing that a truck hits me. There's a glint of life to me still, I guess; the eyes are guttering but not quite dark; you know how it is with the zoms. So this shape bearing down on me; I'm even reaching out a little to it. Or I *think* I reach; maybe nothing of me actually moves. It smacks my head, and yeah, hell yeah, I feel that. Numb as I am, I feel that pain. And its weight rolls over my body, and I break. The pain sharpens, then it stops. So does everything else.

Except it takes a while to come out of it, to be Jemmy again, you know? I'm dead, but I'm still riding the maddie. So instead, there's this super-intense nothingness. So intense Jemmy can't re-enter me—you know, like when they say to meditate or shit, and your mind wanders? Well, I'm not a mind; nothing's wandering, or wondering—there's only a slow, patient awareness of the nothing. Until yeah, there are shapes of things again. Because for a brief while, suddenly, I'm like this mist rising over the street. Hanging, and thinning, and then gone.

I can make out what's below me, by the way. While I'm the mist. There's no sound. And I don't feel, really. At peace? Is that what I am? Detached? I see bodies, some of them dead, some with the last breath draining from them. Others roaring and pinballing, or burning. I hang there, watching. This isn't the cricket park, right, it's Flea Town, but all tore up. The cobblestones have been clawed out of their beds. The street is like a buckled granite river.

And yeah, it's on fire. Fire soothes the cold in you. Zoms with lighters, with matches, they *will* light you or themselves on fire. We living-torched a car on fire, it looks like here... Yeah, I may have been in on that? Been blown clear before the ride hit? I came in toward the end of the dude.

But then it is the end. The mist fades and I'm gone. I stay gone, I don't know how long. Only that eventually, I'm Jemmy.

CHAPTER EIGHT: YEAR ONE INTO YEAR TWO

"We can find all manner of things within our memory. It's like a pharmacy, or a chemist's laboratory, where the rummaging hand will fall with equal likelihood on a soporific drug or a dangerous poison."

Marcel Proust (translation Derek Kannemeyer), *La prisonnière*

"Everything possible to be believ'd is an image of truth."

William Blake, "The Proverbs of Hell"

YEAR ONE INTO YEAR TWO, FIRST PERSON:

Jody, Elise, Andrew, Lisa, Matt

I.

Andrew came by. I'd been half-hopeful he'd weasel out.

His greeting was so tender! To recall to me our "official intention," possibly: to know and trust each other; to be better siblings? But how could I commit to that without taking a good look at the missing piece of me? Maybe not then, depending on what we found.

But I showed him my house, and I served him tea; we chitchatted, idly exchanging views; I let him set the pace. And soon enough, he turned refreshingly direct, as if everything so far had been to satisfy the courtesies—which from his perspective I knew wasn't so. I liked that he was sensitive to my side; that he understood what my side was.

He asked about The Day. The last things I remembered. How I'd spent the morning, he presumed it would have been with Brian?

I said, in point of fact, I was conspiring with my friend Lisa. On a... project of hers. "That's fine!" he said. "So why not fix your mind on that project—on what led up to the lacuna—and steer yourself to its brink?"

I said, "What a good idea!" I didn't say, Duh, obviously. Or, Dude, why do you think I invited you and your big bulletproof van *over* here? If not to sideswipe me *by* that brink?

"And you?" I asked instead. "Anything in particular you'd like to remember?"

He said, "Now you're being polite."

"No," I said. "It's small talk, but it's for my benefit. Frankly, Andrew, it's not easy having you here. And then I'm always nervous, before."

"So small talk helps."

"Not usually. No."

"Well, then," he said. "Let's just take the pills."

So we clinked our mugs. We lounged on our facing sofas and went under.

II.

And once again, Lisa was at my mother's house picking me up. She hugged Brian hello; I kissed him goodbye. "Wish us luck," she said. "I'll have her back in a couple of hours."

"All very mysterious," replied Brian. Lisa put her fingers to her lips and mouthed *Shh...*

She drove to the park, and we sat in the car and got our stories straight.

"Okay, so this dude..."

"Bradford Brower."

"So he's kidnapped... Parrot-napped your neighbor's African grey."

"Not my neighbor, in fact. Nick's neighbor."

"You don't know him, then?"

"Bradford Brower? We've met, but no, not really. Even Nick doesn't know him well, he apparently isn't around that much. He knows the separated wife."

"Jenna Brower."

"*Mrs.* Brower, to her face. She's not the first name type."

"And the parrot is hers."

"Totally. You need the previously-ons. Mrs. Brower goes to Haiti. Mission trip, she's big with the good deeds, is Mrs. B. 'Nick,' she says, 'can you look after Loulou?' Loulou's the parrot."

"Got it."

"Nick loves the parrot. The parrot's a hoot. 'But Mrs. Brower,' he says, 'what about your husband?' 'Nick,' she says, 'Mr. Brower is in and out the picture, he has his own man-hovel of a place, I don't know what he's up to half the time, and half the time when I do, I wish I didn't.'"

"So they're not really separated? They have some froufrou hipster arrangement?"

"They're separated *now*. Since this incident."

"Since about two weeks."

"She says no way they're reconciling."

"Because he stole the parrot."

"Well, in his view it's his parrot also, except not. She's the mama. The parrot has learned a few phrases he's taught it. 'Pluck me and roast me!' it says sometimes."

"So he's taught it mean things."

"Vicious things, fake sweetly. 'You dumbass birdbrain!' And with his wife gone and him needing money, Mr. Brower thinks, why not sell the parrot?"

"But Nick tried to stop him?"

"Well, Nick happens to be there. In the bathroom, so the Brower dude doesn't know. So he's hauling the cage out into the hall when here comes Nick. 'Mr. Brower, you can't take that parrot; I'm responsible for that parrot.' And Nick, you've met Nick; he's like seven feet tall and built, so the dude looks him over and tries to reason with him. 'It's my parrot too, he needs exercise.' Whatever. 'I'm sorry, Mr. Brower, no,' Nick says. 'Please, you have to talk this through with Mrs. Brower. I don't want to get in the middle, but blah blah.'"

"But the dude takes off with the parrot anyway?"

"No, no, he hands the parrot to Nicky! Says, fine, he'll do that, the wife gets home next week, they'll discuss it. And Nicky says, 'Thank you, blah blah, I'm so relieved, blah blah'— and then the stupid little doofus just hangs the cage back up— bills and coos with the bird, who's sort of ruffled and growly, 'Such a silly polly!'—but basically he just locks back up and goes."

"Stupid *big* doofus."

"Yeah. The guy's waiting for him to leave; he slips in, boosts the parrot."

"And he still has it."

"Well, Nick has second thoughts, so he checks back, 'Oh no!' and he reports it stolen. The police come by the man-hovel. 'I'm the husband; I'm *tending* to it.' They ask, 'Oh, so you're not *appropriating* it?' And he figures, fine, I'll *tend*, I can *stall*, I'll chivvy her into exhaustion and *then* sell it—so he says, 'No, I swear!' The police go, 'Well, okay, then. Just see you don't.' When Mrs. Brower comes home, of course, she pitches a fit. She tells him to stuff it."

"The parrot."

"Up his ass."

"The parrot."

"Except she'd be incapable of saying *ass*, she'd say, 'Stuff it up your you know where.'"

"Don't you like her?"

"Not much. But the parrot does. And the thought of that bully..."

"Yes. So Nick thought..."

"Oh, the man's maintained *possession*. For now. He's fending his wife *off*. But he also still needs his money, like *yesterday*. Plus, he has no parrot-tending skills. Or interest. So..."

"Damn, he'll kill the poor thing."

"I think he knows. So he needs a buyer, fast. Nick says the fucker's put the word out."

"And I'm the buyer."

"The hot as shit, oh-I-do-hope-you'll-take-my-daddy's-check buyer."

"Oh, don't worry, Mr. Brower, *big smile*, let's go right now to the bank, *wink*, cash it together, *bat eyelashes*, that way you'll... Oh, *giggle*, then a drink to celebrate? Sure!"

"While Nicky and I, unbeknownst to Mr. Bradford Brower, have a set of keys—"

"Excellent!"

"—that his wife found in a pocket, and who's the dumbass birdbrain now?"

"Oh, this check isn't valid? Oh, *swoon, flutter*, there must be some mistake..."

"And we reunite Loulou with her mama."

"So how do I *know* he has an African grey to sell? Can we run lines?"

The whole, magnificent morning, in all its oft-told detail. I won't say it was a waste of an MGM—it was exhilarating. I *bewitched* the guy. The stratagem worked brilliantly—not perfectly, but improvising our way past the rough spots was the best part. And Lisa and I, the Trouble Twins, together in triumph again. But after we returned the parrot to Mrs. Brower, and Nick had smooched me his thanks—more enthusiastically than a soon-to-be married girl should enjoy being smooched, but I'd earned that smooch—as Lisa drove us back to Brian, the big hole took me. We skirted the time between and she dropped me off in oblivion. For what, an hour, more—honestly, I don't know how long—I floated in perfect blankness, and then I woke.

III.

My father is a nutjob, which can be fun.

For instance, lifestyle choices? We've moved to a truly seedy neighborhood. It has a distinctive smell, diesel, dog poo, Indian cooking, that I'm beginning to find comforting. Mucho concrete, beaucoup busted windows. Rows of dirt-strip yards. Rusted out machine parts in the weeds. And he enrolls me in a school so vile that it's amusing. Classmates more or less my age, but with the bodies of adolescents, the brain power of lint, and the social skills of hyenas.

None of this is because we can't afford better. We can. This is because better would be "profligate," what with the world about to end, and "in fact a terrible preparation" for my future life. What with the world about to end.

I do some schoolwork, well enough to be left alone. Pops says to consider the place day care and to practice my invisibility. My "real education" is *his* job. It's "more useful and more urgent." Meaning survivalist indoctrination. "Theoretical, but also practical." Meaning weapons and wilderness training. Scads of it. Okay, it's way cooler than school.

So on weekends we're in the woods. Hiking, fishing. Camping, hunting. The *weather* is bad, you say? Even better! Don't be scared of rain! Oh, you'll need to be *careful*, some-times—a blizzard, for example, could kill you *dead*. But listen: this is how to shelter from one, Elise, and how you melt the snow to drink. Oh, and lightning, or a hurricane? Be careful! They can kill you *dead*. So you find a low spot, Elise, not by a tree but not too isolated either. You keep moving. Crouching low to the ground. Et cetera. Check, Dad. Check. Got it.

And after sunset, and at dawn, we spar for an hour, in the backyard. Dad let slip once that's why he chose this dump: for its big yard, its perimeter oak trees. Said while putting up a privacy fence too, mind you, because, *priorities*, Elise. We do ju-jitsu. I get my ass kicked. We duke it out with staffs, blunted knives, fungo bats. I get my thighs whacked. If they *could* see in, even *these* neighbors, he's right; we'd have social services down on us. The old wackjob.

Now, though, he is also composing, I kid you not, weird stories. I like weird stories. But his are *creepy* weird: they're about *us*. People he's related to, people he knows.

I found a file folder in his study.

Where I knew I shouldn't be, but hey, I go where I shouldn't. I'm curious. Anyway, he lets me. Like if he trusts me, that'll deter me. So it's his look-out, yes? He should know me better. And which I knew I shouldn't read because I did assume it would be "inappropriate." But it had a photograph of my aunt Jody stapled to it! And I've never spoken to her, although I know a lot about her, and she waved to me once, across a room. So I perused it, obviously.

To be honest, I didn't understand most of it. It's in two parts. First, his letters to my aunt Jody, which, *her* privacy, so I respected that. But part two? So confusing! *And* it freaked me out. There's this state, e.g., called Tudoria, which is and isn't VA, peopled by people with our names, e.g., my aunt's and her boyfriend's, and my pops is, like, foretelling their horrible weird futures.

I'm in it too, which, Ew! Especially since, okay, that title? He calls part two "The Book of Headaches." So these headaches: are they us, then? Me?

Typical prediction as regards me, fyi: when I'm fourteen, I'll run away from home. And I want to say, "Oh, so you think I'll wait till I'm fourteen, Daddy?" But of course *don't* say. Not that he'd stop me, probably. Good training for when the world ends, running away from home.

"Know your limits and capacities, Elise," he says. "So you can stretch them. And know your weaknesses, to outflank them. Promise me, sweetheart. Because we must stay ready..."

Well, I'm quick. I'm tough. I am four strong, lean, brown

limbs. I can read our street sign from a block away and decipher a whisper from the far side of a playground. I can crisscross our house and yard in the pitch dark without a sound. I can dance like the wind and run till you drop. Plus, I waste time reading comic books without much liking them. I do crave pizza. I miss my great-grandma. Cats make me sneeze. But I'm not easily rattled. I don't need you, probably. I like my body. I like to make it do things, to figure out what it can do and almost do, and then to work it and work it till it does that too. Can *you* do this? Or this? Bet you can't.

I can.

IV.

My two experiences under my sister's drug—we also split her last pill—have not, in kind, been anything like what Jody led me to expect. Oh, as remarkably *vivid* as promised—which I had not believed possible, and which makes me aghast at Jody's stupidity in seeking to relive, so augmented, the sear and the howl of a car wreck's impact on her bones and her skull. May she ever, for her sanity's sake, keep flinching from that moment.

The first did resemble a memory, and it may, quite shortly, be one: it was set in the near future. It may help to explain that I was "recalling" meeting Millar. Not our encounter yesterday but the tête-à-tête I intend us to have, soon, at a bar, no Jody, to size each other up; to decide if we're allies or enemies. In fact, I met in such a way, although Jody still does not know it, with Brian; I liked him. Interestingly, Millar is very much the same physical type as Brian. At the same time, in its accoutrements, this so resembled one of my visions—complete with blurry hovering lights and bright shadow-shimmer—that I wrote it up for "The Book of Headaches."

Vision Millar wished me to preach at Jody. *Dissuade her from this mad quest!* Does the real Millar know the half of it, I wonder? But I agree with him, and I have preached at her.

The second, which I also wrote up, was stranger still. It began with a recited preamble, one whose sense defeats me, though I was purportedly its author. What, pray, do I make of this?

> *Eastbrough is the fictional capital city of the fictional state of Tudoria, located where Virginia ought to be, and co-opting most of its history. Her geography is not always Virginia's, and her population centers are dispersed about its cocked green witch's hat in altered ways.*
>
> *"Tudoria" is a ridiculous word, as ugly to my ear as the coinage "Virginia" must once have seemed: take "Virgin," lipstick it with a Latinate suffix, et voilà. But rhyme it with "gloria" and "euphoria" and one begins to hear the jangle of a state song. About her, the world resettles. Washington D.C., ever her neighbor, views her from across what it insists is still the Potomac, and Washington must be obeyed. West Tudoria, Semper Liberi, turns a spiny back, having seceded with the renunciation of the Northwest Territory. Hooking down from Maryland, the Eastern Shore breaks off south of Onancock into a claw, resizing the Chesepiock Bay. The mouth of the James grows enormous. Beach towns and clifftop towns, shipyard towns and river towns plug its gap-teeth; quaint little Jamesport brags about how it was once our colonial capital. The James stays navigable beyond Eastbrough— a city twice Eastdon's size, and set closer to Tudoria's shores, as to her mountains; for if the Blue Ridge remains the Blue Ridge, the Appalachians the Appalachians, her Piedmont hills march down its north bank almost to our skyline, to be called the Copperwoods.*
>
> *Beyond them, Charlottesville, Lynchburg, Roanoke, all the misty rest, have flounced off somewhere equally else and carved new natures; but I shan't adventure there, nor into any of that borderland of shadows. Grant me only Eastbrough—this city of my imagination; of my arbitrary*

heart's ache; transmuted out of the glittery dark matter of my life of memories.

Back in Australia, when I was very young, I was a pageboy at the wedding of my father to Jody's mother. For many years, I believed I remembered it. During the reception, in a tent with clear plastic panels cut into one side like dormers, he hoisted me upon his shoulders, and we danced. His breath smelt of champagne and cake—its waft rose from his mouth up to mine—I laughed and swallowed it into me—as the night's wheeling windows glinted over us and were gone; blank canvas then framed skies; for the stars to wink at us, spin, and vanish.

"Rubbish, Andrew," my mother said when I told her this memory. "There was no tent. There may have been dancing, but you couldn't have been among the dancers, because we weren't at the reception, only the wedding. He broke with his bloody family over it! I suppose there might be some other such occasion you're remembering, but I can't imagine when."

On my first X7 trip, I spoke of this with faux-Millar. "For some of us," faux-Millar said, "it's often like that. Our memories are our heart's pet lies."

On my second X7 trip, it was in Tudoria, constricting about me, to the specifications of my memory, my fancy, my desire, that I began to set—and populate—a tale. Altering with it, by the same forces that altered it, and that altered the people herded with me inside it. So I was Stan, its declamatory narrative voice; and so I became my sister; and soon there were a cast and crew of us, hunted and haunted, inhabiting it utterly.

Still deep within the trip, I stepped out into a screening room. I *watched* my documentary of us: an exposé of a failing world, an ode to our shared life. *Yes*, I said. I stepped back in.

Because the world's world is immense, and we are tiny stood against it. But not so the world of our senses, our aspirations, our memory, which tightens into this balled yarn of our real world—our world, to each of us his own. To discover and claim myself, me and mine. In brave, new, ridiculous Tudoria.

Would we all make it? Would we thin to fantastic shadows, or banalities, or both? Most colonists to a new world die. False starts and false steps towards the vestiges of history, a story's tropes, the worn patterns of a life. I X7-lived it. I X7-narrated it. In, out, and back in.

Declaring, "Here is where I'm from. These are my people. See what we did to each other! This is the world I warp into a gobbet of itself, and how it warps me. This is who I am."

V.

Jody, Nick, and I are from Connecticut. Nick brought me to Eastdon, and I brought Jody.

Nick's mom is my mom's sister. She came with us from Jamaica. She married, had Nick, and divorced. He grew up as much at our house as my aunt's. I ask to have no children of my own: I'm good with Nick and Jody. When Nick first enrolled at U. of E., a recruited walk-on on an academic scholarship, he used to call me homesick. Classes were fine. Basketball wasn't. He's tall, not that gifted—if still, ahem, Black—but he can be klutzy, and he couldn't bring himself to care much. The people were fine. Except *so* White. The town was fine. He just didn't know anyone. He missed us all. Missed me. The usual stuff.

In the end, he adapted. I came down anyway, partly because I missed him too, but also because I didn't get into any of the vet schools I applied to. I'd been working at an animal shelter back home, knowing exactly what I wanted to do in life, and when no one would let me do it, I got despondent. Eastdon Medical had a veterinary nursing program. I didn't want to be a vet's *nurse*, exactly, I'd have resented the shit out of the world, having to settle for that, but regular nursing might be okay. If I could take a few veterinary nursing courses alongside... And hey, Nick was there. And Jody was saying, "Hey, I'll come too."

Now I'm stuck worrying about them both again. Jody's been a mess since Brian died, but I'd really hoped she was improving. Nick's piddling away his twenties, amiably directionless, no big deal—only suddenly he's now saying how he's started to *forget* things.

The alarm bells are rattling my skull.

And so I've called a conference. Jody, Nick, Millar dude: we need to talk.

VI.

My aunt Jilly isn't circling the drain yet, as she's taken to putting it, but you can hear the little wooshes, from time to time, of the plug having popped loose and the water plashing its fingers. Her memory is worse too, at about the same stage of a descent into cuckooland.

Rather than look in on her, I've moved in, mostly. It's a tad much for me, to be honest.

But what truly unnerves me isn't what's happening to her. It's that the memory part might be starting in on *me*. And if you're paying attention, what you've heard talk is happening all around town.

And beyond? Maybe, the whisper goes, across the world?

"Aunt Jilly," I asked. "You reckon what you've got is catching? Because I keep trying to come up with these scraps of things... and I poke and poke at them, and I can't even riffle the air of them. It's like the whole last year from high school has hightailed it, and most of whatever the heck it was, I did after that, before I got married, five more years, maybe. And even my *Berry*, aunt Jilly, twenty-seven years and more, I'm holding on tight as I can, but I swear..."

"Matthew," she said. "You know that package I asked you to put aside? The one the nurse at the clinic gave me for safekeeping?"

Well, I did know, although I needed the connection explained to me, with what we were just talking of. And aunt Jilly answered, "Oh, there may not be a connection. But open up the package and let's take a look-see..."

I phoned that nurse later to see what she wanted me to do with them. And she did say, What a coincidence, she'd been about to call us, and could she come tomorrow, please? But by that time, I'd opened it and found the two score pristine white tablets, and me and aunt Jilly had each taken one. And suddenly—like a magic trick—there was this road trip I took with Berry, out west to California and the Grand Canyon, I mean exactly as if it were happening all over again, all around me. And when that nurse and her boyfriend, Jody and Millar, showed up at our door, believe me, I had to be talked into giving back that package. By my aunt Jilly, as a matter of fact, who hugged Jody as if she were family, while the girl hugged and hugged her back and wept for having stayed away so long.

We came to an agreement in the end. Jody will help me out with aunt Jilly. And we'll get to keep a quarter of the pills. And nothing will be said about it to anyone.

VII.

I say, "We've piddled around enough. We're at a crossroads, and as Nick's surrogate mother, and Jody's sister and keeper, and as Mother Hen to our circle, it's on me to call it. Every card on the table, and let's thrash out where we stand."

"Lisa and I have talked," Millar announces. " I know someone who can help."

I'd dropped by Jody's place and found her and her brother in an X7 trance. Not good. I grabbed Millar to make an ally of him. But Millar hemmed and hawed. He's starting to worry about his own mind. His own memory's slipping. He's taking pills again.

When Nick starts stumbling into furniture, busting up a foot and toppling lamps, he's seriously flustered by something. I asked. He doesn't know what's happening to his memory.

Memory loss patients, once again the business of the clinic, have overflowed it. There are cases all over my hospital ward. I told Nick this and brought him here. Yesterday he ingested one of the magic mushroom pills, with Jody downing another one to keep him company, as Millar and I stood watch. The results of which blew Nick away.

It seems that a last shipment of X7s came in on the day that testing was suspended. One box got opened. Jody stole some and re-crated the box as intact. Before the lab could catch the discrepancy, she hid a forty pill sleeve with Jilly Simmons, who gets to keep a share.

I'm fine. Danny's fine. That leaves at least six of us twenty-eight tablets to stave off how much of an assault, on who we think we are? If that's a godsend, it's an inadequate one.

"I think, in fact," Andrew says sententiously, "that what we're up against may be the beginning of the end of the world as we know it. You're right, Lisa; it's not enough."

But Millar has already called a friend, from his undergrad days in Charlottesville, a girl he says he trusts implicitly, who has a Chemistry degree and went into pharmacology.

"You think this person can reconstitute the formula?" Andrew asks. "That's a long shot."

I've been researching too. "No, it might not be. Once the

tests stopped, once the extent of the crisis began to be suspected, some things have begun to be leaked."

"Leaked? What do you mean, leaked?"

"Oh, and suppressed, but once something is out, you can't
suppress it entirely. Who knows if we can trust it, but there
are versions of the formula for this drug cropping up in several
places. Often wildly divergent, but if we have a sample..."

"Who the hell leaked it?" Jody asks.

"Who knows? Someone connected with the trials, and the
research lab was cited as being talked to, though. Did you ever
know a Jacob Corrigan?"

"Dr. Stubble?" says Jody. "That poseur Dr. Fucking Stubble? No way!"

"Lisa," says Millar. "Let's print out every formula you've
got. And I'll go talk to TGF."

It had taken him some time to track her down. She's
moved, out past the far east end of the city, to a cottage down
a private road in the woods. Our first thought was to descend
on her en masse, give it to her straight, no hedging or hesitations, but the way things play out it's me and Millar.

They've talked on the phone, and she knows we're coming.
A gangling, square-faced, caramel-skinned girl, who introduces
herself as Kitty, answers the door. They're eager to help, she
tells us, excited, in fact, but... TGF isn't herself these days.

Kitty shows us into a bedroom. TGF is apparently the girl
in the bed. There's another who looks very like her, who has
to be her sister, sitting on the edge of it, tending to her.

"Millar," TGF says. "Who'd have thunk. It's okay; it's not a
fever; I think it's in my mind, actually. I just feel... hot and cold
and disoriented? Like I need to lie down and... list things?
Catalog the room, you know? I lie and say the names in my
head to calm me."

"Tiff. It's so good to see you. You've no idea."

"But Millar, I don't think I can help you. This kind of

work," and she waves vaguely at the pills he's brandishing, "was never my strong suit anyway. And I've lost some of that part of me. But my sister—"

The other woman goes over to Millar and shakes his hand. "Hi," she says. "I'm Edie. I've heard a great deal about you."

Tiff laughs. "Oh, she's heard everything. You'd be surprised."

"Millar, Lisa," says Edie, "this is right up my alley. I can do this."

CHAPTER NINE: YEAR TWO, MAY

"This pestilence was so powerful that it was communicated to the healthy by contact with the sick, the way a fire close to dry or oily things will set them aflame."

Giovanni Boccaccio, *The Decameron*

"We will dance again. We will sing, and we will laugh, and we will be together. But we must accept that it will take a while. In part because the disruptions have been so sweeping, in part because they haven't been sweeping enough. So many who still survive are too damaged to be made whole, and the sheer number of them is dangerous. They are without faith, they are without trust, and they may never again be otherwise."

Library of Virginia, *The 5 Year Report*

YEAR TWO, EASTDON:

Lisa

I.

When the call came to the Simmons house, Lisa answered it. She was there mostly to be with someone, because these days everything worried her sick. Jody; Nick; the dangers of her not taking the medication and the others taking so much; their dwindling supply of the foul stuff; Edie's lack of progress synthesizing more. The goddamn imminent collapse of the world.

Jody was walking Jilly around the garden. Stranding Lisa with Millar, who had a thing about telephones. A thing opposite to her thing: he loathed talking on them, so he sat unmoving as Jilly's landline screeched at them; she hated the noise, so she shoved by to pick up.

"Is Matthew Simmons to be available, please?" the voice asked. Weird accent.

"I'm sorry, he isn't," Lisa answered. Matt Simmons was, as usual, away somewhere, working. Out in the country, at the haven of some rich folks' toy farm. Pretending the world was still all cook an' curry. Keeping calm, carrying on.

"I have a message for Jody Barker," the voice continued in standard American.

"She's out back. I'll see if—"

"Please don't. I don't wish to talk to her personally."

"I'm sorry?"

"She might recognize my voice. I'd prefer to proceed cautiously."

"Look—"

"Tell her I know what she did. The missing X7. This isn't blackmail. I've always known."

"You're inept at proceeding cautiously. I'm a total stranger. We're on a telephone."

"Ah. Yes, sometimes my thinking is... fitful. But you're *au courant*, yes?"

"I'm what?" She had put him on speakerphone now, so Millar could overhear.

"I have more of the medicine. I understand you may be trying to make more."

Lisa said nothing. She looked at Millar. "It's the doctor," he whispered.

"Okay," said Lisa. "That would be helpful. Why do you wish to help us?"

"I wish I could help everyone. But I know about you people. Jody. Kearney. You."

Her? What did he know? How could he possibly? But if he had more of the drug...

"What do you suggest?"

"A meeting. You. You're Lisa, yes? I give you my word; I mean no harm. Bring a friend, if you like. One only, please. Not Jody Barker and not Millar Kearney. At least, not yet."

He named a place: a park, quite close. The statue. A time: soon, within the hour.

"Okay. We'll be there," she assured him. Calmly. Showing no fear.

But she felt fear. This weird guy knew her name.

"Take a pharmacy girl," Millar said as soon she'd hung up. "We'll have to call right now; they'll barely have time. I'll do it."

And without fuss, he did call them. And was succinct and authoritative. *You or Edie. Here's where. Avoid this area; it's gotten dangerous. Take care on the roads; there are rough spots. But come quick.* Perhaps, in a crisis, Millar was the kind to shape up and be a man? Perhaps, after all, he could be counted on? Still shaking, Lisa went to him. He reached his arm out. She lay her head on his shoulder. She leaned. Without fuss, he held her.

Jody was at the French doors with Jilly. Jilly hung low over her walker, panting.

"What's happened?" asked Jody.

"Tuesday!" said Jilly. Mostly Jody interpreted for her. Sometimes she didn't bother.

"Thanks, sweetie, I'll take it from here," Jody said instead. Millar pecked Jody on the cheek, and Jody took Lisa from him. In her arms, Lisa felt both very fragile and very loved.

Perhaps, it occurred to her, she should append a "Lisa" to her worry list.

II.

It was Kitty who came. Lisa was glad of it; Kitty relaxed her. She was a bit like a baby giraffe. And though her first thought had been *Danny*, or *Andrew*, she recognized that Millar was right: a pharmacy girl because there might be information at stake here that Edie needed.

But Kitty had not come into the city for a while. The array of homeless (or of those Lisa preferred to think of as homeless) startled and dismayed her. Spotting Lisa, she stopped dead: a young man in rumpled winter clothes, cataleptic, lay slumped on the first bench; a woman and a teenaged girl huddled close on another one, almost as immobile, shivering in the seventy-degree heat. Lisa had barely noticed them; these people were everywhere.

"I thought—"

But Kitty didn't finish the thought. There was a third bench, vacant, but like Lisa, she made no move to sit on it. Nor did she come any closer to the statue than Lisa had, to see if their doctor might be there: two more shabby sad sacks were sprawled face down at its base.

"How was the drive?"

"Fine. Not fine, actually. I saw too many, mmh, people. Like these."

"You found a parking place okay?" Pure change of subject. Lisa had come on foot and had avoided too many people like these en route to heed them now.

"Can't anybody help? Yes. There's plenty of parking. The city's empty."

"It's emptier, yes. No, no one, I'm afraid. Our friend Danny has ferried a few vanloads to the hospital emergency services, where he works. But they're overrun."

"The hospital? Is *Danny* how this doctor knows us, maybe? Millar said he knew things."

Lisa shivered. She hoped not. "Danny? No, not possible. Well, he may *know* him, but—"

Kitty nodded. It didn't matter. "So, where *is* this guy?"

Lisa's cell rang, which was disconcerting. Recently, it had rarely worked.

"I'm fifty meters west," the voice hissed. "Start walking. We'll meet halfway."

III.

The man approaching them did not at all resemble the Dr. Corrigan whom Millar had described. A wild, full beard, a pair of shades that hid half his face, a baseball cap he was tearing off to swat the air with, at something Lisa thought probably wasn't there. A head shaved stubble-bald. Millar said he'd disappeared from the research facility without explanation, but then that kind of thing happened these days. Meanwhile, Lisa wasn't sure if the look was a bad disguise or if the doctor was now a crazy person. Or both.

"Lisa," he said to her. "And you are?"

"Kitty. And you?"

"No," said Dr. Corrigan. "No names. Follow me to my vehicle, please."

This was an SUV, tinted windows, parked in pointing distance across the jogging track.

"We're not getting inside that," Lisa told him as they neared it.

"Necessary. To talk privately. And chop chop, please, there are eyes."

"Fine," said Kitty. "But I get the driver's seat."

"Yes, yes," he said. He took the passenger side. Lisa climbed in the back, sweeping aside bags of clothing, some newspapers, a week's worth of food trash. One long blond hair. The car stank, not with a six months of homelessness ripeness, but with a good, rich reek.

"I drove around after we spoke," he explained. "To air it out."

"Very considerate of you," said Kitty. "Do you have the X7?"

"Kitty has questions about the formula," Lisa added.

"I may be *like* this, let me say first—a bit irrational, I mean—*because* of what I've taken. And how much of it. Not just the X7, which, yes, is what I have for you. But the X6. And way too much of the X8, which in retrospect, I don't quite trust. But which for a while seemed to be making the X7 expendable. Very few false memories, you see. Far worse side effects, though—from which I suffered, to a degree, even with the 7. Still, made it easier to get at the X7 supplies, right? Even now, to some degree, if you know how. But the thing is. The thing is..."

He appeared to have forgotten what the thing was. He closed his eyes. He pressed his fingers to his temples and opened his mouth. He gave a long, piercing scream, as if to drive the ruckus from some mobbed and muttering rumpus room inside his head.

"The thing *is*, I used to be quite certain that there was no authentic enduring and evolving identity without memory, that memory to a large degree *was* identity, and it didn't much matter if the specifics of the memory were true or false—because duh, we falsify our memories, that's what they're *for*, we draw upon our store of them to create a story, to supply parables, to guide us through the now. If they're accurate, their integration *is* less ticklish, but what's frankly *more* important is to make them *vivid*, for example, as I'm sure you know Andy Warhol would wear the same scent for three months, then never again, so that if he wished richly to *reinhabit* a certain period of his life, he had only to open a bottle of it, the cologne served as a time capsule. Others keep journals. Pffft. Or rely on the *common* memory, which is, of course, *most* of what keeps us tethered; what others tell us by their every action is the reality of what this world *is* and who we are and our place in it. If our personal, individual memories are intense enough, we can, of course, *challenge* the group perceptions, which to some might indicate a kind of psychosis, but I don't think so, my feeling is that *this*, if we wish to tap into our full human potential, is what we must strive to *exploit*. Since the X's superiority is rooted in the intensity of its memory jolts, to *my* mind damn the torpedoes, the virus is a *gift* if it forces us to use it, personal persistence is all very well but is it enough: don't you see that once I *remember* more, I *am* more? *We* if there is a we become *more*. And so what if we need time to *learn* to integrate them and *be* that larger self? We can learn, we will learn, we *will learn*. Except now, I'm less certain there *is* a we. *Yes,* it must surely be that I *personally* haven't learned, that I haven't *yet* learned, that I may *never* learn, but whoever this I *is*, this I is personally less confident than the I I *was* was that any of this is possible. Oh, by the way, here's the formula. The *virus* is the enemy, though, isn't it? Not the drug, the drug is merely dangerous. You'll see that what they told me formerly was an evasion, they omitted one of the active ingredients, and I'm not certain that this still isn't a fudging, not that I know what *of.* So you see, I'm not sure I can go on as I have been? Without the common memory and its checks and balances? I need a, shall I say, support group? So what I want to know is, the gift of these pills is *not at all conditional on your response* but what I'm *asking* is if your group will have me...? Because these people who are just everywhere recently, just *everywhere*, why isn't anyone doing anything about them? I want to know, they were people once, they could still *be* people if... That cataleptic blond girl by the tree we walked past, did you see her?"

The barrage stopped. He evidently expected an answer. Lisa and Kitty, who had long given up trying to make sense of his oration, wanting only to shield themselves from its noise, rewound the last sentence to themselves to consider.

"No," said Lisa. Of course she hadn't noticed the girl; she refused to see any of them.

"Yes," said Kitty. "I saw her. She seemed more alert than, actually, than—"

"I knew her, you see. When she was *her*. Which she isn't, quite, now. But with the X—I crush it up for her, you see— maybe she could be, not her, but *someone*? I honestly don't know. I *will* keep trying, whether or not your group will have me. You girls are pretty. Are you taken?"

"I'm gay," said Kitty. "And yes. Yes, I am."

"None of your business," said Lisa. "You've brought us the drugs?"

"Yes, here," he said and plunged his head down between Kitty's legs to extract a plastic bag from under her seat. "There are a couple of hundred, I think. But you're very pretty, Lisa. I think you could like me."

"Thanks for the drugs, Dr. Corrigan," Lisa answered, snatching the bag from him, checking inside it. "But I think not."

"Oh well," he said. "Get out of my car then. Go on, be off with you, the damn pair of you, so I can go fetch my friend back from the tree. *She* used to be pretty, you know. *And* healthy."

"Thanks, Dr. Corrigan," said Kitty. As she climbed out he was already clambering over to the driver's side, and had pulled yet another bag out from under the seat. She held the door open a second to watch him pop a pill and swig some water. She said, "You've been very kind."

She shut the door. The girls stared at each other. The car window rolled down.

"You get in touch now if you change your mind," Dr. Corrigan said pleasantly, normally, to Lisa, with a broad and a serious smile. "The name's Jakes, by the way. I'm not always like this, you know. I do apologize." And then he chuckled, and he winked.

Lisa did not ask how to get in touch. She had no intention of getting in touch, not even for more drugs. Edie had better crack the damn formula; that's all there was to it.

"He sounded normal at the end there," Kitty said. "And that wink. Do you think some of it was an act? Though I can't imagine why."

Lisa didn't know. She thought not an act, but she didn't care. The sun was going down. It was no time to be out of doors. Kitty would drive them to Jilly's, they would call the others and convince whoever could come to come round now.

Things were happening. They needed to talk all this out. Since apparently they were a *group*. Time, bandmates, to start acting like one.

CHAPTER TEN: YEAR TWO, AUGUST

"After the war, they won't recall they ever were human."

> Howl, in Hayao Miyazaki's film *Howl's Moving Castle*
> (after the novel by Diana Wynne Jones)

"How do you place a city in quarantine? Or a state? Surely the whole state would be safer?

"By the time we ask such questions, it's too late to act on them; it had been too late from the start! Travelers from Eastern Europe carried the EEML virus all over the globe. Whatever the national tendency to pin the virus on us, to call it EVML, or the Virginia flu, we were only where it was most concentrated. Viruses mutate. Eastdon scientists were the first to identify this latest mutation. We were forcefully instructed that in the EEML, the cataleptic stage was rare, rarely prolonged, and rarely terminal, so it *was* probably our fault. And then came the Rampages. In smaller or greater form, this new horror of the memory loss virus revealed itself to our whole country, our entire world, almost at once. Eastdon won out by a day or by up to three weeks."

> Library of Virginia Commission, *The 5 Year Report*

YEAR TWO, EASTDON

Blog Entry, @mekim&chris: Library of Virginia
Commission *5 year report*

The Rampages began on an ungodly hot day in late August. It was as if the heat reached inside all the cataleptics at once and flipped a switch.

But late August? Had so much time passed? Where did we lose track?

Regular trash pick-up went the way of mail delivery. For a while, emergency crews swept the streets of the human rubble, but as the tally of the infected mounted, the pool of willing sanitation workers shrank.

Kim's brother Mike was on a crew. He lasted ten days. The bodies would wake and claw at him. Their exposed skin had hardened, Mike said. It was leathery and corrugated—but scratch or cut it, and the flesh would, quote, "glow like squishy hot radioactive jello." Not even rats or bugs would touch it. The crews wore protective gear, but even so, constant proximity would aggravate their own infection. All those sanitation workers were *already* sick, did you know? They signed up because signing up got them nearer the head of the medical helpline.

Plus, restored health and a good service patch could earn you a spot in the county retreats.

But since earning it mostly got you sicker quicker, as it did Mike, the system crashed. Next thing we knew, the brink-of-dead people were left to rot, or to harden and irradiate, in the gutters and the alleyways. With all the other uncollected garbage.

In spite of everything, the world *has* kept turning, in

stumbling drunk fashion. Other emergency services, like the food distribution trucks and the memory medicine vans, have been semi-reliable. You don't get *much* medicine, and it's surplus early generation, or so Mike heard, but it helps. The food's sort of edible. I'd have said: we're quarantining, but we're coping.

Until one ungodly hot day in late August.

Shapes that had huddled comatose since the spring—how could they not be *corpses?*—began to jerk into life. Not the more recent sprawls. It wasn't their time? But bodies nobody had seen stir, let alone take nourishment, for weeks, or heard one loud moan from, began to howl. Presumed missing neighbors who had lain hidden indoors for months rose up, shambled out, and joined in. The howling was unearthly, in pitch, in volume, in its duration. It was like an all-day cat-fight choir.

Chris, our fifteen-year-old, ran to an upstairs window to look. Kim and I yelled, "Be careful!" but we looked too. House doors were open. Folks we once knew *as people* shuffled out to clutch and howl with the gutter bums, that tribe of lumps that we'd sometimes see lapping at our drain water! I watched a lump stand and wobble. She steadied. She joined the howl.

And then the pitch changed. The whole dissonant chorus went up a dissonant half-octave. After a ten count or so, they broke apart like panicked deer—they flailed, they fell, they lashed out blindly at whatever was in reach, whether it moved or didn't move. They battered into walls, parked cars, each other, trees—still howling. But once they detected anyone like us—we were told later that it was the body heat they were drawn to—the living people, like us, if we were out among them—they, what, "coalesced'"? They *blobbed*, but as if with purpose. The blobs *targeted* us, to be blunt. People, animals, anything with the warmth of breath.

No answer, when we called the cops. Ditto the cavalry. Downtown, a guardsmen corps *did* protect those who matter, the immune. The city's de facto ruling cabal. They're stretched thin, so, yeah. Justified. A well-armed citizen militia, if our block had such an element, might have protected the rest of us. Ramboed out to gun down our sick friends and neighbors.

But no, no local Rambos. The wannabes cowered like the rest of us sensible cowards. In horror, in self-preservation, and in terror. In sane and simple shock. We did hear of one locale where there was carnage. It was on both sides, though: being shot at with little handguns proved to be an irritant. It *drew* them. A block from us, or so we heard, some idiot snuck out to the end of his walk to get better *photographs*. Of *course* they killed him.

The formerly domestic animals, that first go-round, had it the worst. There were a lot of them, orphaned cats and dogs, not sick, just cut loose, scavenging and begging. They wouldn't touch the flesh of the infected, however starving they themselves were. They sniffed. Maybe they nudge-nosed a fold of cloth. But soon enough, they would back away, growling. When the bodies rose and came at them that first time, they froze like rabbits in the headlights. The mobs got to pick them off. The pets who survived got smarter, fast.

So that was the Rampages, Wave One. It crested for less than six hours, as it turned out. Most of us humans, unless we were out of doors and too dumb to run, managed to survive it. Or too dumbstruck: even looking from the window, it was hard not to freeze. So we stayed out of the way, letting the animals bear the brunt. We prayed it would pass. Then we prayed that it *had* passed. But holy shit, just a few days later (two? six?—I lose track of time), it started up again and was *worse*; it persisted; it was tidal: oh we hid, but there was no escaping the noise. The storm waves of howling. No ebb to it either, just a kind of leveling before the next surge, gathering and rising, then rising even louder and wilder. Three days of that. Yeah, now everyone says "the zombies." Black humor. Sometimes helps, mostly doesn't. To us, they're the howlers.

The Wave Two howlers targeted occupied buildings: inhabited houses, open shops, the help centers. Body heat again? Was that how they located us? That was the guess, yes, but if the cataleptics (official term) could think and plan, why the days of reprieve? Why the sudden concerted surge? As if an alarm clock had trilled, *Get to work now!*

Also, if the heat *was* a factor? This was August—hot days were common—why had the creatures waited?

Eastdon became ninety percent unsafe. Unsafe is a limp word. We're talking war zones. Every half-well person with a lick of sense threw a few possessions together and flew the coop, and those with more than a lick of sense fled without packing. If, that is, unlike me and mine, you had a notion where to flee to. There *were* quiet neighborhoods, apparently. High ground is better than low ground. Private estates, MacMansions in big wooded grounds are better still. Trees, lakes, and distances hide your living heat and stench. Me and mine and the rest of us little people might go beg refuge, now we know that. Hey, super-rich philanthropist buddies!

It's been hard not to feel paralyzed. We aren't immune, after all. (That test the French figured out for immunity? Big deal if it won't lead to a cure. If you're losing your memory, like us, Q.E.D., you're infected.) But a *lot* of people, like us, did get stricken less badly. So we'd felt like the lucky ones, riding it out till the world turned the corner. *This*, though—this three-day Zombie Apocalypse, it's getting called, when the bodies rose up and rioted—that wasn't our designated corner. Turns out we had merely been the complacent ones. All we felt now was blindsided.

We're still here, though. They didn't rip us to bits or set fire to us. (Oh, yes, fire, did I say? The howlers burned half our block down.) After Wave One we barricaded the windows. During Wave Two we turned up the A/C—and yes, the power held! In a rickety, clackety way. We blasted every bit of cold air we could. The creatures pay no attention to noise. They're so loud they wouldn't have heard our pitiful machinery whirr even if they did. If heat drew them, shouldn't cold repel them? And it worked. But when it was over, and we *did* venture out? The infected bodies were everywhere. You don't so much step around them as trip and fall on them. I guess we eventually got too much exposure.

So yeah, we are all getting sicker. Every day another hole in the head.

We do try, though! We also get these odd manic jolts

recently, and we ride them. We tell bad jokes and groan. Chris plays us his guitar. Kim makes up lyrics and they duet. I've written *this* thing. Even if it's taken a few days to get it said right. To, as Kim says, bear witless.

Wave Two receded two weeks ago. Eastdon's semi-functioning population has gone from real down to a real downer. (Take that, Kim!) Not so many plucky survivors. More folks fleeing as far as they have gas to get. From what I hear of the rest of the country, there is no safe haven.

Oh, yeah—the law has changed! We're allowed to execute the highly contagious not-dead people before they rise again! They don't take kindly to it, though. Even if you win, the bodies don't go away, they just lie there rotting and stinking. And if *they* win, so do you. Anyway, the rumor is that the bigwigs have been figuring out the signs and preparing responses. If and when a Wave Three hits, they'll be ready. Or readier.

The other positive is that the disease doesn't progress that fast. People had it for months, for a year, there were *stages*, there was catalepsy, before they got like those zombie howlers. And we two and the kid aren't *that* incapacitated yet. We're just not ourselves any more, I guess? Temporarily? The city has run double the medicine vans this week. Maybe the double pills will slow it? Sometimes, the way they give us nice little memory jolts, it seems they must be stronger than Mike said. So we haven't given up hope.

We're just worried is all. We don't really know where to turn.

The help centers?. No one at home there recently.

Three weeks ago? Two? Four? Time gets so hard to keep track of.

It's another really hot day today, the PSAs say. I can't tell. Myself, I feel kinda cold.

Yep. It concerns me too.

CHAPTER ELEVEN: YEAR TWO INTO YEAR THREE

"who cowered in unshaven rooms in underwear... listening to the Terror through the wall."

Allen Ginsberg, "Howl"

"All roads in my mind take me back in my mind,
And I can't forget you, won't forget you,
Won't forget those days."

Chris White, The Zombies, "Beechwood Park"

YEAR TWO INTO YEAR THREE, EASTDON, HALE COUNTY, HEARTWOOD:

Jemmy, Danny & Joyce, Andrew & Elise, Millar & Jody, Danny

I.

We were in Rhino's pigsty of a basement. More of a pigsty now than when we used to rehearse the band there, yeah? Back when there were gigs to play.

"It stinks in here, Rhino," I say.

"Nah, Jemmy," he says. In his dirty tee-shirt and his skivvies. "That smell is you."

On Tuesday, they sent a dozer crew through his street. Could have rendered the stench more piquant, I guess? Yeah, Danny says that's about all the body bagging the city will still get done: when the no-hopers flopping down in the road make a neighborhood impassable.

"So we can go check on the dude?" Nick asked when Danny provided the Rhino intel.

"My thoughts exactly," chorused Danny.

So here we came a-motoring, yeah? Because Danny and Nick are too soft-hearted for their own good. Rhino's a frigging lost cause.

So, yeah, the smell, Rhino is claiming, is *me*, when Nick's phone rings. He puts Lisa on speaker. She's three blocks away, which may mean ten minutes. To find a way around.

"Who's Lisa?" asks Rhino, who even had to be reminded who *Danny* was.

"A way around what?" asks Nick.

"Nick, just be at the door waiting! We'll need to haul ass."

"You're leaving?" says Rhino. "Well, nice seeing the back of you."

"No," goes Lisa. "You're coming too, Rhino, for fuck's sake!"

Which, really? But Lisa's the brood mother, so we half-dress Rhino, and we arm-twist him out onto the porch. He's clutching his axe, and he's a frigging, squirming handful.

And holy fuck, the noise out here! It's frigging *choral*! I can't even count how many *keys* it's in. But right on cue, here's Ma Hen, ordering Nick and me to haul ass out to her van.

"Danny," she yells, "you take Rhino!"

"What the fuck is happening, Lisa?" I ask.

"Get *in*, Jemmy," she says. "Just *look*!"

She points. I look. Every local stiff the baggers missed is on its goddamn *feet* somehow. And howling, though most of the noise is coming from farther off. Oh, and they're, I swear to God, body slamming!

"This is nothing," Lisa says. "You should see the surrounding blocks."

Rhino has had enough of this. I've loosed him, and he's brandishing his axe at Danny.

"Put down the damn guitar and get *in*, Rhino!" Lisa yells. "They will *swarm* you."

I offer you my adios mental snapshot of our doomed ex-front man Rhino. He's in a filthy bathrobe. He's giving Lisa this giant snort—like a, yeah, *rhino*. It turns into a fit of coughing. "Wusses!" he says, coughing. "Sheep!" He slams the door on us and on whatever else is out in the pasturage.

Rhino's sicker than the rest of us put together, but yeah, he *still* denies there's anything much awry. Like: *what* body-slamming cadavers? Like: *what* howling?

We have no choice. We ditch him.

And then, what a ride here, man! Like crosstown through hell during a street rave! Twice, we have to squeeze by a real, literal fire.

"Here" is Jilly Simmons' house, yeah? Or what used to be her house; her body's in a box in her nephew's truck. Good old natural causes, he says. But which he's fretting with big wet sobs about, because the truck is parked out on the street, waiting for him to drive his aunt Jilly to the cemetery, which how can he, or do we think he can? So yeah, *his* house now, this poor Matt dude's. In a gated community no less, with pricey de luxe private bagging, he says. Apparently, he's been voted into our gang of seven. Who are also us four, plus Jody, who moved in here to give Jilly hospice care, plus her boyfriend, Millar. We're pledging implicit allegiance while fires lick the foot of the hill. While the howling, still as loud as fuck, but also kind of floaty from up here, right, like almost a cool vibe? It starts to go a little hoarse. It sharpens into shrieks.

What I'm listening to, mostly. The others are arguing over what next, what now...

Surprise, though! The crisis turns out to be temporary. No slow fade; the din just cuts off to silence. Mid-note, bro! We peek through our upstairs window. There are a few first-wave corpsicles who have made it up to the viewable vicinity—it's weird how they move, right? It's like a pied piper is playing games with them, yeah? Or the devil's playing three fiddle tunes at once, and they can't decide which strain's theirs. They keep doing that for a half-minute, but in silence. Then they stop and drop, like the devil's said, "Wait, I've broken a string."

So we've had a reprieve—but none of us believes it will last.

Okay. Where the frigging heck next, then? Matt Simmons's

posh country seat? He's been out of town till recently: duty-bound, he says, since they've paid him, to finish a project for this rich family who got trapped in India when the borders closed. Yeah, and casting a covetous eye on the joint, says Millar. That too, Matt admits. But there are *managers*. They won't *leave*.

Still, he might be able to negotiate? Could we give him some time?

Do we *have* time?

"Crap," he says suddenly. "I'm going for it. I've got to do right by her."

And the dude just takes off to bury his poor auntie! Wacko, but mucho endearing, right?

Millar reads Jody's face, the way couples do that, and he speeds off after him. He has his phone! Jody can call him with the scoop!

So then we're the gang of five, yeah?

Nick, surprisingly, is who has the notion we five glom onto. In the meanwhile, to try this big charming 18th-century house, at the top of Old Eastdon Hill, at the easternmost part of town.

"They do climb, but their instinctual swarm is toward lower ground," claims Nick, ticking off the pros on his fingers. Nick has had his nose buried in the news and the community watch posts. "It's in a residential neighborhood, yes, but an old and small one, not dense with zombies."

Lisa gives a little moan. We've been avoiding "zombies."

"On two sides, what's more, unlike at our present location, the proximate neighborhoods *aren't* residential. They're industrial or they're administrative."

Which is so Nick. The zombies bust out into an apocalypso, and he greets it with words like "proximate."

"And fourthly, it's an isolated dwelling in a park ringed by woods..."

Nick would clearly, in Nick talk, *expostulate further*, but Jody and Lisa are already sold.

"Yes!" they say. "The Cricket Club Lodge!"

We try to call in this scoop to Millar and Matt, but there's no signal. The lines are down for two days. One day later, when we do reach them, the second wave breaks.

II.

Much, much later, in some kind of hospital, Jemmy will be shown a document labeled "Intake Transcript, January." He won't know what to make of it. He recalls almost none of what he apparently, some time back, told them. He was under treatment, of course, and he'll be under treatment now, too, naturally, with precautionary measures in place, as his responses are assessed and approved or disapproved. Yeah? he groggily asks himself. If he isn't, yeah, dreaming this?

III.

They reach the cemetery just before dark. Matt is relieved to have made it in time, but chains are across the gate.

"Jesus H. Christ!" he exclaims. "This is where her plot is! They *knew* I was coming. How the fuck could I have got her here any sooner?"

"Matt," says Millar. "A city cemetery? Today? A dangerous place, maybe?"

Matt says nothing. He climbs back in the truck. He drives them to a county cemetery.

The gate is chained and padlocked. A sign says, DANGER!! STAY AWAY!!!

Matt rattles the chain and howls. A dog howls back. Millar has heard enough howling for one day. And it's gotten late. "Tell you what," he says, as Matt slams the driver's side door behind him and slumps down, nonplussed. "I have some friends who live out this way, in the woods."

"The pharmacy girls? I could bury her there, you think?"

"Perhaps. Really, they need to be in on whatever the group decides anyway."

Matt has met Edie once and Kitty more frequently. Yeah, they might help.

He drives. Ten minutes of silence, except for a couple of phone calls that fail to find a signal. The coffin bounces and rocks as they turn onto a gravel road. Matt thinks he hears Jilly's head bumping up against the lid. He takes the driveway curve too sharply, and the truck's back doors fly open. The coffin shimmies between two sacks of dried goods and a clattering tool cabinet and careens out. It bumps, it slides, and they all come to rest.

IV.

"So they're at the Wolker estate now, your people?"

"They are. It's a decent choice, I think—"

"It's better than decent, Danny. Genuine woods. A very isolated house."

"And it's inside your protected zone, I think?"

"Ah. I was wondering what you knew of that."

"The difference between here and five blocks from here is startling, Joyce."

"It's only just inside, mind you. We *may* have to retrench. We *hope* not to abandon it. It's a good natural barrier, the Wolker estate."

"Understood. But the caretakers also worry me. One of the reasons we could talk our way in is that they're both sick. A Jody and Lisa tag-team can get unstoppable, but they didn't have to try. That old couple is going to need, well, looking after."

"And watching."

"I'm sorry?"

"You're worried that they won't just be a burden; they'll be a danger."

"Correct. Listen, Joyce, these are my people. I understand that the government needs the immune types like me, or we'll all go under—"

"We do. But you're not *proven* immune yet. Low susceptibility isn't the same thing."

"Okay. But I've been around a lot of very sick people."

"You have, Danny. And Hospital Roving Services is important work too."

"Is it? I've been helping those who it's too late to help."

"You're getting them off the streets before they crash there. That matters to the healthy."

"What do you guys do with them, though? After we bring them in? You've been studying them, haven't you? Someone said you're working on what triggers them."

"Need to know, Danny."

"And if you do figure out how to trigger them, then what?"

"Need to know, Danny. But you're right; if you *are* immune, and you likely *are*, we could use you here. That's when you'll need to know."

"So, how long before my results are in?"

"Not long. It would be quicker if you stayed on-site and quarantined."

"Yeah, but no."

"Well, then. A week after the first test, you'll get the second. And a vaccine, if you pass it. There are almost always some trace impurities. A month later, we retest."

"Five, six weeks? Seems like a long wait to me."

"Necessary. Anyway, it gives you time to get your group settled and fully functioning."

"Fine, but don't bullshit me, Joyce. Without help, nowhere

in the city will be safe. And it's not just that the rampages are getting more severe, and lasting longer, and spreading farther afield, and that the numbers of the infected just keep swelling. It's that town life isn't designed to be self-sufficient. You don't grow your food, people sell it to you. You have supply lines."

"We still have supply lines."

"Oh, adequate ones? And it's got to stay safe enough for genuine commerce; safe enough for us to come up out of our bunker and forage."

"We're managing, though, considering where we might be."

"That's not the view from my side of the siege. Look, Joyce, I need my crew out of town, on their own land, somewhere long-term. Where they have a chance to fend for themselves."

"Some of them already are out of town, you say."

"Millar and Matt and his dead auntie, yeah, funny story about that..."

"You said. Exasperating, I'd call it. Closing the cemeteries for fear of the word *zombies*. Some of the safest places around, cemeteries. No human body heat at all!"

"Yeah, well. Millar and Matt. Not my crew, but they matter to Jody, so... With the pharmacy girls, out by the airport. Yeah, in a woods cottage. With some scrawny fruit trees, even. And with Matt's dried goods, and sure, they could put in more vegetables, keep chickens. Small drawback: they aren't doing that. Bigger one: the pharmacy girls are more infected than the rest of us. Anyway, their place isn't huge. Listen, I know you didn't date Jemmy for very long—"

"Two weeks and change. No more or less than either of us wanted. I like Jemmy."

"But it was long enough to see how he looks up to me. He's my little brother, Joyce. I can't let him down. Or let Jody down, for that matter, or Lisa or Nick. These are my people."

"I'm sorry about your parents."

"Yeah. I should have—I just didn't get my—Yeah."

"So now you're here. But you have conditions."

"So, yes, I'll sign up for your war effort. But number one, you'll give me longer than just five or six weeks to get our affairs in order."

"Three months. Deal."

"And next, you—we—keep helping my tribe once I... abandon them. To settle in here."

"Special treatment for your posse."

"Or I don't sign on."

"Well. That's the deal most people insist on, I suppose. *I* didn't. I just got to work."

"Well, good for you. What would Eastdon have done without you?"

"Gone under, possibly, in point of fact. Very well. You have your deal, Danny. But we have conditions too."

"Meaning what?"

"They can't know. Because if they know, other people might know. Will know."

"Who can't know? And will know what, Joyce?"

"Your people can't know we're playing favorites, that we're saving them. As others die."

"I won't say anything, Joyce."

"You won't have to. They, your posse, will see us saving them when some near future wave breaks through our perimeter and hits the lodge. As one *will*, of course. Also, they're hotheads. The news of our assistance will not be suppressed."

"Yeah. Yeah, I guess I get that."

"Secondly, once we've made sure they're away from the crazies, and settled, and coping, we ease up on the help. We can keep an *eye* on them. Step in if there's an *emergency*. But they will have to figure out their own communal survival strategy. We can't nanny-state them."

"But their memory loss—"

"The drugs don't cure it, exactly, but they do, we're convinced, stabilize it. They may already be stable."

"Or they may not be."

"It's variable, true. Do you have faith, right now, as they are now, that they can make it?"

"If they don't deteriorate. Yes. Yes, I do."

"Then first, we supply you with more drugs. Let's make sure we *get* them stable. They may not even realize how low they're running, your hotheads. Top up their stores. Offer them some truth if you have to. We'll clean up the loose ends later. If one or both the caretakers can be saved, or maybe rebuilt as someone else, you have permission to try that, but first, make sure your own people are..."

"Wait. Clean up the loose ends?"

"Look, just feed them a cover story. Not important what. And this is going to sound weird, but keep them zonked. Until we get them out and clean up after ourselves."

"Keep them *zonked*? On the X7?"

"The X9. They'll still function. They might not know quite *how* they do. This is no time for half-measures, Danny. Right now, zonked is worth the risk. Shore them up, once and for all, and you shouldn't lose them."

"Shouldn't."

"It's variable."

"I could lose them to the drugs too. Jody is already..."

"Yes. Can't be helped. Watch over her."

"Got to be careful with that. Keep some distance. I feel like that has to be Millar's job. Can we maybe make sure the lines of communication stay open? She needs the dude, I think."

"Between the Lodge and the pharmacy girls' place? I don't know if you're a nice guy or a sap, Danny. Without our help, Jody would almost certainly disengage from Millar."

"I'm being a nice guy, Joyce. I won't be staying anyway, so Millar... Millar should..."

"Jeez, Danny. Anyone else you want us to play Cupid and

226

Santa to?"

"Absolutely! I need Jemmy to live through this. And Lisa. And yeah, Big Nick."

"That was *intended* as sarcasm. But fine. We may need Millar's crowd, eventually, anyway, when we get your main group out of the Lodge. Andrew Barker has a compound set up an hour out of town. Some of us don't trust him. Or any of those nutty, delusionally infected survivalists with their big armories. I may not be permitted to protect him. The estate Simmons has been working on could be our primary."

"Holy crap, Joyce. Who *are* you people? I didn't even mention Andrew—"

"He and his daughter checked in at the lodge this morning. He probably hopes some of you will take off for his compound with him. They won't."

"How much aren't you telling me? Because it's like you're this all-seeing eye, and you have some great mastermind plan already in place or something. And you're stripteasing me your little glimpses! Have I said anything you didn't already know?"

"All in good time, Danny. A nice idea, though, the stripteasing you. Stay single for me."

V.
Closed captioned drone video. Andrew Barker's compound, the evacuation.

> *(Howling. Crackle of flames. Sound of gates shuddering and bouncing.)*
>
> *(Armored truck engine revving. Machine gun rattle.)*

AB: Steer *into* them, girl! Not around them. Yes! Better!

> *(Crunch of impact. Tires squeals. EB yelps and sobs. Machine gun fire.)*

AB: No! Bear left. To the bridge.

EB: Left is where they are! I can—

AB: No, you can't. That's what they want!

EB: What they want?

AB: Just do it!

(Tires screaming as the truck corners.)

EB: Jesus, daddy, I steer, you shoot!

AB: Then steer, fuck you!

(Howling rises in intensity. Engine roars. Sounds of impact and engine stalling as bodies fall under the wheels. Machine gun fire. Engine starts back up. Acceleration noises. Howling diminishes behind them. EB whimpers.)

EB: You were right. The bridge is clear.

AB: How did the fuckers know, Elise? How did those fuckers find us?

(Silence, except for the measured purr of the engine.)

AB: Well, well, well. Look up there. Following us. Eye in the sky.

VI.

Given that everything is terrible, Millar can't believe their luck. In three, four ways!

First, the woods cottage is proving to be a genuine refuge. Periodically, the foghorn will sound from Foghorn Rock, but otherwise, it's pre-pandemic quiet. Just the five of them and trees. The happenstance that brought him and Matt here was a happy one: there's room enough, once they figured out they could use the truck and the cars as storage pods; the lodge is just as full; they can't afford to lose contact with their pharmacy crew; they have fallen into a way not to.

Second, Edie has come sideways at the X recipe, and stumbled on a way to make it work. The formula notes Corrigan gave them were as much a hindrance as a help—had been, Millar suspected, deliberately corrupted—but she'd made some educated guesses, and she'd cracked it.

Third, he's getting to spend time again with Tiff, one of his favorite people ever, and it turns out he adores this new girlfriend of hers, this Kitty.

And fourth, the lines of communication between them and the lodge seem always or almost always to be open. They can be without power for hours, yet if they call the lodge, or try, who knows, to Skype there, somehow it will thrum back on, so that they can.

So Millar has been talking with Jody again. They talk often—if that's what it takes to get the power working, all the better—and they've been telling each other how everything is terrible.

Millar fears it's taken too long for Edie to crack the formula. They have the ingredients; Edie can compound her X-variant, but not in large enough quantities to bring someone back from Tiff's kind of brink. Kitty and Edie say, don't worry about us, give ours to Tiff, but if they do, he fears they'll lose Kitty too. Edie, he, and Matt are in better shape than the other two, but not in good enough shape to go without.

To save the caretakers, Jody fears, they will have to reconstruct them as other people. There's not much there any more, though the woman, Sarah, is nicely susceptible to suggestion. Danny, who seems, miraculously, to be immune, and who is still working with Hospital Roving, has somehow gotten hold of enough of the drug for all of them.

Yeah, Jody might be abusing her supply. She's aware. Everything's just too hard for her otherwise. "Especially without you, Millar."

"You've got Danny there."

"Fuck Danny. I want to fuck *you*. Or at the very least snuggle. I'd sleep sounder."

"Both options is my vote."

"Yeah... Danny's out of our league now anyway. Lisa

doesn't seem to get that yet."

"Lisa?"

"They're sharing a room. Good for them, but it can't last. He's dropped hints, big ones. About duty and the like. Once he's done all he can for us, Danny's going to leave."

"I thought Lisa might be immune too?"

"Nope. Just slower to succumb."

Millar frets about the longer term. They should be together, all of them, but where? Matt wants them to try Heartwood but fears it might be too late, that the managers—who weren't medicating but weren't sick either, the last time Matt saw them—will have filled the place with their own people. Didn't Andrew, Millar asks hazily, propose an alternative site?

"Yep, but he's here now," Jody tells him. "His compound got overrun."

Millar sighs. "But the lodge is still safe enough?"

Jody hesitates. Harlan worries her. "From the mobs? Yeah. No incursions yet."

"Good," says Millar, reading her perfectly. Who worries him is Tiff. "Here neither."

Later, after the woods cottage goes up in flames, and Tiff, too tenuously human, dies, and Kitty, too heartbreakingly faithful, dies with her, Matt brings Millar and Edie to Heartwood. The estate isn't merely abandoned, it's set up and supplied and ready to be moved into, as if someone has spruced it up for them, as if it's been lying in wait. There are no Marie Celeste-level signs of earlier occupation—no half-eaten meals, no overturned chairs—but the managers clearly were here until, what, a week ago? Or someone was; maybe half a dozen someones. The clean-up was careful, but there are names scribbled on cereal boxes, a crisp shopping list in a coat pocket. Matt looks through other pockets and finds a driver's license. Tom Jarvis. Son of one of the managers.

So why did they all leave, and for where? Should Matt, Millar, and Edie be afraid?

But one thing is clear: it wasn't zombies who turfed them out. The place is immaculate.

Matt and Millar share the same suspicion. A not rare side effect of the X7 is paranoia, which they know, so they don't air or indulge in this suspicion. They need this refuge; they'd like to enjoy it guilt-free, please. If they were Andrew, they would voice the thought with glee: *So Danny is looking out for us.* Well, Danny's a good guy, thinks Millar; Danny will do right by the evicted people. Millar imagines Andrew's snort. His indomitably self-righteous chuckle.

Meanwhile, though, they're going to need Edie. As ready for them as Heartwood has been made, the day-to-day work is a lot for Millar and Matt, and Edie is still in shock. For two weeks, she has stayed pretty much out of her mind: zonked on her homemade maddies, compulsively listening to Millar's taped interviews with Tiff and Kitty, reading and re-reading Millar's notes.

And then she's done with them. "Here," she says to Millar. "Hide them from me."

In the morning, she's quite literally a new person. Poised and efficient; scripted, re-drafted, and copyedited. It creeps Millar and Matt out. It's an enormous relief.

Now it's Christmas, and Millar is telling Jody (yet again) that the whole crew should be together: that the lodge won't be secure forever; that it's time for them to come out to Heartwood. There's room for everyone, and they need everyone. "Yes," says Jody. "Let us know when to be ready, and we will be. But be careful. The roads are still trouble."

At New Year's, Millar has barely settled into his chair before the link goes down.

"You can't come," Jody has had time to say. "Not now—we'll let you..."

There follows a month of silence. No phone service, no internet. Millar is sick with worry, and not just for his friends and for the state of the world. He's actually forgetting some of them! So he doubles up on his note-making. He recites his careful histories to Matt and Edie. They need to remember too! When, finally, they do get through to the lodge, it's Andrew who answers, sounding both cheery and groggy. Millar reminds him who he is and who and where they are. Andrew *needs* some reminding. A month out of contact is just too long!

"Jody? Jody's fine. She can't speak right now, is all. But no, she's fine. Swing by and pick us up, and you'll see for yourself."

"We can pick you up? That's it, no worries? What has changed, Andrew?"

"Oh, it's just that things are quiet now. It seems like a good time."

"Well, what the fuck *has* been happening? At New Year's? This whole last month?"

Andrew chuckles. "Well, wouldn't you like to know? Us too, actually. Our memories are vague. *All* our memories. And they're contradictory."

"Of the *month*? The entire *month*?"

"New Year's, we had an incursion. A big one, and yet none of us can recall the details. We disagree about what we do recall. Oh, Harlan died. For some reason, Sarah, that's Jenna Brower now, thinks she pushed him off the roof. Not a useful delusion, so we re-educated her. It's more likely he went full zombie and *I* killed him. Or that the cattle did. The rest of the month, we all agree, *blurrily*, has been uneventful." He chuckles again. "In short, we have been *benevolently*, quote unquote, *tampered* with. Play it again, Uncle Sam—am I right? Oh, and Danny's gone."

Millar doesn't understand. Does he need to, though? "We'll be there ASAP."

In the event there will be weather difficulties. So Matt balks. And Edie insists there are things to fix first, inventory to acquire, spaces to make ready. ASAP proves to be sixteen days.

VII.

Harlan had been responding to treatment, but not well enough. He had gone right on succumbing, if Danny was honest, since the five of them moved in here. Sure, the drugs Joyce got them were keeping Harlan's body alive, if not his mind, but the virus managed that trick too, in a weird way. It made you look comatose, or be comatose, while it changed you. Harlan wasn't comatose. The drugs held him upright. But the sickness was still changing him.

The trees bothered him. He would hack through the woods to the cricket pitch, swinging an axe and a sickle. He would sprawl, face-up, midway between the headstones—Jenna-Sarah said he had dug up the bodies once, a year ago, after Jody asked him about those graves. To confirm that there *were* bodies, and that it wasn't maybe the Beale treasure. Yep. Two caskets. Two bodies. But something else had been buried down below them, once. Or so he was convinced. He'd found a gold ring. If it hadn't been for the pandemic, he would have found a way to get that whole strip dug up.

Now, even sick, Harlan was obsessed. He slept there in the fall sunlight, like Smaug on his hoard. But *getting* there, through those trees, those damn trees, really bothered him.

On New Year's Eve, he didn't make it back. He rose, apparently, from the stubbled grass, and went around the circle of the frosted meadow, setting fire to the woods.

Danny should have been ready. Those graves gave even him the shivers. Not just their zero body heat: he felt ghost chill. Eventually, that cold was bound to get to Harlan. It did. He trapped and wrapped himself in hot flames of his own making. And he died.

Within half an hour, the grounds of the estate were thick with howlers, drawn there.

Their own local rampage had begun.

Within an hour, there were helicopters, drawn also. No need to call Joyce. There were armed men by the truckload. This wave, after all, was localized, and it was local. It could be contained. There were orders, from on high, to contain it. So they would contain it.

Within two hours, it was contained. Within three, the lodge was emptied of its people.

Danny helped empty it. He kissed a few zonked brows. He left with the troops. It stayed empty for a month while Joyce's people sanitized his people.

Meaning you all, my friends. Meaning more drugs. She bedded you down and wove you a tangle of cover stories. After a few weeks, we drove you home groggy. I tucked you in to wake up heavy-lidded. Y'all: I am so sorry.

Still, the bargain held. They all, except Harlan, got safely to Heartwood.

There were new folks in the lodge within a week. They liked it. There was even a parrot!

CHAPTER TWELVE: YEAR THREE

"I've had some narrer shaves and lively rides before;
I've rode a wild bull round a yard to win a five-pound bet,
But this was the most awful ride that I've encountered yet."

A.B. "Banjo" Peterson, "Mulga Bill's Bicycle"

"I'd give it to you if I could, but I borrowed it."

Syd Barrett, Pink Floyd, "Bike"

YEAR THREE, HEARTWOOD:

Elise

I.

The first time Elise discovered the shed on the river island, it housed a girl's bicycle. Not new, but sturdy; an all-terrain bike, she thought, and a perfect size for her. It even seemed to be in good working order. It was hard to say how good because the island was shore to shore with trees.

To try it out, she would need to get it across the river and into the meadows. Which was going to be a challenge. She'd been able to wade a lot of the way over today—the water was low right now—but she'd still had to swim ten yards or so, fighting a mild current. Not all that dangerous a feat; she swam well. But she wouldn't be able to while dragging a bike. What had the other girl used? (*Sita* was the name stenciled on the frame.) A raft, maybe?

Well, she'd leave it for now. She splashed across to where she'd stowed her clothes, to pull her jottings book from a shorts pocket and make some notes. She needed a plan.

II.

Five days later, she had one. She wasn't sure it would work, but she knew who she'd ask for help—and this very day, since who could say when the drought might break and the river rise. And she knew what she'd do if it panned out and she liberated that bike. Tomorrow, she hoped, before anyone got wind of what she was up to and stopped her.

Okay, Elise knew she wasn't ready to run away from home yet. She wasn't even ready for a proper test run. But she did need to research the area beyond the farm. Just to look around for a spell without going too far. No farther than, say, easy bicycle range.

Fortunately, her homeschooling mentor this week was Big Nick. He might be the only one of her housemates who could or would help her, at least without interfering or blabbing. He was tall, and he was strong, and she knew how to talk to him. So after lunch, ambling back out into the fields, she told him what she wanted; he laughed and said, "Why not?" Until sloshing and stumbling, wading all the way (except the two times he sputtered under), he followed her out to the island. Together, they got the shed door off its hinges and laid it out flat in the water. If they each gave a hand in support, yes, it would float. They maneuvered the bike out onto it. They buoyed it. Awkward as hell, but manageable, if Nick could avoid slipping and near-drowning. "You're sure this is okay?" she asked again. He was cute as a big old bug, stripped to his shorts and his sneakers, all glistening wet. He gave the confident macho chuckle she had aimed to elicit; he jumped right in. Elise was already in. She grasped the other end of the door, put her shoulder under it, doggy-paddling. Nick had to half-lift his end, reach out closer and closer to the center of gravity, just to keep the contraption steady, but somehow he kept his stride even, and they made it to the big flat rocks halfway across without major incident. The bike did slide off in the water, once, at the end, but Nick pivoted to seize it. They hauled it back on its pallet until Nick said, "Now we park it, and we reattach the door." "Sure," Elise replied, the hard part past; the river got shallower after the flat rocks. "No hurry."

So they did that, and they dawdled over the task, chattering away about anything and everything—her homeschool project for the week, for example, edible wild plants, she was thinking. Maybe cultivated ones too? Because Nick could totally help her with that. "Ha ha," he said, as if she were teasing, which she hadn't been.

It wasn't hard to get the bike ashore from the halfway rock. They stashed it near a stand of trees to dry. Sweet, dear Nick. She felt like kissing the boy. If he were Jemmy, she probably would have done, on the cheek or something, just to gross him out, but with Nick, it wouldn't have been quite a joke. So instead she curtseyed, in her soaking shorts and her bikini top, and he gave her back a sweeping bow. Adorable. She waited till he was out of sight. She stripped and hung her cutoffs over a branch, squeezing out water. She grabbed a book and an apple from her studies bag. She shinnied up into the high leaves.

III.

The bike's tires were flat, but she'd made time, right after supper, to slip out, get back across to the shed, and fetch the pump she'd seen on a shelf. She'd inflated them, had found no leaks, and this morning she slipped the pump into her studies bag to bring with her .

She'd packed a few other things too—lunch, a survey map, a handgun, a pocket knife, a towel she could wrap the very uncomfortable seat in—nothing that would weigh her down. She wasn't going far. The rain wasn't due till midnight or so. She'd be fine. She'd get off-road when she could, might even hide the bike and hike some. Just a look-see.

There had once been a stile you could climb, to cross a minor road into more fields. Some of their farm's perimeter was protected by the river, but not that stretch. One of the first things her people had done was to knock down the stile and fence off the area; Jemmy, whose job it was to patrol the fences, checked it daily for signs of a breach. But there was still a wriggly way out through the woods to that same road. She'd marked the trail in her jottings book; she visited it regularly to keep it in her memory. The bike had to be carried through some of it, but it was negotiable. By eight-fifteen she was in open country, pedaling. Free, free at last. Till after forty minutes of slow climbing, not a soul on the road, nothing but fields, she spotted a green path up into the still higher hills. Her legs were strong. She could handle it; coast back down home after. Treat herself to a nice long descent. She steered, puffing, wobbling, where her nose pointed her.

And when she came to a fork, and a trail sign, *Bone Caves one mile*, up a much rougher, narrower footpath, she laid her bike under the cover of a bush, and she walked. Birds were whistling behind and in front of her, a call she didn't know. It was a beautiful morning.

The caves weren't hard to find. They were inhabited. The way opened out suddenly, and there was the cliff face. A man and a woman, maybe fifty or sixtyish, sat out on a brushless outcrop of rock, in deck chairs, for all the world as if they were waiting for her. The woman held a shotgun, not yet hoisted toward her. Elise stopped dead. The woman gave a whistle, like a bird whistle, and from back down the trail came an answering whistle. A boy a few years older than Elise emerged from the dark of the trees, wheeling her bike.

IV.

"You don't come one step closer, now," the man warned her. And then to the boy. "I dunno, Merle. You think it's safe to touch that thing?"

"I swabbed it down," he answered. "Swabbing works on

239

non-organics. I told you."

"Too late now anyway, I guess. You've *been* touching it."

"Quit the tizzy. I'm keeping it."

"Little girl," said the woman, "we ain't never got sick yet. And just for your information, we ain't planning to get sick. Are you sick, little girl?"

"If you touch me, or you touch my dead body, I guess you will find out," said Elise.

"It don't have to come to that. Just step over there a ways so our boy Merle can get safely by you. Then we'll let you turn around and skedaddle on home."

"Wait a minute," said the man. "You got any other presents for us in that backpack of yours before you go?"

Elise said nothing. She waited till Merle was by her with her bicycle, and at rest next to his parents on the shelf of rock before extracting the bicycle pump.

"Here," she said, tossing it. They dodged as if it were a stick of dynamite, the woman knocking over her deck chair and sending the shotgun skittering. "Sorry. If you keep the bike, you'll need it."

The woman, not pacified, had already retrieved the gun, was swinging it toward her. "Woah," said Elise, hauling out her own gun, cocking it, "we're all friends here."

The boy laughed. "Doesn't exactly seem like it."

Elise laughed too. It was hard to, though, and the noise was clattery and unconvincing. "Well, we can try to be, anyway."

She backed off two paces. She dangled her gun hand down and curtseyed. The woman nodded and lowered her weapon; the man bowed back at her. Not as adorably as Nick had, but Elise would take it. Deliberately, recklessly, she turned her back on them. She sauntered away. Reaching the safety of the trees, she broke into a juddering, suddenly sobbing scutter. And ran, downhill through the scratch of foliage, the entire mile to the footpath sign. Where at last she looked behind her, listening for the whistle of an unfamiliar bird.

The walk back took all day. The food she'd brought felt meager. Her shoes pinched. Her ass hurt from the dumb bicycle seat. Once, she saw a horse and cart off in the distance, clopping her way. She hurtled as far and as fast as she could into the woods until it was safely by.

V.

It was dark outside and through much of the house. Lights shone in the dining area, though. Good, she was starving.

"Where the heck have you been?" her aunt Jody, the only person still at the table eating, asked. Which struck Elise as kind of funny, a nervous funny: of all the people whom she might have expected to hold her to account, her aunt wasn't one. Her aunt was rarely coherent enough. But she didn't actually seem that upset.

"Andrew, Reds is back," Jody shouted, but her father had heard and was at the door.

"I told them no need to worry," he announced. "They wanted to send a search party, some of them. They're out looking now, I believe. That Nick was quite distressed. So you didn't run into anyone?"

"Not a soul," said Elise. Dad was positively jolly. She was going to get away with this.

"Well, I trust you, darling. I raised you to look after yourself, and I'm going to let you do that. No need to go racing around after you; I told them that. I'll signal them back."

He fetched a rifle and went to fire the shots. Through the door blew a soft spatter of rain.

"Where the heck were you, anyway?" Jody repeated.

"Up in the hills. Almost getting myself killed. Came through it, though."

241

"Well, you do always prepare. Good job too. It's a danger-ous world out there."

"Yeah. I learned a little something about that."

"Worth the trouble, then. Hey, you even beat the rain."

"Rain's nothing. Yeah, not going to log it, though, I don't think. I think maybe I'll make up some lie for Brian and forget about today. Let the course of time swallow it."

"Smart," Jody cheerfully agreed. "Not everything is worth the anguish of remembering."

Elise sat down by her. No, not everything. Sometimes she did love these people, though. Sometimes they did feel like family.

Okay, deep breath. She piled her bowl with stew, and she ate.

CHAPTER THIRTEEN: YEAR FOUR

"What's that, girl? Timmy's in the well?"

Apocryphal, attributed in jest to the TV show "Lassie"

"We will be told, once the world is stable again, by those who survive to tell us so, that we could have and should have done more. That we should have gone out, for instance, into those small struggling rural communes, to assess how they were coping and to assist them. How many such communities, in fact, had we helped set up, because of their members' hard-earned patches, or their ties to us of blood and friendship? But then we left them to it, barely keeping body and soul together. Let us pray they will survive to resent our apparent passivity, so that we may apologize. So that we may explain the obstacles we faced. They may listen; during the first three years, the obstacles were indeed often insuperable. But by the fourth year? Were we cautious, or were we lax? We moved, I would contend, too slowly. We could have and should have done more."

Library of Virginia, The 5 Year Report

YEAR FOUR, HEARTWOOD:

Elise, Jemmy, Edie, Lisa, Andrew, Jody, Matt, Millar

I.

"Who the fuck are you?" Elise asks the girl Jemmy is tugging toward the stepwell.

"What the fuck, Reds!" Jemmy exclaims. "You're nine years old or something. Speak nice, can't you?"

"Excuse me, miss," Elise says. "I don't believe we've met. My name is Elise, though this turd and most of the turds around here taxonomize me by hair color. And who the fuck are you?"

Lisa's dogs bound around her, their tails swishing. The girl, maybe twentyish, and she looks Indian, appears mildly confused but not frightened; there's not much affect there at all, in fact, just a placid dopiness.

"Jeez, Jemmy, is she cattle?"

"From crude to rude! Look, girl, I'll explain later. Nick needs help right now."

"News flash, Jemmy. Nick always needs help."

"If you want to be useful for once in your life, come with me to the stepwell. Nick's banged his head. He sent me to get help."

"And you fetched a zom?"

"I was looking for your father."

"And the difference escaped you?"

By this time they're almost at the wellhouse. Behind them, they hear a shout.

"Jemmy! Jemmy, wait right there, asshole."

The three of them make a mirroring swivel, with Elise spinning to peer over her left shoulder and the other two pivoting right.

"Nicky's in the well!" Elise yells back to Edie.

"Come on, Edie, he really is. Anything else you have to say can keep."

Jenna Brower, lagging far behind Edie, stops and heads back where she's come from. ("Useless old biddy," Jemmy thinks, still turned to wait.) Edie puts on an impressive burst of speed. Reaching Jemmy, she takes a moment to catch her breath. Then she slaps him full in the face.

"Ow! What was that for?"

"What do you think, pervert?"

This is all too much for the zombie girl, who bursts into tears. She cups her hands over her ears as if to shield them from the noise she's poised to make, and she launches into a wail. The dogs howl with her. The three of them fuel each other, spur each other to a sparring cacophony.

Jemmy takes the zombie girl in his arms.

"Shh," he says. "It's okay; it's all right."

The sobs quiet a little. Edie yanks Jemmy viciously away and flings him, *Ow*, to the ground. She takes the zombie girl, who has quickly re-amped the volume, into her arms.

"Shh," she says. "It's okay. It's all right."

"Jemmy!" says the zombie girl, disengaging. She bends to him and helps him to his feet, the dogs circling and hopping. She caresses his face. Edie, utterly disgusted, stands watching.

"Cattle don't say names," Elise points out. "Hey, do the dogs *know* her?"

"She's in recovery," Jemmy replies gently. "We've been rehabbing."

"Pervert," repeats Edie, no less bitingly, but under her breath this time.

"I haven't touched her."

"But it's the plan."

"Hoping to touch a girl one day, when the time is right, is perverted, Edie? I don't think so. Besides, who had I got a prayer of touching around here before? You, Edie?"

"There's me," says Elise.

"Ugh. Wash your mouth out with soap and water, girl."

Elise giggles. Jemmy pushes past her into the wellhouse and finds the flashlight. "Nick?" he calls out.

There is no answer.

II.

Up in Lisa's room, she and Andrew are out of the shower and dressing, chatting happily about nothing much, when they stumble and bumble their way, amiably and without escalation, into one of the usual arguments. The water pressure has been so low for a couple of days now, has Lisa noticed. Oh? Well, it often is, isn't it? I don't know, Lisa, not like this; I suggest we may prefer to be careful. Careful...? In case this is finally *it*... It...? Don't be coy, you know what I mean. Etc.

A week later, when the patterns have repeated a few times, Lisa will be less patient and less tender. Today she pushes herself onto the tips of her toes; she kisses him on the lips.

"Would you stop bloviating about how the world is ending," she asks. "It's not helpful."

"Helpful, is it? You want helpful, you prepare for what's happening if you've got the eyes to see. Not what you *want* to happen."

"Except we're so geared toward fending off your imminent improbable *doomsdays* it blocks *out* what there is to see. You must recognize that, Andrew."

"We're geared, as you put it, towards makeshift daily survival. When the real shit goes down, apocalypse apocalypse apocalypse, this place is not going to hold."

"Stop saying that stupid word! Anyway, it's not the apocalypse. There's shopping."

"Pocalypse. Pucker lips."

"*Crisis*. Contagion. Calamity. The real shit *went* down. What we *need* is to rebuild."

"Shore up the Stock Exchange. Vote Republican. Have kids."

"Have kids?" Lisa sighs. She *has* her two. They worry her. "I nominate Edie."

From outside they hear a wail. Andrew talks casually over it. It's probably just Jody.

"You pie-eyed Pollyanna." He ruffles her hair, kisses her forehead. "No one remembers *how* to rebuild. Everyone's faking it, Lisa. Ashes, all fall down again."

"What was that noise? You squint-eyed Jeremiah. Who around here makes a noise like that?"

"You, a few minutes ago."

"Ha ha. Seriously, who is that?"

The windows are too well boarded up for them to see. They finish dressing, and he follows her down and outside. There's no one.

"Okay, so we're in a holding pattern," says Lisa, urging him further into the open, beyond the first barn, still looking. A pretty day still. "But people are going to start to remember."

"Which people, us? We are now and will remain doped up and damaged."

"Edie's kids, then. Is that Mrs. Brower? No contagion runs and runs. It gets worse, then it eases off. Hey, Mrs. Brower! What *my* eyes see is it's been tapering for months."

They reach Jenna. She's pushing a wheelbarrow loaded with medical supplies. "Let me, Mrs. B.," Andrew says, taking it from her. "Where am I going with this?"

Mrs. Brower explains: Edie, Jemmy, the zombie girl...

"Woah, way to go, Jemmy!" Andrew interrupts to say.

"Ugh, *Jemmy!*" Lisa interrupts to say.

"No, he's very respectful of her," Mrs. Brower assures them and continues the explanation: Nick, the stepwell...

"Nick!" says Lisa. "What do you mean? Is he all right?"

"That's all I heard, that he's in the well," says the older woman.

Lisa rummages, muttering, through the supplies, what's there, what else she might need.

"But I'm sure he's okay, they were more squabbling than scurrying. I fetched the wheelbarrow, though, in case. We need a house wheelchair."

"Well, the wheelbarrow will do fine if he's dead," says Andrew.

Lisa loathes the man. Furious, meaning every erg of it, she wallops the back of his head with the flat of her hand, Stooges-style. Andrew misreads the geniality quotient. He chortles and makes the *Nyuk nyuk nyuk* noise. They're getting on so well! But here they are at the wellhouse.

"Hello?" calls Lisa.

III.

What Jody loves most about the maddies these days, is that they make the world coherent. What she sees under their influence becomes, briefly, blessedly, all that there is to see.

Or almost all. Oddly, they also anchor her to the present, which is usually such a struggle to keep hold of, so small against the welter of her memories and fake memories.

Sacked out on the bed she shares with Brian, his last maddie rifled from a drawer and dissolving into her, she sees the room about her as she failed to see it when she woke this morning: as an appalling mess. Brian is a virtual absence; it's his "room," he no doubt spends the night here, he's scattered some of his stuff around its spaces, but the imprint of his body, of his attention, is so light she can barely feel it. This is her space, her wallow. It is rich in the smells of her neglect. She wonders uneasily to what degree they truly consort; of course, she knows the answer. But she wants such a connection. And if Brian didn't want it also, would he still be around, as difficult as she is, as hard to love as she is?

All this in the interval as her eyes begin to flutter; as wider and wider awake, she boards the dream plane. The room softens its hold. Its bearing walls recede but glint—if she wished, she wonders, might she refocus her attention, escape back?—oddly reluctant to let the moment of coherence go. But she has arrived; the memory place is pushing through, so palpably that it hurts. She's out of the habit of such sharpness, except when there's a maddie in her. Her awareness has to adjust to it, to this dominance of the single here, the only now.

Her father is on the cusp of death. She has flown back, this morning, from med school to watch its waves break over him. At present, though, he's in his sun porch wheelchair, surveying the great elm tree at the far back edge of their lot. They've talked sometimes about the face-shapes in its limbs and leaves, the Rorschach of their staved-in bulges and recesses, these mouths and eyes the wind and the sky make pouring through. *The eyes are glazing over*, he remarked once, which made her shudder... Well, he does look baddish today, but not *so* bad, really. Sure, as if he may croak any moment, but not *this* moment; for this moment more, he is doggedly alive; he is his stubborn self. She grasps both his hands in both of hers and feels his presence strengthen back to her.

"Brian was just here," he tells her, hoarsely, raggedly. "With Andrew and Ben."

"With who?" she asks, not recognizing the names. "Are

those his violinist buddies?" Brian had said something about having his violinist friends come play for her father. "Dad, are you all right? Have you been crying?"

"With *who*?" shrieks her older self, the echo amplifying and distorting.

As suddenly she remembers: she shares her room with *Millar*. Brian is dead; she killed him; how she killed him is what she has prayed, eight years and more, to know. But this? *Her* Brian? With *who*, with—how could Brian even *know* Andrew or Ben—is that even possible?

"Jesus, Jody," she thinks, hard, at the girl in her vision, "for God's sake, ask him!"

And the past being the way it is these days—mutable—she will ask, and she does.

IV.

Nor has Matt Simmons come to the wellhouse. He, too, is in the elsewhere of a maddie—not that he uses the drug as casually as Jody, or as needily. But he's one of the unlucky souls who get the migraines when it's too long out of their system. So he remains lightly dependent. And anyway, he does treasure his highs and is as adept as anyone at tailoring them to suit him. What he prefers is to marry his trance state with a literal dream; to ride the drug into his REM sleep.

He has a favorite trick. There's no whiff of memory to it. Oh, he's remembered wonderful things, under the influence of the maddies, true memories and almost true memories and a few sweet, plausible, what-if-wow-if-only lies; and he's grateful for everything he has received, the facts, the falsehoods, the fantasies; even the regrets, the unmet aspirations. To have had some of his vast, lost self restored to him, and so vitally, is more than he deserves. (He has watched enough of himself in action to make that judgment.) But there came a point, a while back, where he demurred. Frankly, to *keep* remembering was depressing him. No matter how much more of his past there was, how suddenly warm its breath, it had been lived. It was done with; the truth of it was dust; it was time, as it is always time, to find what needs doing here, right now, and be busy doing it.

But there is one dream that settles him. It's the flying dream. Everybody has dreamed it, yes? But not as Matt has dreamed it, and has learned, at will, maddie willing, to summon it. Feeling himself, the spread of his hands turned to pinions, step out onto the air; the currents roll with and under him. To drift as naked and sinuous as the angels, donning a haze of sunlight for a robe! What he dreams again today (but is it a dream? as always, it's too real to be a dream—look, below, near the wellhouse, the housemates are assembling) is of becoming an utter lightness, a feathery slight strength. He remains himself, a man, yet nimble as a bird, banking, rising. He takes to the faintly troubled air above the farm. He senses the far tug of the hurricane. In spirit guise, he lunges to meet its fringes. It is moving upon them fast, hours ahead of schedule, and it is huge. Far away yet, but gathering. His voice is a bird's rough caw; he sounds it, wheeling on the delicious winds, sea-rich and rumpled. High over Heartwood Farm he circles, gliding, sinking, soaring; sipping at the cocktail of its smells and tangs; both mounting it, like a lover, and of it, like a self.

Sshh... He sheds the words and thoughts of it.

He rides. He is.

V.

Exit Jody, girdled by bees.

She has summoned them (or perhaps, seeing her in the yard, they have come to her of their own volition) to shepherd her to Andrew—and somehow, they seem to know the way.

While it is customary to treat the luminous daze of the drug as a slumber, to lie in one spot for the duration, traveling only mentally, it isn't requisite. Once its brand of disorientation becomes as familiar to you as it has to Jody, it is possible to move through the shared world, mistily seeing that world, even as one goes deep into the other. Jody, in fact, sleepwalks, or tripwalks, fairly often these days. It's an annoyance for her housemates, who feel they must watch over her, or at least watch out for her—at the best of times, she is inattentive, and maddies are her *very* best of times; but there you have it. She has been known to narrate the experience as it happens, like a sports event; she may invite your commentary. And should there sound a call to action, she may try to act upon it.

Today, for instance, what her father has been telling her is monstrous. They have browbeaten a sick, sick man! And while she is furious with Brian, and annoyed by Ben, anyone can see that the true villain of the piece is Andrew—who lives with her here—who is somewhere near at hand.

So she will not wait. Anyway, her old man is sleeping, all she's doing is sitting with him, and she can do that anywhere. So she will find her half-brother, right now, and she will have it out with him. Girdled, if need be, by bees.

VI.

Which brings us, at last, to Brian. Or to Millar: perhaps, after all, he is Millar.

He alone remains within the house, shuttling between the records room and the logging room, fetching files. He has a pet project, which requires some note-taking and much reading.

Because: all these meticulously shelved tales! He's been collecting them for longer than his friends recall—he has some of Danny's testimony, for example, he has Kitty's, he has

TGF's. The cumulative weight of them is immensely satisfying—the richness with which he is archiving their lives. He knows them, these people—patches of their preserved history, at least—better than they know themselves. Which is only a fraction of a fraction of everything they are and have been, he accepts that—but how much of it they have themselves forgotten! Edie's marriage, say, an abrupt catastrophe: in the wake of a worse catastrophe, she abandoned all memory of it, giving herself over to her sister Tiff's memories—of Kitty; of Millar himself... Who Jenna Brower once was, before Lisa, Nick, and Jody renamed her; and for whom... How Jody, in her visions, has eventually seen, or intuited (or falsely conjectured?), the back story of her father's will. That he was bullied before he died, by Andrew, Ben, and Brian, into a disposition of his property that they worked out between them—what Andrew and Ben thought they were owed, and what Brian, nobly or overzealously, agreed they were owed. Her mother, Jody then realizes, must have known of it also. How, finding these revelations hard, Jody has, several times, refused them.

It's incumbent on someone, surely, to stand sentinel, to know such truths; and he's pored over the logs so often that their memory is in some places permanent.

Now he's compiling a short shared history, which he calls *The Heartwood Chronicles*, of the house's denizens. He sorts through the bits and pieces they've borne witness to; selects a few choice segments each, not too many, to package and present. He's worked on this, one person at a time, for quite a while now, though he recognizes that he may not ever finish: he forgets what he has done and has intended; spends time, some days, rereading, startled by how much is unfamiliar; there is always so much to re-examine, to rework and update. Still, the base testimonies are in place for everyone but himself. He's put off editing his own; it doesn't seem scholarly to include them.

Or perhaps they're the ones he can't face, and he's just making excuses.

Today as he speed-reads through, it strikes him that the section on the Rampages-slash-Hellfest is out of place and distorts the balance of the rest. Not that the colonists' eyewitness accounts and confused half-memories—unnaturally confused, for many of them—of the months when the rages of the virus were at their most brutal, and the world threatened to go under, are without value. But there is much documentation of this period out there already, and their own fuzzy, contradictory accounts need a discrete kind of study. He wonders if this is the first time he has had this thought. He checks his notes. No, indeed; he has written about this problem; has merely been reluctant to trust his impulse and follow through on it.

He excises the section, to place its pages within a new folder: *Chronicles of the Rampage Months*. As its own volume, he will be able to do the peculiarities of the subject justice. Maybe the Heartwood text would be better served by the in memoriae: Tiff, Danny, Kitty, and so on. Though some of that material would go better with the new volume...

The way Matt Simmons works on the storm cellars, obsessively and beyond all logical impulse, Millar returns to what he has achieved so far. He does so now, as the rest of them, all except Matt and Jody, help carry Nick's moaning body from the wellhouse dark into the wide white daylight, to lay him out to be patched and fretted over, in the high, dog-scampering grass.

CHAPTER FOURTEEN: THEY ARE REMEMBERED

"In memoriam all
Who were once whole selves,
Who were loved, and who made their marks, and are forgotten,
We, who are ghosts now, set this marker:
Stones. Tumble and tangle of stones. Of earth, of cluttering vines.

In memoriam all
My own once selves,
Who lived, and who made our marks, until they fell forgotten,
I, as I follow them, set this marker:
Breath. Tumble and tangle of breath. Of sky, of sputtering lines."

John Boggenpoel, "Cairn Song"

"The dying are like tops, like gyroscopes—
they spin so rapidly they seem to be still.
Then they fly apart...

The soul's like all matter:
why would it stay intact, stay faithful to its one form,
when it could be free?"

Louise Glück, "Lullaby"

IN MEMORIAM

Jacob Corrigan

Dr. Jacob "Jakes" Corrigan, who died this week at the age of thirty-five, was, in the course of his short life, a nine pound baby, a bedwetter, a mama's boy, a toddler like any other, a target of bullies, a bully, a reciter of prehistoric animal statistics, a fount of knock knock jokes, a video gamer, a choirboy, a math whiz, a briefly pudgy adolescent, a classics wiz, a terrific lacrosse player, a dove hunter, a prep school valedictorian, a competitive water-skier, a BMOC, a serial polygamist, a sham party animal and cradler of barely sipped microbrewery stout, a reader of other people's mail, a pretty decent poker player, an asshole, a totally and devastatingly smitten new man, an absolute sweetheart, an asshole again, a driven and cocky med student, a covert napper, a hotshot young doctor, a slightly stodgy dandy, a not quite so hotshot no longer quite so young doctor, a sporter of stubble, an espouser of the whole stubble aesthetic, a not always scrupulous but gung-ho medical researcher, a sampler of experimental drugs, a sufferer of uncharted side effects, a conspiracy theorist, a whistleblower, a campaigner for truth and justice, a heretic, a zealot, something of a mystic, and a very late developer of scruples. Among, of course, many other things.

It is possible that he died a martyr. He himself may have thought so, at any rate; but paranoia and hallucination are now confirmed side effects of the drug he was helping to test, and helping himself to, so it's quite likely he was delusional. In his delusional state, he developed certain suspicions about the origins of the disease that he was treating, and of its peculiar relationship to the drug in question. He found that he had contracted this disease, against which this drug was in some ways extraordinarily effective and in other ways extraordinarily unreliable; and saw that the side effects, not particularly common but more common than was acceptable, were often alarming; and determined that he suffered from them. His response was to take the formula public, which (since he wasn't certain what the formula in fact was) he did in several variant forms, always with warnings about its dangers and its limitations and the people he suspected of being responsible for its propagation. He understood perfectly well that his postings and his transmissions would more often than not be interfered with and garbled, but what else could he do? He died in a fall from a great height. It is not known whether he jumped, or was pushed, or stumbled, or believed himself able to hop from cloud to cloud.

But here he is in mid-air, his trigger finger on a crucifix he has recently, for the first time since he was a not particularly cherubic choirboy, taken to wearing again. His lips are moving and his eyes are closed; he is softly, inaudibly, reciting, under the high howl of the wind's breath. He has not always fought the good fight. He knows this. He has begun, belatedly, to try, but he doubts it is enough. He has lost little of his memory; he knows very well who he has been. He asks God to forgive him. He does not wish to feel himself hit the ground, so he seeks, and finds among the temporal shadows, a present time where he might pass out first. Now that's curious—

Jenna Roy Brower

A few years after Nick Trifflett leaves for college, we lose contact, and this tale he has tagged me to passes me by. Perhaps I perish: many do. Perhaps I am sixty-something years old now with a healthy memory: some do get lucky. Either way, all I am to you, I guess, is Sarah Oldchurch's black-skinned shadow; all I have contributed is a mischievously borrowed name.

Nick's cousin Lisa found me a starchy, prissy old woman, and yes, I came to seem one, sometimes. I wasn't always so. I divorced three husbands, and before I was rid of the first, there was a married pastor to whom I bore a child that the second one stole. But my progeny and the getting of them can stay their own stories—let *my* story be the pale we won't go beyond. Did they tell you I'm a folklorist? African American tales. Or African diaspora. Haitian oral tradition recently. Honey, some of them will curl your toes. I go on mission trips, I carve out a little time, I collect. I tell my stories, they tell me theirs; I sing for them, they make their music. Did I say I'm a singer? I had a career, ask Nick. Jazz and blues. Nick knows all about it. Fine drummer he may well be, but Nick has never recorded, not in a studio, not yet, leastways. I did, many times.

On one spoken word record—Lisa's father played on it—I laid down five folk tales that my mother, and her mother, and my mother's mother's mother herself in one case, granted me the keeping of. Plus a sixth one I filched from our family history. I fought with my sister Lilian about that, and about other things: a man, my stubbornness and hers. There was once a girl so lovely (I used to think of this as *my* tale) that at the sight of her, hardly a thing in the world but lost all sense of what it was doing. Cats wagged their tails like giddy dogs. Dogs stood on their hind legs and whistled Dixie. Cocks crowed at the scent of her, and flowers opened at midnight, thinking she was the sun. And oh, the menfolk. They were the worst, honey. A girl that fine—fifteen years old, and fresh as new-perked coffee—why, she was just begging to be dragged off into the bushes and taught what was what, was what, was *what*, however many times it took. Fortunately for her, however, she was so lovely they just stood there frozen, all the man-thoughts in their little heads clogging the machinery of them, eyes wide and the wheels spinning.

Well, such a state of affairs couldn't be allowed to endure. There is a what that is *what*, and that little girl had best learn it like everyone else. So when they recovered a tad bit from the luminosity of her presence, when all that was left was the trailing whiff of her, her glow in the gleam of their eye, these menfolk set to muttering and to strategizing. If but one of them could get to her—humanize the goddess out of her—the spell would break, and she'd be just another dumb bitch to trample under their heel. Unfortunately, unfortunately for *them* anyway, she left the mob of them transfixed, unable to lift a finger against her, nor any other body part neither.

But unfortunately, unfortunately for *her* anyway, these men had two big items in their favor. One was time. Wasn't no one could stay quite that breathtaking forever. She would come into her mortal age, like everyone else. And besides that, you know how time operates: how soon we get used to the way things are. They had seen her, now. Newness is fleeting. All they needed was to wait out the shock and dazzle of her, and then—oh boy, *then*—they would take her *down*.

And the second thing they had going for them was good old human nature. Because most of us aren't like those menfolk, but one idea in their evil little heads. Most of us are whole human beings, both sexes and all ages of us. That lovely girl had family, and she had friends. And of course her family and her friends didn't see her the way the gawkers saw her! The girl they knew was an everyday sweet kid with foibles and flaws and a name. So this one evil man, he noticed that, though he found it hard to credit. Like, wait a second, could a creature that beautiful really be just a *mortal*? And then he realized: why, this could be his way to *get* to her.

Who knows, maybe he even had good intentions. They could be human beings together! She would convert him to humanness!

So he came at her widdershins, so to speak. Palled around with her playmates, partied with her people. Contrived himself an invite into her house. Was soon so caught up in the role that he forgot himself and fell for her sister. Whom he sweet-talked into bed and treated like crap, all the while stealing sidelong glances at the untouchable sister as if it was no big deal—until the day might come that it *wouldn't* be. You know, habituating himself.

And came the day it wasn't. Oh, she was still a stunner. But listen now, would she get out of his damn way while he gave her dumb bitch sister a piece of his mind? Because putting herself in his *way* like this, she was no goddess but only an interfering little trollop. In the middle of which thought, he swiveled and switched his quarry, leering as she shrank into a scared ordinariness. And he hauled her off under the trees.

Might have gotten away with it, too, if the world hadn't changed since your grandma's grandma's grandma first told this tale. It took us a few millennia, but we modern women-folk, we don't stand for that bat guano. No more, O Lord. For out behind them comes the dumb bitch sister with her cocked and loaded shotgun, all poised to teach that evil cuss a lesson about the difference between power and blind arrogance, which one he thinks he has and which one he has. Except lookee here, the interfering little trollop sister has beaten her to it—for up swings a can of mace and a square-toed cupid shoe, and she is showing that man *pain*.

Folk tales got to change with the times, my mama told me. We learn from our elders, and we learn from our experiences, and we tell it to the world anew until we get the ending right.

So this one's my mama's styling of it. Her moral still happens to be my moral:

Arm yourself, girl.

That was one of the folk tales on my folk tale record, or the short version of it. But I was younger then, and maybe it was truer in the wish than the living. Maybe it's not always as easy to be as strong as you tell yourself to be. I put up with plenty in my time, I regret to confess.

Still, what I wanted to say was I no longer go by Brower. I never did for very long: seven disagreeable years. Roy was the name I was born with, recorded under, and reclaimed once I got back my dignity and my parrot.

Jenna Roy. *Ms.* Roy, if you're young enough to be my grandchild.

So anyone who wants the other is welcome to it.

Fiddle with it, soul sister. Fix it, refit it, and refine it. Go get your ending *right*.

Ben Ungar Clayton Barker Ungar: a disclaimer

At two, Ben Ungar, Jr., loses his biological father to the state penitentiary. The prosecution witnesses hold without wavering to their testimony; the accused, who in his flap to concoct an alibi has lied and lied, the worst of his lies being those he told Ben's mother, fails to mount a credible defense. (Ben may ask, but he is still too little to be told the details.) But for these reasons, and some equally hard, more private others (his aunt Ilana falls silent again), Ben's mother divorces the scumbag, excising his family name from the family papers.

At nine, Ben Clayton, a testily unruffled child, who wants

only to be let alone, thank you, to be allowed his own solitary time, please, so he may construct Lego aliens, and their space-ships, or else take household devices apart and reassemble them, acquires a new adult male in his life. This is not unprecedented, and at first, Ben pays scant attention. But this new man, who is White, reels Ben in. In part because he is wealthy, in part because he sticks around, darn near half the days of most weeks, for over a decade. And he treats Ben Clayton almost like a son.

When Ben is twenty-three, this quasi-father, who is dying, names Ben the fourth of his four full and equal heirs; among the other three is a may-I-call-you brother, Andrew Barker, who moves in with them for a few months. Ben, too, takes the name Barker, although it's soon clear that the foremost and next most equal heirs, the White wife and her daughter, have no wish to share it or anything else with him. Ben's mom, Flora Clayton, has been left her house and a modest annuity, with which she is absurdly content: this disgusts Ben a little. But for two years, in attempted gratitude for his own prefer-ment—perhaps even a bit out of love—Ben Barker struggles to adopt the persona and direct the business affairs that have been bequeathed to him.

But since this is not who he truly is or wishes to be, when the Innocence Project takes on the case of Ben Ungar, Sr., calling into question his involvement in the crime of which he was convicted, Ben Jr. seizes the opportunity to switch alle-giances again—to reclaim the identity that was stolen from him. He quarrels with his mother, he reconciles with his birth father. Whom he spends his Barker money to exonerate and free; until it seems likely that he will succeed.

Whatever world affairs may intervene (or not) to thwart him, whatever vision Andrew Barker may believe he has experienced, of his ex-stepbrother's capitulation to some vague and terrible plague, is not, Ben Ungar, Jr., wishes to attest, the business of anyone in these pages. He has no quarrel with Andrew Barker. Nor with Jenna and Bradford Brower, to whom he once delivered newspapers. Certainly not with Lisa Huttongold or Nick Trifflett, amicable minor characters in his life story during much of the course of it. Not even, really, with Jody Barker, who might, if she wished, have consented to be his sister; and who, having decided otherwise, may most amicably go fuck herself. He merely asks to be the central figure of his own tale, and not this cipher of a bit player he seems to be in theirs.

He consents to no continued reductionism: no further bending of his shape to suit their saga's purposes; no cozy memorial pieties. Let, he says, the reader beware: any resemblance between him and the shadow-thin depiction of him that you'll find here is coincidental.

Jill Winifred Simmons

Jilly Simmons. JWS. Jill W. Simmons.

I'm like a teenager—doodling my initials during math class and practicing my signatures. I remember that age. Because of a pill I took? I'm not so clear any more, but I do believe so. That is also maybe why I write my name over and over. The need, I mean, to re-imagine who I am. In high school, who might little Jilly Speight turn out to be one day; latterly, who it is I've spent my life as. As Jilly Simmons. That I have been Mrs. Jill Winifred Simmons.

In this life, it turns out, that I have made. A good enough life.

My husband's brother's boy, Matthew Simmons, who tends to me, he frets over me more than I do myself, I believe. I do forget things. I've forgotten *many* things. But I am still in here. The *here* part is a problem, admittedly: the body is going bye-bye even faster than the mind.

What helps is to be conscious of it. It's my daily task if you like. To be aware of myself, may I say it as? Within the constrictions? To move about while I can. Testing my stiffness of joints; the knot in the muscles. Before I'm pent like Ariel in his pine, if you know your Shakespeare. Only his eyes moving, and the blood, slow as sap; the heart bumping at the chest. Only the mind minding. A bit wild, in fact, inside the trap of him.

So, now that my old pal Jody Barker's here to shadow me, I go walkies in the garden. Just to drag these roots and this hard bole of me from tree to tree. Place a hand on the rough of some bark. Stand, feel my breath, look. Who knows, do *you* know: any gasp could be my last. Oh, and birdsong! I've finally learned the sparrows from the mockingbirds, the cardinals from the blue jays, if you can believe that. You hear that? *Vulture*... Or fine, if I fall over, ouch, splat, well so what, so be it—I'll lie and watch the wind fool around with the limb tops. Reckoning whatever it finds to reckon on its abacus of leaves and sunlight. All the innumerables, all the inexhaustibles.

We all pass this way, Jody. I ask only to set a meager few of my terms.

Today I had been intending to hike into the woods there, where the path stops. Where the nettles poke up from the scrub. But it's looking like a long way, if you must know.

Possibly my body doesn't wish to move that much more as yet.

So I close my eyes awhile to fix them on the map of it.

Yes. I believe this may be the way to travel it.

Into the trash trees with me then, step by mental step. On into the imaginary firs: pushing through the minor dark. To come blinking to the hemlock by the creek. (Whose shadows wave, wave me on from the other side...)

And I shall stand over its small babble in proprietary

fashion; and I will peer across the ravine toward those farther woods. To babble a few things back. Running my words for them softly on the tongue until they're clean.

Only to say from my small throat into this lovely fall of evening what there is left to say. Repeating what there's always been to say, until the breath and the voice are gone.

CHAPTER FIFTEEN: THEY REMEMBER

"Wherefore they banded together, and, dissociating themselves from all others, formed communities... and lived a separate and secluded life, which they regulated with the utmost care."

Giovanni Boccaccio, *The Decameron*

"We live by each other and for each other. Alone we can do so little. Together we can do so much."

Helen Keller, from a stage performance featuring her with Anne Sullivan

Selections from "The Heartwood Chronicles"
continued

7. *Narrowly or broadly, characterize your Heartwood Farm
   life.*

Elise Barker

Hey, Brian, want to hear something? I cried today! I
asked, and no one, not even my dad, can ever recall me
crying. I know no one remembers *much*, but still. Doesn't
it sound unlikely?

The strange thing is, here's what made me cry. I only
brimmed, I guess, I didn't sob or anything, but when I
wiped my hand across my face, it came away
legitimately wet. Which is fairly awesome, actually, and
made me go, *Wow, I'm crying!* Which made me laugh and
cry at like the same time.

Anyway, for homeschool, I was discussing with Lisa
about how I want to be more animalistic and less
dependent on technologies, right? I've told you that. And
to live in the present tense, remembering mostly
through sense memory, like the animals? And she said
that in point of fact, it's been demonstrated that animals
almost certainly do have episodic memory.

So I asked what that was, and she explained that they
remember episodes and events just as humans do, and I
started crying. I didn't know why! Neither did Lisa, she
thought it might be because I was so happy for the poor
little animals, but as soon as she asked that, I realized
that no, I was ticked off. I've been working so hard to
learn my territory, you know?—this farm?—by
thoroughly habituating myself to it, the way I thought
the animals did?—and it turns out that they have
episodic memory! Not fair!

And when I told Lisa, "Oh, I thought it was they had
highly developed senses and paid sharper attention," she
said, "Yes, that too, but you can't simply *tell* yourself to.

You can't just say, I'll have as many receptors for smell in my nose, for example, as a dog does. A dog has two hundred million, and you have five million." Which is a really interesting fact, and in case I haven't said this, I do like my homeschool time.

So, okay, I realize, I can't smell like a dog...

Oh ha ha, very funny.

So I can't smell as *expertly* as a dog, but five million receptors is not nothing! I do have a more evolved brain, right, meaning I can figure out how to make the most of what I have? Because I've decided that even if animals have episodic memory, I need to get along without it, so I will. I already tour the farm daily, for example, so that I can maintain my knowledge of it. And I have this roster of secret places I have to find, a rotation of them. I allow myself to not visit them until I forget them, so that when I rediscover them I can see how long it took—I leave visit pads, so I'll know when I was last there.

Today, for example, I found a shed on the river island. Yeah, the one almost to the far shore, but it *is* ours; there's a *Private Property No Trespassing* sign. So yeah, I had no clue about the shed, but there's a note in the window, from me, claiming ownership of it, and a padlock on the door which I understand immediately I have to figure out how to open—to find my visit pad and log the date of my return. It took me less than a *minute* to find the combination. And the visit book tells me I was last there nineteen days ago, so I barely had time to forget it.

Pretty good, huh? What do you mean?

I *like* to talk. I'm not sullen! I just don't always have much to say about the questions you ask. But yeah, sure, I'm in a good mood.

Possibly because I actually cried today, and I think that's totally awesome. So, yeah. Yay, Elise.

Edie Driscoll

Good day. We have power back. Which is a joy for us all, but is life or death wish for Jenna and me. Away with the brooms and the washtubs! Twelve loads of laundry, and let's vacuum the rugs! Dancing a *jig*, we love our work so!

Jenna's writing a chain gang song for Sunday, by the way. She's going to make you sing a free-the-slaves hymn.

If one of you strong male handyman types doesn't figure out the wind turbines before the next big outage, I swear, we're running away from home.

Write that down.

Matt Simmons

This is my evening log-in. I've pretty much followed my schedule today: some storm cellar work, but mostly *pisciculture*, as Edie's calling it. I told her I needed to spend time on the two ponds in the next week or so, and that's how she wrote it: *pisciculture.*

I'm not sure I'm doing the fish pond part right, to be honest, but the bluegills are in, and now it mostly wants fencing off to keep the livestock away. The largemouth bass will go in in the spring, and we'll see how it all works out. This was a working fish farm of some kind at one time, though, I believe, so we have a shot.

But I also visited two islands. That second pond's really more of a channel off the creek. About as far away from the farmhouse as you can get, but worth exploiting. I mean, for more than the deer Andrew and Reds have been culling when they drink. I call it Goose Pond because sometimes there's geese. And we've left them alone so far, so maybe they'll keep dropping by. Anyway, I thought I'd take a look.

I don't know, Andrew thinks *not* migratory, but pond-hoppers, from the tributary, or even the James. Does it matter? I mean, if enough of them pass through, don't they become food supply? Don't we want that? How the shit are we supposed to know all this stuff, Brian?

Anyway, I walk the perimeter. But also, I go see the island. We have a rowboat, did you hear? Jemmy helped me haul it out. Yeah, it's in good shape; we left it moored. So Jemmy goes back to what he's doing, and I row out there. No surprises, it's just a patch of ground, a good spot for a picnic. Only now that I'm out on the water, I think why not row downstream a ways, take a look at that bigger island, you know, where the river demarcates the property line?

So I do that.

This one's more impressive. Thronged with trees, most of them big. So guess what I find, totally hidden by them? A *hut*. Well-made, but this low roof. Kid-sized. There's a padlock on the door, snapped shut. So I take the circuit, and I spy a small window at the back, awkward to get to, but I figure I can manage a peek through. But it turns out you can't see a darn thing.

You know why? Someone has taped a sign on the inside that takes up the whole space: STAY OUT. PROPERTY OF ELISE BARKER, BECAUSE SHE FOUND IT FIRST.

Now ain't that something? That girl.

Jenna Brower

Okay, logging in, what is it, December 12th? I'll start with a recipe if you don't mind. I got compliments on this one. I don't get a whole lot of compliments in this house, I liked the feeling. Could be Lisa was just in a good mood today—it was Andrew's magic manly fingers, or it was the animals who deserve the credit, and next time I try the dish, she'll hate it. Or it could be it was sarcasm. I'll allow the possibility. But I've written down the recipe, just in case. It's all things we can get pretty regular—see?

Put it in the log and I'll have it where I can find it in two places, in case the recipe stack gets tossed again like someone did that last time.

Make sure to include about the special ingredients for Lisa's portion. Though maybe I should blend in the arsenic with a bit more rosemary—actually, let's double the quantity of each. Don't say anything to her, mind. It's by way of an experiment—to see if she notices the flavor enhancement before she croaks.

Jemmy Jaronsky

No available women. Not available to Big Nick or me, at least.

Big problemo, in my book, bro.

Lisa Huttongold

Today we were at the barter market. Once again, I discovered how hard it has become to interact with those outside our small group. I'm not talking about the haggling, which I have never enjoyed but can manage. We have good product. If what we want is available, we can get it; if it isn't, we have, between us, a better sense of what will be of use to us and what won't be, and its market value, than most of the people we're dealing with. We do all right.

But I fear that this world has become a seethe of simpletons and scoundrels.

Of those who have survived to still frequent it, at least around here, most are like us: partially memoried. I find it astonishing how many proficient amateur pharmacists there must be, capable of compounding an effective memory drug—until I remember that, of course, there were professional pharmacists also, and one fully stocked lab might supply hundreds of customers. We had trouble nailing down an effective formula, but others may not have. The internet propagates many lies, but the truth is also out there. And with some persistence, it's traceable.

But merely having a modicum of your memory restored can't suffice. People need resources. We have more than most, which makes us vulnerable. As reflexively as I squabble with Andrew, he's right about this. You are also right, Millar, when you say almost no one is organized enough to take advantage of our vulnerability. People might like to come after us, but they don't know how. If they hatch plans, they forget them. They have insufficient means to implement them. They live too much like animals, from day to day, focused on the next meal and the next sleep—and they're vulnerable too, of course—more so, most of them, than us.

There are also the unmemoried out there. Few genuine zombies, except when the social services come around, with their security escorts and their sympathetic health workers, asking about our needs and our amenities, offering us their ideas on more cooperative living. They always bring tame zombies. "Guaranteed against catalepsy, wild dog, and rampage of all kind. We'll provide you with a starter kit of a hundred maddies just to place one of these poor lost people under your protection." Oh, they get takers; why not? What turns my stomach are the *virtually* unmemoried. The drones, I've heard them called. Brought just far enough back to perform some tasks. Not so far as to make them uppity, or particular. You see those types more and more.

And then there are the memoried.

Two kinds. Those who are only now crawling out of the woodwork: the hermits and the hillbillies who never got close enough to the infected to get sick. Who need something from us now, but not that much; who are cautiously beginning to test the troubled waters. I have my eyes on those. I've had Red taking discreet pictures, and I've set up a gallery. I want to see if any of them come back later, newly diseased. So far, so good, though I know it's not proof of a lot.

The second kind weren't susceptible to memory loss. They're the five percent, the immune, the members of the fifteen million who didn't heed the call to join the government but stayed behind to help their people or to plunder those who weren't their people. The more I see of them, the more grateful I am the government enticed most of that sort away from us. We can't compete, Millar. There are any number of the desperate they can conscript to do their bidding. And I'm sure some of them are honorable, and that there are other checks and balances, that the government is more and more alert to them, and interested in the greater stability. Yet if they get it in their minds to look hard at us? Our best defense may be to not seem vulnerable.

I used to think Andrew was crazy to insist I carry my gun, and that we go in always by motor vehicle. Around here they're back to horse and cart—why draw attention to ourselves and what we have? But I see some of them gauging our strength, Millar. Our smarts, our readiness to fight, to flee. On barter market day, although it rarely lasts—there's too much else to think about—I unload wondering if I should, like right now, go with Andrew and Red to the range, and shoot till my hand and my eye know what my heart refuses to: how to by God end you.

Andrew Barker

I worry about our capacity to defend ourselves.

We have the weapons. BTWC, I stockpiled, and I trained, and I got them ready to bring. As I did my whole store of necessaries, from beans to barrels to batteries. You all know I'm the principal reason that we're to some degree prepared—an insufficient degree perhaps, but we have a chance—to face whatever is to be faced. Yes, Matt Simmons too, but I had another place in mind if you weren't already set up here, and yes, Edie for the drugs, we've all played our parts. But I'm talking about the bad times that are coming, Millar, not just the bad ones that have been.

And who else apart from my daughter, and perhaps Matt Simmons, and a few days out of most months Lisa, would you trust with our weapons? And how long before I can get you all to train on an almost daily basis, to make their use second nature?

I'm not going to belabor this point. I'll keep it clear and succinct.

Hey, I'm talking to all of you. The Heartwooders.

We drill. Or we die.

Jody Barker

I like it here. The bees. The enabling of me. How I can chillax while y'all scurry about ensuring we survive. And *you.* Why do you put up with me, dude? It's a puzzle, but thank you. In case I hadn't said. Not just you, but mostly you. Totally thank you. Not sure if I'm the queen bee or the lucky lottery winner or the canary in the mine or the jester in the stocks sometimes, but thanks.

Nick Trifflett

Dear Sir or Sirs, or Madam or Madams, or Ms or Mses—
    Heartwood has challenged me emotionally, physically, and intellectually; it has forced me to be adaptable and to grow. I have learned what it is to be a part of an authentic community. A community of trust and fellowship, where we depend on each other and know that our faith will be rewarded. The people here are like family to me.
    I feel that when and if I'm given the opportunity to pursue new challenges elsewhere, I will have been rigorously prepared to meet those challenges.
    I assure you that if I am selected for your program, whatever the fuck that program may be, wherever the *hell* it may take me that isn't, please God, *here*, I will do my very best to reward you for your confidence in me.
    I look forward to hearing from you.

8. Relate an experience that illuminates the character of a housemate.

Andrew Barker

My daughter Elise.
    She taught her class today. Gave her report, if you prefer, on this week's homeschooling. But it's teaching, and I'm glad she's encouraged to think of it so. She takes a topic most of us know nothing about, or that we've forgotten everything we knew about, and she doesn't

merely lecture. She incorporates Q & A, and discussion, and drilling, and today she gave a quiz, which at the start of the class I would have failed. Fine, she's my daughter. But I'm proud of her. And if she *were* able to retain her grasp of it—yes, Lisa, I hope the fog *does* lift one day and reveal to us all we have lost, and we shall know it, hallelujah, but let's be real—if one day it's possible to have access to the whole shebang of ourselves, she'll be a superbly educated young woman.

Okay. So let's see what I can still manage.

Firstly in American Sign Language? Then Heartwood Alphabetic Cypher, then a couple in flashlight Morse Code. You'll have to imagine me doing them, btw, it's a test for you too:

Please.
Food and water.
Something's wrong.
Ssh. Predator. Prey.
Left. Right. Forward. Back.
Help. Now. Be careful.
Run.
I love you.
LOL.

Edie Driscoll

Millar, I have to say, I do not get what you see in Jody.

Lisa's pretty. I'm pretty. Simplify your *life*, dude.

You know how she likes to walk around the house while she's tripping, recently? Here's my Jody impression—I'm not sure it's humanly possible to do the eye-flutter—oh, you say *Jody*'s human? *really*?—but Jenna and I have the walk down...

You like that? A little sashay and wiggle? See, we can do that for you, if that's your thing.

Apparently, for today's stuporama she was the Princess of Stupidville. You know how she can see you and know exactly who you are and where she is, at the same time as she's away in la-la land, and she incorporates you somehow into both places?

"Mrs. Brower," she mumbles—we're in the kitchen—
"you may serve the scones and clotted cream a half hour
early this afternoon."

And then, so that we'll feel sorry for her: "I'm so
unhappy, Edie. Daddy's very sick." Intoning it now, like
a hack actor in a bad film. "If he dies..."

I can't help it. I say, "If he dies, you'll be Queen, your
Highness."

Her eyes uncloud. She looks right at me like a
normal person. Except very confused.

"What?" she says.

Lisa Huttongold

Mine is a very verbal family. Not a one of us who doesn't
have some skill with words. But Nick is the nonpareil. I
doubt there's a word he's ever encountered he hasn't put
to use. And not to be a show-off either—though he *is* a
show-off, he's like a juggler who'll work whatever you
throw at him into the act—but really, it's more for the
sheer love of it, for its play of sound and meaning. And
tone, he adores tonal shift. In a casual conversation even,
he'll toss these off-the-cuff jazz riffs into the air like a
collision of fireworks.

It's been his week to work with little Red. You know
how most of us let her set her own curriculum? Probably
we ask what it is but then we let her be—we maybe just
sit with her once or twice at mealtimes, or we get to the
weekly presentation fifteen minutes early to be sure
she's cool. Nick, I don't know if you've noticed, but he
gets into it. And because she does pay attention to who's
assigned to her—you know how she'll pick an area of
study where we might be of use to her—she's fully alert
to his interest. So when this week he suggested that she
study the elements of rhetoric—anyone else, she'd have
told us, no, I'm doing edible berries again, I've forgotten
too much of it—she actually said, "All right, sure."

Not, "What possible use could that be to me, Nick?"
but "Sure."

Apparently, he was startled. You know you won't

remember any of it, and so on. But she told him she hoped to broaden and limber up her ways of thinking. Well, then, of course, he was thrilled. He's spent an hour or more with her every day. And okay, she seems to be having some harmless fun with it, though it surely won't make any lasting impact, she'll forget it all in a month; but the difference in Nick has been palpable. He's been almost happy, which won't last! Not once he falls back into drudgery. Nothing but work he feels crap at. No, of course he's *competent* at it. Competent *enough*, anyway. We eat just fine. But Nick's like his cousin Lisa. He frets! So *I* fret!

I guess what I'm pleading for is more feed-the-soul time for him, Millar. He and Jody are the two I'm most scared of losing. Jody's the opposite problem—she's as happy as a pig in shit, much of the time. But she's going to self-indulge herself into mindlessness unless we do something. We need to have an executive committee meeting about this, Millar. You, me, Edie, possibly Andrew, if you think we can stop him perverting it to his own purposes.

I don't, as you know, believe the world is ending. I don't even think Andrew does, not in the imminent extinction of the species sense. What we're figuring out, isn't it, is how to adapt to a shifting social model. Well, in the long run, none of it will work if we're not somewhat attentive to the needs of the individual. *Nick's* needs, and *Jody's* needs, Millar. Help me.

Jemmy Jaronsky

May I ask something on the subject of Danny? Because Danny *should* be our housemate, and I've been fed BS mumbo jumbo about why he isn't. Granted, I remember next to nada about the lodge era. But I am a hundred percent positive he didn't just ditch me and embark for friggin' Washington to be ordered about by friggin' Uncle Samwise. Not unless someone convinced him I was a hundred percent dead. And Lisa's version is just as big a crock.

There's something someone's not telling me or that no one remembers, or ever knew. The Danny story is still to be told.

Elise Barker

Does anyone ever share about *your* character? Might I?

I find it very sweet how Brian encourages us to call him Brian, so his confused druggie girlfriend, who has forgotten that his actual name is Millar, doesn't unhinge herself still further trying to cope with annoying facts.

He's also the only person apart from my father to call me by the name I prefer, my actual name, Elise.

But the flip side of this sensitivity of Brian's is his mania for separating the world into piles of data, this fact here, that fact there—and since who could keep up with all that, mostly he gets trapped behind himself, straining under the accumulated weight of what's no longer there.

I must sort the past into its piles! Here, there, here—sorry, not now, dear, I can't stop! The dude looks like he hasn't slept properly in months.

Hey, Brian, I know my whole philosophy of life is the exact opposite of yours. But dude, I worry about you. Let a day or two *go*.

Jenna Brower

I'd like to say something about Edie. Edie is a kind, kind person. You know how Eggy hasn't been doing too well, these last few days? Probably just an upset tummy, he ate a mouse who disagreed with him, or something—not enough for Lisa to have any time or patience for him, she says he's just older and fatter, mostly. But he's been throwing up a lot, and he's been moping. And it's cold out, and all he's much wanted is to stay in his cat bed in my bedroom.

Ssh, so this is a secret. Edie gave me the day off today and covered for me. I haven't done a lick of work all day.

"Jenna," she said, "it's not just Eggy who's in the dumps, is it? Or who's getting to be a senior citizen. I think you need to take one of those detective novels you like so much off the shelf and head on up to your bedroom and take a reading and a cat bonding day."

So I've been lounging in an armchair with a book. And Eggy's been in my lap purring his sweet fool head off. Most all the darn day.

First day off I've had since I can remember. Not that any of us has days off around here. Or would remember, necessarily, if we did.

Matt Simmons

Reds is about the slipperiest and the spookiest young woman I've ever met.

It's cute; I'm not saying anything different. But if the home invaders come for us in the middle of the night, she's who they'll have to watch out for.

You know how last night I slept in the south storm cellar to get a feel for any problems I might have overlooked? Sometime before dawn I get restless; it's stuffier in there than I'd anticipated. I need some air. It's a fine moonlit night. I figure I'll take a stroll and clear my head.

Well, I hear this owl-hoot from the fringe of the woods, and I look up, and a face pops out from among the leaves.

"Hi, Matt!" she says.

Well, I know it's Reds, of course, but I can't help it, I swing up the lantern to see, and for a moment, it's at precisely the right angle to shine clear upon her. Brian, I swear, so maybe she's not naked as a jaybird, but she'd get leered at at the pool with what she's wearing.

So I let out this "What the hell!" and I drop the lantern. I mean, I avert my eyes just as fast as I can. "What the hell you doing half-naked up a tree in the middle of the damn *night*?" I say.

But all I hear is this evil, I mean *evil* laughter—you know, a Halloween laugh?—and a brisk rustle of leaves.

When I look up, there's a sway of branches about ten or fifteen feet above my darn *head*. And that's *all* I see.

That girl.

Jody Barker

You. Insecure and irked. You're nervous about us; it's sweet. Asking, "So what *is* your type?" Didactic and sentimental, I say. "Thank you, but without taking the piss, what's your type?" Dude, nothing. They've had zilch in common. They're cute, smart, and boys. Do I have to have a *type*? Do *you* have a type? Just cute, smart, and girls, right? *See?* The type changes, dude. Right now it's didactic and sentimental. I find I'm very fond of didactic and sentimental. Your mouth goes into that twist of a smile it gets when you're manfully struggling to remain annoyed and stern whereas, in fact, I have you wrapped around my little toe and wanting to lick whipped cream off it. No, it's cute, I like it. Get down and grovel, smart boy. Go ahead, lick away.

Nick Trifflett

I used to have such a crush on Jody. Okay, in large part because she's hot. But she's still hot, or she would be if she weren't so lost to reality. She was this super-competent, vital force of nature, and now she's your girlfriend. Sad, really.

Sorry.

I wasn't actually being sarcastic for once, until that last bit.

She remembered who I was right off the bat today. She talked to me like a friend. There are stories in her head, inhumed in a morass of falsehoods, of course, but true stories about us, me and her and our group of friends, many of which I've forgotten. She retaught me a couple.

Oh God, this place.

CHAPTER SIXTEEN: HE REMEMBERS

"No lamp was burning as I read,
A voice was mumbling, 'Everything
Falls back to coldness,

Even the musky muscadines,
The melons, the vermilion pears
Of the leafless garden.'

The somber pages bore no print
Except the trace of burning stars
In the frosty heaven."

Wallace Stevens, "The Reader"

"All memory can do is scream for touch."

Kathy Acker

IN MEMORIAM:

Millar

Year One.

Millar does know that Elise is right about him, as TGF was right. The past is past, and sometimes he needs to let it go. (And not just the shockingly stupid bits. So many of those! Good riddance, away!) But he *has* let go so much of it. Before Edie's Hale County cottage, he never kept a daily log; what he chronicled was his recent and ancient history, polishing the lens of memory. But then, late in year one of the crisis, as the virus wormed into him, he was robbed of the keys to his storeroom. He'd had a childhood; he'd been a teenager and a new adult, but what he had left unrecorded he was losing access to. And the X7, though life-saving, was patchy, willful, and treacherous! And yet, since he now had Jody, he felt well compensated. He was, if anxiously, in love; she, in her own complicated fashion, began to return his love; the world might be in freefall, but he'd exchanged his storerooms for a palace, where, often enough anyway, he got to dally with her in their emperors' new clothes. He'd never felt more alive. But then, during...

Year Two

Millar found, bit by bit, that he was losing his more recent past also, and soon, too, this recent present. It was odd, though—

282

learning how to surf the three weeks at a time which, by year's end, were all he had left—there was something exhilarating to it. To the evolving competencies of mastering what was possible; and then to how the stories might be vanishing, but the feelings affixed to them did not. He might not remember (did not, in fact, remember, any more than Jody did) the fall day when they had gone apple-picking, how they had abandoned themselves to the pleasure of it, and of each other, holding hands and watching the sun go down; he might not remember scores of similar shared pleasures. But then whoever had, whoever did always recall the details of such moments, which bind us together and are gone? We recall rather that we are bound, luxuriating in the rub of the binding, and Millar and Jody *did* keep hold of that feeling; somehow, they *stayed* bound. Even with Jody at the lodge, and him elsewhere—at Edie's, Tiff's, and Kitty's place, then at Heartwood—apart for longer than their working memory; they knew, somehow, that they were coupled. There were many days (mostly forgotten) when for whatever reason, Skype functioned, and they spoke, shyly, tenderly, frankly, and knew they missed each other; that they longed for and *loved* each other. Astonishingly, their union held; and...

Year Three

brought them, once again, to a shared bed. Forget the heartbreak of finding her so changed. Of having to change to meet her. The *ache* of her seared him. And that Valentine's Day maddie trip! After six months apart—including one wholly out of contact, fearing her irretrievable loss—he took a pill before fetching her from the lodge. The Eastdon weeks he relived were their miracle: she wasn't just *with* him; she was in love with him. "Move in with me," she said. Oh, he'd *never* forgotten; they had honeymooned. But was it *all* as the X7 told it;

was every *detail* so? Millar is vaguely, privately religious; Jody is not; she stood him against a wall and knelt to him. Taking him in her mouth, she riffed, languorously and mischievously, on the Lord's Prayer, hallowing the name of something other than the Lord. If false, so needy; true or false, sacrilegious; even if true, just *memory*. He missed Jody, physically and with his whole being, and it was natural, he supposed, that the drug took him down such pathways, but what he wanted was not the fantasy of her but the fact. He was worn thin by the fantasy. Persuading Matt to make the difficult trip back in, unplowed snow and rampaging cattle be damned, it was time to go get them, *now*, all he truly wanted, needed, was Jody, whose flicker shape-shifted and flamed in him and singed. When the real woman ran into his arms, crying *Brian*, he became Brian; he would be her fantasy if she could be his fact. The *feeling* roiling him then was as potent as any X7; it was fiercer; it was volcanic. Their third year was hard, and its joys hard-won. But as he logged each new hard day, treasuring its flawed salvage, he tendered himself to it; to this shared life's *now*; toughening.

Year Four.

The days slip less darkly into the dark now; he has made his accommodations. This is what it has become to remember; to live with purpose; to love. She still buoys, still sustains him. Neither he nor Jody recalls the day of their reunion. Millar wrote of it, yes, but carefully. (Of *course* he edits things. Who would not? Or he fails to find time to report at all: time is just so short.) Weeks ago, beyond memory's edge, Jody woke in the night and asked, "Who are you? And don't say Brian because you are fucking *not* Brian." And he answered, "No, I'm not Brian. Trust yourself, Jody; who am I?" So she thought. She said, "I don't know. I do love you, that I do know. *Because*

you're not him? Is that one reason? You're him for me, right?"
He said nothing. She said, "What's your name?" He told her,
and she laughed, in startled recognition—yes, Millar! Never
Edie's Millar! Hers. She knew him; she held him, and they
slept. Like so much else in their two lives, that night is gone;
and yet they are bound, or more bound, each to each, because
of it.

In Memoriam
But nothing will be remembered. The last forgetting, whether
fast or slow, is total. All we have, I, you, or Millar, most loved
in life, no one, one day, will ever again feel love for. It will be
gone.

The Fallen Leaves
So red, so yellow, so orange. So dappled on the trees' high
limbs. So bright, once, on the ground.

CHAPTER SEVENTEEN:
THEY REMEMBER

"Live for today, not for that blur
Of smoke coming out of your ass.
So what if you aren't what you were?
You got here by riding that gas."

Jemmy Jaronsky, "The Be Do Be Song"

"I thought I knew me yesterday,
Whoever sings this song."

Robin Williamson, The Incredible String Band, "Ducks on a Pond"

Selections from "The Heartwood Chronicles"
continued

9. *What are your identity issues? How do you now*
   characterize yourself?

Jenna Brower

Ah. Well, we are immortal souls, Brian, and we need to
have faith in that. Here on planet earth, as Edie likes to
put it, I'll take it day by day, thank you, learning to be
Jenna, the kitchen wench slash cat lady. Anything much
else is a long walk off a short pier.

Lisa Huttongold

It's an interesting question, Millar, but not, I think, a
useful one. We all know the maddies rewire us and
rewrite us, but what the devil doesn't? Anyway, this isn't
the kind of introspection we gain much by engaging in
right now. It's a luxury for later, or let's hope it will be.
   If you're hoping to identify who among us is in
psychological difficulties, I can help with that. Jody is.
Nick is, for his own reasons. The two people I love most
in the world. I'd appreciate suggestions as to how to help
them, since I'm at a loss. Or have I made suggestions?
Have I asked for your help in implementing them? I
forget these things, sometimes, Millar; I'm quite aware I
do. I would so appreciate your help. You might think a
little harder about your girlfriend's needs than you seem
to, by the way. I accept that she's a hard nut to tackle. But
isn't it your duty to try?

Matt Simmons

Who do you reckon is going *near* that one? I'm not
touching it with a ten-foot Balkan.

Yeah, Nick's line. He thought he had to explain it to me. When I didn't smile. Which I found a little insulting. Nick can *be* a little insulting.

I'm doing my best to hold it together, Brian, just like us all. Give it up, man.

Elise Barker

What, like my new age second baptism Native American name?

I am the Student Who Instructs.

I am Future Girl.

I am a Reluctant Synecdoche Of Hair.

Nick Trifflett

Well, I'm not the person I thought I'd be. Nor anyone I much care to be. Which is possibly the way of the world and the fact of your average life, as some sanctimonious asshole farted at me, this morning as I was bellyaching to my mirror. Don't worry, I beat the crap out of him for it, just as I did yesterday, and no doubt will tomorrow. Fucking wiseass asshole.

Jody Barker

I'm a kid; there's a mall with an arcade where my friends and I go to watch cartoons. *The Cartoon Zone.* We hang out, we migrate from room to room. TV room, film room, handmade room, foreign language room. This one show, under its closing credits, the characters vote on the episode, Reset Button or Continuity Show. They say, *Reset!*, and the next episode, no one has aged or has to deal with their amputated limb or murder rap or whatever from before. But sometimes they go, *Continuity!*, and it's built-in. Then later, there'll be a Continuity Reset Day, where they've decided they hate aging and amassing baggage, so they spend the show tossing out rejected attributes. My life exactly. Except I get no vote. No one does. *Reset! Continuity! Continuity Reset! Deal with it!*

Andrew Barker

You'll never manage to learn the half of who I am, Millar. *I* may, but *barely* half.

Last night, after working on this document, I had a memory dream. My dreams, to judge by the shreds they leave, are rarely vivid or persuasive, and the exceptions don't stay persuasive for an instant. In my teens, I had dreams in which I could leap, through cityscapes of fog-smudged moonlight, for hundreds of yards—and every night I bought into them, telling myself, *See, it's true! It's real!* And every morning, they winked out under me. A vivid adult dream, so compelling that I record it in my journals as having startled me awake, was of a field at sunset, with, on the horizon, two elephants, one watching the other ride a trampoline. Wow, but not exactly plausible. You don't reassess your concept of reality because of it.

But now I find myself dreaming of a trip back to Australia to interview for a job—there's a girl involved, a crazy hope to see her again. And I'll look up a friend while I'm there; oh, hey, I've done so; as I walk, I'm thinking about the dinner we've just shared. Mostly it's the walk up to and into the campus that I see, a harbor and a curve of sea at the foot of the hill below me and tall trees and thick air here at its summit; and the interview, which I dream every word of, knowing I have a shot at this job, *wanting* it, even—I hear myself talk about the places I've been from, and why the America I've come to has left me restless. But then I'm withdrawing my application for all the practical reasons, and it's all so plausible, meticulous, so charged with the sensual verities that *prove* it. When I wake, I can barely find my real self enough to disbelieve it. And yet, for the life of me, when I finally manage to, I don't get what it even has to do with me.

If I did see myself in it, though, would I rewrite my

past to incorporate it? If a drug had heightened it, would I?

So are plausibility, memorability, vividness, *any* of the subjective responses, proof of anything at all? And what factual stance, what cool, dry, clear, objective eye has ever known anything but itself? Anything but a flat and affectless dimension, where no one—*no* one—*lives.*

We're self-liars, Millar, all of us. We spin stories to order who we are. We root one in memory and recast ourselves to try the fit; we try it out on our friends and lovers; we shift and watch them shift—deceiving ourselves, perhaps, more than we fool each other. We settle on our working truths, our best simplifications, and build to the skies on them. Until under us, like an impossible leap, our arc of self collapses, or it carries us across.

Like you and Walt Whitman and every other non-zombie you've ever met, I am large, I contain multitudes. Eeny, meeny, no not that one: we make our best guesses, and we seize hold till we're ready to die for them. I've made mine. My articles of faith. And I'm ready to stake my life on them, b/c there's no other way. And that's what I have to say in re my identity.

For the slightly less short version, also read my other answers.

Jemmy Jaronsky, *singing*

I am what I am.
It is what it is.
We be who we be,
And that's show biz.

You put on your clothes.
You do what you do.
It goes how it goes:
Do be do, do be do.

Do be do, do be do
Do be do, be do be

Here's a sock, here's a shoe.
Go be you, I'll be me.

That's all I got, man. Little insta-ditty.

Edie Driscoll

I know who I am. You may take that claim any way you like.

I have a working hypothesis as to who I've been. Ditto *that* claim.

We are who we are *right now*, Millar. The rest is a construct. Some people, when they discover that what they've believed about themselves is false—where they've come from is a lie, how they got here is a fable— their world is sent into chaos. Now, yes, I can be hurt; I can be destroyed. But as a *self*, or a balancer on the beam of self, I don't believe I'm shakable.

I'm the person who *is*: here, now. That person is a constant improvisation, a response to stimuli, received from the here and the now—and, yes, from personal and public memory. Our constant, human task, as we move through the moments, is to turn them into breath and being. Or into dance, or song, or whatever the art of our being uses for a voice, if we want to be fancy about it. That's the impulse toward, not just surviving, I guess, but *mattering*, and I guess we do all need a little of that. Just not too much of it is my take, because the being *needn't* matter, and it needn't, in any fancy way, even "mean." It just has to inhabit its breath. Then let the rest fall into the place it finds.

So that when and if I discover I *am* shakable, my task will be to inhabit and move through the moment of being shaken.

I discover. I accept, except it isn't passive. We steer into our identity, as we discover what we stand for and believe: we work to *intend* a self. Maybe we manage to live by that intention; maybe we fail to. Either way, we're self-creating creatures. We have no control of the *materials* we forge ourselves from, but why should that

291

matter? The sculpture that's waiting in the stone is different for whoever works it. We *become* as we are *being.*

The End. I have spoken. I have earned a cookie.

The testimonies presented in this document have been edited for length and for clarity. In some cases, the respondents provided direct answers to the direct questions given as section headings; in others, the editor selected from remarks made in the course of a more general conversation. Andrew Barker's responses were submitted in writing, as were most of Jody Barker's and three of Nick Trifflett's. All other commentary was made orally. The editor's intention is to offer a coherent if limited portrait of the Heartwood colonists at a particular period of their collective history. Although there was some effort made to confine the interviews to a concentrated span of time, that is to say, the last two months of Heartwood's first full year, the additional material was collected over a longer period, between 3/8/2 and [5/27/4, currently]. For the original interviews, and for the extensive library of additional testimony, see the Colony's unedited files.

Millar Kearney, editor

CHAPTER EIGHTEEN:
THEY ARE REMEMBERED

"There's a somebody I'm longing to see
I hope that he turns out to be
Someone who'll watch over me"

Ira Gershwin, "Someone To Watch Over Me" (music by George Gershwin)

"The château caught fire
The forest caught fire
The men caught fire
The women caught fire
The birds caught fire
The fish caught fire
The water caught fire
The sky caught fire
The ash caught fire
The smoke caught fire
The fire caught fire
Everything caught fire
Caught fire, caught fire."

The Maid's poem, Eugène Ionesco (translation Derek Kannemeyer),
La Cantatrice chauve

IN MEMORIAM

Danny's Tale

Danny Jarowsky may or may not be dead: not one of the unreliable narrators of the Heartwood story knows. But as always, they are willing to hazard their best guesses.

Lisa, usually such an optimist, believes she saw him on the verge of death, inevitable death, about to be overwhelmed by the hordes of the crazed. He sets out from the lodge, several of the witnesses agree on that, under the illusion, or in the knowledge, that he is free of the virus and can outsmart the rampagers while drawing them off. And in this way give momentary respite to his besieged friends. But the diversionary dogs he sends baying and crashing into the zigzag of the woods return unscathed, and as he makes it to the car he left parked at the end of the drive, he finds rampagers lying needily in wait. Maybe he forces a way inside the vehicle, but how far can he possibly get? It stops, swarmed. It begins to rock. It rolls and it tumbles; a door tears open... Lisa's version of his story is elaborate and utterly conjectural, built upon half-glimpses and perhaps-memories and impossibilities. (What dogs? These that she adopted at Heartwood Farm?) It is as if she knows a price must be paid to earn this survivors' tale of theirs that she has such faith in, and she has decided that Danny, who has in any case vanished, and whom she loved dearly enough for his loss to serve, should be that price.

Andrew, the avowed skeptic and conspiracy theorist, who had little personal connection to the man, is hopeful that Danny weighed the odds and struck out to join the others of his kind, the world's new elite, the fortunately immune. Of course, Andrew doubts that all such immunity is sheer good fortune: there is no question in his mind that the epidemic was engineered, and that its engineers will have ensured their own preservation. But he wishes Danny luck as he heeds the call to join them—Danny is probably naive enough to believe in the sincerity of their appeal for help. While Andrew cannot know how well Danny will have fared in this endeavor, he has consulted his angels on the matter, and their fuzzy indication is that Danny will do his best, as always, to brighten the world around him, to be a good little goldfish among the sharks.

Both Lisa's and Andrew's theories are self-interested, bolstering some larger narrative they have constructed to map their window-fogged world-view, as are the cozier speculations of Danny's brother Jemmy. But it is Jemmy's theory, without any greater concrete evidence to support it, that Millar finds more seductive. By this accounting, Danny did indeed, as Lisa posits, make his break in the hope of saving his friends, but because he was genuinely immune and had all his wits about him, he was successful; and rather than abandoning them once he was free of the lodge, he stayed close by, to watch over his tribe, a kind of local government guardian angel. Those systems that continue to operate could not do so without folk like Danny—people who would naturally remain protective of their infected friends and strive to find positions of power from which to keep track of them. Why do you think Heartwood Farm has remained so untroubled by raiders and plunderers? Clearly, the government takes sides. It has taken theirs.

There is so much for the Dannys of this new era to do! Jemmy worries over all the hats he must be wearing. Danny was always smart. He might have lacked a little ambition, but his brand of competence never escaped notice; even before the crisis, he was rising out of the low-level administrative staff position he had taken at the hospital. For all Jemmy knows, he's back there, and running the place. Look, here he is, peering out a ninth-floor window. The James River crawls below him. How quiet and how empty the city seems! Who still lives in Eastdon, Jemmy wonders? The memoried, the mindless, the memory-drugged? Danny's desk is piled with papers. But one file, a report on rural survivors, hard-scrabbling at the edges of his administrative zone, lies open to a list of names and a few dozen satellite images. How different Heartwood looks from that vantage point! How peaceful! As indeed it is, with Danny monitoring and restraining the ragtag threats to it. Yes, Danny thinks. It may soon be time to pay his friends a visit... But first, there is work to be done. Reports to be read—most excitingly on the progress of the virus, which research suggests is weakening its hold. Needs to be assessed throughout Eastdon and the counties; resources to be allocated. He sits back at his desk and sets himself to tackling it all.

Sometimes as he steers a tractor through the far fields, Jemmy imagines Danny's eyes on him, a benevolent god. And fantasizes a brotherly reunion: its clasp of arms and well of tears, its refuge of small safety. And sometimes, out of pity for Jemmy, the other gods of wish and wonder have mused on how they might nudge and nip the twists of this tale to assist him.

"Sita Patel's Crew"

is the slogan scrawled across the base of a tee-shirt Jemmy has found in Sita's backpack. There's a photograph, full-color once

but blurry with wear now, splashed above it, of nine college-
age kids in a state of high intoxication, and in various stages
of over and underdress. Or no dress, for two of them, as far as
Jemmy can tell, if you don't count a solitary flip-flop. Sita is
one of the overdressed, in a frothy, heart-buttoned wedding
gown, combat boots, a tiara. The printed legend above the
photo says PLAGUE PARTY PICS, from which Jemmy guesses
that this is one of a series of tee-shirts made to commemorate
the same event. No doubt all one-offs: a Dave Green's Crew, a
Cyndi Barlow's Crew, one each for whoever they all are—cost
being not much of an object when you're about to die. Sometimes—it happens, sometimes—Sita has hung on to this
backpack through the disintegration of her self and her improbable pilgrimage home. But little else from inside it has
survived. A broken smartphone; a bag of unwashed underwear;
an anthology of contemporary poetry, its edges charred; a very
old apple core; an immaculately garment-bagged sari. But a
tag inside the side pocket confirms Sita's name, at least.
Jemmy re-teaches her it. He shows her the tee shirt. She places
her hand on the picture. "Your crew," says Jemmy. "My crew,"
she agrees neutrally. The odds are that most of them are dead.
Still, it's a place to start rebuilding her. He goes to unwrap the
sari to show it next; gently, she prevents him and slips it back
into the bag. She opens the poetry book instead, turning away
from him, as if she doesn't wish him to see what she might
choose to peruse. After a half-minute of silence, he sneaks a
peek anyway. It's the fly-leaf, and the page is blank.

For The Plague Dead & Dying:
by Kitty Boggenpoel, from Millar Kearney's files

1. During Wave Three week we lose the internet, the TV,
and the phones. All the prattle, until the voices go dead, is

of the Zombie Apocalypse. Some of it is still gallows humor, but mostly it's pitched too shrill. Spokespersons respond with the usual pablum. *These are sick human beings, nothing more. There will be no apocalypse.* They're cut off mid-BS. The lights flicker and recover; they flicker and they fail.

2. We five are out at Edie's cottage, down a private road in the Hale County woods. Our only neighbors, Edie's landlords, fled months ago. No way are we venturing onto the public roads, to gauge the damage or wind up as part of it. But one day, far away, the Foghorn Rock siren begins to sound. For eighty minutes; then every hour, on the hour, for ten minutes: so regulated a signal that it has to be official. *Keep away*, it must surely mean.

I say, "Are they dumping them there?"

Millar shakes his head. "We need to know more."

Matt says, "My truck radio?"

3. Our only radios are in Matt's truck and the two cars, mine and Edie's. Why hadn't we thought to try them? And there *is* a station broadcasting— canned classical music, mostly, but with intermittent reminders to tune in for the news update at noon. Which turns out, that first day, day four, to be mere blandishments: *Stay in your homes, barricade the doors and windows, we have forces on the ground.*

But the next day's news is meatier. *We're clearing the population centers, quieting the rampages, treating the not yet hostile; we are sequestering the violently ill in detainment camps. Stay home, barricade the doors,* etc. The Eastdon detainment camp is indeed on Foghorn Rock.

Those already taking refuge there have been cleared out and are receiving treatment; they may just have had their lives saved. But for the "violently ill" (i.e., the very, very ill, who are very, very violent), Foghorn Rock will be a graveyard. There's no manpower to care for them, no resources to cure them. "Cure" being a euphemism; the depleted self, we're told, can be rebuilt, but only as someone else; little of the original person survives.

Tiff, whom I love, who is one of the not yet hostile, might still be "saved" by such treatment. For how much longer, I do not know. And to what end, if she ceases to be Tiff?

Of the others of us, Edie, Millar, Matt, and I, I am the sickest, the tetchiest, and the least herself. But I'm fine, really: the maddies may yet rescue me back to being Kitty. Remembering more shreds of what I've been and who I've loved. And am losing. Have almost lost.

4. I look at my friend Edie, and I am angry, or I am, so help me, lustful. She is too like Tiff. Why can't she just *be* Tiff? In anger, in love, in lust—in loss of myself—I have had trouble keeping my hands off Edie.

5. I ask Matt Simmons to escort me to Foghorn Rock; I wish to observe the unloading of these violently ill human beings. Or let's say, *zombies*. I want to see what Tiff the incipient *zombie* has coming to her. And Matt says no. The gas in his truck is too valuable to expend in this fashion, even though it's not three miles, even though he has canisters of spare fuel locked in the back. So is the gas in my own damn car too valuable, apparently: we must marshal our resources.

"We could hike," says Matt.

"Are you nuts?" say the others.

It's only when I lose it, "Fuck you, I'm going, and I'm going tomorrow," do they listen. All right, Kitty, you may take your own fucking car. Matt Simmons will ride shotgun.

6. Day seven. The roads are quiet as the grave. It's nice. We talk. An amble of deer bars the Wykeham Creek bridge. But we sit. The sky is cloudless. There's bird chirrup.

I ask Matt about his aunt, who died, who Matt buried under the trees that fringe our yard. He worried about the ground not being consecrated, which touched me, so I told him about my Indigenous ancestry, and offered to perform a Lakota ritual. We've been buddies ever since.

(Millar, appalled: *Kitty, you made that whole thing up!*

Me: *Well, duh.*

Tiff: *Matt needed her to, Kearney, you prig.*

Edie: *Hi, Matt.*

Matt: *I needed her to, Millar, you prig. Kitty, it was lovely. Thank you.*)

"You loved her a lot, didn't you?" I say now.

"Yes."

"So you couldn't just leave her body behind."

"No. I left so much in the rush, but..."

"Yes. If it were Tiff..."

"Kitty, I hope this won't upset you, but Tiff propositioned me."

I laugh. "Tiff claims to be polyamorous and promiscuous," I tell him. "It's her fantasy."

"She said," he says, "that she intends to, uh, have everyone in the house before she goes, and did I want first shift."

I laugh. He laughs more nervously. "She tells me that too," I tell him. "I hold her awhile, which is about all she'll stay still for. If she asks again, hold her."

He looks uncomfortable but shrugs. "Okay."

The last buck ushers the last of the fawns into the woods.

7. Public access to Foghorn Rock is via a north bank footbridge, but there's a gated south bank road skirting the railway line. Do we drive to the footbridge, or park near the south gate, and trek the half-mile to the south bank vehicle bridge?

"Both entrances," Matt points out, "will be barricaded. There might be armed guards."

"Yes," I say.

"From the footbridge, at least we'd see the island."

"Also," I remember with a laugh. "I may have some Foghorn Rock luck due me. I brought Edie here in the fog."

8. And what do you know? There's a bus unloading. We back up to skulk behind the curve. I climb out with Tiff's camera. Click: six officers in asbestos suits. (To protect against infection? Against fire? Since the zombies are firebugs.) Click: two score honking but otherwise placid cattle. (Tranked up?) They moo with the siren; they paw

at each other. The officers busily, gently surround them. Click: six lumbering sheepdogs herd their flock onto the footbridge.

I adjust Tiff's telephoto lens. A face, vacant of everything. Another, so effaced of self that it and the first face seem as alike as deer. A third, fourth, fifth, a cluster of empty faces. An officer, looking round, spies me. *Stay there*, he gestures. He swivels his bulky suit up the hill. Matt is out of sight, around the bend; I could run for it. But I wait. As the officer approaches, she removes her headgear—he's a she. Gorgeous, in that typical South Asian way. Often makes me gulp.

"It's okay," she says, "you're not in trouble. Are you infected?"

I nod.

"Don't worry," she says, "I'm immune. We all are. The suit's just precautionary."

I nod. Matt drifts to join us. We chat awhile. She tells us what they're doing, which we already know, that we should keep away, that they're sequestering these people.

"Look," she says. "I presume you have the drug? Keep taking it. If you hang onto enough of your memory, you'll make it."

"I thought they were supposed to be violent," I say, pointing. They're shuffling across now like a raucous, incurious tour group.

"They're needy," she says. "Violent when they feel abandoned. Or when they're attacked. Or somehow triggered. Right now, they're calm because we're helping them."

"That's all it takes?" I ask.

"No," she admits. "It's unpredictable. When one is, let's say triggered, let's say into a tantrum, others pick up on it. It'll escalate into a rampage... So they're medicated."

"And that's what will happen to us if we don't take the drugs, or we got started on them too late," I say. "We'll get violent and murderous."

"Not necessarily," she says. "With large numbers, they set each other off."

Matt says, "But it takes just one to start it."

I say, "They think you're helping them. You're not helping them."

She says, "No. We're helping us."

She says, "After the meds wear off, they rampage. Nothing to set fires with; not much to rip to bits. Trees, each other. Well, some do make it up the rock to the electric fencing. Zap."

She smiles. "I'm Joyce."

She says quietly, like a confidence, "I'm wearing down a little."

She whispers, "When we bring in a new crop, the ones from the day before are dead."

She says, "They're bringing new fencing today to make repairs. Stronger grade. The back gate's bottle-necked. So we brought our busload round the front."

She says, "I like it, though. It's gentler, somehow, walking them in over the river."

Matt says, "If I pray for them, will you two ladies join me?"

We hold hands. Matt prays, *For the plague dead and dying, everywhere. For the people crossing this footbridge, to their deaths. May someone who loved them live to remember them with kindness. For Joyce, who has no course but to lead them to this brink; for your servants Matt and Kitty, who stand here helpless, abandoning them to it. May somebody remember us, too, with kindness. Lord, have mercy on them. Lord, have mercy on us all.*

9. On the drive home, Matt says, "I'll forget this day." An intention, not a regret.

One perk of this illness: it's easier to fudge an unpleasantry: to will it gone. But I'll write this day. To remember.

10. "Power's back," says Edie, exhausted. Tiff's in the tub, steamed red and splashing. When I kiss her on the lips, she pulls away, the way she does sometimes, not understanding, not herself. So I kiss Edie as a surrogate, and our mouths open as she yields to me. We fold into each other.

"Edie," I say, "remember me with kindness."

"Kitty," she says, "don't you go dying on me too."

I nod to acknowledge her. I push her from me. To say, I make no promises.

Tiff Driscoll's eulogy: by Millar Kearney,
appendix to *The Heartwood Chronicles*

I had the good fortune to spend some time with Tiff
Driscoll before she died. Her conversation, what there
was of it, was not usually coherent, nor was it entirely
hers—often it would have degenerated into mumble
without the promptings of Kitty Boggenpoel, her partner,
and Edie Driscoll, her sister, who appeared to be already
familiar with every story Tiff might wish to tell. And who
were eager to help her rediscover its turnings.

But Tiff has always meant a great deal to me, and I feel
the loss of her. I find that I'm grateful for what bits and
pieces have come through—not intact, but in their mirac-
ulous fragments. Despite Tiff's memory loss, and my
own; despite the fire that took her life, and Kitty's, and
Edie's selfhood; and did not take my notes and transcripts.

The Heartwood Chronicles are not the place to tran-
scribe this cache. Tiff is no longer of our number. I do
have a project in mind where her tales, also Kitty's, also
Danny Jarowsky's, might fit better. But *my* voice does
belong, even if I've been obliged, in my role as objective
editor, mostly to quiet it. Only in this appendix shall I
allow myself, briefly, to bear witness, and it will be to tell
of Tiff. I wish to honor, in her name, the many people
we've all lost, and to hold up her loss as the one that
affected me the most gravely. The *Chronicles*, after all, are
a memorial as well as a living testimony; to our erosion as
well as our survival.

So if I simply list, without narration, some of what I
learned or relived as I recorded her memories, that strikes
me as only fitting: it is in the fragmentary swirls that she
resides. I think, for example, of her growing up in a
college town in Appalachia, a judge's daughter; of her
night swimming in the mountain lakes, and how if not for
a boy whose name she never knew, she might, one time,
have drowned; of her resentment at having to wear her
sister's cast-offs, and how she took to splashing them with
drink and mutilating them, so as to be given her own. Or
I recall that she knew exactly who Nick, Danny and Jem-

my were—she'd seen that band a dozen times and danced to them—they were great, right, Kitty? And a lot about Kitty, and more than a little about me. Let me admit that I was mocked fairly mercilessly (if affectionately; I'll stress the affection) for my general ineptitude when we were a couple: in matters of social graciousness, of housekeeping, of romantic ease and sexual suavity. And that Tiff took credit for releasing me back into the world in much better shape than she found me; also that she was justified in every syllable of her claims. Some of the last words* I heard from her, I might add, were high in praise, for the gentleness and the humor with which I took correction, and the suavities she said I rose to. I was both pleased and embarrassed by the familiarity Kitty and Edie showed with those tales.

I may never grow used to how Edie will sometimes refer to that same store of stories as if she had been my partner in them.

I caught myself looking at her today at lunch and seeing Tiff. Jody was at my side, fortunately. With that astuteness she has never entirely lost, she cupped my face in the grounding gesture, and waited till I'd returned to the present, and to her; then she kissed me. What lesson Edie took from this, I'd rather not imagine. I fear for her the day the illusion fails.

Lastly, a confession of sorts. During my later sessions with Tiff, hoping to stir her into anecdote, I sometimes leafed with her through old photograph albums. Neither Kitty nor Edie liked this tactic. Sometimes it worked, but more often it caused Tiff to moan and jitter, even to erupt into a rage. It got so I only tried it when the two of them weren't around. They never forbade it, exactly, but if it wasn't working, they would urge me to stop. But I was curious; I wanted to understand what exactly might be provoking such a response. Was it the frustrations of lost memory; was it something about the way photographs distort the focus—we see what the camera points at and we forget the rest; was it the memories themselves? Most likely that first one, I surmised, but I kept, when I got the chance, delicately pushing. Tiff was no longer fully Tiff, of course. Kitty warned me against treating her like my lab rat.

304

Was this what I was doing? Could I really have been so callous?

At any rate, on the day of the fire, rushing in to rescue from the smoke and flames whatever I could, I saw that one of the piles Tiff had made and poured accelerant over—she was in the sentient wild dog stage; she'd been medicated enough to escape catalepsy—was composed at its heart of photograph albums. I was astonished at the intricacies of the bonfire material she had thrown together under and all about them, and she had made three other stacks around the cottage, but photograph albums lay splayed open, unhinged, all through the largest pile.

Which may not mean much. Perhaps these were the combustibles she found closest to hand. And anyway, the whole thing may be a grief lie; I found no time to write about what I saw that last day, nor do my notes hint at a lapse of tenderness in my care for Tiff; and there is no one to confirm or refute my memory's charges. Still, to my shame, they are what I remember.

*Her *first* words to me were, "Hi, shy boy. I'm Tiff." Her *very* last words were, "The multiverse has cat doors... I'm so cold, Kitty... Don't let me eat the goldfinches." Her last *sounds*, as I abandoned her to the flames, were moans, howls, and a high, hurt animal chitter.

I have these truths, at least, in writing. I am, right now, reading them.

CHAPTER NINETEEN: YEAR FOUR

"Presentiment—is that long Shadow—on the Lawn
Indicative that Suns go down—
The Notice to the startled Grass
That Darkness—is about to pass—"

Emily Dickinson

"What do you remember, thinking back?
... Even at dusk in the deep chair
Letting the long past take you, bear you—
Even then you never leave me, never can."

Archibald MacLeish, "Ever Since"

YEAR FOUR, HEARTWOOD:

Matt, Lisa, Andrew, Jemmy, Jody, Elise, Edie, Nick, Millar

I.

When at last Matt Simmons lurches awake, alone on his cot in the south storm cellar, everything about his situation—even before he knows who or where he is—feels eerily, utterly wrong. He has overslept, of course. This is one of the first realizations on which he can fix. And just as the flying dream is freeing, the long withdrawal from it, across a shadowland of normal sleep, where it weakly, intermittently persists, is a kind of shrinking—back into a stiff, physical discomfort. This is a simultaneous realization: that he is no longer flying, high in the unfettered sky; that, barred from heaven, he mortally hurts. Each of these insights, to its own degree, perturbs him. But they feel familiar. The wrongness is something more than them.

He swings his legs over the bed's edge and clutches his hands to his brow. Slowly, his head a spilled bowl by some process beyond his understanding refilling, he re-enters himself. Yes. He has overslept by a good length of time, and no one has come to find him. His watch and a few bulkier totem items are set out on a chair; a pocket flashlight is stashed in his right boot. It's after suppertime, in fact. Well, there's food here, if need be. He lights a table lantern and shuts off the flashlight; he struggles to dress. Every Heartwooder knows this grogginess—they all have a good amount of saved memory, but waking into it is a slow, disorienting process.

Why on earth has no one come looking for him?

Before checking outside, he makes his way into the men's locker room, relieves himself, splashes water on his face. By the time he has climbed the steps and is pushing at the hatch, he feels ready to take a hard look at what's out there. He knows in his bones he may not like what he finds, and congratulates himself on this knowledge: forewarned is forearmed. Usually, of course, there are simple, harmless explanations that one hasn't thought of.

It may be bad. It won't be bad.

Wind and darkness. The darkness is wrong. He remembers about the hurricane, realizes that it's the storm's darkness: not fully arrived yet, but well on its way—which is by quite a way too soon. They were supposed to have till before dawn to prepare. Who messed up, the weathermen, the PSA channel crew, him? Does this mean the system will pass through faster? And why aren't his housemates in the storm cellar, taking shelter?

He steps outside. He sees no one, hears no one. Only the wind, gusting loudly now, a shivery high keening in the tops of the trees, a low, bony creaking of the limbs, of the thick, inflexible trunks. What is he supposed to do? Stumble around out here solving this?

Screw it. Did *they* search for *him*? Any one of them? Because he wasn't hard to find, damn it. No pelting rain yet, barely a few drips, so he could make a dash for the main buildings, but why should he? He returns to the storm cellar. He lifts the hatch, he climbs back in. Will he bolt it shut? No, he can give them that at least: he'll wait a while yet for that. If they still wish to come, let them come. He'll be here at the foot of the stairs. For twenty minutes. After which they'll have to bang and holler. He hopes and trusts they'll come. That there's a simple, harmless explanation that hasn't occurred to him. Or it may be bad. He hopes it isn't bad.

II.

"Eastdon's a good hour away. There are closer hospitals."

"Not routinely operational ones. Nor that I remember the way to."

"You remember the route to Eastdon?"

"I'm not sure. But Eastdon's the city. There'll be signposts. Once I'm in the vicinity, I can get there. I used to drive to that hospital every day. SNAG, Andrew."

"Look, Lisa, this might not be the best idea. Edie thinks..."

"Edie may be right. We may be able to treat him. But if there turn out to be complications—and I'm the nurse, love, I assure you there may be complications—it's more likely that we'll fail."

Andrew says nothing. He mulls the differences between a vision he once had and this reality. There are many. Nick died there, but here, in the world, he may not. He checks his angels. They don't want Lisa to leave, but it's more that they're nervous about it than adamantly opposed.

"I'll go with you," he announces finally.

"Jemmy will be with me. We'll be fine."

"Number one, Jemmy's bringing a zombie girl no one but him knows, and who trusts no one but him. Which can't be useful baggage. Number two, you may not remember the route. Jemmy flat out insists he doesn't, and you sound less than sure to me. Number three, and please listen hard to this one, Lisa; there's apparently a real mother of a storm just hours away from us. If things go wrong, the more of us there are, the more help we have coming through it. Number four, even if things go right, we'll be a long way out of our comfort zone for an uncomfortably long time; in the morning, the more familiar faces around us, the more likely we are to weather *that* moment. Number five, my truck's armored, and we'll be armed—"

"Okay, okay. We can use the help. Right, Jemmy?"

Jemmy's still hunkered next to Nick, with the zombie girl guarding his back. He doesn't lift his eyes from Nick's face to answer. But Nick seems to be on a decently tranquil ride. For pain meds, all Edie had to offer was aspirin and ibuprofen. In the end, they decided that with luck, a maddie might take the edge off.

"Sita's not a zom," Jemmy replies. "She's never been cattle. She's a human girl who lost her memory. Which we're working on."

"Fine. But you could still use the help, right?"

"Fine. But the quicker we get out of here, the better our chances, so—"

"You're right. Let me tell Elise, and I guess the others, and we'll get going."

"I'll pack some food. Lisa shotgun, Sita and me in the back with the cot?"

Later, waking, Matt will not notice the missing cot. Andrew and Jemmy had turned lights on, even, and he hadn't so much as stirred. It was early in his trip, and he was many miles away, above the tree line of the Gingerwood mountains.

"Sounds like a plan. Down 808 to 5, all the way to 219, and in through Chigoe."

Jemmy recalls the last time he passed through Chigoe. Well, not through it, and not him exactly. He died there, a year ago now, a maddie told him. He stifles an inclination to shudder. He squeezes Sita's hand and checks his watch. Two, three hours of light. They need to move.

III.

As Jody and her bees swarmed up to the group at the wellhouse, intent on letting Andrew know what they thought of him, neither Andrew nor anyone else had paid her more than brief attention. Jody girdled by bees and caterwauling at her wretch of a half-brother did not constitute a crisis. Hey, here's Crazy Jody; she's got a bee in her belfry, so what else is new? They had tightened their ring around their injured housemate and ignored her.

Maybe Lisa took a moment to think her usual thought: *Jody's worse every day, she needs help, if I don't do something, and soon, who will? But Nick is even more my charge...* In this house, there was generally something more urgent, and with luck more straightforward, to divert one's purpose. Nick's case was urgent, and to Lisa, at least, straightforward. The percentages said to get him to a hospital. This was Nicky. She would get him to a hospital.

Only the dogs slunk away, as far from the fray as they reasonably could, eying the bees.

Only the new girl, the one whom, even in his concern for Nick, Jemmy was insisting they not call a zombie, cried out when Jody began to wail.

"The walking dead girl's freaked," Elise had said.

"She's unmemoried, not dead," said Jemmy. But he, too, was more concerned for Nick. He didn't feel guilty—Nick had decided without any help from Jemmy to be an idiot—but he did feel responsible. Nick was Jemmy's concern, no less than Nick was Lisa's. "Take her for me for a while, will you, Reds? Talk to her quietly and sweetly."

"Come with me, unmemoried South Asian American chick," said Elise and tugged the girl off toward the dogs, with whom she seemed to share a strange affinity. They excited and stilled each other. Okay, so they clearly knew each other. "Do you have a name?"

Jody shoved into the ring of housemates, filling the space the two of them had vacated.

"You made my daddy cry!" she screamed at Andrew. "He's *dying*, you bully!"

"Are you with our father now?" Andrew turned to ask. "You're tripping, right?"

"Yes, I'm with him. He *told* me."

"May I speak to him? Will you take a message?"

"You leave him alone, asshole. He's sleeping."

"Then please, stop screaming. You'll wake him."

Jody paused, needing to weigh the logic of this. Edie took her by one arm, and Jenna Brower took her by the other, ready to steer her from there if Andrew and the rest were in agreement. Andrew nodded yes. Edie fished something from the wheelbarrow.

"I don't need drugs, Edie," said Jody, submitting with punctured flap to the stewardship. "I need to talk to Andrew."

"Not now, though, okay? Nick's hurt, didn't you see?"

"Nick is? Puppy Dog boy! Nick's hilarious. He'll be all right, though, right?"

"We don't know. We hope so. Andrew and Lisa are seeing to him."

"Andrew is? Oh. Well... Can I talk to Brian, then? I mean, Millar?"

"Oho, Millar, is it?" said Edie. "Okay. Millar it is."

And with the bees spinning up and away, they led Jody off toward the house.

"Okay, fun's over, Sita, back to Jemmy with you," said Elise, from where she stood apart.

"All right," said Sita.

Elise called the dogs to her. Let the others tend to Nick. She was going to follow the bees.

IV.

Jody is at a loss. She wants to demand that Brian explain what the hell he thought he was up to, making deals with Andrew to pressure and manipulate her father. At a time when all the man requires is rest, and about the only comfort they have to give is their support! But then she remembers that, yes, that's right, this person isn't Brian at all. He's Millar. Both Brian and her father died a long time ago. The guy she lives with is called Millar.

"I don't know what I want to say to him," she tells Edie as they walk.

"Are you still tripping? Try untangling your feet."

This is a standard joke; Edie enjoys confusing Jody. But Jody is too preoccupied to faze.

"I'm more almost resurfacing. Anyway, there isn't much happening. My father's still asleep; I'm dozing in the chair next to him."

"Are you kidding? You're asleep?"

"In fact, I'm dreaming."

"You get to peep in on your dreams? What the heck is *that* like?"

"Pssh. Trip dreams are drippy. My mind wanders."

Edie and Jenna exchange glances. They ponder the oddness that is Jody.

"Come on, Edie, I know you dated him. Help me out here."

"Well, Jody, what's worked best for you in the past—"

"I've remembered who he is before?"

"It happens. What works best is you tell him you know who he is. And you thank him. After some cursory, tender reunion chitchat, you take him up to your room and you fuck him."

"I do?"

"Jody, I haven't a clue. I'm suggesting that maybe you should."

Well, Jody acknowledges to herself, maybe she should. But Edie doesn't think much of her, does she? She's Millar's sex doll, or she's pointless.

"Still," she says out loud. "Hardly Millar's fault."

Par for the course, thinks Edie, failing, yet again, to follow Jody's shifts of thought. They find the hallway, left, all the way back, left again, down. She swings open a door. Millar is behind it, his arms a swag of files, another file between his teeth.

"Your name is Millar," Jody says.

Millar makes what might be a noise of assent.

"Thank you," says Jody. "May I start by saying thank you?"

Unable to articulate a response, Millar attempts a grunt. File papers spill from his mouth. He and Jody bend simultaneously to gather them up; they bump heads. It's an old-school rom-com. He sets down the other files, and they embrace. Edie watches without embarrassment, but with more than a twinge of jealousy. She has *got* to get herself a zombie boy.

Jenna pulls the door shut. "Kitchen," she says.

"Coming," sighs Edie. What a day. Thank God there's wine.

V.

Maybe it's the combination of the madeleine and the three ibuprofens. Maybe it's the maddie itself, featuring Edie's new, slightly experimental formula. For whatever reason, Nick's ride today feels sweetened and scented. Not so much better or worse than the usual brew, because there are trade-offs, but refreshingly different.

For one thing, it's less intense: he's at a slight remove from the action, which is fine. He's with Mrs. Jenna Brower Mark One, his neighbor lady, back when he was growing up. So far, he's merely showing her how to navigate her new computer.

Which is less dull than it sounds—as always, the old new is the new quaint, which never fails to amuse him—and oh look, they're surfing one of his favorite old quaint websites! It occurs to him about now that his mood is quite remarkably jolly. No doubt it's a purely chemical ebullience, but so what? He likes it. He's about equally in his teenage body as in Andrew's truck, able to toggle back and forth, the way Jody has learned to do. Though not in the *pain* of his body, sort of floating above it, like a departing spirit. Which he doesn't believe he is yet, but he's cheerfully open to the possibility of.

For another, he's peculiarly aware of his sense of smell. Barnyard stink precluded, Nick's never been much of an olfactorist, and the novelty is pleasing. So Mrs. Brower wears perfume! He wonders if she always has. The fact that he can identify certain of the components (lavender and sandalwood) suggests latent capacities to which his subconscious, at least, has paid attention. The roses in her table vase smell surprisingly listless—they look good, but the scent has leached off, or perhaps been bred out of them—but the table itself has richer redolences than he might have expected, of both wood and varnish. Even, he fancies, from its sunlit dusts. Oops, Mrs. B. wishes to ask him a favor. Her manner has become almost apologetic; she is talking in circles.

She is asking about his college options. She will take a while to get to her point.

Meanwhile, back in the truck, the new girl has slipped a hand inside Jemmy's shirt. Jemmy, by now monitoring Nick less keenly, is slumped dozily into her, until the touch of her skin on Jemmy's skin prods him back to alertness. Jemmy's face collides into kaleidoscopics, of blanched red guilts and hungers. Reluctantly, he places a hand on her wrist and tugs. She resists the disentanglement. Jemmy groans. Nick's best guess is that the vixen is tweaking and toying with Jemmy's nipple. Jemmy remains strong. He extricates the arm. "Soon enough, I hope," he whispers to her. "But you need to be Sita again first, okay? An equal self?"

The girl seems to consider this and assent. In any case, she nods and resettles herself, her head on Jemmy's shoulder. Jemmy, by contrast, looks a little sick: he has won out over his baser instincts, but his baser instincts have decided he's an idiot. He places the hand the new girl hasn't claimed upon Nick's forearm: his fear for Nick's fate will shame him into strength.

Up front, Andrew and Lisa worry about the storm. The skies are dark, they observe, much earlier than expected. We'll make it there, probably—we're nearly at Chigoe, though we're going to have to steer around this part, *look* at these burned-out buildings!—wow, this many?—but let's hope there'll be no issues getting into the hospital. Will we be expected to pay? Insurance is mostly defunct, the responsibility of public hospitals to the public is moot, resources are limited. How do they staff the place? Will they even treat Nick? If they won't, his chances will be worse than if we'd stayed at Heartwood, and why didn't we plan for that possibility? (Nick feels his pulse race and stutter as he listens and begins to wonder the same thing.) And whether they treat him or don't, we are not going to be heading back tonight. What are our options, and how might we ready ourselves for the disorientations of the new day? Separately, unwilling to admit it, Lisa and Andrew are having second thoughts.

Mrs. B., meanwhile, is at last coming to her request.

She knows that Nick is considering U. of E. She senses it isn't his first choice, and she doesn't want to influence him unduly, but he hasn't ruled it out, has he? Nick has not. Well, if he does go to Eastdon—she may not have told him this, but her people are from Eastdon—it would be so useful to her if he could look up somebody for her. And pass on a message.

Observing, remembering, Nick realizes that this must

have been the precise moment he decided on a college. Well, why not? Would any other choice, for any other reason, have been less capricious? U. of E. was okay. His life has been his life. It will continue or it won't.

"Right or left?" Andrew asks Lisa.

"Try left," she says.

They're looking for a back way to the old Emergency.

A siren sounds, and then another. The rain has begun to gust. All at once, all around them, all the streetlamps go out. In front of them, though, a block away, there persists a wash of light: could that be the hospital? So unpromisingly quiet, so dimly lit?

"There," says Lisa, hoping.

They steer uncertainly toward it.

VI. From Jody's set of top ten Eastdon histories:

#8. The Chigoe Slave Museum; Its Relocated Ghost

A Slave Museum should be excluded from a list such as this. We have set out to commemorate Eastdon's non-violent history; the violence of the city's slave legacy, as with its Civil War history, was on an epic scale, chronically and unflinchingly cruel. However, even more than the Civil War, slavery is so integral to Eastdon's history that there are few city sites that are untouched by its specter. And the story of this museum, so tokenistic and trivialized a monument, is ultimately less about the violence of our heritage than survival in its margins.

If I may be permitted, I'll sketch some of that heritage, since to fail to do so, especially in this tokenistic context, would be an abomination. Eastdon's was the most important slave market in America. After 1808, we no longer imported our slaves from Africa: laws were passed to ban that atrocity, which was now prosecuted as piracy. But the need for slave laborers being greater than ever, we bred them, with Virginia as one of the very greatest of the slave-breeding states. Slavers poured in to ply their trade, and Eastdon bustled and blossomed and took pride in it.

The slave market heart of Eastdon was in Chigoe. The name is Native American in origin. Appropriately, though, the insect word we've corrupted it to derives from a West African language. We call the area Flea Town now, and we say, "It Hops!" Where perhaps a quarter of a million of the negro faceless (not for a hundred fifty years yet African Americans) were bought and sold, there are now night clubs, fine restaurants, and boutiques—the old slave age buildings burned when the city did, set to the torch by the fleeing Confederate army in 1865 to spare it from plunder—and as it was resettled, it was reborn real pretty.

Somehow, tucked around the corner, there was set aside a tiny preserved half-street, not of pre-Civil War buildings, but restored soon after in the good old style of things, where eventually, in the 1950s, a house was opened as a private museum. It's neither professionally staffed nor publicly supported. It exhibits mostly folk art and family kitsch. There are some decent informational posters and historical artifacts, but the museum's goal—which, with simple, cutesy sincerity, and touching, aching incompleteness, it achieves—is to tell the tale of an expiring clan.

There's also the ghost.

Henry Bartholomew, who describes himself as the "part-owner and steward" of the property (and is disappointed that the African American community is less interested in being part-owner with him than in ousting him, if the funds can ever be found, in favor of something much grander and more solemn), is tired of talking about the ghost. The ghost is not what he wishes to be known for. But he did speak to us, and at some length, because of a personal connection that my friend Lisa came to claim with him.

Lisa's cousin Nick was good friends, back in Connecticut, with a woman who was born and raised in Eastdon. One Mrs. Brower. It was partly to pay her a service that he came to study here, and since Lisa followed him, and she brought me, all three of us might be said to have come, in part, because of her. This woman had a sister with whom she quarreled and broke. The sister remained in Eastdon when the other left, eventually becoming Mrs. Henry Bartholomew, and the pair of them never spoke again. Nick came south with an olive branch—a cache of family letters and photographs—and a message: Lilian, let's forgive and forget, and be friends.

But it was too late. Lilian Bartholomew had died six months before.

Lisa had accompanied her cousin on his visit to the Bartholomew house, and when I expressed an interest in the museum, she secured me a private tour. The old man, still very much in mourning for his wife, had been touched by Nick's remembrances, and now displayed many of the pieces he had brought. Lisa and I had both met his sister-in-law also, and that we were able to reminisce about her was enough for him. He opened up to us.

The ghost was real, he assured me, though not threatening. A little Black child, perhaps seven or eight—it appeared less often now since Henry's wife had died. A fine, fine mother was Lilian. The boy would stand at the top of the stairs, in wait for them, a shape of darkness in the darkness—even a dim light would dispel him. You might not see him, but you'd feel his hand take yours. A cold breath would pass through you, but you wouldn't shiver from it—perhaps "cool" would be a truer word than cold. And you know, he almost never showed himself until their children were gone from the house. It was as if he had waited for the couple to be childless.

And here's something you might not credit, he added, as if confident we had believed it all till now. This ghost once haunted another house down the street. There was a Black woman living there too, but she moved. So the ghost moved, moved four doors down, to them.

I don't know that I did credit it, for all that I gasped and goshed to Henry. But I wanted to. I wanted this whole lovely, lively strip of Eastdon to be haunted. I wanted to believe that some dogged, suppliant residue remained after the horrors that had been perpetrated here for half a century and more. I don't like the notion that we can do anything we like, we humans, to each other, to the world, and act as if it's over and forgotten. Oh, we need our facility to excise and smooth over, to dissemble, but man, we abuse the shit out of it.

Henry Bartholomew's inadequate little monument should depress me: this private house with its peeling wallpaper, its too ordinary, too tacky displays. It doesn't, though. I find it charmingly personal. I find him charmingly personable. And on reflection, I'm not sure that "personal and inadequate" isn't, after all, the best, the truest memorial.

VII.

"So how many for supper? All six of us, or four?"

Both numbers strike Edie as tiny, especially since two of them are the cooks. When you're used to serving ten, day in, day out, one minor meal, one main meal, there's something about six, or four, that makes you wonder if you need to bother.

"Or two maybe, once the two of us settle for some salad greens and a slice of pie."

"Jody and Millar will be down later for midnight leftovers, my guess is. We've got to get something on the table anyway, I reckon, so we might as well make for them."

"I don't know. I'd lay odds Little Red won't show either. No one skips meals like her."

"Matt, though."

"Maddienapping, Andrew said."

"But he would want us to go get him."

"Yes, he would. But just for tonight, excuse the language, Jenna, I don't much feel like being his fucking servant. If he can't show up on his own, screw him."

"Fine. Salad greens, pie, and wine it is... Still, sorry to be practical about it, Edie, but we're going to have to do a little work first. Or we'll hate our lives in the morning, leastways if we lose power. Which is likely."

"Matt thinks we might lose the whole house."

"A whole other set of problems. He's got the storm cellar stocked for that eventuality. Meanwhile, we'll be fine in the basement. And the lovebirds can scurry bare-assed down and join us, or else stay up in their room dying happy. That's their concern. Ours is to be ready for the normal grind. To be alive tomorrow and needing to be fed and with a roof over our heads."

"Fine... Not the fire pit, though."

"Not tonight. Get a bunch of things going on the regular old stovetop, be ready to put 'em on ice when the storm hits and the power goes."

"Damn it, though. No rest for the wicked."

And they begin, for a while, to work. To sort through what they have and what they need to use, what won't keep on ice or in the cellar if the power goes, what this and that and the other might go best together. It's exactly what Edie hadn't wanted to be doing.

"But speaking of which...," says Jenna.

"Sorry?"

"Speaking of the wicked, Edie. There's something I've been meaning to tell you."

"Jeez, another zombie?"

"Something newer. Started when I freaked out this morning..."

"About the horses."

"Well, only in part. But I wasn't sure yet, so I didn't say. Except it just happened again. While we were gathered around Big Nick."

"Okay. Something happened. So spill."

"This is going to sound better than it is, maybe."

"*Spill.*"

"Well, then... I may have started to remember things."

Edie empties her arms of pots, peels off a latex glove, and turns.

"You *what*?"

"Twice now. No maddies. Just spontaneous, like."

"Jenna, are you sure? Because that's *stupendous*—"

"No, Edie, you don't get it: it's awful. I was a wicked person, Edie. Oh, I may have been strong, impatient, confident, other things too, I'm sure. But if what I'm remembering is true, I was someone I... Sometimes, I was someone you're not going to want to know."

"Okay, now wait a minute. Sit."

"Because this morning, I, well, it wasn't that bad, just a tad bad, and it startled me, but..."

"Jenna—"

"But this last time—"

"Jenna, is this about the parrot?"

"The parrot?"

"Is this about your parrot you loved, but didn't really, and didn't realize you didn't till—"

"You know about the parrot?"

"And so do you, Jenna! Know about the parrot. Most of the time. But you forget."

"So I didn't just now remember?"

"No, darling."

"But it's real? The parrot?"

"I'm afraid it is. As far as I can tell, it is. You had a parrot. And yes, you abandoned him."

"Oh."

"I'm sorry, darling."

"Oh. And the boy I killed, I knew that too?"

"The boy? Oh, the one you pushed over the cliff? I don't think that one's real, dear."

"Mario Ruben. Sarah saw them pull him from the water. Till Nicky moved, I thought..."

"His name is new. That's exciting. But it doesn't make him real."

"I don't think I want him to be real."

Edie studies her friend's face. Of course it can't be real. Can it? Of course it can't be. Not *Jenna*. No way it's real! But what, holy Jesus, if it is?

She has a terrible, sinking, exhilarated feeling: a true piece of new memory! If so...

But how can she let it be true? Can she do that to Jenna?

Screw making food for tomorrow. Tomorrow can wait. Tomorrow does wait most days. "Well, then, dear," she says. "If you don't want it to be real... Real for Sarah, because no *way* it's real for Jenna, is it, darling? You know that, right? That *you're not Sarah*? Okay, then... Well, let me pour some more wine. And what say we go to work on that?"

Edie's third glass, Jenna's second. Just a sip while she thinks. Actually, she *has* thought. Secretly, it's a small fear of hers, in fact: some old lost self coming home to roost, saying, *Move along now, I'm the one you* really *are, remember?* But this isn't that, is it; this is about Jenna.

Think. She needs to tread very carefully.

"Okay, sweetie, let's say it's a true memory. This old you, this Sarah, has come to call. How do we *greet* her? She's not you, but she is your neighbor. To whom we must show charity? So we ask the context. The exculpatory detail: this boy's meanness, your fear of him—look, I *know* you, Jenna, they're *there*. How do we approach this to recall it, next time, the proper way?"

Jenna looks doubtful. "You mean, to persuade myself I was the victim or something?"

"Well, or it was an accident, he was careless. I don't *know* which, Jenna. Tell me."

Jenna's memory is cloudy. But this feels devious. She doesn't know, she doesn't know!

Edie sips. She is right about this. This is *Jenna*! And tenderly, grimly, she waits.

VIII.

Elise is back where she was this morning: across the brook at the far reaches of the west meadows, Lisa's dogs in tow, following a storm of bees. Seemingly reluctant to settle anywhere near their hives, they've taken over a cluster of honeysuckle vines. Elise looks right and sees the horses over in the next field; there are geese along the riverbank; all the loose animals of the farm are somewhere in view. She's not sure what this is proof of. How can animals, whatever the acuity of their instincts, gauge where to be safest from a storm that won't hit for hours yet? She doesn't entirely trust their judgment. She doesn't understand it well enough to.

But nor is she prepared to dismiss it. And with her father away and the attention of her housemates elsewhere, this may be the perfect time for her to prove to herself she has the guts and the smarts she thinks she does. Not to survive full-time in the wild; not yet. But if such is her long-term goal and ambition, she should at least be able to weather one lousy mother of a storm.

She has perhaps two, three hours to think this through and prepare. Those two rocks she picked out aren't near here. Still, maybe there. Or she knows a good ditch, but can a ditch, no matter what it has for walls and drainage, be the way to go? Wind, flood, lightning, how do you plan for all three? No caves about, of course... Does she have notes? Can she get online?

If not the rocks, then maybe a thick, low tree? There are plenty of those. The taller ones will take any lightning there is, right? She'd rather not mess with lightning...

Time to weigh the risks. And to provision herself to survive them. And for the aftermath.

A shiver of fear goes through her. Suddenly she feels very uncertain and very small. Does she understand what it is she's risking? Is she really, really going to do this?

Yes. She does. And yes, she is. She is really going to do this.

Okay, then. She needs to move.

There's also, perhaps, a little shiver of a thrill? Oh, yes, I am one crazy mofo?

Well, maybe. She grimaces at herself; she chuckles it away. No posturing, no dither.

She moves.

IX.

Millar and Jody have not jumped into bed, only stretched out on top of it. This is Millar; this is Jody. So they've been talking. The truth is, these are the days Millar most lives for, when Jody turns briefly lucid: when, for a while, she knows him and cleaves to him, when he can claim to be, for a while, himself.

"Tell me who I am," she says, and he begins, very straightforwardly, to recount the story of her life. She doesn't need much help—she knows all the stories and many more—just a guide-light through the true ones, this path, not that; or else I'm not sure right here, but we'll pick it up on the other side of this stretch of thickets. As they talk, she repeats some of his phrasings to fix them a little more firmly in her map. When he arrives at Brian, and his death, she tugs him by: let all that go, for now. When the tale reaches Millar, she slows him down, wanting to be tender with this part of it. He won't let her prettify it, though—why she chose him, how she has treated him—he wants neither to blame nor to extenuate, neither to simplify their disparate, sometimes desperate motives nor to overcomplicate them. The task, no doubt, is impossible: the way shifts beneath their tread. But there is no other way, and they can feel it, sometimes, dankly, thornily, as they stray or they go straight.

"How have you remembered all this?" she asks, in wonder, more than once.

"I have a *lot* of documents. I look at them so much they're rarely far out of my memory. In some ways," he admits, "I know your story better than my own. Perhaps I care more."

She blushes; she has no wish to be adored, and too much devotion tends to the icky.

"No, no," he says. "You misunderstand me. Not just *your* story, though it's true I know it best, but all of ours here— because they can be just stories, and I need such stories. I can't know my own life well enough for me, not any more, to care to look at it, which is fine. I know it well enough to orient myself. But I've let my addiction to it go."

She doesn't really get this. She'll take his word for it. She is drained, buzzed, and hungry. She missed lunch, she tells him, has had no more than bread and honey and fruit all day, and now this wine.

"Let's go down to the kitchen," says Millar. "They must be making supper right now; we could help."

For the moment, though, she doesn't move.

"So you're saying," she asks, "I'll forget everything again by morning?"

"Not so much forget," he says, "as you won't know where to look for it."

"I'll forget where to look for it."

"There are corners of you you keep returning to. That you get lost in."

"And yet such a small life, really." Such an ordinary life, for the times they live in. No more of a puzzle or a maze than anybody's. She pulls a sour, embarrassed face. "I think I care more about your life."

He laughs. She's teasing. It's pleasant to be teased.

"What's that?"

Something, a tree limb, has thudded on the roof above them. At last, they notice that the wind has risen, that what was a spatter of rain is becoming a rattling yowl.

"That's right," cries Jody. "We're under a storm watch! Supposedly it may take the house."

Millar lifts the curtain, and they press their noses to the

window. Fidgety with wind, it presses back. Nothing beyond it but the rain, the darkness... Abruptly, from off its left edge, a sheet of loose plywood yaws and clatters at them, dangling across the face of the pane, and they startle away, shrieking into laughter. Quite inappropriately, and both at once.

"If the house goes," says Millar and nuzzles her neck, "I doubt we'll make it."

"I don't feel like going downstairs yet," she decides, falling across the bed again, light-headed, buzzed. "Well, if we all die, at least your records will survive, right?"

"Oh, we have cookies!" Millar exclaims, remembering. "Mrs. Brower made cookies yesterday; she gave me some; they're in that jar there." A flare of older memory rises in him, and he grins. A red vase, ringed by candles. Jody, and cookies.

"People will be able to read about us," continues Jody. "We may have forgotten ourselves, mostly, but maybe you've made it so that history won't."

Millar thinks of the mess in which he left the records room. He'd been in the middle of some things, and then he spilled that folder. Then knocked loose more of them while grabbing Jody's files—knowing he'd need to consult them, that she'd want him to tell her her story, and that the stacks of back-up boxes upstairs wouldn't help much, being more an archaeological site than a navigable archive.

"Oh yeah," she says, nodding at the sheaves of her strewn around them. "I guess mine may be lost, though. When the roof goes, they'll blow away across creation. I'll be forgotten!"

She laughs again, so happily tipsy, so languidly lovely. He does too. The idea of anyone reading through their files is absurd, suddenly. Who, any time soon, would care? And really, why on earth should they care either?

"We'll all be forgotten, Jody," he says. "Or even if someday not, because of the files, we'll still be remembered wrong. Completely reimagined. They'll tell any story about us they want."

"Okay, I think I'm ready; we've got time," she answers, as the night retunes its note, and all the trees at once begin, operatically, to sing. "Let's take off our clothes and do this."

He turns toward her, a hand outstretched.

"Cookie?" he asks.

POSTSCRIPT: UNTIL THEY ARE NOT REMEMBERED

"For the living know that they will die;
But the dead know nothing,
And they have no more reward,
For the memory of them is forgotten."

The Book of Ecclesiastes, 9:5

"Farewell! We lose ourselves in light."

Alfred, Lord Tennyson, "In Memoriam"

IN MEMORIAM, YEAR TWO, OCTOBER

Kitty Boggenpoel

Back when I was six years old, my parents dragged me, kicking and crabby, to a crosstown mardi gras party. But it turned out to be fun for all the family, with cocktail party clatter there, rec room rompage here, and cake, beads, crazy hats for all. My father visited us in the kids' room, exclaiming over the cartoons on the VCR and kibitzing with the card players. I can't say I paid any heed, at the time, to what parent prattle might be springing up around me, but when (courtesy of a magic potion concocted by my friend Edie) I revisited that party, the morning of the fire that killed me, I found my attention more drawn to it than to the cards.

Although I grew up in Eastdon, in the Fridge Park area, both my parents were come-heres. My mother, part Lakota, hailed from the Midwest. She met and married my dad in Europe. His family was originally from Cape Town. He's a shade or two darker than mom and me. Most people can't place him racially.

There in the rec room, though, he fell into conversation with a man recently returned from South Africa, who could. Yes, dad agreed; he was indeed South African! A Cape Coloured, in fact, or used to be. And yes, the place was beautiful.

"But Cape Coloured," the man said, cautiously, politely. "Is that the polite term?"

"No," said my dad, "Cape Coloured is considered derogatory, but I've claimed it."

"Yes," the other replied. "Besides, the Blacks and the Coloureds I saw were not exactly unhappy. They're surely among the most fortunate of their kind in all of Africa."

"You thought so?"

This was well after Sharpeville, the Soweto school shootings. I know that history now, having gone through a phase when it felt important to know it, when I considered my neglected "heritage" to be a significant part of me. I never exactly renounced that judgment, but with time it took its proportionate place. The past is never entirely past. But the present, I came to see, had to strive for a certain independence from it.

But this man—Spencer, he introduced himself as—apparently had little concern for historical context, or at least no awareness of how, or why, my father's sense of it might be different from his. A "spectacular country," he thought South Africa. A "fortunate people," he thought its apartheid-era Africans.

"You do realize," my father said, "that someday soon they'll rise up in open revolt?"

"The Blacks? Oh not at all! No, if there's trouble, it'll be the outside agitators."

"The outside agitators? Is that what they told you? The Whites?"

"They didn't have to!" Spencer protested. "Or yes, they did say it. But just looking at them—oh, anyone could see it."

"At the Blacks?" said Dad. "That might depend on the circumstances you saw them in."

"Oh, you can claim that. But fundamentally, they're happy. Why wouldn't they be? About all they do is smile and move slow!"

"Oh yes? There may be reasons for that."

"Yes, there are. Why would they rock the boat? When they like the boat."

My father took a sip of his wine. Spencer took a sip of his wine.

"You may be right," Dad said. "About the outside agitators. Since it's illegal for anyone but Whites to own guns."

Spencer took a sip of his wine. Dad didn't. Spencer put down his glass.

"Excuse me," he said and moved, politely, away. His son, a nice boy I remember thinking, was watching the VCR, and Spencer went to kneel protectively by him.

In the end, of course, they were both wrong: the dismantling of apartheid was imminent, but was achieved without insurrection—who was Dad to know, he'd been gone a lifetime. There came a collective sense that rocks were looming; that the boat which all South Africans occupied together was about to smash against them; that it would be wise to jump and find another way.

Thanks to Edie's witch brew, I retrieved, that last day of my life, a rich assortment of early memories. I was struck, however, by no greater revelation than this one: of how itchy in his brown skin my father had felt here in the new South. Although during the car ride home, as my parents rehashed the episode, I began to sense that he might feel unassimilated anywhere. He'd also spent time in Europe, and the US was his fourth country. There was no place he was from any more, or that he'd still *feel* from if he went back there.

But then, don't those of us who *are* from a place sometimes feel just as out of joint in it? As subject to its shifts and swirls of *us* and *them*? To the creep and rush and fast fade of the tide of our times, always swarming and going out on us, always stranding us in some new present?

A self, and the ghosts of a self. Losing and recasting our

wild thread of life.

My parents took off for the UK the fall before I died. They'd scored a coup: twin visiting professorships. But then the world got weird; UK phone and email communication faltered; error messages sputtered into silence; I was battling not to forget. *(Let them, somehow, be healthy. May they, somehow, remember me.)* They'd put most of their possessions in storage, but my father, at my request, gave me stewardship of his unpublished manuscripts. He wrote poetry as an avocation, and those, not the academic work, were the pieces I had wanted. He took with him mostly just the poems in progress. As the cottage went up in flames around us, his poems, one poem especially, were the last things my mind went to. Who knows who and what will survive these times, whatever does survive? And I confess, I wrote a little too, and had shelved my files with his. No one, perhaps, who didn't know me, who doesn't know him, would much value any of our writing, but somehow, I realized then, I had hoped it might outlive us just a little. That *his*, at least, might.

There's a pyramidal cairn in Forest Ridge Park, near the old azalea gardens that my father and the Friends of the Park were working to restore. The poem whose lines came to me was set there and played with the theories about it, what it might be a memorial to. Was it some kind of Civil War thing, or Reconstruction era Black thing, or was it a WPA project, using leftover granite from the stairs and paths—or an amusement park relic, perhaps? In the early twentieth century a trolley line had its terminus here; there was a Ferris wheel and animal entertainments; somebody suggested that the pyramid guarded the bones of a much loved black bear. One of my dad's Friends of the Park projects, a year before my parents left, had been to tear the vines and the poison ivy from it and see if they could find a plaque. But there was no plaque.

In that fire, I lost my partner, whom I treasured, but I'd

been losing Tiff for so long. I lost my life, which I had treasured, but I was exhausted enough to feel release. I relinquished the sprawling novel of us, treasuring as flame-glimmer my small pages of it, but I still wished. *(Let Millar get out with his archives; Edie with her lab gear; Matt with his awkward tenderness; safe and whole with their love of us; with their difficult sanity.)* A riffle, here, then elsewhere; gone.

All this as I freed Tiff, who was immovable, from Edie's arms. As I spoke my truthful lie: "Go! I've got Tiff!" As we clasped and turned from them. The last place my thoughts went, through blaze, smoke, pain, and loss of breath, and the quieting of Tiff's clutch, was to the glitter of my father's papers, and that puzzle of a cairn. And in a parting swirl, in the flame-tear and tangle of its vines, to what had housed it: a park, this town, our life I'd loved, a world.

Stories and images I'm no longer there to sift the sense of. Let the ash and the air make of them what they will.

ACKNOWLEDGMENTS

I dedicate this novel, with much love, to Sally. Sweetheart, if we were Millar and Jody, I know you'd want us down in the basement two hours before the storm hit, but hold on a sec, so I may raise to you this oatmeal cookie toast.

Thanks also to St. Catherine's School, where I taught for decades. I began *The Memory Addicts* during an aughties summer break, but it wasn't until I was granted a three-quarters teaching load and had my first two periods free that it became a draft. Using my classroom for studio space, I churned it out during six months of first periods. I'm grateful to James River Writers, in whose Unpublished Novel Contest that draft placed second; it was the plan to submit there that inspired me to plow through. While I can't bring myself to thank COVID-19 for anything, it was in the pandemic year of 2021 that I fished out the novel to rework and finish it. I'd like to thank Elise Hitchings for her essential first round of editorial feedback, and Bryce Wilson at Atmosphere Press for his stellar work on the final drafts.

ABOUT ATMOSPHERE PRESS

Atmosphere Press is an independent, full-service publisher for excellent books in all genres and for all audiences. Learn more about what we do at atmospherepress.com.

We encourage you to check out some of Atmosphere's latest releases, which are available at Amazon.com and via order from your local bookstore:

Dancing with David, a novel by Siegfried Johnson

The Friendship Quilts, a novel by June Calender

My Significant Nobody, a novel by Stevie D. Parker

Nine Days, a novel by Judy Lannon

Shining New Testament:.The Cloning of Jay Christ, a novel by Cliff Williamson

Shadows of Robyst, a novel by K. E. Maroudas

Home Within a Landscape, a novel by Alexey L. Kovalev

Motherhood, a novel by Siamak Vakili

Death, The Pharmacist, a novel by D. Ike Horst

Mystery of the Lost Years, a novel by Bobby J. Bixler

Bone Deep Bonds, a novel by B. G. Arnold

Terriers in the Jungle, a novel by Georja Umano

Into the Emerald Dream, a novel by Autumn Allen

His Name Was Ellis, a novel by Joseph Libonati

The Cup, a novel by D. P. Hardwick

The Empathy Academy, a novel by Dustin Grinnell

Tholocco's Wake, a novel by W. W. VanOverbeke

Dying to Live, a novel by Barbara Macpherson Reyelts

Looking for Lawson, a novel by Mark Kirby

Yosef's Path: Lessons from my Father, a novel by Jane Leclere Doyle

ABOUT THE AUTHOR

Derek Kannemeyer was born in Cape Town, South Africa and raised in London, England. His recent books include a poetry collection, *Mutt Spirituals,* a five act play, *The Play of Gilgamesh,* and a hybrid non-fiction/photography book, *Unsay their Names*, about the 2020-2021 fall from grace of the Lost Cause statuary of Richmond, Virginia, where he has spent most of his adult life. *The Memory Addicts* is his first novel.

For much more (his website is a labyrinthine folly), visit him at www.petalridge.com.

CPSIA information can be obtained
at www.ICGtesting.com
Printed in the USA
LVHW041245090323
741071LV00002B/120

9 781639 884094